# SPECIAL MESSAGE TO READERS

## THE ULVERSCROFT FOUNDATION
**(registered UK charity number 264873)**
was established in 1972 to provide funds for research, diagnosis and treatment of eye diseases. Examples of major projects funded by the Ulverscroft Foundation are:-

- The Children's Eye Unit at Moorfields Eye Hospital, London
- The Ulverscroft Children's Eye Unit at Great Ormond Street Hospital for Sick Children
- Funding research into eye diseases and treatment at the Department of Ophthalmology, University of Leicester
- The Ulverscroft Vision Research Group, Institute of Child Health
- Twin operating theatres at the Western Ophthalmic Hospital, London
- The Chair of Ophthalmology at the Royal Australian College of Ophthalmologists

You can help further the work of the Foundation by making a donation or leaving a legacy. Every contribution is gratefully received. If you would like to help support the Foundation or require further information, please contact:

**THE ULVERSCROFT FOUNDATION
The Green, Bradgate Road, Anstey
Leicester LE7 7FU, England
Tel: (0116) 236 4325**

**website: www.ulverscroft-foundation.org.uk**

# WEDDING BELLS FOR LAND GIRLS

Summer 1942. Britain is in the depths of war and the Women's Land Army is hard at work looking after the farms while the men are away fighting. For Yorkshire Land Girls and firm friends Grace, Brenda and Una, romance in wartime comes with a host of challenges. There's a wedding to plan, but married bliss is threatened when the time comes for the groom to enlist. With lovers parted, anxious women have no idea whether they'll see their men again. And while single girls dance and flirt, will they be able to find true love among the men who've stayed behind?

JENNY HOLMES

---◆---

# WEDDING BELLS FOR LAND GIRLS

*Complete and Unabridged*

# MAGNA
*Leicester*

First published in Great Britain in 2018 by
Corgi Books
an imprint of Transworld Publishers
London

First Ulverscroft Edition
published 2020
by arrangement with
Transworld Publishers
London

A catalogue record for this book is available
from the British Library.

ISBN 978–0–7505–4772–7

Published by
Ulverscroft Limited
Anstey, Leicestershire
Set by Words & Graphics Ltd.
Anstey, Leicestershire
Printed and bound in Great Britain by
T. J. International Ltd., Padstow, Cornwall

This book is printed on acid-free paper

For all the Land Girls and Lumber Jills
of World War Two. May they live
on in our memories.

# CAST OF CHARACTERS

## LAND GIRLS

***Brenda Appleby*** — worked at Maynard's butchers before she became a Land Girl

***Hilda Craven*** — warden at Fieldhead House hostel

***Joyce Cutler*** — farmer's daughter from Warwickshire

***Jean Fox*** — worked as a bank clerk before joining the Land Army

***Poppy Gledhill*** — the youngest recruit and ex-mill worker

***Kathleen Hirst*** — former hairdresser from Millwood

***Grace Mostyn*** — daughter of Burnside's pub landlord and blacksmith, married to Bill

***Una Sharpe*** — former worker at Kingsley's Mill in Millwood

***Elsie Walker*** — former groom from the Wolds

***Doreen Wells*** — until recently, worked in a department store

## BURNSIDE VILLAGERS

***Maurice Baxendale*** — owner of a car repair garage

***Bob Baxendale*** — Maurice's brother and

caretaker at the Institute

*Lionel Foster* — owner of Hawkshead Manor

*Alice Foster* — his wife

*Shirley Foster* — their daughter

*Jack Hudson* — Bill Mostyn's best man, serving in the Royal Navy

*Cliff Kershaw* — landlord of the Blacksmith's Arms

*Edgar Kershaw* — his son, an RAF gunner recently shot down over France

*Esther Liddell* — village post mistress and church organist

*Edith Mostyn* — Land Girls representative, widow of Vince

*Bill Mostyn* — her son, owns and runs the family tractor repair company


## BURNSIDE FARMERS

*Joe Kellett* — farmer at Home Farm

*Emily Kellett* — his wife

*Henry Rowson* — shepherd

*Peggy Russell* — widow

*Roland Thomson* — farmer at Brigg Farm

*Neville Thomson* — his son

*Horace Turnbull* — farmer at Winsill Edge

*Arnold White* — owner of Dale End Farm, Attercliffe

*Hettie White* — Arnold's daughter

*Donald White* — Arnold's elder son

*Les White* — Arnold's younger son

## ITALIAN PRISONERS OF WAR

*Angelo Bachetti*
*Lorenzo Marino*


## TOMMIES

*Private Cyril Atkinson*


## CANADIAN AIR FORCE

*Squadron Leader Jim Aldridge*
*Flight Lieutenant John Mackenzie*


## OUTSIDERS

*Alfie Craven* — Hilda's son
*Howard Moyes* — associate of Alfie Craven
*Clive Nixon* — associate of Alfie Craven

# 1

'Hop up on to the pillion seat,' Brenda Appleby told Una Sharpe. She kick-started Old Sloper and felt the thrum of its engine beneath her.

Una climbed on board. She and Brenda wore identical lilac dresses with frilled necklines and flared, knee-length skirts. 'Thank goodness it's stopped raining.'

'Yes, what would Grace say if her bridesmaids turned up at the church looking like drowned rats?' Brenda eased the motor bike out of the stable yard on to the driveway of Fieldhead Hostel just in time to spot their friend and fellow Land Girl, Joyce Cutler, carrying bridal bouquets through the front door.

'Hello, Joyce. Who's getting spliced?' she called with a lively smile and an exaggerated wink.

'Not me, worse luck.' Joyce placed the two sprays of white carnations in the back of a green van then glanced at her watch. 'Shouldn't you two visions of loveliness be down at Burnside helping the bride to get ready instead of wasting time talking to me?'

'Don't worry, Sloper will get us there in two shakes.' Brenda was confident of the bike's ability to transport them to the village on time. She and Una would sail along the winding lanes, ignoring barking dogs and avoiding puddles left by overnight rain. They would arrive with cheeks aglow and hair whipped back by the wind, and there would still be plenty of time to help Grace into her wedding dress then tidy themselves up before all three made their grand entrance into St Michael's Church.

'Have you remembered your bridesmaids' shoes?' Joyce noted that Brenda and Una wore sturdy brown lace-ups.

'Here, in the panniers with our headdresses and gloves.' Una patted the canvas satchels strapped to the pillion seat. 'Don't worry, Joyce; we'll make ourselves presentable as soon as we get there.'

Joyce smiled as she imagined the unusual spectacle of Grace Kershaw's two attendants kitted out in their silk dresses riding down the narrow main street and into the yard of the Blacksmith's Arms. *Typical Brenda to buck the trend*. 'Just don't crash the darned thing,' she called after them.

'Hold tight, Una,' Brenda warned.

Una gave Joyce a wave then followed instructions. 'Ta-ta, we'll see you in church!'

And off they sped. Brenda crouched forward over the handlebars, boyish in spite of the frilled dress, with her short, dark hair and tanned skin. Una was smaller and had a daintier look — dark auburn hair catching the sunlight, slim arms wrapped around Brenda's waist in anticipation of the twists and turns in the bumpy road.

Joyce stood beside the van until the bike disappeared from view. She glanced down at her dark green jersey and corduroy breeches, half regretting the group's decision to attend Grace's wedding in full Land Army uniform. Yes, it would be satisfying to form a guard of honour up to the church door and the girls would be happy to show their pride in serving King and Country in wheat field and hay barn, henhouse and milking parlour. And yet . . . Joyce brushed a stray piece of straw from her sleeve and straightened her tie. And yet it would have been nice to have dressed up in her best frock and fashioned her long, thick brown hair into a French pleat; nicer still to show off her shapely legs in her one remaining pair of nylon stockings and her high-heeled shoes.

★   ★   ★

Brenda and Una soon left the hostel behind. It was ten in the morning and the sun was already warm on their faces. There was blue sky overhead and green fields to either side, rising steeply towards rocky horizons. The slopes were criss-crossed by low stone walls and dotted with grazing sheep. Nearer to the road stood tidy, well-kept barns housing hay, tractors and other farm machinery, next to solid houses with narrow windows and doors, where the inevitable dog strained at its long chain as the motor bike cruised by.

'What's the betting that Grace is a bundle of nerves?' Brenda called over her shoulder as she slowed down for the junction that took them into Burnside. 'We'll have all on to calm her down.'

'I've got butterflies myself, so goodness knows how she feels.' Una took a deep breath to calm herself as they rode under ancient copper beeches that formed an avenue into the village. They came to the first row of houses with a post office at the end of the terrace, next to the Village Institute and opposite the pub and blacksmith's, which was where the bride lived with her father, Cliff Kershaw.

Easing off the throttle, Brenda steered the bike into the pub yard then came to a halt. Though it was a Saturday morning in early June 1942, there was no hustle and bustle. Instead, a sense of still, silent anticipation filled the air, as if the village held its breath before the day's big event: the marriage of Mr Bill Mostyn, owner of Mostyn Tractor Repair Company, and Miss Grace Kershaw, publican's daughter and Yorkshire Land Girl.

Una slid off the bike, then delved into one of the panniers for two pairs of white, open-toed shoes. Brenda, meanwhile, drew out cotton lace gloves and floral headbands. Armed with these accessories, they crossed the yard and entered the building via the open door of the blacksmith's forge.

'Hello!' Grace's brother, Edgar, intercepted them on their way into the house. He was dressed in RAF uniform, with no sign on his handsome face of the troubles that had plagued him six months earlier. 'Don't tell me you two came here on that.' He jerked his thumb towards Sloper.

Brenda breezed past him into the kitchen. 'Of course we did. And I'll feel badly let down if you haven't parked your Spitfire on the back field.'

'Hello, Edgar.' Una squeezed by with a shy smile.

'No Spitfire, I'm afraid. Anyway, I fly Lancasters.' Privately he thought that letting high-spirited Brenda anywhere near the controls of a fighter plane would be a big mistake. 'They've given me forty-eight hours furlough but I had to promise to leave the old girl in her hangar.'

'Never mind, we're glad you're here.' Una smoothed the panels of her gored skirt then took off her brogues. Sliding her feet into a pair of court shoes, she discovered that they were far too big.

'Here, silly — those are mine.' Brenda snatched them from her then realized a shocking omission. 'Oh, dearie me, we forgot to bring a hairbrush!'

'Calamity.' Edgar smiled wryly as he drew a comb out of his top pocket. 'You can borrow this if you like.'

'No, ta — it'll be covered in Brylcreem. We'll borrow Grace's brush. Oh, and we forgot lipstick as well!' Brenda wailed.

'Can't lend you any of that, I'm afraid.' Edgar's mouth twitched as he put the comb back in his pocket. 'Shall I let Grace know you're here?'

He was about to mount the narrow stairs to his sister's room when he spotted a green van pull up in the yard and saw Joyce Cutler open the driver's door. She went straight round to the back and lifted out two baskets of flowers. 'On second thoughts, you two go on up while I help Joyce with those.'

He left the house in a flash, leaving Brenda to raise a conspiratorial eyebrow. 'See that, Una? The moment Edgar claps eyes on Joyce we don't see him for dust.'

'Aah!' Una went to the small window. 'They're both blushing. Joyce has dropped one of the buttonholes . . . Edgar's stooping to pick it up. She's turned red as a beetroot . . . '

'Here, let the dog see the rabbit.' Brenda pushed Una to one side in time to see Edgar replace the carnation in the basket. A look passed between the blushing pair — Brenda would have called it a look of unspoken longing, except this was down-to-earth, steady-as-you-go Joyce and buttoned-up, war-damaged Edgar Kershaw they were talking about.

⋆ ⋆ ⋆

'Ta,' Joyce said. 'I've got more flowers in the van: two arrangements for the church, plus three bouquets for the bride and bridesmaids.'

'Let me help you with them.' Edgar leaned in and lifted out a large spray of pink roses in a silver vase. He handed it to Joyce then pulled out a second, identical arrangement. Together they crossed the road.

'So how is life treating you?' Joyce struggled to keep her voice steady. The last she'd heard, Grace hadn't been certain that Edgar would manage to get leave, so it had taken Joyce aback to see him stride out of the pub, large as life. Not that she'd expected to be told. After all, he was his own man and she was an independent woman — without ties or responsibilities. 'Are you well?'

'Fit as a fiddle now that my leg's finally stopped giving me gip,' he assured her.

Neither mentioned the dark time in the autumn of the previous year when his plane had been shot down over France and he'd lost his co-pilot and best pal in a ball of flame — a period that had seen him stricken with inexplicable guilt and struggling to find a good reason to go on living.

'I'm pleased to hear it.' Joyce entered the church before him. 'And I'm glad you made it back home for Grace's big day.'

He nodded briskly. 'The raids on Cologne are over for now but they'll need me back pronto for a new push — I can't say where.'

'Of course not.' Joyce heard enough details about the war on the wireless news to know that the RAF was engaged in constant heavy raids all over Germany. 'Were you involved in the campaign to hang on to Malta?'

Another nod was accompanied by a faint flicker of the eyelids.

'Sorry — I shouldn't ask.'

'No, it's fine. Malta's in safe hands for the time being. The Allies on the ground are bringing Jerry down like tame pigeons.'

War talk sat oddly with the rich calm of the church interior. Multicoloured shafts of light streamed in through the stained-glass windows and the mellow scent of pine resin mixed with beeswax rose from the pews and the ornately carved pulpit. Joyce and Edgar carried the roses

7

down the central aisle and placed them by the altar. In a niche behind the choir stalls, Esther Liddell, the grey-haired organist and village post mistress, kept her back turned as she rearranged sheets of music in preparation for the service.

'Not long to go now.' Joyce tweaked the flower arrangement that Edgar had set down. 'Do you know how Grace is coping with her wedding jitters?'

He shook his head. Joyce was the one person in the village whom he'd genuinely looked forward to seeing during his brief leave, but now that they were together, he felt tongue tied. She still had that quality of quiet calm about her that he remembered from December — a restfulness that had soothed his bruised spirit. And he loved her rich voice emerging from soft, full lips; her fair, smooth complexion; the mannish uniform that only served to emphasize her feminine curves. *Steady on*, he told himself. *Now is not the time or the place.*

'This is the biggest day of a girl's life.' Satisfied with the roses, Joyce accompanied Edgar back down the aisle. When she reached the church porch, she picked a buttonhole from the basket she'd left there. 'Would you like me to pin this on for you?'

He nodded and watched her slim fingers attach the carnation to his lapel. 'It's good to see you, Joyce,' he said quietly. Then, as she finished with the flowers, he took a step back and turned with a dip of his head and a military click of his heels before heading through the gate and across the road without looking round.

8

Inside the pub, Una hovered at the bottom of the stairs while Brenda went up and tapped on Grace's door.

'It's only us,' Brenda called softly.

There was no reply.

'Grace, are you there?' She knocked a second time.

Feeling a small stab of alarm, Una followed Brenda up the stairs.

'Yes. Come in.' Grace's answer came at last — subdued and hesitant.

Brenda pushed the door open and saw the bride sitting at her dressing table. Her wedding dress was only partly zipped and she was shaking from head to foot. 'Look at you!' she exclaimed. 'Less than an hour to go and you haven't put on a scrap of make-up.'

'I'd only make a mess of it if I tried.' Grace turned on her stool to show Brenda and Una her trembling hands. Her wavy blonde hair was swept up to reveal her long, graceful neck. The demure, calf-length dress had a high neckline and long, narrow sleeves edged with lace.

'Never mind; that's what Una and I are here for — to get you ready for your big day.' Recognizing what needed to be done, Brenda zipped Grace up then turned her towards the mirror. 'See how beautiful you look,' she murmured, her hands resting softly on Grace's shoulders as she studied her reflection.

'Yes, who needs lipstick and rouge with a face like yours?' Una saw the bride's shoes nestled in tissue paper in a cardboard box on the narrow bed and brought them to her. She crouched down to help her slide her feet into them. 'You always look the bee's knees, even when we're out in a field, up to our ankles in mud, digging up turnips.'

Grace gave a wan smile. 'You're only saying that.'

'It's true,' Brenda insisted. 'You're a da Vinci painting come to life.' There was no one like Grace for serene, classical beauty. 'You're the envy of every girl at Fieldhead if you did but know it.'

'But am I doing the right thing by marrying Bill?' Grace blurted out the question that had been on her lips since she rose at dawn after a sleepless night. She caught Brenda and Una's startled expressions in the mirror. 'I know — I've left it a bit late in the day to change my mind, haven't I?'

Brenda tried to brush the doubt away with a breezy response. 'It's a woman's prerogative, isn't it?' She glanced again at Grace's reflection. 'But you're not serious, are you?'

'No. Yes. I don't know.' Caught in a helpless whirl of emotions, Grace was on the verge of tears. Part of the problem was that she'd known Bill for so long — they'd grown up together in Burnside and been playmates, fishing for tiddlers in the beck or climbing trees in the copse at the back of the pub. Romance had only come into the picture at the age of fourteen or fifteen, once they'd started attending village hops and beetle drives at the Institute. In fact, she could remember the exact moment when everything had changed — she and Bill had been dancing a Scottish reel and he had caught her around the waist and swung her off her feet. She'd landed breathless and laughing then looked straight into his eyes. His arm had still been around her waist, their lips had almost touched.

'Don't worry. Everyone gets the jitters on their wedding day,' Brenda assured her. 'I know I would.'

'It's only natural,' Una agreed. She picked up the bridal headdress from the glass-topped dressing table: a velvet band festooned with white silk flowers that would perch beautifully on top of Grace's upswept hair. There would be no veil since clothing coupons hadn't run to the purchase of the necessary length of gauzy fabric. It had been hard enough to scrape together the points for the dress material itself — she, Brenda and Joyce had added their coupons to Grace's, which wasn't strictly in accordance with wartime rationing rules but who would be mean enough to snitch on them for an occasion like a wedding? The bridesmaids' dresses had proved more of a problem, which had eventually been solved by an under-the-counter acquisition of twelve yards of white parachute silk. Una and Brenda had dyed it lilac in a big vat on the hostel stove, then spent many hours cutting and stitching in their spare time after hay had been made, eggs gathered, pigs fed and cows milked.

'But do I love him?' Grace's plaintive question filled the small room.

Brenda frowned as she took in the cross-stitched pictures of poppies above Grace's bed. Wherever she cast her gaze, the plain white-washed walls displayed examples of a younger Grace's craft skills — pressed flowers and clover leaves in small frames beneath an intricate marquetry picture of a sailing ship. The iron bedstead was covered by a patchwork quilt, the starched pillow cases were edged with daisy embroidery. What a leap it would be from this old-fashioned, nun-like space to married life with Bill Mostyn. 'Of course you do,' she faltered.

'Why? *Why* do I love him?'

Una stepped into the silent breach. 'Because you'll always be able to rely on Bill. You can trust him and know that he won't let you down.'

Brenda nudged her with her elbow and tutted. 'Hush — Grace isn't thinking of buying a second-hand car!'

'No — you have to be able to rely on the man you marry.' Una defended her opinion with flushed cheeks. That was the thing about her Angelo — though he was an Italian prisoner of war presently working hundreds of miles away in the Greenock docks, she would trust him with her life.

'I do know that,' Grace agreed. 'I'm not saying that Bill is unreliable. I'm only trying to get clear in my mind the reasons why I said yes to marrying him.'

'Because he's the best-looking man in Burnside?' Brenda chipped in. 'Call me shallow, but that would be good enough reason for me.'

12

'Because he's kind,' Una added, using her own elbow against Brenda hard enough to knock her to one side. Trust Brenda to put her foot in it by calling to mind the time last winter when she had set her own cap at Bill.

Her fellow bridesmaid was not to be put off. 'And he drives a nice car and owns the whole of Mostyn Tractor Repair Company now that his old man has kicked the bucket.'

Grace put up her hands in surrender. 'All right, you win,' she said with a sigh. It was time to dismiss her doubts and pull herself together, to go through with what she'd promised. 'That's enough about how I'm feeling. What about you two?'

'Nervous as a kitten,' Una confessed.

'Tip-top,' Brenda contradicted. 'Who wouldn't be? The bride is beautiful, the sun has come out and the church bells are starting to ring.'

As she spoke, a loud peal of bells woke up the slumbering main street. It coincided with the arrival of twenty Land Girls in the back of a lorry borrowed from the Canadian Air Force base on Penny Lane. They piled out on to the pavement in breeches and jumpers, felt hats tilted at jaunty angles — Kathleen Hirst and Elsie Walker among them. Kathleen spotted Una at Grace's bedroom window and waved up at her. Elsie stayed in the lorry to hand down rakes and pitchforks to the waiting gang.

'The guard of honour has arrived,' Una reported to Brenda and Grace. She spotted Joyce handing out white buttonholes to Jean Fox and the two new girls, Doreen Wells and Poppy Gledhill.

13

'Oh, Lord!' Grace drew a deep breath. 'I mustn't be late. Brenda, lend me a hand with my make-up. Una, are my stocking seams straight? These shoes feel much too tight. I'm sure I've gone and bought the wrong size.'

\* \* \*

The groom had decided to leave his car at home and walk arm in arm with his mother the short distance from their house at the bottom end of the main street to St Michael's in the centre of the village. There they would meet his best man, Jack Hudson. Jack and he would escort Edith down the aisle to the empty front pew on the groom's side. Jack would sit with her to keep her company while Bill waited at the altar.

He heard the familiar click of the garden gate shutting behind them as they set off and the sound of his steel-tipped heels clipping the pavement. His mother leaned lightly on his arm.

Edith Mostyn had taken a long time to dress, even though she'd chosen her outfit weeks before — a slim-fitting grey linen suit with a heathery tinge that would sit well alongside the brides-maid's lilac dresses. Bill's mother cared about such things. Her blouse was made of deep purple silk to match the shallow-brimmed hat perched to one side of her head. A delicate black veil hung over the brim to cover half of her face.

'How do I look?' she'd asked before they set off.

'Champion,' he'd told her in the reassuring tone his father would have used.

And now here they were, walking up the street under fresh green lime trees and silver birches, recognizing every crack in the pavement and every moss-covered stone in the wall. They passed the first of two street lamps and a pothole in the road where Neville Thomson's cart had come to grief a week before — the wooden axle had broken and the cart's load of horse muck had spilled across the road. It had stayed there for two whole days, causing a terrible stink, until Maurice Baxendale had loaded it into the back of his van and driven it away.

Bill's mother gripped his arm a little tighter as they reached the second lamp post and spied the Land Girls gathered outside the church. As the local Land Army representative she was anxious for the girls to be on best behaviour throughout the day. She needn't have worried, for the moment they spotted the groom and his mother approaching the church, they formed straight lines to either side of the path and raised their pitchforks and rakes to make a ceremonial arch. Edith gave a stiff smile as she processed beneath it.

The bells rang loud and clear as Bill and his mother shook hands with Jack in the church porch. The best man was bursting with pride in his chief petty officer's uniform, resplendent with braided cuffs, with his white cap worn low on his forehead. He winked at Bill as they entered the church. Heads turned. The women assessed Edith's outfit while the men waited impatiently for things to get under way. At the front of the church on the bride's side, Edgar sat and stared

15

straight ahead, his emotions unexpectedly stirred by the pealing bells and the solemn face of the vicar taking his place with Bill at the altar. Now they must wait for the bride.

★   ★   ★

In spite of the last-minute rush, Grace stood ready in the pub yard before the bells fell silent. Una and Brenda fussed at her dress and adjusted their own headdresses — smaller, less elaborate versions of the one Grace was wearing — while Joyce dashed across the road to hand the bride her bouquet.

'Your posies are waiting for you in the porch,' she muttered hastily to the bridesmaids before hurrying back to take up her position among the ranked Land Girls.

Grace looked around for her father, of whom she'd seen neither hide nor hair all morning. Where on earth was he?

'Wait here. I'll go and find him.' Interpreting Grace's anxious glance and knowing that Cliff Kershaw wasn't in the house, Una ran towards the forge and discovered him there, his jowly face mottled from the build-up of nerves, his celluloid collar buttoned tight around his neck, watch chain looped across his broad chest over a brown three-piece suit. 'Hurry up — Grace is waiting for you,' she told him.

He glanced around at the tools of his blacksmithing trade — bellows against the wall, empty furnace door hanging open, leather apron slung across the anvil, hammers of varying sizes suspended from iron hooks — and seemed to draw comfort from them. 'I don't know why a wedding has to come with all this faff,' he muttered in a voice thickened by cigarette smoke, alcohol and old age. 'Especially when there's a war on.'

'The 'faff' is what it's all about, Mr Kershaw.' Una smiled and squeezed the old man's arm then led him out of the smithy. 'There's Grace — now, doesn't she look lovely?'

'The spitting image of her mother on her wedding day,' he mumbled, too low to be heard. Struck by the similarity, he strode ahead to join his daughter.

Strains of organ music issued from the church as Grace took her father's arm and the bridal party crossed the empty street. Joyce, Kathleen, Elsie and the rest formed the arch for a second time.

'Rightio, here we go!' Brenda murmured as Grace and her father paused nervously in the porch. She signalled their arrival to the usher, Maurice Baxendale, who passed the information to his brother, Bob, waiting by the organ pipes, who in turn prompted Esther Liddell.

Bill cleared his throat and cast a look of panic in Jack's direction. He saw his mother with her chin tilted upwards, swallowing hard and already fighting back tears. Then, inside the porch, he glimpsed a woman in a white dress next to a stocky, balding figure. It was Grace and Cliff. The wedding was about to start.

As the organist struck up the 'Wedding March', Grace held her bouquet at chest height like a shield and breathed in the fusty smell of dust rising in the summer heat. She turned to her father and smiled.

# 2

'I'll let you all in on a little secret.' Jack Hudson's best man's speech drew to a close. He'd listed Bill's good points — his generosity towards his pals (he'd never, in all the years Jack had known him, missed paying for his round of drinks in the Blacksmith's Arms), his decent and fair way of conducting business (everyone knew they wouldn't be over-charged or short-changed when Bill Mostyn mended your tractor), his willingness to shoulder sole responsibility for the firm after the recent sad death of his father (a gentle nod at this point towards Edith, who acknowledged the respectful reference with another stiff smile). 'In spite of all the nice things I've listed,' Jack concluded from the head of the long table running down the centre of the Institute hall, 'and this is a big 'but' — Bill is a devil for being the first under the shower after a Saturday-afternoon football match. He may be a gentleman on the pitch — no foul tackles when the ref's back is turned — *but* if Bill finds himself at the back of the queue for a shower in the changing room afterwards, he won't think twice about shoulder-charging his way to the front. He sends bars of soap, loofahs and what have you flying in his rush to get there.'

'That's right!' The Baxendale brothers banged the table. 'He does it every time.'

'You hear that, Mr White — the Institute needs

more showers.' Neville Thomson from Brigg Farm added his raucous twopenn'orth. 'The two we have aren't anywhere near enough. And the water's always cold by the time I get there.'

Arnold White leaned back in his chair, resting his hands on his sons' shoulders. 'I don't hear these two boys complaining.'

'That's because Donald and Les always shoot straight off home after a match. They can have a shower at your house any day of the week.' Maurice followed young Neville in putting his head above the parapet. Old man White was a fast-talking, hard-headed farmer who resented any hint of criticism. And the fact was that he, along with the Fosters of Hawkshead Manor, had control of the Institute purse strings.

Though it was the natural choice of venue for wedding receptions, Saturday-night hops and Christmas pantomimes, the fifty-year-old Village Institute building was showing its age. Limewash flaked from its walls and the leaking central-heating pipes left rusty puddles on the wooden floor. The red velvet curtains across stage and windows were faded, the room was still lit by gaslight and, more to the point, the changing-room facilities were definitely below par.

'I'll put it on the agenda for the next commit-tee meeting,' Arnold grunted as he thrust his weight forward and the front legs of his chair thudded down. The fifty-eight-year-old widower gave off an air of prosperity in his dark, double-breasted suit and expensive silk tie. 'But there's a good deal of costly plumbing involved in that sort of thing, so don't build up your hopes.'

Jack tapped the table with the end of his knife to restore order. 'You're sorry I brought it up, eh, Bill?'

'Yes, move on,' the groom prompted with a good-natured grin. 'But I'll thank you not to let on about any of my other bad habits.'

'You mean leaving the toilet seat up and the lid off the tin of boot polish, shying away from spiders in the bath . . . ' Jack counted off sly examples on his fingers.

'Hush, Grace doesn't need to know any of this until after her honeymoon, poor love.' Joyce's intervention drew smiles from everyone.

'Anyway, taking a shower isn't a crime.' Brenda spoke from her seat next to Una near the top of the table. 'In fact, in my opinion a man can't be too keen on personal hygiene — especially not at close quarters, if you know what I mean.'

She raised an eyebrow at the innuendo, which was greeted with a laugh and a few suppressed giggles.

'Move on, Jack,' Bill urged again. He clasped Grace's hand reassuringly. These speeches took some getting through, though the bride's father's had been mercifully short and sweet, ending in a toast, and Bill had restricted his own to the obligatory thanks to bridesmaids and ushers followed by more deeply felt compliments to Grace. Now, once Jack had stumbled to the end of the speechifying, the room could be cleared to allow a four-piece band to set up their instruments and the dancing would begin.

* ★ ★ ★

'How do you think the day went?' Grace was anxious to hear Joyce's answer as they sat together in a quiet corner of the bar. It was early evening, after the band at the Institute had packed up and left, prompting the remaining wedding guests to repair to the Blacksmith's Arms. The pub door was open and late sun streamed into the low-ceilinged, oak-panelled room.

Joyce, who had changed out of her uniform into a summer dress of green printed cotton, squeezed Grace's hand. 'Swimmingly. It couldn't have gone better.'

Grace's mind flew back over the day's events — the solemn march up the aisle with her father; Bill's pale, serious face as he'd made his vows; the new Land Girl, Doreen Wells, jumping high in the air outside the church to catch the bride's bouquet. 'What about the speeches?'

'All tickety-boo,' Joyce insisted. She glanced towards the bar to see Grace's father at home behind his row of beer pumps — jacket off, sleeves rolled up, serving with a genial smile. Edgar was there too, looking relaxed as he pushed pint glasses over the counter towards Bill, Jack and Maurice. 'I'm glad your dad made mention of Edgar. It showed everyone how proud he is of him.'

'Yes, Edgar's come on a long way since Christmas.' Grace stared fondly at her brother. 'I haven't had much time to talk to him, though. And before we know it he'll be back in action

22

and I'll have to start worrying about him all over again.'

'I noticed the two White brothers squirm when your dad praised him.'

Grace scanned the room for the White contingent and spotted them in a snug alcove next to the ingle-nook. Arnold and his two sons had been joined by a late arrival in the shape of Donald and Les's sister, Hettie, who had stepped into her mother's shoes after Mary White's death ten years earlier. Hettie White was now in her mid thirties, the oldest of the three siblings and a force to be reckoned with; a handsome woman with strong, symmetrical features and a sweep of almost black hair lifted back from her high, wide forehead into a fashionable chignon. 'Why — what did Dad say to offend them?'

'It wasn't so much what he said as the long sideways look he gave them. Donald's got himself a bad name for avoiding conscription a couple of times.'

Living away from the Land Girls' hostel, Grace sometimes missed such gossip. 'Oh, on what grounds?'

'The first time around it was because he claimed he had polio as a child.'

'And did he?'

Joyce shrugged. 'More recently it was because he told them he was a Quaker and a pacifist.'

Grace raised her eyebrows in surprise. 'But the Whites are Catholics.'

'You and I know that but the authorities didn't cotton on, so they accepted his excuses and made him join the Home Guard instead. It's a safe enough bet — everyone knows there's not much call for buckets of sand and stirrup pumps in this neck of the woods.'

Grace nodded thoughtfully. 'It can only be a matter of time before Les gets his call-up papers, though. What is he now — twenty-one or twenty-two?'

Joyce shrugged her shoulders. 'Something like that. Meanwhile, rumour has it that Brenda has got her eye on him so the poor boy had better watch out.'

'Like a lamb to the slaughter,' Grace agreed. A glance across the room at Brenda, Elsie and Kathleen in a huddle with five Canadians told her that Les White was safe for now. 'You know the queer thing about today? I expected to remember every detail but the fact is it's mostly been one big blur.'

'Nerves will do that to you.' As Bill left his pals at the bar and headed in their direction, Joyce stood up. 'Well, Mrs Mostyn, I'll love you and leave you,' she said.

Grace gave a small gasp of astonishment at the sound of her new name then glanced down at the thin band of gold nestling next to her diamond and ruby engagement ring. 'How long do you suppose it'll take me to get used to hearing that?'

'How long is your honeymoon?'

'Two days. Bill and I have to be back at work on Tuesday.'

'Then I predict that's how long it'll take you to forget you were ever Grace Kershaw.' Joyce

24

smiled down at her then brushed Bill's shoulder lightly as she stepped aside for him to sit down. 'And may Mr and Mrs Mostyn live happily ever after.'

⋆ ⋆ ⋆

'You look worn out.' Hilda Craven, the warden at Fieldhead, had joined Bill's mother at the tail end of the wedding celebrations to help supervise the girls from the hostel. She sat down beside her and patted her hand. 'Why not go home and lie down?'

Edith shook her head. 'Not until Bill and Grace have left for their honeymoon. Grace is upstairs getting changed into her going-away outfit.'

'Then come outside and sit in the sun with me.' Hilda's insistence was kindly meant. Though she and Edith didn't always see eye to eye on Land Army matters — Edith being strict and sticking to the letter of the law while Hilda liked to fuss and mollycoddle the girls — today the warden's chief concern was to look after her old acquaintance. So she stood up and led the way. 'Come along, no arguments.'

Edith followed obediently and soon the two women settled on a bench beside the wide smithy door. 'I can't stay away for too long. I have to keep an eye on Poppy and Doreen. They haven't had time to settle in properly yet.'

'They'll be fine,' Hilda insisted. 'Doreen for one can take care of herself. And Joyce or one of the other old-timers will look after young Poppy for you. Now, tell me honestly, Edith — how are you feeling about Bill and Grace getting married? This isn't what you and Vince originally hoped for, is it?'

Hilda's characteristic bluntness raised a frown on Edith's carefully powdered features. Twelve months ago — a year that now felt like a lifetime — Edith and Vince's sights had been set on an alliance with the Fosters, the landowning family whose daughter Shirley had looked like a bright marriage prospect for the up-and-coming Mostyns. Now all that was dissolved into dust. Within weeks of Bill revealing that he and Grace had been secretly engaged for months, Shirley had got herself hitched to an RAF squadron leader. Worse still, Vince's heart operation in the week before Christmas had only lengthened his life by a few short months. He'd passed away on Easter Monday and now she, Edith, was left alone to see her son married and about to fly the nest. 'Perhaps I wish they'd waited a little longer,' she said with a sigh.

'Young ones don't go in for long engagements — not these days.' Hilda didn't have to spell out that the reason for this was the war and the all too present threat of being killed in action. Imminent danger had brought about many a tumble in the hay followed in short order by a headlong dash to the altar. 'At least you can rest easy that Bill and Grace's feelings are genuine — one look at the pair of them together tells you that. And they've known each other long enough.'

Ordinarily Edith would have kept up a barrier

against Hilda's frank observations but today she didn't protest. With her hands folded on her lap and with the loud hum of conversation and the chink of glasses drifting out through the door, she gazed wearily ahead.

'Grace is a lovely girl — I don't think Bill could have chosen better.' Her companion went blithely on. 'She's always ready to lend a helping hand, maybe a bit quiet and studious for some, but just right for your Bill, who's smart as can be and steady with it. If you ask me, it's a match made in heaven.'

As they talked they noticed Bill drive his car up the street, park it in the yard then hurry into the pub. Soon afterwards Jack, Bob and Maurice emerged from the smithy armed with old tin cans, which they tied to the back bumper along with a 'Just Married' placard. There was some good-humoured banter and time for a quick smoke before the sneaky trio disappeared back inside.

'Are you ready to wave off the happy couple?' Hilda asked Edith.

'As I'll ever be.' Preparing herself for what could not be avoided, Edith stood up. She had a vivid memory of Vince on his deathbed giving his blessing to the marriage then reminded herself that he was here in spirit, looking down from above. The thought brought her a grain of comfort as Bill and Grace walked arm in arm into a pool of golden, late-evening sunshine.

Bridesmaids and groomsmen accompanied them into the yard followed by dozens of guests ready to clap and cheer them on their way.

Brenda, Una, Joyce and Kathleen threw the remainder of the confetti as Bill and Grace got into the car. At the last moment, Bill turned and walked towards his mother to embrace her. He held her slight frame close to his chest and murmured a heartfelt thank-you before he released her.

The pain of letting him go brought tears to Edith's eyes.

'You'll be all right?' he asked.

She nodded and drew her veil over her eyes.

'I'll telephone you as soon as we get to Attercliffe.'

'No need,' she said firmly. 'This is Grace's day. Look after her.'

She saw him off with the others, heard the rattle of tin cans over cobbles, noticed Grace in her royal-blue going-away dress lean out of the window to wave goodbye to her father and brother.

The car approached the junction and the hubbub subsided. As the wedding guests filtered back inside, Edith gathered herself to walk down the straight, narrow street towards her gleaming, modern but empty house.

* * *

'So, Poppy — what do you make of our Canadian friends?' Brenda collared the new-comer after they bumped into each other during a visit to the outside ladies' toilet. Both were tiddly after a long afternoon and evening of celebrating. Brenda's lilac silk dress was creased

28

and she'd cast aside her Alice band headdress. Poppy, meanwhile, looked cool and fresh in a pale blue dress with a demure neckline and a nipped-in waist.

'They're different,' Poppy admitted. The question had brought a flush to her pale cheeks.

'Yes, I've noticed you admiring them from afar.'

'I've only ever seen men like them when I go to the flicks — Clark Gable, and so on.'

'But they're not American, even though they sound similar. Still, I wouldn't be surprised if we do get the Yanks camping out over here now that they're finally about to get their sleeves rolled up in the Far East.' Brenda walked Poppy across the yard towards the pub. There was something about the young recruit that made Brenda feel she needed looking after, like a tender plant that should be watered and protected from rough winds. After all, Poppy had just turned eighteen and had taken Una's place as the baby of the gang when she'd shown up at Fieldhead a week earlier. 'There's plenty of room for them at Beckwith Camp, now that the Italian prisoners have moved on up to bonnie Scotland.'

'I thought the Canadians had moved into Beckwith?'

'That's right, but they don't fill the whole of the POW camp. A lot of those Nissen huts are still standing empty.' Brenda paused outside the door to offer Poppy a cigarette.

'No, ta. I don't.'

So Brenda lit up and leaned on the door jamb, flicking the spent match to the ground. 'You're sharing a room at the hostel with Joyce and Doreen. How's that working out?'

'Fine, ta. Joyce is teaching us the ropes.' In her first working days Poppy had learned how to groom Major, the Thomsons' cart horse, and to muck out his stable, then to collect eggs at Horace Turnbull's hen farm on Winsill Edge. For an eighteen-year-old canteen worker in one of the big Millwood woollen mills who hadn't known one end of a pitchfork from the other, this was good going.

'Yes, you stick with Joyce — she'll look after you.' Brenda blew out a narrow cloud of blue smoke. 'And take a word of advice from another old hand: the safest place to admire a Canadian is from a distance, the way you are now.'

'Why is that?' Wondering why Brenda didn't seem to follow her own advice, Poppy sensed a story behind the words.

'It just is, that's all.' Brenda threw down her half-smoked cigarette and ground it underfoot. She'd gone as far as she wanted to with that topic of conversation. 'Come on, Pops — let me introduce you to the best man. He's a much safer bet.'

They went inside into a fug of smoke and bursts of laughter as the evening tipped towards uninhibited enjoyment. The moment Les White spotted Brenda's return, he launched himself in her direction, almost tripping over a chair leg and regaining his balance by grabbing hold of his brother, Donald, who brushed him down then re-launched him. Les arrived at Brenda's side, swaying unsteadily.

'Hello, Bren — I wondered where you'd got to.'

'We were doing what a girl has to do, weren't we, Pops?' She laughed at Les's evident embarrassment. 'I mean we were powdering our noses.'

'So, will you dance with me?' he blurted out. 'Come on, Brenda. As soon as Donald has set himself up at the old Joanna, can we have a dance?'

She smiled and nodded as she noticed the piano in the corner of the room being wheeled out and saw Les's brother open the lid. 'There you are, Jack!' She seized the best man's arm as he squeezed by. 'Meet Poppy Gledhill. Pops, meet Jack. You two will get along swimmingly, I'm sure.'

And then she was gone to help Les clear away chairs and tables to create a small space for dancing, leaving Poppy lost for words in the face of a surprised Jack Hudson.

'I'm sorry . . . ' She gestured towards Brenda. 'I mean, you don't have to.'

Jack took in her flushed cheeks and flawless, pale skin. She came up to his shoulder, and was slim and supple as a willow wand, with wavy, fair hair and blue eyes flecked with violet. 'I certainly don't have to but I want to,' he replied as he gallantly offered her his arm. 'Is that a waltz that Donald's playing?'

'No, it's a foxtrot.'

'A foxtrot, eh?' They reached the already crowded dance area and took up the ballroom hold. 'I've got two left feet so I'll have to rely on

31

you to show me how.'

Poppy smiled up at him and blushed. 'I'm not very good either.'

'Then we'll learn together. Ready? One-two-three, one-two-three.'

'That's waltz time,' she reminded him with a tap on his shoulder. 'The foxtrot has four beats to the bar — one-two-three-four, off we go.'

★　★　★

The problem for Brenda was that she was drawn to Canadians like a moth to a flame. Or rather, to Jim Aldridge, the squadron leader at the Penny Lane HQ, who had dealt with the whole horrible mess concerning John Mackenzie, his second in command. Mack the Knife, as Brenda now thought of him, had turned out to be as violent and unscrupulous as Bertolt Brecht's stage villain when he'd attacked her in the changing rooms after the Land Girls' Christmas show. She still avoided the word 'rape', though this is what he'd have gone through with if Kathleen hadn't come on to the scene and stopped him. With her fellow Land Girl as a witness, and with Joyce, Una and Grace's support, she'd found the courage to report her attacker and Aldridge had believed her unhesitatingly. Mackenzie had been put under military arrest and sent away, never to be seen or heard of again.

Since the Mack the Knife incident, Brenda's and Aldridge's paths had seldom crossed. She saw him occasionally at a church service and once or twice when she'd been sent on an errand and had ridden Old Sloper along Penny Lane to the old isolation hospital, now commandeered by the Canadian Air Force authorities. He always acknowledged her with more kindness and respect than she suspected she deserved, for she carried a victim's guilt with her wherever she went. After all, she had flirted openly with Mackenzie and perhaps given him the wrong idea. People in Burnside still looked at her quizzically and some judged her harshly, she could tell. *They believe I brought it on myself,* she thought with a sickening thud of realization. *In future, I must watch my p's and q's.*

But it was like telling a leopard to change its spots — there was no altering Brenda's outgoing nature and *joie de vivre*, her tomboyish sense of adventure and love of taking risks.

Some of this went through her mind as she danced the foxtrot with Les, though she tried to bring herself back to the here and now by teasing him about his ballroom-dancing prowess. 'You must have had lessons,' she chirped as he led her effortlessly in the military two-step that followed the foxtrot. Donald played with gusto, thumping out the bass notes in a heavy marching rhythm. 'Have you? Did your dad send you to classes to keep you off the streets?'

Les's cheeks coloured up. 'You must be joking. Dad would far rather see me covered in mud, playing in goal for the Burnside eleven.'

'Dancing is strictly for sissies, eh?'

He swept her across the floor regardless 'Something like that. Our Hettie was the one

33

that taught us behind his back. Dancing and piano. She must have reckoned they were good ways to impress the girls.'

Brenda spotted Les's sister still sitting with their father by the fireplace. There was a strong resemblance between the two, despite Arnold's white hair being set against the jet-black tresses of his daughter. Both were tall and spare, with deep-set, dark eyes that gave off an intense, often critical stare. Arnold had taken off his jacket and sat in waistcoat and shirt-sleeves, while Hettie's late arrival meant that she wasn't as festively dressed as the other wedding guests. She wore a tailored two-piece costume in finely woven, plum-coloured linen, teamed with a white blouse and black court shoes to give a prim, bank-clerk effect. 'You don't say! You mean there's a fun-loving side to your dragon of a sister?'

Les tilted his head to one side and had the grace to bark out a laugh. 'Yes, though it might not look like it from the outside. Anyway, enough about Hettie. How is the Land Army treating you? I hear they work your fingers to the bone?'

'Oh yes indeedy — we lift hay bales and follow the plough from dawn till dusk.' Brenda gave an exaggerated sigh. 'We scythe and we dig. Roland Thomson out at Brigg Farm even has us mending stone walls if he gets half a chance. Not to mention rat-catching up at the Kelletts' place.'

Shy Les ventured a compliment. 'You look well on it, though.' He thought Brenda's looks were striking — she was someone you would always notice in a crowd, with her dark hair cropped short and her lively, laughing features.

But he was wary of her in case her teasing turned into contempt.

'There's no call for callisthenics or health and beauty classes when you turn your hand to farm labouring. I gave all that up when I came to live at Fieldhead.' Brenda enjoyed the sensation of Les's hand placed firmly in the small of her back and let herself appreciate his features close up. His style was clean cut, his chin shaved so close that his skin almost shone. His eyes were clear grey and his fair hair neatly parted, his only defect being a nose that was slightly too large for his face. On the whole this gave him more character and improved his manliness, she decided.

The music stopped and couples drifted back to rejoin their drinking companions. Brenda spared a thought for Grace and Bill, who must have arrived at their honeymoon destination by now. She mused briefly on how it would be for Grace later on in her first shared bed and hoped that the reality of married life wouldn't come as too much of a shock.

'Drink?' Les said, breaking into her thoughts.

'Oh, yes ta!' Though Donald had struck up another tune, she abandoned the dance floor and followed her partner to the bar, feeling Hettie's intense stare burning a hole in her back as she did so. 'It's a Dubonnet for me, please. But be careful — the Dragon is watching us,' she said with a wink.

Les laughed again before ordering the drinks. 'I'll tell her if you don't watch out.'

'Tell her what?'

'About the dragon tag.'

'And will she come breathing fire all over me?' Brenda took her drink. She liked that laugh and set herself the task of drawing it out of him for a third time. 'Ought I to take cover while I can?'

'Oh no, don't do that.' He set his pint glass back down on the copper bar top and unexpectedly took her in a dance hold to whirl her back on to the floor. 'This one's too good to miss,' he explained. 'It's a Glenn Miller number — 'Chattanooga Choo Choo'. It came out last year — do you know it?'

'Do I know it? I sat through *Sun Valley Serenade* twice without a break. 'Pardon me, boy, is that the Chattanooga Choo Choo?'' As they launched into the dance, Brenda began to sing an uninhibited version of the famous song.

''Whoo-whoo!'' Les raised his arm to twirl her then drew her back to him. They danced on cheek to cheek, disregarding the stares of other couples such as Jack and Poppy and Joyce and Edgar. When the big band number finished, they stayed on the floor and went straight into a slow waltz, after which Donald stood up and declared that it was his turn to dance.

'Les, you'll have to sit and tinkle the ivories for a bit. I've done my stint.'

No sooner said than the brothers had changed places and Brenda was left high and dry without a partner. She looked around the room and saw that they were short of eligible men. Jack had handed Poppy to an eager Neville then made a beeline for Una, while Doreen had boldly claimed Donald as a partner. Maurice was still

36

propping up the bar with his brother, but the two Baxendales were a bit over the hill for Brenda's taste. There was nothing else for it — she would have to ask Squadron Leader Aldridge to dance.

Deliberately toning down her usual bravado, she approached him with a flutter in her stomach. She needn't have worried — Jim Aldridge greeted Brenda with a smile and said he would be honoured.

'You look as if you're in the pink,' he told her, holding her in a gentlemanly way — not too close but not stiffly. 'I guess Land Army life must suit you.'

'It suits me better now that summer's here,' she agreed. 'No more frostbite and chilblains, thank heavens.'

'We're all glad of that,' he agreed. 'Even though we're used to a few months of sub-zero temperatures back home.' Polite and warm at the same time, Aldridge let Brenda know that he was glad to dance with her and establish that there were no hard feelings after the John Mackenzie episode. 'What's your favourite summertime activity?'

'Do you mean work or play time?'

'Either.'

'All right, so what I love most of all about living out here is the chance to set off on Old Sloper on a sunny Sunday morning.'

'Old Sloper?'

'My motor bike. I'm up with the lark and set off up the dale then over the top to Attercliffe. Often I don't see another soul. There's just me and hills and blue sky — oh, and sheep!'

'Sheep,' he echoed. 'I didn't have you down as a genuine country girl.'

'I'm not,' she admitted. 'I worked in a butcher's shop in Northgate before I joined up. I could tell you the difference between shoulder of lamb and pork loin at the drop of a hat, but if you'd asked me how to pick out a Herdwick sheep or a Gloucester Old Spot, I couldn't have told you for all the tea in China.'

*What a waste.* Aldridge imagined Brenda behind a butcher's shop counter and quickly decided she had too much spirit and originality for such humdrum work. He suspected that it was the same way with a lot of the Land Army girls and saw that the outbreak of hostilities had in a strange way liberated many of them. 'And what will you do after the war ends?' he asked. 'Will you go back to . . . ?'

'Northgate.' Brenda shrugged her shoulders. 'I'm not saying yes, I'm not saying no. We'll have to wait and see.'

He nodded as the slow, sedate waltz came to an end. 'I guess that's true for everyone. At this point in time none of us can plan very far ahead.'

'That's right — we can't.'

They smiled and separated. Les upped the tempo for one of his big band favourites while Poppy extricated herself from gangly, over-eager Neville, only to be swooped upon by Maurice. Meanwhile, Joyce acknowledged that it was time for Edgar to go back behind the bar to help his father. Furthermore, it was clear that Donald had no intention of loosening his hold on voluptuous Doreen, dressed to kill in a purple halter-necked dress.

No one could plan the future; tomorrow the Allies might re-take Burma or else Rommel's offensive to the west of Tobruk might succeed. Who could tell?

'Come on, Kathleen — let's dance.' Brenda seized her Fieldhead room-mate by the wrist. 'I'll be the man. Elsie — you dance with Joyce. Don't be shy. This is no time to play the wallflower — life's far too short for that!'

# 3

Light summer rain began to fall as Grace and Bill arrived at their honeymoon destination. They'd driven for an hour along Swinsty Edge, through the hamlet of Hawkshead then over the high moor to Attercliffe, basking in welcome silence after the hubbub of the wedding reception and the raucous send-off engineered by Jack, Bob and Maurice. Some time earlier, at Grace's request, Bill had stopped the car in a lay-by to untie the rattling tins from the bumper to allow them to drive on in peace.

'Better?' he'd asked as they'd set off again.

'Much,' she'd said with a sigh. Even on her wedding day she was loath to draw attention.

So they pulled up outside River View without ceremony — a smartly dressed young couple who had booked into the small bed-and-breakfast retreat for two nights. The Victorian house stood next to St Luke's Church, with its square Norman tower, over-looking the village green to the front and a fast-flowing river to the back. There was one shop on the triangular green and a pub called the King's Arms next to a narrow bridge, plus a cluster of stone houses and a weather-worn market cross.

Bill stepped out of the car into the warm drizzle, taking off his jacket and holding it over Grace's head as they walked up the short path. They entered the house, trying their best not to look like newly-weds, wanting no fuss from the hotel owner — a sharp-eyed, stout woman with a broad face and a mannish haircut.

'Mr and Mrs Mostyn?' she enquired peremptorily. *Just married.* She registered their status at first glance, even before she spotted stray flakes of pink and white confetti in Grace's fair hair.

'That's us,' Bill replied, slipping his jacket back on.

Grace's heart skipped a beat as she tried not to blush at the sound of her new name.

'Welcome to River View. I'm Mrs Marion Binns. Breakfast is between eight o'clock and half nine. I can do you an evening meal, but it'll be extra.'

'That'll be fine with us, thank you.' Bill retreated from the tiny reception hall to fetch the suitcases, leaving Grace to face the landlady's continued scrutiny.

'Will you be wanting a Sunday paper?' Mrs Binns enquired with the worldly air of someone who knew that reading a newspaper did not come high on the list of newly-weds' priorities.

'No, thank you.' Grace looked down at the brown and green striped carpet then up at some narrow stairs leading to the bedrooms. She glanced nervously at the formidable Marion.

'Tomorrow is Sunday. The village shop will be closed but I think you'll find you have everything you need in your room.'

'Yes — thank you.'

*Shy and proper. Lovely looking. Doesn't have a clue what she's let herself in for.* 'There's a good walk from here up to Lingfield and back.

41

That's the one most visitors start off with. You can't go wrong — just follow the river all the way.'

'I know it,' Grace said quietly. She suffered badly from the directness of the woman's gaze. 'I've hiked here many times with my rambling group.' *Come back, Bill. Don't let her stare at me a moment longer.*

He carried the suitcases down the hall, hair, face and shoulders wet from the rain, saying that the drizzle had turned to a proper downpour. 'Let's hope it clears up before tomorrow, eh?'

Mrs Binns came out from behind her desk. 'I wouldn't bank on that, if I was you.' The stairs creaked as she led the way up two flights and along a narrow landing. 'June can be a tricky month, weather-wise.'

Grace walked ahead of Bill and had first glance of the room they would share. It had sloping ceilings and rosebud-print wallpaper, with heavy net curtains at a small arched window. There was a navy-blue rug on the floor and the iron bedstead left just enough room for a mahogany wardrobe and wash stand complete with porcelain ewer and basin. Even before she entered, she heard raindrops on the roof and a wind sighing through the oak trees overhanging the churchyard.

The landlady stood to one side to let Grace and Bill pass. 'Breakfast doesn't include bacon,' she advised. 'My food coupons don't run to that this week. But there'll be two eggs each, fresh from the farm up the hill. Would you like them poached or boiled?'

'Poached, please.'

'Boiled.' They answered together then heaved a sigh of relief as the door closed and Marion Binns' heavy tread retreated.

'Blimey, I wouldn't fancy going ten rounds with her.' Bill rolled his eyes and set the suitcases down on the floor. He found the room small and cramped, something of a let-down. 'It's not up to much, is it?' he said as he followed Grace's disappointed gaze.

'No, but I wasn't expecting the Ritz.' They'd agreed in the early stages of planning their wedding that the honeymoon would be low key. That way, most of their savings could be used as a deposit on a house, which they could move into straight after they were married. Things hadn't gone as they'd hoped, however. Though they'd scoured the adverts in the local newspaper, a suitable house in Burnside had not come up for sale in the months between January and June and they'd had to settle on a temporary move into a rented terraced house next to Bob Baxendale, who doubled up as church warden and caretaker at the Institute. It wasn't ideal, but both Bill and Grace had agreed to make the best of a bad job.

'I'd bet a week's wages that Mrs Binns hasn't spent a penny on this place in the last thirty years.' Still disgruntled, Bill took off his jacket and hung it in the wardrobe.

A strong smell of mothballs wafted towards Grace as she sat on the edge of the bed. She wrinkled her nose then chuckled.

'What's funny?'

'Your face.'

'What's wrong with my face?' He hitched his braces off his shoulders and sat down beside her.

'Nothing. It made me laugh, that's all.' *Here we are, a married couple on our wedding day, complaining about decor.*

Bill had the grace to smile and take her hand. 'Perhaps we should've forked out a bit more money and gone to a nice hotel in York, or spent a week at the seaside. That's what I'm thinking.'

Grace shook her head. 'I couldn't have got the whole week off. They need me back at work on Tuesday.'

'I could have swung it with Mother if we'd wanted.' However, he already knew that Grace wouldn't have wanted special treatment and he quickly let the subject drop. 'Everyone had a good time today, didn't they?'

'Yes, Joyce says it all went swimmingly.'

'So far so good, then?'

Bill's tentative remark made her study his face more closely. She knew his features so well — classically straight and symmetrical, with a slight cleft in his chin, the firm line of his mouth, lips not too full, and the deep set of his brown eyes. Yet today there was something different — a flicker of uncertainty that mirrored hers perhaps.

'Your face,' she said again, this time in a whisper. She touched his cheek with her fingertips.

He clasped his hand over hers and pressed her fingers against his skin. 'Are you happy?'

Grace nodded. They'd come to the part of the day that couldn't be planned.

'I give you my promise to make you happy every day from now on. I never want you to be sad.'

''For better, for worse,'' she reminded him as he kissed her palm. Her heart fluttered at the touch of his lips.

Strange how effortlessly she enslaved him without even knowing she was doing it. All she had to do was to speak soft and low, to look earnestly into his eyes and let the corners of her mouth curve into a gentle, hopeful smile. He kissed her wrist then drew her to him.

'We will be happy,' she promised. In spite of everything — the war, his father's recent death and mother's grief, her own self-effacing nature and the difficulty Bill sometimes had in showing his true feelings.

She felt small and perfect in his arms. He picked a piece of confetti out of her soft hair. Then he kissed her lips and felt the length of her body relax into him.

This part, the unplanned part, was happening. There were faded rosebuds on the walls, the sloping ceiling pressed down, the bed shifted as it took their weight.

He lay with her and felt her tremble. He touched her neck, her shoulder, her breast.

The years of knowing him melted away. She was in the moment and it was strange and unfamiliar, like stepping from a height into mid-air, trusting that she would not crash to earth. She touched the hollow at the base of his throat then ran her fingers over his smooth skin, along his collarbone towards the bunched

45

muscles in his shoulder.

Her skin was impossibly soft and white. Her grey eyes trusted him. Now everything changed. Nothing was the same or ever would be again. Breath came short, kisses were hard. She held him tight and knew with diamond-bright certainty that she loved him more than anything on this earth.

★  ★  ★

'I wonder who'll be next to waltz down the aisle?' Brenda tossed the question into the air at breakfast time next morning. She faced Una and Joyce across the long trestle table in the large dining room at Fieldhead. To her left sat Kathleen and Jean, to her right Elsie and newcomer Poppy.

'Not me!' Kathleen, Elsie and Poppy chorused their answer. An early morning sun cast bright, slanted strips of light through the long Georgian windows. There were other signs of faded splendour in the room, including an Adam fireplace at one end and ornately carved plaster cornices. The floor was solid oak but the official-issue tables and tubular-steel chairs were utilitarian. Kathleen and Elsie declared there wasn't a man left in Burnside that they would touch with a bargepole.

'Not since Thomas Lund was called up, anyway.' Kathleen recalled the handsome clerk with the cheeky grin who was currently sweltering out in the North African desert. 'I had a soft spot for him, I don't mind admitting.'

'And Jack Hudson has to answer to Lord Mountbatten, worse luck,' Elsie added. Late in the night, she and Jack had gravitated towards each other then danced into the wee small hours until Cliff Kershaw had chucked out the last of the revellers and shut up shop. 'His ship sails for Gibraltar next week.'

'Poor Elsie!' Brenda hadn't been the only one to notice the strong mutual attraction between the pair: Jack proud and dapper in his royal-blue uniform; Elsie transformed from lithe, practical Land Girl into glorious, gamine femininity in a daringly short emerald-green dress with a sweetheart neckline and a string of cultured pearls. 'That's a pity,' she commented. 'If there wasn't a war on, I could see you and Jack making a go of things. What about you, Poppy — is there a young man pining for you at home?'

Poppy's pale face turned bright red as she pretended not to hear. She went on spreading a thin layer of butter on to the heel of a loaf that Una had handed her.

'Try some of this home-made plum jam.' Una pushed her ration Poppy's way. 'Go on — you need feeding up.'

It was true; it looked as if a breath of wind would blow Poppy over. At eighteen, her figure was slender to the point of boyishness, with a tiny bosom and waist, slim hips and straight thighs. Her baby-blonde hair was hidden beneath a checked blue and white scarf tied turban-style around her head.

'Don't worry; you'll soon fill out with the grub Ma Craven dishes up.' Brenda did her best to make the new girl feel at home. 'Won't she, girls?' Less willowy than Poppy, she had a wiry strength and her face and arms sported a healthy tan. 'Before you know it, you'll be chucking hay on to the wagon with the best of us.'

'You will.' Una remembered how it felt to be the rookie recruit. Her own arrival at Fieldhead in the autumn of the previous year had been attended by a dozen question marks — will the other girls like me? Will they make fun of me? How will I tell one end of a cow from the other? Like Poppy, she'd come into the Land Army straight from working in a woollen mill, with no knowledge of the countryside and a head full of doubts about whether she would survive the tough Land Army regime. 'Don't worry, we'll look after you,' she promised.

'Ta.' Poppy's voice was high and breathy. 'But I'm stronger than I look. I worked in the canteen at Kingsley's for two years without missing a day.'

'Good for you.' From across the table Joyce gave her a reassuring wink before offering to clear away people's plates. She'd been quieter than usual at breakfast, reliving the walk she'd taken with Edgar after they'd slipped away from the party. They'd crossed the field behind the pub and entered the copse hand in hand. Hardly a word had been spoken as they'd woven their way between the silvery trunks of the birch trees and glimpsed the clouds drifting across the face of the moon.

'It looks like rain,' Edgar had murmured, keeping her hand fast in his. Tall and thin, with his head tilted towards her, he'd stared intently into her eyes.

'We could definitely do with it,' she'd replied. 'Let's hope we don't have a repeat of last year's heatwave.' She'd felt linked to him at a deeper level than their words conveyed. She'd wanted him to go on holding her hand for a long, long time.

But today Edgar was packing his bag to rejoin his squadron. This good, gentle, sincere man would follow orders and fly out from his base on the north-east coast. He would drop bombs on civilian targets in Essen, Bremen and Berlin.

'Are you all right, Joyce?' Brenda stood to help her carry the dishes into the kitchen.

'Yes, ta.' Once before, in a different life lived on a farm near Stratford-upon-Avon, Joyce had opened her heart to a man. She'd been engaged but her fiancé, Walter Johnson, had been killed in action. Soon after, in an effort to dull the pain, she'd applied to join the Women's Land Army, who had snapped her up and sent her to Yorkshire. *Ideal Land Girl material*, was what Central Office had told Edith Mostyn prior to her arrival. *Joyce Cutler was born and bred on a lowland sheep farm. She's strong and sturdy as they come.* 'I'm champion,' she told Brenda as they stacked the dirty plates beside the deep stone sink. 'What are you planning to do with your day off?'

Brenda considered her reply. 'I fancy putting Sloper through her paces. Do you want to come along?'

Joyce smiled. 'No, but ta for the offer. I have to

49

wash my smalls and mend my socks.'

'Are you sure? That doesn't sound like much fun.'

'I'm certain. A quiet day after yesterday's wedding jamboree will do me good.'

So Brenda donned her second-hand, army-surplus-stores jacket with its pilot's fleece collar and belts and buckles, then sailed off up the dale while Joyce settled down to domestic chores. Back in the dining room, Una stayed to chat with Poppy and a few others while Doreen Wells made a late, bleary-eyed entrance.

'Blimey, Doreen, you look like death warmed up.' Jean Fox spoke bluntly as usual. From the beginning she'd seen little to admire in Doreen's swanky, attention-seeking manner. They were polar opposites. Where Jean was thin and apathetic, Doreen was curvy and animated. Jean was a born pessimist and complainer, Doreen always looked on the bright side. In Civvy Street men had seldom noticed the mousy bank clerk, whereas Doreen's dark, sultry good looks drew admiring stares wherever she went.

Doreen lowered herself gingerly into Brenda's empty seat. Her beautiful, heart-shaped face was pale, her dark blue eyes shadowed and her long, black hair pulled back severely into a low bun. She was still in pyjamas and barefoot, as if she had just crept out of bed.

'Tea?' Kathleen offered to pour her a cup from the big brown teapot.

Doreen nodded then winced. 'Ouch!'

'Headache?' Jean whipped out the question with a tilt of the head which suggested that it served her right. 'Mrs Craven doles out the aspirins around here. But don't expect any sympathy for a hangover.'

Doreen's eyes flickered shut and she bit her bottom lip. 'I might have overdone it a teeny bit,' she admitted in a croaky voice. 'But it was fun while it lasted.'

Una grinned at Kathleen and Elsie. They'd all seen Doreen cavorting with the Canadians and Donald White. There'd been deep-throated laughter and frequent glimpses of stocking-tops as she twirled and kicked up her legs in a seductive can-can, throwing herself into a dance with a French Canadian airman from Quebec. They'd watched Jim Aldridge step in to restrain his pilot while Brenda sat on the sidelines for once, watching Les White play the piano. Then, after the Canadians had made an early exit, Doreen had thrown herself at Les's brother and stuck to him like glue. At the end of the night, opinion among the Land Girls had been divided. Some were won over by her devil-may-care activities while others cringed with embarrassment at the uninhibited display. One thing was certain: no one at Fieldhead remained neutral about Doreen Wells.

'You're paying for it now, though.' Jean voiced her sour disapproval.

Doreen sipped at her tea but refused bread and jam. 'Ugh!' she groaned, the corners of her lips turned down in exaggerated disgust. 'What time is it?'

'It's five minutes to nine. You're out of luck;' Mrs Craven took the porridge pot off the stove

51

half an hour ago.' Jean delighted in mentioning food to an obviously queasy Doreen, who stood up abruptly then scraped back her chair.

'I need fresh air,' she gulped, resisting all offers of help before rushing from the room.

'Who's sorry now?' was Jean's parting shot.

Kathleen had had enough of Jean's meanness. 'Not Doreen,' she shot back. 'She only made the biggest conquest of the night. Why should she be sorry about that?'

'You mean Donald White?' Elsie was quick on the uptake. 'Yes, I did notice that.'

'He couldn't take his eyes off her,' Una agreed, abandoning Jean along with Kathleen and Elsie, who had made plans to hike up to Winsill Edge together that morning. She followed them into the large, tiled entrance hall. 'Good luck to Doreen, I say.'

Kathleen sat on the bottom step of the wide stair-case to lace up her brogues. 'Yes, and in answer to Brenda's question, those two will be the next to 'waltz' down the aisle, you mark my words.'

Elsie sat next to her and followed suit. 'You mean Doreen and Donald? But they hardly know each other.'

'It doesn't matter. Eyes can meet across a crowded room . . . '

'And, flash! The magic happens.' Elsie laughed then glanced up at Una, hovering nearby. 'Someone here knows that better than anyone, eh, Una?'

# 4

''Calling all women!'' Brenda's voice rang out over the small turnip field at Home Farm. She wielded her hoe like a spear and marched Una and Elsie out of the farmyard on to the exposed ridge overlooking Burnside village. 'Come along, girls — we're here to answer Lady Denman's rallying cry!'

Una and Elsie shouldered their hoes and followed her in true Land Girl fashion.

Joe and Emily Kellett's farm was more run-down than ever. Thistles and chickweed had sprung up between the stone slabs in the yard and nettles flourished in the hedgerows. Every worker's heart sank to see her name on the rota and the words 'Home Farm' written in Edith Mostyn's neat hand in the column next to it, for they knew that the old farmer was a hard taskmaster and that these days his frail wife scarcely ventured out of the house to moderate his ill temper and unreasonable demands.

Still, Brenda, Una and Elsie had a job to do this Monday morning and they would do it to the best of their ability.

'Once we've cleared all the weeds we can take a breather.' Elsie vaulted over the gate into the field and immediately got stuck in. She envisaged unpacking her fish-paste sandwiches in the shade of a hayrick then pouring herself a cup of good, strong tea from her thermos flask. 'After that we'll go back to the house and find out what the old so-and-so's got lined up for us this afternoon.'

Una too got straight to work with her hoe, digging up the weeds and heaping them at the edge of the field. 'There's a cool breeze today, thank goodness.' After a few minutes she paused to take off her jumper and roll up her sleeves. When she set to again and stooped to pick up a bundle of uprooted weeds, she gave a sharp intake of breath. 'Ouch!' Examining the palm of her hand, she saw the first red blotches and raised skin of a nettle sting.

'No wonder they call us the Cinderella Service,' Elsie remarked glumly. 'The powers that be don't even shell out enough money to buy us gloves.'

Brenda leaned on her hoe and looked down into the valley, across fields of sprouting turnips and yellowing wheat. 'They don't mention that when they recruit you. Or the fact that you'll be working knee-deep in cow muck half of the time.'

That was how their morning had begun — cleaning out the milking parlour after Joe had finished milking. The filthy work with spade, brush and hose was one of the worst around, not made any better by the old man keeping his beady eye on them until he was finally satisfied.

'And all for thirty-eight shillings a week.' Elsie found a dock leaf growing in a nearby ditch and handed it to Una. 'Here — this will help take the sting out of it.'

Una crushed the leaf to release the sap then

dabbed her hand. Meanwhile, Elsie and Brenda worked their way along the first row of turnip shoots. She soon joined them, then all three kept their heads down and their hoes turning the soil until the sun had risen high in the sky. They didn't pause or look up from the back-breaking work until they heard Joe call from the gate.

'Missy!' he yelled, his gnarled hands clasped over the top bar. He was dressed in his all-year-round tattered overcoat, tied around the waist with string, hatless and with his thick white hair uncombed. 'I want you.'

Brenda frowned and looked at Elsie and Una. 'Which 'Missy' would that be?' she called back.

'The little dark one. Come here.'

Elsie immediately split from the trio and started up the hill.

'Not you — you!' Joe stabbed his finger towards Una. 'I need you to cycle over to Brigg Farm with two buckets of pig swill.'

'Charming!' Brenda muttered to Elsie as Una put down her hoe. 'What's the betting we'll still be expected to finish this job by dinner time, even though there's only two of us?'

Despite a twinge of guilt about abandoning them, Una welcomed the break. She left the field then fetched her bike from behind the dairy, letting Joe hitch two zinc buckets full to the brim with potato peelings, old cabbage leaves and sour milk curds over her handlebars.

'You'll have to manage without lids,' he instructed. 'Try not to spill any.'

It would be a fine balancing act, she realized. The contents of the buckets slopped around as she wobbled off along the rough farm track on to the road. Once on the smooth surface, she was able to free-wheel down the steep hill and over a hump-backed bridge, then cycle on through the village before taking a left turn towards Brigg Farm. The buckets tilted and a little of the rotting mixture spilled on to the ground. Una sighed and cycled on, intending to ignore Maurice's approaching van and tooting horn.

The bespectacled car mechanic braked and leaned out of his window. 'Where are you off to this fine day?'

She was starting to gag on the foul smell. 'Sorry, Maurice, I can't stop — the sooner I deliver these buckets of pig swill to Roland Thomson, the better.'

'I'd offer to help.' He turned up his nose and shrugged. 'Only . . . '

'I know — it's an awful stink.'

'Rather you than me,' he said. *These Land Girls deserve every penny they get paid,* he thought as he drove on. *Some of them don't look sturdy enough to cook a chap a decent dinner, let alone plough a field or dig a ditch.*

⋆　⋆　⋆

Poppy's first morning at Brigg Farm was not going well. She'd been given the task of harvesting hay with a scythe, despite never having handled such a thing before. It had seemed simple when Joyce had stood in the field behind the barn and demonstrated to her and Doreen the action of swooping the scythe in a downwards curve and Poppy had listened to the satisfying swish of the blade through the tall grass. But when it came to her turn, she couldn't seem to keep the scythe at the right angle and there'd been no swish and fall. The grass had stayed defiantly upright.

'Not like that — like this.' Joyce showed her a second time. 'Look, Doreen's getting the hang of it. Try to copy her.'

Poppy felt frustration form a lump in her throat. She raised the scythe above her shoulder and brought it down — there was a second failure, then a third, and a fourth.

'I know; it's not as easy as it looks.' Joyce adjusted Poppy's stance while Neville strolled out of the farmyard to perch on the gate and enjoy the show.

'We'll be here till midnight at this rate,' he'd crowed.

Poppy felt six inches high. Why could Doreen get the hang of it and not her? The glory of the glamorous shop girl wielding a scythe was something to behold. Her glossy dark hair partly hidden by a red paisley scarf and her white Aertex shirt revealing her smooth, strong arms, she raised the blade above her head and with a svelte twist of her torso brought it down at just the right angle. Swathes of long grass fell at her feet and she moved on — raise, twist and swing, again and again.

Neville, however, seemed to have eyes for none but Poppy. 'Crikey O'Reilly, would you look at that!' he chortled, a flap of ginger hair flopping down over one eye. 'Stand well back, Joyce

57

— she'll have your leg off if you're not careful.'

Poppy grunted then went on failing with the scythe until at last Joyce relented. 'Doreen and I can manage here. Why don't you ask Neville if there's a job in the stable that you can help him with?'

*Out of the frying pan into the fire.* Poppy didn't relish the prospect of Neville telling her what to do but she followed him anyway.

'I enjoyed that — you gave me more laughs than Buster Keaton and the Keystone Cops put together.' He grinned as he entered the tack room next to Major's stable. The grey shire horse flicked a bored ear towards them then returned to his hay net.

*I've had enough*, Poppy thought. 'I didn't notice you offering to lend a hand.' In a rare gesture of disgruntlement, she pulled off her scarf and tucked it firmly into the pocket of her dungarees.

'Why should I? Dad dishes out the orders. My job is to look after the horse and cart, plus Lady M over there, the rest of the pigs and the chickens.'

Poppy glanced across the yard to the three red hens and one black one pecking seeds from between cracks. She liked the look of them, but not of the enormous sow thrusting her snout through the gaps in her wooden sty. 'Why do you call her Lady M?'

'It stands for Lady Macbeth. She rolled on her first litter and killed every one of them stone dead.' Neville took a few seconds to enjoy Poppy's dismay. At sixteen, his main source of entertainment lay in teasing and flirting with the newest Land Girl recruits and since Una had made it plain at the wedding reception on Saturday night that she was still spoken for, he'd begun to seriously consider transferring his attention to Poppy. 'Lady M will be for the chop herself before too long. But take my word for it, you won't want to be anywhere near when that happens.'

Preferring not to pursue the topic, Poppy staggered backwards under the weight of an enormous leather horse collar that Neville had taken off its hook and foisted upon her. He then unbolted the stable door and led Major into the yard before tethering him to an iron ring attached to the stone wall. 'Hang on to that collar while I fetch you a box,' he instructed. Poppy felt her legs start to tremble. This was a huge, heavy piece of tack for a gigantic horse — his head was unbelievably large, bony and whiskery. One eye was brown and the other a greyish-blue. The pale one stared at her holding the collar, as if to warn her, *Don't come near me with that.*

She sagged and shook as Neville placed a wooden crate next to the horse. 'Step up here and pop that over his head while I fetch his reins and bridle,' he ordered with a casual jerk of his head.

'Rightio!' Poppy took a deep breath and stepped up. Major eyed her balefully and stamped his hairy hoof. She lifted the collar high over his head, expecting him to pull away. To her surprise the cart horse was good as gold,

59

standing motionless as she lowered it. She brushed the palms of her hands together and stepped down from the crate.

'Blow me down!' Neville exclaimed when he returned with the horse's bridle slung over his shoulder. 'I'd have put money on you not being able to manage that.' Out of the corner of his eye he saw a figure on a bicycle pedal up the lane. Recognizing Una, he thrust the bridle at Poppy. 'See if you can work out how to put this on,' he ordered, almost falling over himself in his hurry to greet his old favourite.

'Hello, Neville.' Una smiled as she got off her bike.

'Here, let me take those.' He sprang to help, unloading the buckets from the handlebars and carrying one in each hand to the pigsty, where he promptly tipped the contents into the trough.

'Hello, Poppy.' Una saw the new girl struggling with the horse's bridle and obligingly showed her how to put it on. 'This is the brow band and this part loops behind his ears. These are the blinkers. Stand still, Major — there's a good boy. First you have to slide the bit between his teeth.' She accomplished the task then reassured Poppy. 'It seems tricky at first but you'll soon get the hang of it. And by the way, if Neville teases you, ignore him.'

Neville put down the buckets then sauntered over. 'Are you two girls talking about me, by any chance?'

'Why — are your ears burning?' Una winked at Poppy. 'I was telling her you were a decent sort deep down. You looked after me when I first arrived at Fieldhead and you'll do the same for her.'

'If she behaves herself, I will.' Neville reckoned that Poppy was only a year or two older than him and definitely his type of girl. He decided then and there to take her under his wing. 'I'll show you how to hitch Major to the hay wagon for a start.'

Despite the farm lad's brazen manner, this time Poppy was glad of the offer. While she listened and watched attentively, Una climbed the stone steps into the hayloft above Major's stable and found a quiet corner to sit and reread her latest letter from Angelo.

It had been delivered to the hostel on Friday and she'd read it three times that evening before storing it with the others in the wooden box that her beloved beau had carved for her soon after they'd met. She'd kept the box hidden under her pillow throughout the Saturday, the day of Grace's wedding. On Sunday she'd read the letter twice more and this morning she'd tucked it into the top pocket of her dungarees so that she could read it again during her dinner break. Now she took it out of its envelope and started to read.

'Dear Una.' Instantly she imagined Angelo's deep voice with its heavy Italian accent. 'I am well and I hope you are the same. I miss you every day. My heart hurts when I think of you.' She sighed and, though the words blurred through sudden hot tears, she remembered the next bit verbatim. 'I promise I will not forget you. You must think of me and never forget our times together.' Una closed her eyes and breathed in the sweet smell of newly mown hay. *Times together when they'd kissed and held each other. The time they had made love in the cold winter stable behind the hostel — her very first tender time.* She always wore Angelo's gold cross around her neck, warm against her skin.

'*Mio amore*, do not forget your Angelo. I am with Lorenzo on a new ship. They teach me to weld metal. It is good work but I like better digging a field by your side. How are you? Is the sun hot in Yorkshire? Who digs beside you now?'

Nestled in her bed of hay, she smiled a little at this hint of jealousy on Angelo's part and promised herself that she would put him out of his misery by writing back that very evening. Her letter would wing its way to the shipyard in Greenock and he would be left in no doubt that she still loved him with all her heart.

She brushed away the tears then read on. 'My words in English cannot say how I feel. How long must we wait, *mio amore*? When will we be free?'

'Una — are you there?' Edith Mostyn's clipped, penetrating voice called from the farmyard.

Una jumped up and dusted herself down. She hadn't heard the approach of a car or the short conversation between the local rep and the other girls. 'Yes, Mrs Mostyn!'

'Come down here, please.'

She hastily tucked Angelo's letter into her pocket then descended the steps to find the supervisor addressing Poppy, Doreen and Joyce.

62

'If you have any complaints about your conditions of work, now is the time to voice them.' Edith was dressed in smart fawn slacks and a crisp white blouse. Her fountain pen was poised above a clipboard. 'For example, are you obliged to work longer than your stated hours?'

'No, Mrs Mostyn.' Una joined the group and added her voice to the chorus.

Edith duly noted their answers. 'Is the work expected of you unreasonable in any way?'

Joyce eyed Una, who thrust her shoulders back and jutted out her chin. 'No, Mrs Mostyn.'

'Poppy and Doreen, do you consider that you have received sufficient training?'

'Yes, Mrs Mostyn!'

*What training would that be?* Doreen silently wondered. She'd been whisked out of her department store on the last Friday in May and on the following Sunday she'd arrived at Fieldhead, where she'd been issued with her Land Army uniform and her regulation boneshaker bicycle. On the following day she'd been thrown straight into the mayhem of plucking chickens at Horace Turnbull's hen farm, where the taciturn farmer's toothless old dad had demonstrated the basics then left her to it. Still, she saw by the look on Joyce's face that it wouldn't do to complain.

Edith went down her list. She was going through the motions, filling her day with chores rather than stopping at home. Tomorrow Bill and Grace would return from their short honeymoon; she would put a vase of flowers in the front window of their rented house to welcome them back.

'Phew,' Doreen muttered after the strict rep had finished her inspection then driven away in her shiny Morris. 'What's got into her?'

Una fetched her bike, ready to say goodbye then cycle back to Home Farm. 'Nothing out of the ordinary. Don't worry — she may look like a sourpuss but she has our best interests at heart.'

'You could have fooled me.' Doreen looked in puzzlement at the flat hard stone that Joyce had just presented her with. 'What's this for?'

'It's a flint stone — you use it to sharpen your scythe. You have to spit on it first to get the best results.'

'I can hardly wait. But not until after I've had my sandwiches.' She dug in her heels and made a display of sitting with Poppy on the hayloft steps. 'That's right — we're within our rights to have a dinner break. Beef dripping — yum-yum!'

Sandwiches and hot tea were followed by a quiet smoke. Doreen offered a cigarette to Poppy, who again refused. 'What's up, dearie? You're not feeling homesick, by any chance?'

Poppy nodded and sighed. She thought of her mother at work in the burling and mending department at Kingsley's and her father in his barber's shop on City Road. Her two little brothers, Charlie and Ernie, had cried buckets when she'd packed her suitcase and left the house on Albion Lane.

'I'll be off then — cheerio!' Una called as she walked her bike around the horse and cart, where Neville perched in the driving seat, gazing up at a squadron of Lancasters flying in formation high overhead. The sky was clear blue, with only a few wispy white clouds clinging to the high hills beyond the plain of York.

'Good luck to 'em, wherever they're headed,' he muttered.

Una steadied the bike and studied the fighter planes. 'It's too early to set off for a night raid over Germany. Maybe they're going on to North Africa.'

'Or Sevastopol. I hear there's a big push there.'

'Perhaps.' There was no way of knowing where the brave pilots would drop their bombs or how many of them would return. Una said goodbye to Neville and tried not to think about the war as she cycled on. She kept her mind on the happy events she would share with Angelo in her reply to his letter: 'On the Saturday just gone Grace married Bill at last. They made a lovely couple. Brenda and I were bridesmaids. We wore dresses of lilac silk.'

Una would remind him that the war couldn't last for ever and yes, there would come a time when they were free.

★ ★ ★

'You'll never believe what I heard,' Joyce told Poppy and Doreen as they cycled home at the end of the day. They'd reached Peggy Russell's farm on the single-track road to Fieldhead and stopped off there to deliver half a dozen eggs sent over by Roland, who was a distant cousin.

65

Joyce had braved the fury of Peggy's dog straining at his chain and the old widow had accepted the gift without so much as a thank-you before retreating into her gloomy cottage.

'Roland says there was an unexploded bomb in one of Arnold White's fields over in Attercliffe. A cow stepped on it and blew itself up along with half a dozen others.'

'When was this?' Doreen cycled ahead, eager to reach home first and lay claim to her allotted time in the bathroom. It would be her first bath in a week and she could hardly wait.

'Yesterday. Apparently Les went to the field to fetch the cows in for evening milking. He saw the whole thing — he had to take cover behind a wall because there was shrapnel everywhere.'

'Bang goes the Whites' chances of a bumper milk yield this week.' Doreen's wry remark made Joyce smile. 'It makes you think, though — it could've been one of us.'

'Yes, it could.' Was Poppy the only one to be genuinely disturbed by the news or were the others just putting on a brave face? One of the reasons why she'd joined the Land Army rather than the WAAF or the Wrens had been to put herself out of the way of enemy bombs. She'd imagined that Jerry mainly chose towns and cities as targets, without realizing the importance of sites out in the countryside such as aerodromes, reservoirs and dams. This news about the bomb set her right, however. Now she would have nightmares about slicing her spade into soft earth and hitting metal. She pictured a sickening, split-second realization before the explosion and then oblivion.

As they approached the stone pillars of the hostel gates, Poppy and Joyce drew level with Doreen. All three were surprised to see a man dressed in a suit and trilby hat at the far end of the driveway. He lounged with his back turned against the side wall of the main building, smoking a cigarette.

'What's he up to?' Joyce remarked with a frown. It was unusual for men to visit Fieldhead, and anyway it was almost suppertime, when all of the girls would be indoors.

Instinctively they held back. They watched as a figure emerged from the yard at the back and quickly recognized Kathleen, still in her uniform but with her fair hair hanging loose. She spoke urgently to the stranger.

Doreen was the first to react. 'Look out — we're in danger of breaking up a tryst.'

The man talked back, throwing down his cigarette and taking Kathleen by the arm. He must have said something she didn't like because she pulled free and tried to retrace her steps.

'Uh-oh, lovers' tiff.' Doreen still hesitated by the gate.

The man went after Kathleen. He pulled her by the arm again. She shoved him away and this time made good her escape around the back of the building.

'Does our hairdresser friend have a secret admirer?' Doreen asked as the man slowly followed.

'Plenty, I shouldn't wonder' Joyce acknowledged that the fun-loving Kathleen gave Doreen a good run for her money in the glamour stakes.

'Ooh — do we know who he is?' Poppy too was intrigued.

'I haven't a clue.' Though they'd only caught a back view, Joyce didn't recognize the square set of the man's shoulders or his natty dress sense — the suit had been fashionably cut and the brown shoes were highly polished. 'I don't think he can be local.'

'Then we have a mystery on our hands!' Doreen set off down the drive, followed by Poppy and Joyce. 'But I'll winkle it out of Kathleen at supper, just you watch.'

# 5

Brenda cycled home alone. She'd stopped late at Home Farm to help Emily Kellett collect eggs. 'You go on ahead,' she'd told Elsie and Una. 'I won't be far behind.'

It had taken less than ten minutes to fill a basket with brown beauties; the eggs when she picked them from the long grass behind the milking shed were smooth, speckled and warm. Emily had given her three to keep and thanked her for her help.

'I can't bend down like I used to,' she'd admitted, her grey hair escaping in thin wisps from its plaited bun. But it was something worse than stiff joints that ailed her since the death of her son, Frank, whose frozen corpse had been found on the moor in the dead of winter the previous year. She'd lost what she insisted on calling her 'gumption' — her spirit, her tenacity, plus whatever else it was that had kept her grinding on year after year. Now she was broken, stooped and lined, with no one to nurture and protect.

A grateful Brenda had thanked her for the eggs then cycled off. In contrast to old Emily, she gloried in youthful energy, soaking up the sight of new green leaves fluttering in the sun, of dappled shade and wayside flowers, with St Michael's Church coming into full view as she freewheeled round the bend into the village.

Spotting Les White sitting on the bench outside the smithy with his racing-green sports car parked close by, she decided on the spur of the moment to stop and have some fun.

Les nursed a pint of bitter on his knee. He needed it to calm his nerves after dealing with the clean-up operation in the cow field at home. First thing that morning, he had followed his father's orders and gone out to salvage what meat he could. After some judicious butchery there'd been enough to share out among neighbours. The messy job had taken a lot out of him, however. So here he was with the sun on his face and a drink in his hands, watching Brenda whiz along the road towards him.

'Why so down in the mouth?' she quizzed from a distance of twenty yards. He seemed to have withdrawn into himself since Saturday, to be less at ease than before.

He explained briefly about the landmine and its aftermath. 'The bad news is that Donald shirked his Home Guard duties. The good news is I was able to call in at Fieldhead with extra meat rations.'

'Oh lovely — beef and shrapnel stew!' Brenda braked, hopped off her bike then sat down beside him. Despite the flippant remark, she felt sorry for him. 'You had a close shave, eh?'

'You could say that. Would you like a drink?'

'No, ta. Ma Craven would tan my hide if they found me drunk in charge of a bicycle.'

'One small shandy wouldn't hurt, would it?'

'No, really — thank you.' She preferred to sit and chat. As she'd discovered when she'd danced with him after the wedding reception, Les's quiet, unthreatening nature appealed to her precisely because he wasn't her usual pushy type. He had hidden depths, she thought, and it was up to her to uncover them.

'I had a nice time at the wedding do.' His elbow accidentally nudged her as he raised his glass and took a foamy sip. 'I didn't expect to. That type of big get-together isn't usually my style.'

'But you like to trip the light fantastic?'

As he nodded, a small curl of fair hair flicked forward on to his forehead. 'I'll dance to anything that Glenn Miller or Benny Goodman play. It's the saxophones that really get me going.'

Brenda studied the long fingers that cupped the glass. The more she observed and heard, the more certain she grew that Les was a sensitive sort. *I'm not for him*, she thought in a rare moment of self-doubt. *I'm too loud for his liking.* Then again, maybe she could learn to adapt. 'On second thoughts, perhaps I will have that drink,' she said.

★  ★  ★

The vegetable patch in the walled garden behind the hostel was planted in regimented rows. Lettuce and other salad crops grew to the left of the central pathway while well-established shoots of cabbages, carrots and potatoes were to the right. There were pleached apple and pear trees trained against the south-facing wall and a

71

border of perennials intended to provide flowers for the house. It was from here that the roses and carnations for Grace's wedding had been cut.

'Ladies and gentlemen, I give you the latest score: Doreen nil, Kathleen one!' In a light-hearted attempt to defuse the tension between the two girls, Joyce pretended that her trowel was a radio microphone.

Try as she might during supper, Doreen hadn't been able to discover the identity of Kathleen's mystery man. 'He's no one you know,' or 'Never you mind,' had been the replies to an increasingly frustrated questioner.

Doreen had pressed the point. 'What's the matter? He didn't look the sort you'd need to keep secret.'

Kathleen had ploughed on silently through her mutton stew and dumplings.

'Ah, that's it — she's ashamed of him!' Doreen had concluded, to Kathleen's disgust.

Now she, Kathleen, Joyce, Poppy and Una were making the most of the long evening by tending the dig-for-victory veg patch. *Doreen nil, Kathleen one.*

'But it's only half-time,' Una warned, tying up rampant runner beans with a deft touch.

'And where did you and your beau disappear off to? That's what I'd like to know,' Doreen persisted as Kathleen put both hands to her ears. 'Did you slope off into the woods for a secret rendezvous? Yes, that's right — we've cracked it at last. Kathleen was annoyed because he showed himself in public but they made up in private when no one was looking.'

'You couldn't be more wrong if you tried.' Kathleen's joking resistance turned into irritation. 'There was no secret rendezvous. The last thing I wanted was for him to turn up here at Fieldhead.'

'But he's not a stranger — you do know him?'

'*Did!*' Kathleen retorted. 'I did know him a bit at one time, but not any more.'

'Hmm.' Doreen stood astride the rows of spring onions, hands on hips. 'So he's a bad penny? Come on, Kathleen, put us out of our misery and tell us his name.'

'No, but I will say this. I knew him in Millwood and yes, I did walk out with him a few times — to the cinema and suchlike. But then I found out more about him . . . '

'Don't tell us — he was already hitched!' Doreen guessed. 'Not that I would blame anyone for carrying on with a married man. We all have to grab our chance of happiness in this day and age . . . '

'Cover your ears,' Joyce advised Una and Poppy with a wink. 'Hush, Doreen — there are children present.'

Doreen steamed ahead regardless. 'No one knows that better than me. What am I now — twenty-three? I was twenty when the war started and engaged to be married. My fiancé was at Dunkirk and never got off the beaches. He was mown down by Jerry along with thousands of others.'

Hearing Doreen's sad but familiar tale, a look of shared pain flickered in Joyce's eyes then was gone. 'What was his name?' she asked gently.

'Bernie. Private Bernard Ward of the Green Howards Regiment, God rest his soul.'

There was a short silence, broken by the arrival of Brenda. She rode her bicycle into the yard and caught sight of the group in the walled garden. Tiddly from two shandies, she wobbled down the path towards them and yelled a greeting.

'Hush, keep your voice down! What kept you?' Joyce wanted to know.

'I stopped off at the Blacksmith's Arms — why?'

'Because Mrs Craven's on the warpath about you missing supper.' Glancing towards the house, she spotted the warden at the back door. 'Here she comes now.'

But instead of advancing, Hilda Craven stayed in the doorway with her arms folded. She watched carefully as Joyce took control of Brenda's bike, exchanging a few words with the new arrival before walking it into the nearest stable. Once Hilda saw that all was well, she retreated purposefully down the corridor into the kitchen, where a surprise guest waited.

★   ★   ★

Alfie Craven had taken off his hat and jacket and sat astride a wooden chair in the warden's big kitchen. He rested his forearms on her scrubbed table and glanced up at the rows of tin canisters, earthenware crocks, copper pans and Kilner jars lining the shelves. There was a large gas stove in one corner of the room and two deep sinks, with a plate rack above the draining board stacked with blue and white crockery. 'Now then, Mum — I see you're in your element here.'

Hilda's normally placid face flickered with uncertainty. 'It's hard work cooking for twenty people twice a day, but yes, I'm nicely settled here.'

'Do you bake your Land Girls juicy steak pies with plenty of onions and carrots? They were always my favourites.'

'Yes, if I can get the stewing steak.' After pacing the floor, Hilda sat down and studied her son. His face was a little broader than when she'd last seen him, his wavy brown hair more smoothly slicked back, his expression even more guarded than before. But he was neat and clean-shaven, with an air of prosperity suggested by a stiff white shirt, blue suit and a pair of gold-plated cufflinks. 'What are you doing here, Alfie? That's what I'd like to know.'

'Oh, come on now. Can't a chap drop in to see his old mum once in a while?' He tapped the table decisively then stood up, making his chair rock then rattle back down on to the stone flags. 'What's the matter? Aren't you pleased to see me?'

'I'd have been better pleased if you'd kept in touch.' In fact, she'd had no notion of Alfie's where-abouts over these last few years but she'd always assumed the worst. Her eyes followed him as he reached up then opened a tin labelled 'Biscuits'.

He took out a cheese straw and popped it into his mouth. 'Time's flown. I've been busy.'

'Too busy to drop me a line every now and then?'

Alfie ate another biscuit. 'I did write to you at first — a couple of nice, long letters.'

'Well, I never received them.'

'I sent them to the Fosters' place, addressed to Mrs Hilda Craven, Housekeeper, Hawkshead Manor, Hawkshead.'

'I didn't stop there for long after you left.'

'What happened? Did her ladyship chuck you out?'

Hilda drew herself up and kept to herself the fact that the atmosphere at the manor house had turned distinctly chilly prior to her departure. 'No, I left of my own accord. Live-in work didn't suit me so I moved back into the village and found part-time cleaning jobs.'

Alfie put the lid on the biscuit tin then returned it to its place on the shelf. 'Live-in work didn't suit you, eh? Isn't that what you're doing now?'

'But Fieldhead is different. We're part of the war effort here, all in it together.'

He nodded and sat back down, folding his arms across his broad chest and taking in the changes he saw in her. His mother had never been much to look at but now that she'd sunk well into middle age she was downright dowdy. The hand-knitted fawn cardigan and brown tweed skirt didn't help and she could certainly do with losing a stone or two. Still, what had he been expecting? 'I'm sorry we lost touch, Mum. I didn't mean to. Anyway, I'm here now — that's the main thing.'

'It's been a long time, Alfie.' Seeing him brought back a flood of memories — the long, hard years of fending for him when he was a youngster, living hand to mouth after his father, Willis, had been killed in an accident on Arnold White's farm. She remembered how the early sparks of disobedience in the child had caught light during Alfie's last years at Burnside school and turned into a full-blown, rebellious blaze by the time he was ready to look for work at the age of fourteen. Many in the village had had their fingers burned — Maurice and Bob's father, old Gordon Baxendale, for a start, who had offered Alfie an apprenticeship as a mechanic and had lived to regret it when Alfie had been caught systematically siphoning off petrol from customers' cars and selling it on the sly. After that — and a couple of other similar incidents which ended up with him being sent to Borstal — Hilda had been forced to admit that her son was out of control. From then on he was often in trouble with the police and unable to hold down a job even when he reached his twenties, drinking and getting into fights and then disappearing from Burnside for weeks at a time. Gradually he'd stayed away for even longer periods and only shown up when he was skint. Eventually, at the end of her tether, she'd refused point-blank to give him any more money and, in February of 1937, he'd gone for good.

'A lot's changed,' he cajoled. 'I'm not the tearaway I once was.'

She nodded slowly. 'I should hope not.'

'I've been taking stock of what I've made of

my life so far. It's true that I've got a bit of money put by, but on the downside I haven't managed to find myself a wife and start a family.' He passed off this lie without a second thought; Maureen Wilby and the two daughters they'd had together had long been consigned to history.

'I'm sorry to hear that.'

'No, Mum; when it comes down to it, you're the only family I've got. So I decided it was time to build bridges and here I am.'

'I can't say it wasn't a shock when I found you sitting at the kitchen table.' Hilda's heart still raced. She held on to the edge of the table to steady herself. 'I wasn't sure if you were still in Yorkshire. For all I knew, you could have taken the King's shilling and ended up in Egypt or Burma.'

'Not me. I'm exempted from action because of a dicky ticker. But not to worry, I reckon I've got a few more good years left.'

'What's wrong with your heart?' she interrupted.

'The quack took a listen and said something about a murmur.'

'Like your father.' Hilda had never been sure if Willis's weak heart had played a part in his accident. According to an eyewitness, he'd been working Arnold's threshing machine and had stopped to tinker with the engine without shutting down the whole apparatus. He seemed to have grown dizzy then somehow fallen backwards into the huge, turning drum where he'd been crushed to death. Alfie had been eleven years old at the time — a significant age for any lad to lose his father. 'But if they wouldn't have you in the forces, did they give you a desk job instead?'

'Yes, something like that. But I found out I wasn't born to be a pen-pusher. Sitting behind a desk got on my nerves so that's why I decided to come back to what I know.'

'So this isn't just a quick visit?'

'No, Ma — I'm back for good. Give me the country life any day of the week.'

Hilda wasn't sure how much of the glib account she believed but she started to work through the implications of her son's sudden reappearance. 'So you're looking for work?'

'Yes, I want to find a job here on my old stamping ground.'

The idea of him putting aside his tailored suit in favour of dungarees and wellington boots increased Hilda's scepticism. 'Even if you do, you can't live here,' she pointed out. 'The hostel is for women only.'

He grinned and slapped the table. 'Yes — I can see that would set the cat among the pigeons. It's a pity, though. I ran into Kathleen Hirst on the driveway. She's an old flame of mine — I wouldn't have minded rekindling that little romance.'

'And that's precisely why we have the women-only rule,' Hilda said with a return to her usual firmness. 'Listen to me, Alfie — if you really want to find a job, you might try asking Joe Kellett.'

'Out at Home Farm?'

'Yes. You remember their son, Frank?'

79

'You mean the lad who wasn't all there?'

'Yes. The poor soul was turned out of the house by Joe last winter. He had nowhere to go. Not too long afterwards Grace Kershaw and Bill Mostyn found him frozen to death on Swinsty Moor. Grace and Bill were wed last Saturday, by the way.'

'Get to the point, Mum.' *Good grief, this is what I dreaded — hearing old names, stale gossip, Ma going on and on. But needs must.*

'It means the Kelletts would be glad of an extra pair of hands. They're not managing on their own, even with help from the Land Army.' She paused to observe Alfie's clean white hands and the soft fleshiness of his face. 'It'd be hard work, mind you. And not a lot happens out there — it might be too quiet for you.'

He stood up and took his jacket from the back of the chair. 'Quiet' was precisely what he'd had in mind — an out-of-the-way place in which to hunker down while some trouble in Northgate had a chance to die down. If he set off now and cut across country, he could just about make Home Farm before nightfall.

'Thanks for the tip-off, Mum.' He pecked her on the cheek then headed for the door. 'Peace and quiet is just what the doctor ordered.'

# 6

Grace woke to the warmth of Bill's body beside her. For a few moments she wondered where she was then the floral design on the thin cotton curtains came into focus and she gradually got her bearings. She lay next to her husband in the front bedroom of number 4 Church Terrace. The bedclothes were thrown back because of the summer heat and she could see that Bill's pyjama jacket was unbuttoned, his smooth chest rising and falling while he slept. A lingering shyness made her turn her head away. Then she reminded herself of her new status and stretched out her hand.

He sighed at the touch of her fingertips on his cheek. His eyelids flickered open.

'Good morning,' she whispered.

'Is it?'

The curtains let in the bright sunlight. 'Yes. We're in for another scorcher.'

He drew her towards him and she didn't resist. 'We don't have to get up yet, do we?'

'Not for a while.' They had time to lie together and revel in the novel sensation of skin against skin, his arm under her neck, her hand resting on his chest. The tick of the bedside clock was the only sound in the room.

Bill pressed his lips against the soft mass of her hair. 'Do we have to go to work today?'

She moved closer. 'You know we do. I'm due

81

at Home Farm with Brenda and the new girl, Poppy Gledhill. You have to drive out to Arnold White's.'

'But really, do we have to?' Like Shakespeare's schoolboy creeping like a snail to school, he felt an overwhelming reluctance to get out of bed, but for altogether different reasons. He kissed her again. 'I'd far rather stay here with you.'

Grace made a feeble attempt to push him away. 'Bill Mostyn, you'll get me into your mother's bad books if I'm late for work.'

He smiled and showered her with more kisses. Then suddenly, in one swift movement he raised himself and rolled clear of her on to the floor. 'All right, Mrs Mostyn — you win. What's for breakfast?'

In spite of her dutiful reminders, it was a wrench to see him slide his feet into his slippers then pad towards the door. She pouted then pulled the sheets to her neck. 'Toast and jam this morning. No eggs, no bacon.'

Amused by the reversal of roles, he teased her as he walked along the landing. 'I'm following orders — you were the one who said we had to go to work today.'

He smiled to himself as he went downstairs. 'Happy' didn't cover how he'd felt these last few days. 'Transported' was more like it — taken out of one life into another that bore no resemblance to what had gone before. It was still a blur — the two days and nights at River View under Mrs Marion Binns' vigilant gaze, the days spent walking along the riverside with the wind sweeping across the limestone landscape, the water tumbling between white cliffs, curlews calling overhead. And the nights cocooned in the little attic room, the floorboards creaking, rain on the roof. Grace by his side.

She came down in her cream and pink dressing gown as he cut slices of bread for their toast. The kettle was on the boil, tea leaves ready for the pot.

'Two pieces for me, please. I've a feeling I'll need to build myself up for the day ahead.'

'You reckon Joe will keep your nose to the grind-stone?'

'As per usual.' On the previous day she'd worked her way back into Land Army routine with the relatively easy task of scrubbing out Horace's hen huts, but today at Home Farm was bound to be tougher. 'Brenda says Poppy is finding it hard to cope, poor lamb. We're not sure she's cut out for farm work.'

'You two will look after her, I'm sure.' *Tick-tock* — the clock on the kitchen mantel-piece, like the one in the bedroom, was relentless. 'I'd better get cracking. Arnold's expecting me at half eight and he's a stickler for good timekeeping.'

With a mouth full of toast, Grace tilted her head to receive his kiss. Bill vanished upstairs and she was left to wash up. She hummed a tune as she ran the tap. The sun streamed in through the kitchen window overlooking the playing field at the back of the Institute. She saw Maurice drive his van into the small yard and open up the door to his workshop. The day had begun.

'Listen to me, girls — I've thought of a good way to cheer Poppy up.' Late that evening, Brenda drew Una, Joyce and Kathleen together in a corner of the hostel common room that overlooked the driveway at the front of the house. It was lined from floor to ceiling with old volumes on the subjects of history, science and geography from the days when Fieldhead had been a private school. Worn leather armchairs formed a semicircle around the empty fire grate.

Reluctantly Joyce abandoned her book — an absorbing mystery called *The Wheel Spins*. 'Oh dear, what are you up to now?'

'Don't be like that,' Brenda protested. 'You saw what Poppy was like at supper. She's fagged out.'

'So are we all after a day at Home Farm.' Kathleen pointed out what they already knew.

Brenda stuck to her guns. 'This was different, though. There was one point when Grace and I thought the poor kid was going to burst into tears.'

'Why — what happened exactly?' Joyce's interest was piqued.

'There's a new chap working for Joe — well, new to me. Grace remembers him from the old days. It turns out he's Ma Craven's long-lost son.'

This news silenced the group and they looked at each other in astonishment.

'I know; you're wondering why he never came up in conversation before now. But Grace is adamant that Joe's new helper is Alfie Craven.' As Brenda talked, she gave Kathleen a long, hard stare. 'Ah, I see — this comes as no surprise to you. He's the chap you had the barney with on Monday night.'

Kathleen was puzzled. 'His Christian name is Alfie,' she agreed. 'But when I knew him he went by the name of Watkins.'

'Well, he's one and the same — Alfie Craven, Alfie Watkins — take your pick. We only saw his back view the other night, it's true. But I could've sworn it was the same chap the moment I clapped eyes on him at the Kelletts' place. And he's the blighter who upset Poppy.'

'Why, what did he do?' Kathleen's resigned air showed them that she wasn't surprised at this either.

'He turned the hosepipe on her and drenched her on purpose then made a big show of fetching a towel to dry her down. She didn't know where to put herself. Grace had to step in and tell him to keep his hands to himself. Alfie thought the whole thing was one big joke.'

'So what can we do to cheer Poppy up?' Una hoped that Brenda's reply wouldn't be too outrageous.

Checking that the door was tightly shut, Brenda gathered them round. 'We can play Cupid,' she explained gleefully.

'Who for?' Una's uneasiness grew.

'For Nev and Pops, that's who. Sorry, Una, you've fallen out of favour. Everyone can see it if they stop to think about it — Neville Thomson is sweet on our new girl.'

85

'But I don't think we should . . . ' Una began and was soon backed up by Joyce.

'I agree. Pushing Poppy in Neville's way isn't one of your better ideas, Brenda. In my opinion we need to give her more time to settle in.'

'Spoilsports!' Brenda frowned then turned to Kathleen for support.

'Don't look at me.' Kathleen shook her head then walked to the window. 'Talk of the devil,' she muttered as Neville himself pedalled up the drive. His face looked hot, as though he'd cycled hard all the way from Brigg Farm.

'What's he want?' Brenda was the first to rush from the room, ready to find out.

Joyce soon joined her on the front doorstep, with Una and Kathleen hanging back out of sight.

'Don't!' Joyce warned an excited Brenda.

'Why not? Now's our chance . . . '

Neville reached the house and flung his bike to one side. 'I've come to see Una. Is she in?'

'That's why not,' Joyce muttered. It was clear to her, if not to Brenda, that the young lad's case of calf love for Una was nowhere near cured. 'Yes, she's in,' she told him. 'Shall I fetch her for you?'

'There's no need; I'm here.' Una stepped forward with an uncomfortable feeling that something unusual was going on. Neville didn't have the look of a hopeful suitor, more that of a messenger carrying urgent news. Her heart began to beat faster.

'Una!' he gasped as he leaped up the steps. Breathless, he grabbed her hand and dragged her forward, almost overbalancing her in the process. 'It's Angelo . . . '

'Oh no, please!' *I can't bear it*, she thought. *There's been an accident in the shipyard. Sheets of hot metal, circular saws, sparks flying through the air, hazardous high scaffolding with ice-cold seawater far below.* The blood rushed from her cheeks and she turned deathly pale.

'No, it's not bad news — it's good,' Neville insisted, 'Dad heard it straight from the horse's mouth. He was over at Penny Lane to drop off a couple of sides of bacon. Squadron Leader Aldridge was the one who let him in on it.'

'Let him in on what?' Joyce prompted. She feared Una would fall down in a dead faint if he didn't tell them quickly.

'The Italians are coming back,' he reported triumphantly. 'To Beckwith Camp. Some time next week. Cross my heart and hope to die!'

⋆   ⋆   ⋆

It was Poppy's bad luck to be sent for a third day on the trot to work at Home Farm. It would have been bearable if she'd only been taking orders from Joe, but Alfie Craven had muscled in on the act from day one, making his presence felt at every end and turn.

Lift this, carry that, hose down the dairy — no slacking! The commands were endless, issued in a manner that was a combination of teasing and bullying and seemed reserved especially for her. With Grace and the other girls he was more circumspect and he took care not to do it at all in front of Joe or Emily.

'I see Alfie's made himself at home,' Brenda remarked to Joe as she took a breather before her next task. Morning milking was over and Grace and Poppy were still busy in the dairy, pouring milk from pails into the cooler. The subject of their conversation was clearly visible, dressed in blue overalls and black rubber boots, leaning against the dairy wall. He smoked a cigarette as he watched Bill's arrival in his tractor repair van.

Joe cleared his throat then spat on the ground. 'What's it to you, missy?'

'Nothing. He didn't strike me as someone who'd settle down to hard graft, that's all.'

As if he knew they were talking about him, Alfie stared at them warily through a cloud of blue smoke.

'An extra pair of hands is all I'm bothered about.' Joe's response was typically pragmatic. 'As long as he does as he's told, I'm not complaining.'

'And he billets here with you, does he?' Brenda's curiosity about Hilda's son grew by the hour. Why had he called himself Watkins back in his Millwood days? And what had led him to leave the town and lie low here in the back of beyond?

'Why not? Frank's room was going begging. I've said as long as Alfie doesn't make any noise, he's welcome to board and lodgings. I'll take it out of his wages, mind.'

Alfie threw down his cigarette then sauntered over to talk to Bill.

'He's used to dishing out orders, I'll say that

for him.' Even Brenda had found it hard to stand up to his pushy ways. It wasn't so much Alfie's solid muscle and the low rumble of his voice as the slow certainty of his movements accompanied by a lack of expression in his small, dark eyes. The upper lids were hooded, effectively concealing what lay behind.

'Not here, he isn't.' The old man took exception to the implication. 'Alfie Craven is well aware that I can send him packing the minute he steps out of line.'

Fed up with the direction of the conversation, the curmudgeonly farmer shuffled off to negotiate with Bill. 'My old Ferguson's out of action in the cart shed. See if you can patch her up without it costing me a fortune. And Alfie — go back to the dairy and put a rocket under those two girls. Tell them there's half a dozen other jobs for them to get stuck into as soon as they're done there.'

So Bill took his box of tools and set about stripping the tractor engine while Alfie sought out Poppy and Grace. He chivvied them sarcastically as they lifted the heavy pails of milk and criticized if there was any spillage from the cooler. Then he decided it was Poppy's job to heave the heavy metal churns into position while Grace joined Brenda in the yard.

'I'd better stay here.' Grace was loath to leave Poppy to his tender mercies. 'Rolling those full churns to the door for collection takes two of us.'

Alfie stared impassively at her. 'Please yourself.' His voice dripped with scorn as he turned on his heel and left.

'Ta,' Poppy breathed, already so tired she was scarcely able to think. Her wrists ached from hand-milking twelve cows — an activity that she found distasteful — and she'd taken a few kicks on the shins and swipes of cows' tails in the process. To have had to put up with more of Alfie's taunting would have been the final straw.

Grace took the weight of the first churn then together they rolled it to the door. 'One of these days Joe will see fit to invest in some up-to-date machinery and take the backache out of all of this.'

'That's not what I meant. I mean ta for saving me from Alfie.'

'You're very welcome.' *Poor little chick. She'll have to learn the ropes quickly and grow a thicker skin if she's to stay the course.* Grace saw fit to add a piece of advice. 'You're right to steer clear of Alfie Craven. Bill and I were talking about him earlier, trying to remember the details surrounding his final disappearance. It had to do with the Fosters' daughter, Shirley.'

The names meant nothing to Poppy.

'They're a well-to-do family in Hawkshead. Mrs Craven worked for them as their house-keeper. Alfie had already gone to the bad and was rattling around the village at that time, finding lodgings wherever he could. Somehow he wormed his way into Shirley Foster's affections. She was much younger than him — seventeen at the most.' Grace thought it best to leave the rest to Poppy's imagination.

'Oh, I see.' Through the door Poppy glimpsed Alfie chain-smoking and watching Bill as he

90

worked on Joe's tractor. Bill refused Alfie's offer of a cigarette. There was obviously no love lost between the two men. She nodded at Grace and took the warning to heart. 'Ta very much. I'll do my best to keep out of his way.'

★   ★   ★

Sunday remained Brenda's favourite day of the week and she made sure that everyone knew it. While the majority of Land Girls at the hostel stayed indoors to perform domestic tasks, she would be out and about on her beloved motor bike, which she cleaned and tended with as much devotion as other women shower on their first-born babies. This very morning she'd lifted out the dipstick to check the oil level, taken out the spark plugs and cleaned them one by one, then unscrewed the petrol tank and peered inside to ensure there was enough fuel to carry her wherever she wanted to go. Then she'd taken a rag to polish Sloper's steel exhaust pipe, wheel rims and handlebars. Finally satisfied, she had wolfed down a sandwich for an early lunch then quickly donned jacket, headscarf and goggles, and set off up the dale.

Nothing else gave her anywhere near the same sense of freedom as riding a motor bike. She loved to lean forward into the buffeting wind, to hear the roar of the engine as she opened the throttle and see the tarmac surface of the road speed by in a blur under her front wheel. The more remote her destination the better, so on this fine morning she rode along Swinsty Edge and through Hawkshead — a tiny hamlet of half a dozen houses, with the Fosters' grand hall hidden down a long driveway behind a copse of mature beeches — on over the moor top then down into Attercliffe, with a silver river twisting its way through the new dale. Here there were broader sweeps of green pasture rising up steep hillsides, dotted with sheep and black-and-white cows and intersected by the usual intricate patchwork of stone walls.

*Freedom!* Fresh air filled Brenda's lungs and her heart was eased of all its cares as the steep, single-track road curved down into the valley.

There was a sharp bend ahead and high walls to either side. She braked and leaned into the bend. Out of nowhere a low, green, two-seater sports car with its top down hurtled towards her.

There was a flash of gleaming metal, a squeal of brakes. Brenda mounted the grass verge and rode Sloper headlong into a ditch, where she came to a sudden, undignified halt. Donald White turned off his engine then leaped from the MG and ran to see if she was hurt.

Groggily Brenda extricated herself from her bike. A smell of petrol filled the air and she saw at a glance that Sloper's front fork had buckled under the impact. 'Damn!' she said over and over as Donald helped her to her feet.

'Brenda, are you all right?' A female voice asked the question and a woman peered over Donald's shoulder.

As the world came back into focus, Brenda recognized Doreen, sportily dressed in cream linen slacks, checked shirt and a red neckerchief that matched her scarlet lipstick. Her dark hair was piled high on her head and held in place by shiny silver combs. Donald looked equally casual in an open-necked shirt and dark blue trousers.

'Yes, no thanks to you two!' Brenda perched her goggles on top of her head and shook herself free of Donald's helping hand. 'You must have been doing forty at the very least.'

'Don't look at me,' Doreen protested. 'I wasn't the one behind the wheel.'

'Steady on — it was thirty at the most.' Now that he saw that Brenda wasn't seriously hurt — only a cut to the back of her left hand and a bad graze on her knee where her trouser leg had torn — he was quick to defend himself. 'It was a blind bend; neither of us was to blame. Anyway, at least the ditch gave you a soft landing.'

'But look at the state of my bike,' she groaned. Still suffering from shock, she struggled to pull Sloper clear of the ditch and had to let Donald help her. When they got the bike back on to the road, it was clear that it couldn't be ridden.

'Yes, that thing's not going anywhere for the time being,' Donald agreed. Then, wanting to persuade Brenda that there were no hard feelings, he suggested the best course of action. 'Listen, we're only a couple of hundred yards from home. Why not leave your bike here and walk with Doreen down to the house? Hettie's there. She can give you a cup of tea and clean up those cuts while I turn the car around, drive home and make a telephone call for you.'

Brenda glanced down in surprise at her bleeding hand. Shock must have shielded her from the pain, but the cut looked quite deep, so she nodded and agreed to the plan. 'Who will you call?'

Donald vaulted into the car without opening the door. 'I'll try Maurice to see if he can drive his van out here to collect your bike. If he's not in, I'll try Bill.'

Offering no resistance, Brenda let Doreen lead her down the winding hill. 'You were the last person I expected to see in this neck of the woods,' she muttered. 'Anyway, I was under the impression that was Les's MG.'

Doreen was unabashed. 'It is; Donald borrowed it so he could take me for a spin.'

Ahead of them, the entrance to Dale End Farm came into view. The Whites' house lay at the end of a short driveway with formal gardens to either side and was bigger and more impressive than the run-of-the-mill stone cottages typical of the area. There was Queen Anne styling to the three gables that faced the road. The stone window surrounds were ornately carved and a pair of stone lions flanked the broad steps leading to a porticoed doorway.

'When did he ask you out?' Brenda and Doreen stood aside to let Donald overtake them on the drive.

'Last Saturday, after Grace's wedding.' Doreen took it as read that a well-off landowner's son would be bound to show an interest in her.

'Blimey, you kept that quiet.'

'Luckily he's got the looks as well as the where-withal, so I jumped at the chance.'

Brenda's eyes widened in surprise. 'You don't

94

mince your words, do you?'

The smile became a low laugh. 'Don't tell me you wouldn't do the same. You'd snap Donald's hand off if he asked you out. Come on, Brenda; you can't tell me you wouldn't!' Straightening her face in time for them to join him in the entrance porch, Doreen let Brenda go in first.

As they entered the spacious hallway, Hettie came down the stairs. Within a matter of seconds, Donald's older sister had assessed the situation and taken control. 'Come with me into the sitting room,' she told Brenda as she stepped between her and Doreen, a move that instantly left the Rita Hayworth look-alike out of the picture. 'No, on second thoughts, come up to the bathroom where we can clean up those cuts and grazes without making too much mess.'

Brenda followed obediently while Doreen went with Donald into a study room leading straight off from the hallway.

'How did this happen?' Hettie asked once she'd opened a first-aid cupboard on the bathroom wall and handed Brenda a wad of cotton wool to soak up the blood. She was the taller of the two by a couple of inches, dressed in a pale green dress with a primrose-yellow silk scarf tied around her neck. The outfit went some way towards softening her spare frame and stern features.

'I ended up in a ditch, thanks to Donald.' Brenda winced as the Dragon dabbed her hand with a pad of lint soaked in Dettol. 'If I hadn't taken quick action and swerved off the road, it would have been far worse.'

'Take off your trousers then lift up your leg.'

Again Brenda did as she was told. 'Ouch, that stings!' she muttered as Hettie applied the pad to her graze. Averting her gaze, she caught sight of her reflection in a round mirror above the sink. Her goggles were askew, her hair looked like a bird's nest and there was a streak of black oil from Sloper's engine on her right cheek.

'Now that I've got all the grit out, I can cover it with a clean bandage.' Hettie did this with expert ease then held up Brenda's torn and mud-covered trousers between thumb and forefinger. 'Would you like to borrow a spare pair of slacks from me? They'd probably fit you around the waist and you could roll up the bottoms if they're too long.'

Brenda meekly accepted the offer then sat on the edge of the bath while Hettie went off to fetch the slacks. She heard quick footsteps along the landing but wasn't prepared for the door to open and for Les's face to suddenly appear.

'Oh, I say!' Brenda made a grab for the nearest towel to cover her knickers and bare legs.

Les gasped and backed out, leaving the door swinging open. 'Sorry. I didn't . . . I mean, oh blimey!'

Brenda put her hand to her mouth to stifle the laughter that had bubbled up at the sight of Les's shocked face. 'It's all right, I'm decent now,' she called out as she wrapped the towel around her waist.

'I had no idea you were here,' he called back. 'What are the bandages for? Are you all right?'

There wasn't time to answer because Hettie

bustled back with the slacks. 'I warned you not to lend Donald your car,' she grumbled as she pushed past. 'I knew he would only use it to show off to that floozy and I was right. Try these,' she said in an aside to Brenda, who made sure her new bandage was secure before she slid on the proffered trousers. 'He'd hardly got out of the driveway, probably wasn't even looking at the road with Miss Fancy Pants sitting beside him.'

'I'll bloody kill the beggar!' No sooner had Hettie put him in the picture than Les stormed off downstairs.

Brenda grinned awkwardly. 'I expect it's his precious MG he's worried about.'

Hettie shook her head as she put away the sticking plaster, scissors and bandages. 'No, he's not bothered about his car. It's you.'

'Why, what's Les said?' Brenda quickly got over her surprise and she resumed a careless manner.

'Nothing. I just saw the way he danced with you at Grace's wedding.'

'Oh, I see. Then we'd better go down and show him I'm none the worse for wear.' She led the way out of the bathroom and along the landing.

By the time they got downstairs there was a full-scale row going on between the brothers, with Doreen standing quietly in the background.

'I've telephoned for Maurice to come, haven't I?' Donald yelled. 'What more do you expect me to do?'

'Not drive like an idiot in the first place.' Les hadn't heard Brenda and Hettie's footsteps on the stairs. 'You could have killed her!'

'But I didn't.'

'You bloody could have, though.'

'Keep your hair on. Anyone would think I did it on purpose.' Donald took out a cigarette then offered one to Doreen and glanced up the stairs at Brenda. 'Come down and tell my brother it was an accident, pure and simple; stop him getting into even more of a stew,' he told her. 'By the way, Maurice is on his way.'

Brenda blinked back the irritation she felt. Donald White hadn't covered himself in glory during the morning's events and she recollected other small details that she'd heard about him — that he'd avoided conscription on more than one occasion and that he fancied himself as a ladies' man. And she wasn't keen on the sly smile he shared with Doreen as he offered her a light, as if the whole thing was a joke between them. 'Ta for that. But this is going to put me out of action for a good long while,' she forecast. 'It's not a five-minute job to straighten out Sloper's front fork and patch up the petrol tank. It'll be even longer if Maurice has to send off for spare parts for the suspension.'

'Brenda doesn't like having her wings clipped,' Doreen commented wryly. 'I don't suppose either of you has got a spare motor bike tucked away in one of your nice big barns?'

Hettie looked daggers at her. 'We might look as if we're made of money, but — '

'That's right, we're not.' A new voice joined the argument. It belonged to Arnold White, entering the house with a shotgun under his arm

98

and two black cocker spaniels at his heels. He'd been out shooting rabbits and was in no mood to entertain visitors. 'I don't know what's going on here, but Hettie will put me in the picture. Donald, Les, I expect to see you at dinner, six o'clock sharp.'

It was a clear signal for Doreen and Brenda to leave, but the question was: how were they to get home?

'I'll give you a lift.' Les jumped in with a solution for Brenda, while Hettie told Doreen in no uncertain terms that she must wait in the kitchen for Maurice to arrive.

The blatant snub stung Doreen into defiance. 'No, I have a better idea. I realize the MG is only a two-seater, but Brenda won't mind sitting on my knee, will you, Bren?'

'No, that won't do. You should do as Hettie says and stay here,' Les said quickly and firmly before offering Brenda an arm to lean on. 'Can you walk all right? I'll put the top up on the drive back if you'd prefer.'

'No,' she said. 'I prefer it down for now.'

They were out of the front door and in the car before Doreen could object. Les held Brenda's door open then closed it carefully. Within seconds he had the engine turning and they were easing down the gravel drive.

'Phew, the Dragon certainly has it in for Doreen.' Brenda was determined to keep the tone light above the whine of the engine as they climbed the one-in-four gradient. She glanced ahead to the rugged limestone outcrops on the brow of the hill.

'What makes you say that?'

'She was practically breathing fire back there when she told her to wait in the kitchen. And you heard her earlier: she called Doreen Miss Fancy Pants.'

'That's true, she did.' Les laughed. 'Doreen's not serious enough for Hettie; she'd rather Donald and I went out with girls who spend time in a library and who know how to keep an eye on the difference between income and expenditure. Dad's the same way.'

'But it's not up to them.'

'True. That's why I'm here now.' The car reached the top of the incline and a new vista opened up before them. Limestone gave way to darker millstone grit, trees were more scattered and mile after mile of low-lying heather took over from bright green pastures. Overhead, clouds gathered, threatening showers. 'I'll park in this lay-by and put the roof up in case it rains,' Les decided as he pulled off the road.

Brenda watched him unbuckle leather straps and undo press studs then raise the black canvas roof. Suddenly she was wrapped inside a small, dark space, aware of the painful cut on her hand and the graze beneath the bandage on her knee. Les's face was serious as he got back into the car.

'Hettie lent me these slacks,' she said apropos of nothing.

He twisted in his seat and leaned towards her. There was a question in his grey eyes.

'Ta for running me home,' she said in a low, soft voice.

'You don't mind me doing this?' He leaned closer so that his features blurred and she felt the warmth of his breath on her lips.

With a small shake of her head, she let his lips touch hers then sank into the kiss.

# 7

Edith Mostyn sat in Grace and Bill's sunny front room drinking tea from the delicate Noritake cups that she'd given them as a wedding present. There was a plate of salmon paste and cucumber sandwiches on the occasional table spread with a lace-edged cloth — signs that Grace had made a special effort on her new mother-in-law's behalf.

'I read in the Sunday paper that the Allies are busy building up our defences in the Med.' Bill assumed that war talk was safe territory with his mother and he wanted her to feel at ease. 'We're sending convoys to Gibraltar and Alexandria, ready for 'the big one'.'

Instead of relaxing, Edith looked worried. 'Ought we to be talking so openly about Mr Churchill's plans?'

'Why not? Jack did when I was chatting to him at the reception.'

'And if it's in the papers, it can't be a secret,' Grace added. The change in the balance of power between herself and Edith took her by surprise. Where once she would have smiled shyly and deferred as she sat on the red leather settee in Edith's lounge, she now felt it was her place to play the hostess and express opinions. 'I overheard Jack saying that they're getting men and machines ashore as fast as ever they can. Only last month, his parent ship unloaded LCMs in Norway. Last week his Royal Navy

102

freighter was anchored off Gourock, awaiting fresh orders.'

Edith looked puzzled. 'What are LCMs when they're at home?'

'Flat-bottomed landing craft.' Bill took over from Grace as he watched her top up his mother's cup. 'Jack was lucky to get time off to be my best man. I wouldn't be surprised if his ship is headed for the Straits of Gibraltar as we speak. It's going to be all right, Mum — you'll see. Mr Churchill will soon persuade President Roosevelt to send us even more planes and troops and then Herr Hitler will be on a hiding to nothing.'

'But I worry about our boys meanwhile.' Edith put down her cup and saucer then folded her hands in her lap. She took in the old-fashioned mahogany sideboard and worn upholstery of the easy chairs they sat in — dilapidated furniture that came with the rented house. 'Thomas Lund's mother hasn't had any word of him for weeks. And there are bound to be U-boats and enemy aircraft lying in wait for Jack's convoy when it gets closer to Gibraltar.'

Silence followed as Grace tried to envisage Edgar's role in the conflict to come. How many more missions would her brother have to fly? How many dogfights over the Med against the Luftwaffe and the Regia Aeronautica? A sombre mood built in the room until Bill came up with a diversion.

'They say the Italian prisoners are coming back to Beckwith Camp.'

'That's right,' Edith confirmed. 'I must

103

remember to have a quiet word with Una Sharpe, to remind her that her first duty is to the Land Army, however strongly she may feel about a certain prisoner.'

'Angelo Bachetti,' Grace reminded her. 'I'm sure Una knows how to behave if Angelo is one of the ones who returns. She doesn't know for certain that he will be.'

Edith's frown didn't ease. 'She's a good girl, I agree. But feelings are heightened during times like these. And some of the girls at the hostel weren't keen on her liaison with an enemy prisoner in the first place — Jean Fox for a start, along with Ivy McNamara and Dorothy Cook, who both asked to be transferred soon after Christmas because of it.'

'And good riddance.' Grace had witnessed Ivy's and Dorothy's spiteful actions towards Una and recalled the label of 'collaborator' that they'd tried to pin on her. 'Everyone at Fieldhead except Jean was glad to see the back of those two.'

Edith tapped one hand against the other. 'Still, it's vital to uphold morale. And while we're on the subject, I have some concerns about how Poppy and Doreen are settling in. They're like chalk and cheese; one wouldn't say boo to a goose, while the other — '

'Would scare off a whole gaggle of the blighters.' Bill drew the awkward conversation to a close with a flippant remark. He got up and pulled one curtain across to shade his mother's eyes from the sun. 'Doreen has got bags of confidence. I can see her as a star of the silver screen or hoofing it on a West End stage once the war is over. And good for her is what I say.'

★   ★   ★

Alone in her room, Joyce took out the letter she'd received two days earlier, on Friday the twelfth. It was from Edgar.

'Dear Joyce, I'm writing to you on the spur of the moment — I hope you don't mind. The way I look at it, a chap in my situation has nothing to lose.'

She'd been handed the letter by post mistress and church organist Esther Liddell, who was also a mainstay of Burnside Women's Institute. Esther had hurried out on to the main street and intercepted Joyce as she arrived outside Grace's new house after work. 'Here you are — this came too late to go out with the second post, so I thought I'd hand it to you in person.'

Joyce hadn't recognized the writing so had slipped the unopened envelope into her pocket and not thought much about it until later that evening, sitting alone in the room she shared with Doreen and Poppy.

'The fact is, I spend a lot of my time thinking about you,' the letter continued. 'I remember the things you say and the way you look, but mostly it's the sound of your voice that stays with me. I hear it when I should be concentrating on maps of Europe, radar images and all the top-secret stuff we're involved in day after day. But at the back of my head I can always hear you.'

Joyce hadn't taken much in at first. She'd had

to read the signature at the bottom of the page to find out who was writing this: 'Edgar', written in a neat, forward-sloping hand. An image of him had flashed before her eyes, dressed in his RAF uniform, sitting alone on the front pew at St Michael's and wearing the white carnation that she'd pinned on to his lapel. He'd glanced at her as she'd sat down next to him, his eyes filling with tears when Esther had played the 'Wedding March'. She'd smiled at him then made room for his father.

After the ceremony and the speeches, she and Edgar had danced together then walked in the moonlit woods. Nothing had been said.

'You won't be expecting to read this. And I never thought I'd write it. But as things go, I might not get another chance. So I'll come straight out with it. I love you, Joyce Cutler. There!'

She'd sat on her bed with her head spinning. 'I love you, Joyce Cutler. There!'

*Love!* Love barged its way into her life without warning or invitation, knocking down her defences, battering at her heart.

'I've said it without any way of knowing if you feel the same way. The chances are you might not. But I love everything about you — the way your hands rested in your lap in between playing tunes on the piano for the Christmas show last December, how you took care of me when I was at my lowest ebb, your calmness in the eye of the storm.'

The picture in Joyce's mind's eye flew back to Edgar collapsed dead drunk on the floor of his father's beer cellar, then on to him wandering the frozen moor, seeking oblivion after the torments of war.

'Ought I to put this in an envelope and send it in the post? I doubt it. But like I said, what do I have to lose?'

The writing in royal-blue ink grew cramped and sloped towards the bottom of the page. At Edgar's own admission it had been written and sent on the spur of the moment. Had drink played a part? Was he to be believed? Joyce's hand had been shaking as she came again to the signature.

'I speak this from the heart. I hope that my confession is not a burden to you and that you will see fit to write back to me — a short note to say that you received my letter and a word or two that tells me you're not offended. That's all for now. With love from Edgar.'

A single kiss, a small smudge on the last two letters of his name. Trying to control the thumping of her heart, she'd put the letter away and determined not to speak of it until she'd worked out her response. Now, late on Sunday afternoon, she took it out and read it again.

⋆ ⋆ ⋆

Una had heard nothing from Angelo since Neville's shock announcement on the Wednesday. But it was true: the Italians were leaving Scotland and returning to Penny Lane. Everyone in the village was talking about it — how the prisoners would be back working at the farms alongside the Land Girls, how they would help them with the harvest and charm the birds from the trees.

She'd written her beloved a hasty letter, ignoring any fear that he might not be included in the group of returnees and expressing her joy, telling him it was beyond her wildest dreams to see him again so soon. 'I'd settled in my mind that we would have to wait until the war ended before we could be together, but now this! Oh, Angelo, I can hardly wait!' She'd signed her note and pressed her lips against it, then folded the paper and put it in an envelope. It had gone off in the post first thing on Thursday.

She'd been holding her breath ever since. Did anyone know exactly when the prisoners would arrive? Would they come by train or by road? Was there a list of returnees with Angelo's name on it? No one in the village or on the farms knew the answers. So she went on in a daze of anticipation, going through the motions of collecting eggs, milking cows and cleaning out pig pens, but thinking only of Angelo and how soon he would hold her in his arms.

Now it was almost evening and there was still no word.

★   ★   ★

'Ta very much for the lift, Maurice.' Hoping not to be seen, Doreen slid quickly out of the motor mechanic's van as he drew up in the hostel yard late on Sunday afternoon.

'Any time,' he replied as she shut the door.

*Never again!* Doreen thought. The old vehicle stank of engine oil, and Brenda's broken motor bike had rattled around in the back, all the way home from Dale End Farm. On top of which, Maurice's conversation hadn't been up to much — all about football, as if she, Doreen Wells, could possibly be the slightest bit interested in who the Burnside Wanderers beat in the last match of the season.

She entered the hostel by the back entrance and bumped into Kathleen helping herself to hot chocolate in Mrs Craven's kitchen.

'Wasn't that Maurice's van?' Kathleen enquired with one eyebrow raised. 'Not quite the style to which you're accustomed, eh?'

'Don't ask.' Doreen hurried on, along a dark corridor into the front hall, where she ran into Poppy.

'Hello! Have you seen Brenda?' Poppy asked.

'Why should I?'

'I don't know. I just thought . . . It's nothing. I wanted to ask her advice about something.'

'Well, as a matter of fact, yes, I have.' Doreen relented and steered Poppy into the common room where she seized the opportunity to blow her own trumpet. 'Brenda and I spent the afternoon with the White boys over in Attercliffe. She left before me so I thought she'd have been home by now.'

'The White boys?'

Doreen preened in the mirror above the fireplace, touching up her lipstick and patting her hair into place. 'Donald and Leslie. I'll give you one guess who I was with: the good-looking

109

one, of course. Not that Leslie is bad looking, just not on a par with his brother.'

With Doreen in full flow, Poppy became aware of a flurry of activity on the stairs and soon Kathleen and Elsie burst into the room, quickly followed by Alfie Craven in his Sunday-best suit and trilby hat.

'Alfie's turned up trumps,' Elsie explained while Kathleen looked on disparagingly. 'Look — he's brought cocoa powder for a start.'

'Where did this come from?' Doreen demanded as she took the drum from Elsie and examined the label.

'Never you mind.' In his rapid retreat from town, Alfie had crammed a suitcase full of contraband goods and had made an arrangement for more to follow. Now he leaned back against the door jamb with his hands in his jacket pockets, hat tilted at a rakish angle.

'And these.' Elsie showed Doreen and Poppy two bars of milk chocolate. 'There's enough to go round all the girls — one square each with four left over.'

'But best of all, these!' Alfie pulled a slim packet from his pocket. 'One pair of nylon stockings. Stand back, everyone — these are like hen's teeth. Even I have trouble getting hold of them.'

Kathleen continued to frown at the dubious offerings. 'But where did you get them?'

'Let's just say I ran into somebody who knows somebody and leave it at that.' Alfie was in his element, teasing and flirting but with a hard, calculating edge. He wafted the packet of nylons under Kathleen's nose. 'What would a girl do to get her hands on a pair of these, I wonder?'

Kathleen couldn't disguise her disdain. 'If you're asking what *this* girl would do — not much, as it happens.'

He blocked her way as she tried to slip past. 'What, not even a kiss for old time's sake?'

Quick as a flash, Doreen moved in to snatch the stockings and brush her lips against Alfie's cheek. 'There, I've paid the asking price and ta very much!'

Alfie raised his hand to wipe a lipstick smear from his cheek. He ducked his head to one side then grinned at Doreen as if recognizing that he'd met his match. 'Fair enough. I look forward to seeing you wearing them.'

'You'll be lucky!' she trilled as she swanned out into the hallway and knocked loudly on the warden's door. 'Mrs Craven, it's time to put the kettle on — your prodigal son has arrived on the doorstep for a tea-time visit.'

&#42;  &#42;  &#42;

Brenda had found that Les's kiss was unexpectedly pleasant — soft but long lasting and ending in several more touches of his lips against her cheek and neck. She'd been in no hurry for him to restart the car engine and drive on. Heavy rain had begun to fall and the rapid pock-pock sound of raindrops on the canvas roof had soothed her.

'That was nice,' she said with a contented sigh as they both rested back in their seats and stared out at the blurred landscape. There were a couple of stunted hawthorn trees nearby then a stretch of windswept moor land, dipping down towards Hawkshead and Burnside beyond. 'We could do it again if you like.'

'You mean the kiss?'

'Yes, the kiss. And this drive home, the foxtrotting on Saturday night and the drink outside the Smith's Arms — everything.'

'You're sure?'

She nodded and there was more kissing until the windows steamed up and they pulled apart. Then, as if the physical closeness had opened up a previously locked door, he held her hand and began to talk.

'I'm not very good at this lark,' he began with typical modesty. 'Donald is the one with the gift of the gab as far as girls are concerned. But I do know a good thing when I see it, and that's what you are, Brenda Appleby — a Very Good Thing, with capital letters.'

'Go on — I'm all ears.'

'You're different from anyone else I've known, for a start — more independent than some of the other Land Girls. You're better looking as well.'

'Hmm. Stop right there before I get too big-headed.'

'I mean it. You're modern in the way you do your hair, the way you dress; very forward-looking.'

'For someone who doesn't have the gift of the gab you're doing all right.' *Wrong!* she thought. *Don't be too flippant and put him off. Let him talk.*

He grinned self-consciously. 'It's not just that,

though. You have this peculiar effect on me. I can be feeling down in the dumps about something bad that's happened — the bomb in the cows' field, for a start — but one look at you brings a smile to my face. You don't even have to know I'm there for it to happen; I can be standing in a corner of a room just watching you. And now suddenly here I am, here we both are, sitting together and holding hands, me rabbiting on and you listening and looking at me with those big brown eyes.' *Deep, deep brown, with honey-coloured flecks, heavily fringed with dark eyelashes, always with a sparkle suggesting that the world is full of fun if only you grab the chance.*

'You don't know me very well.' *And likewise, I haven't had time to get to know you.* Brenda decided to put in a word of warning in case Les got too carried away. 'I had a life before the Land Army, you know. And it was different back in Northgate — there were more girls like me. I didn't stick out so much.'

'I don't believe that for a minute. I've spent plenty of time in towns and cities, going around with girls like Doreen. You're nothing like her or any of the others.'

'Doreen's not so bad when you get to know her.' Instinctively she stood up for her fellow farm worker.

'I'm not saying she is. Anyway, that's not the point.' *In for a penny . . .* 'The point is me and you, Brenda.'

Her eyes widened as she thought this through 'What do you mean? Is there a 'me and you'?'

113

'Yes, at least I hope there is. I want there to be.' He'd come this far — banishing deep-seated reticence as they sat in the car, sheltered from the wind and rain. After all, Brenda was worth taking a risk for. 'Will you be my girl? Will you walk out with me?'

She laughed and said yes and they kissed again until the rain eased and she said he'd better drive her home before things went too far.

They sat in easy silence until they reached Fieldhead, to be greeted by a bright rainbow arching over the copse behind the house and by rooks rising from the elms as Les drove his MG up the drive. Poppy, Joyce and Jean watched agog from the window on the first-floor landing then the door opened and stout Mrs Craven emerged on to the step to say goodbye to Alfie.

'Goodbye,' Brenda whispered to Les, leaning over to kiss his cheek before she swung out her legs then slid from the low seat on to the gravel drive. 'I'll see you tomorrow after work. Meet me at seven at the Blacksmith's Arms.'

# 8

Endless June days stretched towards the longest of the year and while there was daylight there was an opportunity for the girls to carry on working outdoors.

'As if it's not bad enough making hay all day long, they make us slave away out here after dinner,' Doreen complained as she straightened up to ease her aching back. She worked on the Wednesday evening alongside Joyce, Elsie, Una and Jean, hoeing the vegetable garden behind the hostel.

'I warned you when you first arrived that it was slave labour.' Jean agreed that they didn't deserve this hardship after a demanding day in the fields and cowsheds. 'But you haven't seen anything yet. Just you wait until the days draw in and there's a nip in the air. That's when Mrs Craven sends us out blackberrying. Last year I fell headlong into a wet ditch and came home covered in mud. That was no fun, I can tell you.'

Joyce was having none of it. 'Yes, but afterwards who stood first in line for Ma Craven's blackberry and apple crumble?'

'Not me,' Jean protested. 'I'm not keen on puddings.'

Joyce laughed. 'Don't believe a word she says,' she whispered to Doreen, who had downed tools and was standing under a cherry tree enjoying a quiet smoke. 'You wouldn't think it to look at her, but with Jean it's a case of why make do with one spoonful of sugar in your tea when you can slip in three on the quiet?'

'Girls, girls!' Sensing a serious argument on the horizon, Elsie coaxed them into a better mood. 'Let's look on the bright side. Those cherries will soon be ripe and the tomatoes in the greenhouse are almost ready for picking. Think what a difference that'll make to meal times.'

Una walked over to examine the tree. Sure enough, the bright crimson fruit hanging from the branches made her mouth water and swiftly turned her thoughts to summer vistas opening out before her — scenes of grapes growing on the vine on Italian hillsides, peaches, oranges, lemons and silvery olive leaves rustling in a sunny breeze.

Joyce noticed the familiar faraway look. 'Any news?' she called across the lettuce and spring onion patch.

'Not yet.' There was still no official word about the returning POWs, only various rumours about them being back in a day, a week or a month. Meanwhile, Una scarcely ate or slept.

'News about what?' Kathleen came into the garden carrying a tray of mugs. 'Are we talking about Jack Hudson, by any chance?' She put down the tray to a volley of surprised, anxious glances. 'Ah, we weren't, were we?'

Jean, Elsie, Joyce, Una and Doreen gathered round, their faces flushed with the effort of weeding, sleeves rolled up and shirts open at the neck. 'Why, what's happened now?' Jean asked edgily.

There was no avoiding it; Kathleen must break the bad news, so she stirred half-spoonfuls of sugar into the mugs and went on falteringly. 'Jack's ship was hit off the coast of Malta at midday on Monday. Apparently a low-level torpedo bomber did for them. The ship was carrying aviation fuel. It blew up and sank in seconds.'

'What about survivors?' Elsie's voice was shaky.

'A few, they think. A mine sweeper found five of them on an upturned lifeboat and took them to Sliema Creek.'

'What about Jack?' Joyce asked.

'He's listed as missing.' Kathleen's voice grew quieter still. 'His mum and dad received the telegram this morning.'

'Do Grace and Bill know?' Elsie thought of Jack's best man's speech at the wedding, so full of life and affection. She remembered how they'd danced into the wee small hours, teetering on the edge of fullblown romance. A mere week and a half had elapsed since then.

Kathleen nodded. 'Mrs Mostyn was at the Hudsons' house when the telegram arrived. She says that neighbours are rallying round. There's a younger brother still at school and an older sister in the ATS.'

While Joyce shook her head in hopeless resignation, Doreen, Una and Kathleen returned to their gardening work, each reflecting on how trivial the bickering over blackberries and sugar rations seemed now. Elsie stood stock still and stared down at the concentric rings swirling

117

gently on the surface of the untouched mugs of tea, holding in her mind a crystal-clear image of Chief Petty Officer Jack Hudson — here one minute and gone the next. Young, proud, handsome and doomed.

★ ★ ★

After just over two weeks in the Land Army, Poppy decided she'd had enough. Life as a Land Girl was not for her.

So she cycled into Burnside straight after work on Wednesday, intending to knock on Mrs Mostyn's door and tell her she was leaving.

*They can't stop me*, she told herself stubbornly. *This isn't the WAAF or the WRNS. We can't be forced to stay on.*

So she stood on the doorstep, raised the knocker and rapped it down, waiting for what felt like a long time before Edith opened the door.

'Poppy,' Edith said in a flat voice. Her face was pale, her brow furrowed. 'How can I help?'

'I'm sorry, Mrs Mostyn, I can't go on!' Poppy blurted out her decision then bit her lip to stop herself from crying.

'What do you mean, you can't go on?' Fresh from Muriel and Harold Hudson's house, where she'd spent most of the day, Edith was at first irritated by the girl's tearful declaration. Didn't Poppy know that there was a war on and they all had to keep a stiff upper lip, for goodness' sake?

Poppy quaked under the severe gaze. 'I want to resign. I'm not cut out for farm work after all.

118

I'd like to go back home to my family. I'm sure I can get my old job back in Kingsley's canteen.'

'Come in, Poppy.' Edith's weary voice reflected the shock of the day's events. But she invited the recalcitrant recruit to take off her coat and hat then sat her down in the lounge while she made her a cup of tea. She stayed in the kitchen while the kettle boiled, wondering how best to proceed.

Meanwhile, Poppy took in her surroundings. The rep's home was spotless. Every surface gleamed, from the round, glass-topped coffee table to the polished parquet floor and the red and green geometric designs in the stained-glass bow windows. Pale grey figurines of dancing girls adorned the low chimney piece and a gold clock in the shape of a sunburst told her that it was already dinner time at the hostel.

'Now,' Edith said as she brought in the tea tray, 'tell me what the matter is, there's a good girl.'

★   ★   ★

The news about Jack hit Bill hard. He'd heard it from his mother, who had telephoned his workshop on Winsill Edge straight after she'd come away from the Hudsons' house. It was late afternoon on a grey, blustery summer's day. 'Harold and Muriel are taking it hard,' she'd told him. 'Muriel's clinging on to the fact that Jack is listed as missing in action, not killed. No one can blame her for clutching at straws, I suppose.'

119

Bill had pressed his lips together and let his mother talk on.

'Apparently the convoy carried on for Malta without stopping to search for survivors. Would you credit it: two of the six merchantmen reached their destination so it came up on the news as a success for the Allies!'

'Who picked up the survivors?' Bill had tried to picture a course of events whereby Jack had been rescued by an enemy vessel and taken off to a prisoner-of-war camp somewhere in Italy or Greece. If that were the case then it was definitely too soon for the Allied authorities to have been informed. Then he sighed at his own version of clutching at straws. The ship had blown up with a cargo of aviation spirit — chances of survival were slim at best.

'I don't know, Bill.' The telephone receiver had felt heavy in Edith's hand. 'Will you tell Grace?'

'Straight away,' he'd promised. He'd driven home slowly and coincided with Grace's arrival at the house.

She'd looked at his face as he got out of the car and known that it was bad news.

It was as if sharp talons had clutched at her throat. 'Is it Edgar?' she'd gasped in the fierce grip of sudden panic.

'No — Jack.'

They'd gone inside the house. Grace had held his hand and listened quietly as he sat in the front room with his head bowed until there was a knock at the door.

\* \* \*

120

'Come with me.' Edith had said all she could to persuade Poppy to stay on. She'd appealed to the girl's common sense and asked her to carry on until the end of the month at least, for wastage of labour was a serious consideration at County Office and the local rep was invariably made to feel responsible. She'd acknowledged that Land Girls were not tied to military law and that most joined voluntarily. But, as things stood, if Poppy were to go ahead with her decision to leave the Land Army, Edith pointed out that the Ministry of Labour might soon transfer her to some other branch of national service, not of her own choosing.

All to no avail. 'I'm sorry, I can't stand the work,' a miserable Poppy had declared. 'It's the cows and the pigs — the muck. I'm not used to it.'

Edith had softened a little. The poor girl probably did well enough in city streets and woollen mills, but the countryside was proving altogether too much for her. 'Do you miss your mother?' she'd asked kindly.

There'd been tears and wet handkerchiefs, and more cups of tea, until Edith led her up the street to Grace and Bill's house.

Grace answered the door and took one look at a red-eyed Poppy, swamped by her dungarees, fair hair hidden beneath a checked headscarf, looking all of twelve years old as she hung back behind a worried Edith. 'Oh dear,' she murmured as she invited them in then led the way into the kitchen. 'Have you had any dinner, Poppy?

Would you like me to make you a quick ham sandwich?'

'Poppy's thinking of leaving us,' Edith reported calmly as Grace sat the girl down on a stool near the sink. 'I thought perhaps you could talk her out of it.'

Grace nodded. 'I'll give it a go. You'll find Bill in the front room,' she said quietly.

Edith slipped away to be with her grieving son.

'What's the matter? Is it Fieldhead?' Grace asked Poppy without any lead-in. 'Don't you like sharing a room with Joyce and Doreen?'

'The hostel's fine.' Poppy's lip started to quiver. 'Joyce kindly showed me the ropes when I first arrived and Doreen cheers me up when I'm down in the dumps. It's not that.'

'What then?'

'It's the cows — they're so big and clumsy; they scare the living daylights out of me.'

'I know what you mean, but you'll get used to them before too long.' Grace was certain there was more. 'And what else?'

'Pigs as well. I don't like their beady little eyes.'

'Poor pigs!' Grace smiled then paused to reflect. 'Come on, Poppy; what's this really about?'

'If I tell you, you won't let on?' Grace's calm, kindly manner drew Poppy out. 'And you won't think I'm silly?'

'I promise.'

Poppy went on haltingly. 'It was last Sunday, after tea. I was taking a stroll through the wood at the back of the hostel. He jumped out from behind a tree and said boo.'

'Who did?'

'Mrs Craven's son, Alfie. At first I tried to laugh it off and walk away, but he followed me.'

'And?' Grace guessed the gist of what was to come, but wasn't prepared for the full extent of it.

'I told him to go away but he wouldn't listen. He caught hold of me and pinned me against a tree trunk. He tried to kiss me and . . . ' Poppy shuddered at the memory. 'Well, let's just say there was a tussle and the buttons of my blouse came undone. His hand went down my front.'

'Oh dear, oh dear.' Grace drew up another stool to sit beside her. 'This isn't silly; it's serious. What else did Alfie do?'

Poppy's pupils dilated and her body shook. 'He put his other hand up my skirt. I couldn't stop him — he was too strong. But then we both heard voices coming towards us and that made him stop. Then he put his hand over my mouth and warned me not to breathe a word.'

Grace stared silently back at her.

'I bit his finger!'

'Good for you.'

'Then I kicked his shins and ran away.'

'Good again. And then afterwards — did you tell anyone?'

'No, I was too frightened. And anyway, Mrs Craven is in charge of the hostel. I can't go telling tales about her son. Besides, I'm bound to bump into him again sooner or later so I'd rather not be in his bad books.'

123

'But what he did was wrong and we mustn't let it happen again.' Grace acknowledged the problem then tried to come up with a solution. 'I've known Alfie a long time. I can have a word with him if you like.'

Poppy nodded eagerly. 'Will you?'

'Of course I will. I'll warn him to steer clear. And you must make sure that you're never alone with him in future. Always stick with one of us if we have to work beside him at Home Farm.'

Reassured, Poppy nodded then took a deep breath. 'Ta, Grace. You're a pal.'

'And I can tell my mother-in-law that you'll stay on?'

Another nod indicated Poppy's new resolve and she stood up, ready to leave. 'I mean it. I can't thank you enough.'

Grace put an arm around her shoulder then led her to the door. 'You're very welcome. How will you get back to Fieldhead?'

'On my bike. I left it in the pub yard.' Eager to make amends for being late, Poppy ran down the path and across the road to fetch her bike. She was already astride the saddle and about to set off when Neville rode his own bike into the yard.

'Ah, just the girl!' he called over a screech of brakes.

'Sorry — no time for a chat!' Poppy yelled back. To date, she'd regarded Neville as hovering somewhere between a mild nuisance and a source of entertainment — either way, she wasn't prepared to linger.

He stopped in front of her and blocked her

way. 'No, but you can save me a ride all the way out to Fieldhead.'

'I can?'

'Yes. Will you take a message for me? Tell Una that the Italians are on their way at last.' He delivered the news with a wink then went on to elaborate. 'Dad heard it from the cook at Beckwith Camp. They crammed thirty prisoners into a single lorry and set off from Scotland first thing this morning. They'll be here in a couple of hours. He asked Dad to sell him a few stones of spuds and a side of bacon on the sly, no questions asked.'

*So it really is happening*, Poppy realized as she edged past. 'All right — I'll tell her.'

Neville was slow to get out of her way. He cleared his throat then mumbled an awkward question: 'I was wondering — will you come to the beetle drive with me on Saturday night?'

Poppy widened her eyes in surprise and wondered if this was an invitation worth considering. Yes, Neville was a young whipper-snapper, but during these days of conscription a girl's choices were sadly limited.

'Whereabouts?'

'At the Institute at seven o'clock.'

'I'll see.' Having delivered her tantalizing reply, she cycled off and left Neville blushing to the roots of his hair.

*A beetle drive?* Poppy thought as she left the village and set off along the narrow road to Fieldhead. *What's that when it's at home?*

★  ★  ★

'Brenda, have you got Sloper back from Maurice yet?' Una burst into the room that she shared with Kathleen and Brenda, flinging down the towel and facecloth she'd been holding while she queued up outside the bathroom. Her dark auburn hair had broken loose from the comb holding it in place and now tumbled across her face.

Brenda, already in pyjamas, sat on her bed, flicking through a magazine. She glanced up nonchalantly. 'Yes, I picked her up yesterday, as good as new. Why?'

'I'll explain later! Get dressed again. Now, this minute. We have to go!' Una snatched the magazine then pulled Brenda on to her feet.

'Go where?'

'To the camp. Brenda, please!'

'Aha!' Brenda cottoned on quickly. 'So, the wanderer returns.'

'Yes. Poppy swears the prisoners will be here soon. If we set off now, we can get to Beckwith by the time they arrive.' Una flung off her nightdress then fumbled to put on her shirt and breeches. Her heart beat fast and furious, fit to burst out of her chest.

Brenda saw that she would brook no argument so she too put on her uniform.

'It doesn't grow dark until after ten so we should arrive there in the daylight.' Una was first out of the door and running along the landing ahead of Brenda. 'Oh, heavens — I can hardly believe it!'

Joyce and Elsie stood chatting at the bottom of the stairs. As Una and Brenda rushed past, they stepped quickly to one side.

'What's the rush?' Elsie called after them.

'I'll give you two guesses,' Joyce said with a conspiratorial wink.

Brenda and Una ran on into the yard, ignoring Kathleen and Doreen, who were enjoying a last cigarette of the day. Brenda wheeled Sloper out of a stable and started the engine. Una hopped on to the pillion seat and they were off with a roar, leaving behind a thin trail of blue smoke.

'Someone's happy,' Doreen commented, absent-mindedly flicking ash from her cigarette.

'Angelo must be back,' Kathleen guessed. 'Let's keep our fingers crossed for Una's sake that he meant what he said when he was here before.'

'Ah.' The worldly Doreen immediately understood. 'Was it love or lust on the handsome gigolo's part? That's the question!'

\* \* \*

Brenda knew better than to enter into conversation with Una as they sped along Swinsty Edge towards Penny Lane. The poor girl had enough trouble catching her breath and Brenda could feel her hands shaking as she clasped her arms around her waist. It couldn't be a pleasant feeling to be so swept off your feet by an intoxicating mixture of hope and fear or to be faced by events over which you had so little control. Brenda had only an inkling of what this must be like.

Take her situation with Les, for instance. Yes,

he was pleasant enough and there were sides to his character that she found fascinating. In fact, Brenda had met him two nights on the trot — the first on Monday, when they'd sat and had a quiet drink at the Blacksmith's Arms, and then again last night, when they'd gone for a spin in his car. They'd kissed and cuddled as before. There was no reason for it not to continue, but when Les had pressed her to go out with him again tonight, she'd suddenly got cold feet. She couldn't say why, except that she felt a strong flutter of apprehension in her chest.

'I'll give it a miss if you don't mind,' she'd told him as he'd dropped her off at the hostel. 'A girl has to wash her hair once in a while.'

His face had fallen for a moment then he'd masked his disappointment and turned his car in the drive. 'Cheerio then. Perhaps we can meet up again at the weekend?'

'That'd be nice,' she'd said cheerfully. 'I'll be at the pub on Friday night with some of the girls. I'll see you then.'

They'd waved and he'd driven off without looking back.

'Nice'. That just about covered Brenda's blossoming romance with Les. Passion didn't really come into it — not for her, at least. In fact, when she thought seriously about it, it seldom did. Yes, she was able to have a good time when she walked out with a good-looking chap and she enjoyed the kisses and the flattery, but something — she couldn't work out what — always held her back. It was like this with Les — blowing hot and cold, hot and cold. She knew he didn't

128

deserve it and she would try her best not to string him along if her heart wasn't in it. *But give it another week or two and then we'll see,* she told herself, with the wind in her hair and Una deep in the excited throes of true love clinging on behind.

'Hold on to your hat,' Brenda said as they reached the long, straight lane leading to Beckwith Camp and she picked up yet more speed. A deep red sky to the west coloured the clouds purple, and slender, silvery leaves on the old willow trees lining one side of the road fluttered in a light breeze.

'There's a lorry turning in through the gates. It seems we've got here just in time.'

Shielded behind Brenda, Una could just see the canvas-topped truck in the distance as the motor bike drew level with the old isolation hospital — a gloomy Victorian building that now housed officers and crew of the Royal Canadian Air Force. Two armed sentries at the gate watched with interest as they rode past.

'Hurry up!' Una urged. There was still half a mile between them and Beckwith.

'I can't make her go any faster.' Brenda had already opened the throttle to its maximum.

The lorry was through the gates and the barrier had been lowered. Brenda and Una saw the truck's back end disappearing between two rows of low Nissen huts. Tall pine trees beyond the camp cast long, dark shadows. Una squeezed her eyes shut and prayed. 'Please let Angelo be here. Please!' At the entrance to the camp, Brenda braked hard. The rear end of the bike swung round and she had to steady it by putting both feet on the ground, giving Una the chance to jump off and sprint towards the barrier.

A British Tommy in full battledress came to meet the excited arrival, rifle at the ready. 'Slow down, miss. Where do you think you're going?'

Una was all for rushing on without replying until he blocked the way with his gun.

'I said, hold your horses. You can't come in here without stating your business.'

'We're from the Land Army.' Brenda had parked the bike and now strode up behind Una.

'I can see that.' The soldier eyed their uniforms. He wasn't much older than Una, with eyes that were too close together and red, sticking-out ears. 'Isn't it a bit late for you two to be gadding about?'

Still Una ignored him and strained to see what was happening. From a distance of a hundred yards she saw a steady trickle of men in grey uniforms descend from the back of the lorry under orders from two other Tommies. The soldiers marshalled the POWs on to the grass verge at the side of the drive where they stretched stiff limbs and gazed around.

'Una's looking for a friend,' Brenda told the guard at the gate.

'She is, is she?'

'Yes. You wouldn't stand in the way of young love, would you?' She thought that if they came clean he might relent. 'She hasn't seen Angelo for months — not since Christmas, in fact. That's an awfully long time.'

The appeal fell on deaf ears. 'Stand back,

130

miss,' the soldier insisted. This time he thrust his rifle against Una's chest and forced her to take two steps backwards. 'You need written permission to come in here.'

Seeing that persuasion wouldn't work after all, Brenda seized Una's arm and dragged her away from the barrier. 'What did you see? Is Angelo there?'

Una gave a desperate sigh. 'I honestly don't know. I think I saw Lorenzo, though.'

Angelo's friend Lorenzo had stood head and shoulders taller than most of the others, recognizable because of his height, his upright bearing and his thick dark hair. His back had been turned and Una had seen the large white circle on his jacket denoting his status as a prisoner.

Brenda glanced up and down the lane then at the sentry still regarding them suspiciously. 'I've got an idea,' she hissed. 'Do you remember the public footpath running down the side of the camp? No one can stop us from taking a stroll along there if we want to.'

So she and Una changed tack and slipped out of sight down a rutted lane used in centuries past by drovers taking cattle and sheep to market. Hawthorn hedges rose to either side and formed a green canopy overhead, obscuring the view of the camp to their right, but they heard Italian voices speaking low and the tramp of boots as the prisoners set off at a slow march towards the huts.

'Oh! Oh!' Una left the track and jumped over a ditch on to a steep bank, only for her ankle to be caught in a tangle of brambles. As she stooped to free herself, sharp thorns dug into her skin.

Still wearing her leather motor-cycling gauntlets, Brenda was able to pull back the vicious tentacles. Then she gave Una a shove from behind so she could reach the stone wall and peer over it into the grounds of the camp.

'Well?' she demanded, one eye on Una, the other on the activity of the sentry who had appeared at the end of the lane.

'They're being marched to their billets.' Una described the scene as six prisoners peeled off from the group. From her vantage point she confirmed that Lorenzo was among them. 'I can't see Angelo, though.'

'Have they all left the lorry?' Brenda asked.

'Yes. The driver's backing it into a parking bay.' Despair sharper than any bramble dug deep and made her heart bleed. 'Oh, Brenda, he's not here!'

From the lane below Brenda offered a shred of hope. 'Perhaps more will arrive tomorrow.'

Una heard an engine cut out then the slam of a door and the sound of feet jumping down from the cab then running to catch up with the group. She climbed on to the top of the wall for a better view. 'Wait — I'm trying to see who the driver is.'

'Well?' Brenda asked again.

Her heart leaped when she saw him, jacket flying open, white scarf flapping. 'Angelo!'

He stopped dead in his tracks then turned, saw her and stood still as a statue. His gaze locked with hers.

'It's me — Una!' She balanced on the wall top, arms spread wide. Two guards ran up behind him. They seized Angelo, he resisted and they dragged him roughly back.

The sentry from the gate had entered the green lane and begun to bark orders. 'Get down from there. You, on the ground — make your friend climb back down!'

Una saw Angelo mouth her name and try to raise one hand in greeting before the guards shoved him into the nearest hut. She felt Brenda grab hold of her ankle and tug at her, pulling her off the wall. She landed awkwardly in the brambles as the sentry arrived.

'Crikey O'Reilly!' he muttered, gesturing first at Brenda and then at Una lying flat on her back in a tangle of thorns. He grinned then lowered his rifle to the ground. 'If this is what young love is all about, give me a pint of bitter and a pork pie any day.'

# 9

It was Les's job to drive one of the family's giant threshing machines out of the neighbouring dale, along Swinsty Edge from Attercliffe to Brigg Farm. Grace, Joyce and Brenda stood waiting for it in the yard with Roland and Neville. The older man glanced at his watch and muttered impatiently while Neville chatted with the girls.

'I was hoping Poppy would be on the list to work here today, but it looks as if I'll have to put up with you three instead.' He blew his nose noisily then thrust his handkerchief into the pocket of his overalls.

'We'll tell Pops that you missed her,' Brenda promised.

'She's coming to the beetle drive with me on Saturday. At least, I hope she is.'

Joyce smiled at the gawky lad's optimism. 'Does Una know?' she teased.

'Una's happy with her foreign chap,' he conceded. 'But I reckon I've got the pick of the rest of the bunch in Poppy.'

His naive enthusiasm made the three experienced Land Army hands laugh out loud. 'Nev must be the only one around here who's glad that there's a war on,' Brenda declared. 'It means there's slim pickings for us girls when it comes to eligible bachelors. He clearly takes his chances while the going's good!'

'Where's the bugger got to?' Roland muttered,

ignoring the jokes and scanning the lanes for a sighting of the machine.

The hiring out of large machinery was the way that Arnold White had made most of his money. Early in the nineteen twenties, shortly after he'd inherited Dale End from his father, he'd bought a steam engine from a family of funfair owners in Scarborough — a major investment — and then purchased a threshing machine to separate wheat from chaff. He'd been correct in supposing that the old days of threshing by hand were well and truly over, even on remote Dales farms, and that local farmers would queue up to hire the labour-saving device. Soon he'd invested in a second engine and then a third, and now it was a common sight to encounter one of his machines chugging up and down lanes throughout the summer and well into autumn, its driver high in the cab with a lad below, employed to stoke the furnace that heated the boiler and produced the steam. The only disadvantage was the length of time it took to get the cumbersome equipment from A to B, due to the narrowness of the lanes and the old-fashioned horses and carts encountered on the way. This was the reason that Les was delayed this Thursday morning — he'd been held up by Joe Kellett's hay wagon blocking the road. Thanks largely to Alfie's inexperience with cart horses, the wagon had ended up in a ditch, spilling most of its hay load in the process. There'd been a swearing match and much heaving and shoving of both horse and cart before Les and his young stoker lad were able to fire up the engine to carry on to Brigg Farm.

Brenda and the others were in no hurry for the threshing machine to arrive. They stood in Aertex blouses and breeches, teasing Neville and taking in the views.

'Nev, I hear you played Cupid for Una again yesterday.' Brenda cornered him against the stone steps leading up to the hayloft above Major's stable, reminding him of the many messages that he'd carried between Una and Angelo during the December blossoming of their romance.

'What if I did?'

'Well, it was big hearted of you, considering your past history with her. So, if you like, I'll put in a good word for you with your new *inamorata*.'

'What's that when it's at home?'

Brenda nudged him with her elbow before he vaulted up on to the steps and she followed him. 'You daft thing — I mean Pops, of course. I can drop a word in her shell-like: get her to say yes to Saturday.'

'All right — you can if you like.'

They entered the loft to a strong, sweet smell of recently gathered hay.

'What's that other whiff?' Brenda wondered as Neville shoved two wooden crates into a corner then covered them with hay. 'It's oranges, isn't it?'

'I haven't a clue,' he prevaricated. 'Alfie dropped them off first thing this morning. He said they were his personal belongings. I said I'd

136

store them for him, no questions asked.'

Brenda frowned. There were definitely oranges in the crates, she decided — a commodity that was in short supply since Jerry had tightened his strangle-hold on goods coming in from Europe and the Middle East. 'I expect he offered you a couple of bob for the privilege?'

'One and six.'

'And is this the first time he's asked you?'

Neville shook his head then pointed to more boxes perched on an overhead beam. 'The smaller stuff's up there. Don't ask me what's inside — I haven't bothered to look. And don't mention it to Dad either.'

*Now I know where Alfie plans to keep the contraband chocolate and stockings,* Brenda thought. It came as no surprise to learn about his shady dealings, and she wondered if this was what lay behind his sudden reappearance in Burnside. 'I wouldn't get too pally with Alfie if I were you,' she warned. 'He's involved with some dubious people, I shouldn't wonder.'

Neville shrugged.

'I mean it, Nev. There are some nasty types in places like Millwood and Northgate, and if Alfie's crossed them, he'll pay for it sooner or later.'

Again he brushed her concerns aside by tutting and giving the boxes a careless kick. 'It's only oranges!'

'And cocoa and chocolate and heaven knows what else — anything on ration that Alfie thinks he can double his money on.'

A stubborn Neville piled more hay on top of

the boxes and no conclusion was reached before they were interrupted by Joyce calling up from the bottom of the steps. 'Yoo-hoo, the thresher's arrived! And guess who's driven it all the way from Attercliffe — Les White himself, that's who!'

★  ★  ★

'You didn't have much to say for yourself when you-know-who arrived,' Grace observed as she and Brenda took up position at the threshing machine and Les went into the house for a cup of tea. Grace had stationed herself at the chute where the separated grains of wheat poured out of the churning drum. Brenda was a few feet away at a second chute, nursing her sore hand but still ready to collect straw, while Joyce stood at the back end of the machine, prepared to deal with the prickly chaff. All three expected to be itching all over and coughing up dust at the end of the day.

For once Brenda made excuses. 'I'm busy. I don't have time for niceties,' she said without bothering to raise her voice above the hiss and chug of the machine.

'Come again?'

'I said I'm busy. Anyway, I'll see Les in the pub tomorrow night. I can talk to him then.'

As grain slid down the chute, Grace collected it in a hessian sack. 'I see.'

'What do you see?' Brenda gathered the first armful of straw then tossed it on to the back of a nearby cart.

'That you're not too struck on Les after all.'

'Who says I'm not?'

There was a pause as Grace hauled the first full sack clear. 'No one. It's as plain as the nose on my face.'

'That's where you're wrong for once.' Brenda dug in her heels. 'Les is a nice chap.' *Nice — that word again.* It slipped out without her thinking.

'And keen on you, too.' Grace had noticed how he looked at Brenda with puppy-dog earnestness. 'Maybe too keen?'

The rhythm of the machine took over and, though they had to raise their voices to be heard, Brenda was at last prepared to share confidences. 'I do like Les — he's good company. And he's deep and brings out the best in me if I give him half a chance.'

'How's that?'

'He makes me less giddy, for a start. We chat about what I did before I came here, when I worked in Maynard's, what I hope to do after the war and suchlike.'

'But?'

'But you're right in a way — Les wants to move things on much too fast. He asks to see me every day of the week and to spend time at Dale End with his dad and the Dragon — lah-lah-lah!' Brenda seized a hayfork then jumped up on to the cart to shift the straw to the far side. 'I'd prefer to take things more slowly.'

'It's a sign of the times,' Grace pointed out. 'Everyone is in a rush because of the war; men especially, but girls too.'

'Like you and Bill?'

'Hardly!' Grace laughed. 'I've known Bill since I was in ankle socks. But seriously, Brenda, do you want my opinion?'

Frowning and nodding, and with the warm sun on her back, Brenda leaned on her fork to listen.

'I think the business with Mac last Christmas set you back more than any of us realized. It was a terrible thing — a girl's worst nightmare — and it put you off men in a big way. That's why you're so slow to take Les seriously; in case he turns out to be like Mac, which he's not, of course.'

Brenda closed her eyes, as if shutting out the memory of what had happened in the changing room at the Institute six months earlier — the Canadian pilot bursting in while she was undressed, the humiliating leer on his face, his hands all over her as he forced her on to the floor. She took a deep breath then nodded. 'I hope you're right.'

'What — that Les is different? Without a shadow of a doubt. I've known him nearly as long as I've known Bill and he's a thoroughly decent sort.'

Brenda shook herself back into the moment then jumped down from the cart in time to gather another armful of straw. 'He comes highly recommended, then?'

'He does,' Grace agreed with a reassuring smile. 'I'd definitely give the poor chap a chance if I were you.'

★   ★   ★

It wasn't until the end of the day that Brenda finally decided to take Grace's well-meaning advice. She approached Les as he stood watching his lad shovel coal into the furnace to get up a head of steam, ready to leave the farm.

'I hope you pay Tiny Tim there a decent wage,' she commented, inclining her head towards the sweating, mop-haired boy. His face was black with soot and he was stripped to the waist and skinny as a rabbit, muscles straining at every shovelful.

'He gets bed and board at Dale End.' Les's reply was unusually terse. 'Plus a few bob pocket money.'

'Blimey, a few bob, eh? What's his name?'

'Johnny Wade.'

'And where did you find him?'

'We didn't find him. His family lives in Attercliffe. His dad joined the army and his mum has too many mouths to feed so he came to us straight from school.'

They watched for a while in silence, each thinking their own thoughts — Brenda disconcerted by Les's closed expression and he disheartened after a whole day of trying and failing to attract her attention.

'Rather him than me,' she murmured against the background sound of Johnny's shovel crunching into the heap of coal and the increasing roar of the engine's furnace. 'I thought collecting chaff into sacks was bad enough.'

Over the far side of the farmyard, Joyce and Grace picked straw out of each other's hair. Both looked worn out as they tried to cough dust from their throats and lungs. Neville lounged on the hayloft steps while his fidgety, wiry father went into the house to find the money to pay Les.

'All set?' Les asked as Johnny slammed the furnace door. He climbed up to the driving seat and checked the dials without glancing down at Brenda. *That's it — she's not interested in me,* he decided.

*That's torn it,* she thought ruefully. *I've kept him dangling for too long and put him off good and proper.*

Out of the corner of his eye he saw her looking up at him, her face covered in dust, with straw in her hair. He felt his heart soften with a tenderness that he was determined not to show. *If she doesn't make a move, I won't either. It's up to her now.*

He pulled an overhead chain to let off a hiss of steam, ready to set the machine in motion until he saw Roland come out of the house waving the pound notes. So he waited for his payment.

'About that drink tomorrow night.' Brenda blurted out the words much louder than intended, attracting the attention of everyone in the yard. 'Shall we try somewhere different for a change?'

Unsure that he'd heard right, he leaned out of the cab. 'What's that?' Ignoring their audience, she stepped nimbly on to the metal plate and softly touched his elbow. 'I said, shall we make a change from the Blacksmith's Arms? How about the Red Lion over your way? I can ride across on Sloper.'

'If you like,' he replied, his heart soaring now.

'But would *you* like?' She couldn't tell from his expression whether or not this had been the right move.

'Yes,' he said after a pause. 'Come to Dale End at seven o'clock. We'll set off from there.'

Brenda took a deep breath, smiled and jumped down to the ground. Roland paid Les. The engine hissed and hooted then trundled out along the track. Across the yard, Grace and Joyce smiled at Brenda and nodded.

⋆　⋆　⋆

Angelo was back! He ate, slept and breathed not five miles from Fieldhead. So near and yet so far.

Una had been sent to Home Farm with Poppy and Doreen but the day of milking and weeding had passed in a blur so that she hadn't paid much attention when Doreen had stepped in between Poppy and Alfie to keep him at bay.

'Steady on,' Doreen had warned when he'd cornered Poppy by the milk churns at the entrance to the dairy. She'd challenged him as she would a playground bully. 'Why not pick on someone your own size?'

'Like who?' he'd sneered back, sleeves rolled up and shirt collar unbuttoned. 'Anyway, she doesn't mind me courting her, do you, Poppy?'

'Yes, she does. Tell him, Pops; he's not to man-handle you.'

Since the incident in the woods behind Fieldhead, Poppy had loathed Alfie's very existence. She couldn't stand the sharp smell of his sweat or the shadow of beard on his unshaven chin, the wiry hair sprouting on his forearms like a dark animal pelt. 'Stay away from me,' she'd told him plainly, shored up by Grace's advice and by Doreen's mocking presence.

'You heard the girl,' Doreen had insisted. 'Keep your paws to yourself, or else.'

He'd laughed and immediately switched the focus of his attention. 'How are you getting on with those nylon stockings I gave you? Are they a snug fit?'

'I don't know — I haven't worn them yet.' Hands on hips, Doreen had batted her lashes. 'I happen to be saving them for a special occasion.'

Meanwhile, Poppy had slipped away to rejoin Una in the milking shed, where the two girls had hosed down the stalls and kept out of harm's way. Now, though, the working day was over and Una was impatient to cycle over to Brigg Farm to find her old go-between.

'I've written a note to Angelo,' she explained to Poppy and Doreen as they left the Kelletts' place together. 'I want to ask Neville to deliver it the way he used to. I pay him sixpence and he sneaks it into the camp for me.'

'My dearest Angelo,' she'd written in a blaze of joy. Then no, she'd crossed that out and started again. 'My darling, precious Angelo. How can we arrange to meet? When will they let you start farm work? Do you know yet where they will send you? Now that you are here, I can't wait. Shall I find a way to visit Beckwith? Tomorrow is Friday and then Saturday is my half day. I'll change the rota so that I can be sent to work at Horace Turnbull's hen farm on the Saturday morning. Perhaps I can arrange to bring eggs for the canteen later in the day and you can be there waiting for me. I hope you think this is a good plan?' She'd run out of space on one side of the unlined writing paper that she kept in her bedside cabinet so had turned it over and tried to control her excited scrawl. 'I long to see you, my Angelo! I will ask Neville to please wait while you write your reply. Until the day after tomorrow, my darling, when I will see you at last!'

She'd signed the letter with a chain of kisses, folded it then put it into the breast pocket of her shirt, where it had stayed all day long.

As they freewheeled down the hill into Burnside, Doreen noticed Una's flushed cheeks. She chose not to comment until Una took the fork in the road leading to Brigg Farm and she and Poppy carried on through the village. 'Why didn't Una give the note to Joyce or Brenda to hand on to Neville What's-'is-name?' she wondered, cycling easily towards the pub and the church. 'Wouldn't that have been quicker?'

'Yes, but Una has to make sure he'll deliver it properly,' Poppy reasoned. 'She needs to see him with her own eyes and explain that it's urgent.'

'Ah!' Doreen glanced at her and winked. 'Out of the mouths of babes . . . '

'I'm right, though.' Poppy had read enough stories in women's magazines to know how such things worked. She forged ahead of Doreen along the main street to where Grace, Joyce and

Brenda stood with their bikes outside the row of terraced houses next to the Institute.

★ ★ ★

'Wait for me!' Brenda called. She said goodbye to the others and joined Poppy and Doreen for the ride back to Fieldhead.

'You'll stop for tea?' Grace asked Joyce, who evidently had something on her mind.

Joyce nodded. She leaned her bike against the iron railings then followed Grace into the house. 'I hope I'm not getting in your way.'

'You're never in my way,' Grace assured her. 'In any case, Bill is staying late in the workshop tonight so there's no danger of us being interrupted.'

She led the way into a small back kitchen where she put the kettle on a gas hob to boil. The hob was the single innovation in an otherwise old-fashioned set-up of cast-iron range, stone sink and open pine dresser set out with Edith's gift of delicate Japanese china. When the tea was made, she brought it to the table and sat down opposite Joyce. 'Now, what's up?' she asked softly.

Joyce sighed and stared down at her work-roughened hands. 'Perhaps I ought not to bother you. You've enough on your plate as it is, what with this recent news about Jack.'

'You're not bothering me.' Grace always had time for Joyce. 'Come on — spit it out.'

Slowly Joyce drew a piece of paper from her shirt pocket. 'I've had this letter from Edgar.'

'You don't say.' Grace's eyes widened in surprise but she kept her voice steady. Then she sat, cupping her tea with both hands, waiting.

'Yes. It arrived last Friday. I haven't answered it yet.' *I love you, Joyce Cutler. There!* The words played like a record turning inside her head, black disc gleaming, bright silver needle following the concentric grooves. She could hear Edgar's voice saying them in a tone of wonderment, over and over.

'He's well?'

'Yes.'

'That's all right, then.'

'Would you like to read it?'

Grace shook her head. 'Why not tell me what it says?'

'On second thoughts, I'm not sure that I ought. I've been sitting on it for nearly a week.' Joyce made as if to stand up then changed her mind. 'I do want your opinion, though.'

'Then tell me.'

'The fact of the matter is that Edgar tells me he loves me.' *There — it's out in the open at last! The words are spoken, but don't look at me like that, as if it's impossible.* 'I know — it came as a shock to me too.'

'It's not a shock,' Grace argued. 'At least, not in a bad way. It's a surprise, yes.'

'At first I didn't know whether or not to take it seriously. I wondered if it was a passing whim and he would regret sending it.'

'Edgar doesn't do things on a whim.' Grace reached out her hand. Joyce, who was usually so sure and down to earth, had become somehow

147

small and vulnerable. 'Believe me.'

'So he's sincere?' All week she'd questioned this and not found an answer. It was why she'd finally come to Grace.

'Perfectly. I guarantee it.' And now that Grace thought back, she was no longer surprised. She remembered the looks that passed between them at the wedding, and, further back, Joyce's quiet strength when Edgar had been at his lowest ebb, the way she'd shown him with her kindness that a decent life could be lived in spite of loss and loneliness.

'He wants me to reply. I don't know what to say.'

'Write to him. You've kept him waiting long enough.'

'I know that. But how can I be sure what to write? I hardly know him.'

'Sometimes,' Grace said after a pause, 'these things take a long time to grow, which is how it happened between me and Bill. But at other times they take place in an instant.' *Love at first sight.*

'And I'm afraid,' Joyce continued without acknowledging Grace's point. 'I was engaged once before — very quick, as you say. I still have the ring.'

'Walter.' In saying the name of Joyce's dead fiancé, Grace opened the door to her friend's pent-up emotions. She watched her head sink into her hands and heard her cry.

'I lost him. What if it were to happen again?'

'I understand. I do. But the real question is: do you . . . *can* you love Edgar?'

Joyce looked up and nodded through her tears. 'I think I could.'

'Then write,' Grace insisted. 'Put him out of his misery and tell him how you feel.'

# 10

It was Hettie, not Les, who opened the door to a disconcerted Brenda. 'Yes?' She blocked the way and made it clear from her stern expression that the visitor was unexpected.

'Is Les in?' Brenda felt the flames of the dragon-sister lick her cheeks but she stood her ground. 'I'm supposed to meet him here to go for a drink in the Red Lion.'

Hettie took in every detail of Brenda's appearance, from the stylish, cross-over blouse and linen slacks to her lively, small features that were free from make-up and her windswept dark hair. 'Did you come across on that motor bike of yours?'

'I did. And I almost took another spill, thanks to a silly sheep and two lambs wandering across my path. I came round a bend and had to brake pretty sharpish to avoid them.'

Still Hettie didn't budge, but stood with the door half closed. Dressed formally as usual in grey twinset and pearls, with a dark blue skirt, she gave no sign that she was about to relent. From a room leading off from the hallway, her father's voice barked out a question.

'Who's that at the door?'

'It's Les's little Land Army friend,' she reported without turning her head.

Footsteps clicked across the tiled hall then Donald came into view. He wrenched the door

150

from his sister's grasp and grinned at Brenda. 'Well, well, if it isn't our dispatch rider, undaunted and unbowed! What are you hanging around out there for?'

'She says she's come to see Les,' Hettie reported stiffly. 'Did he mention it to you?'

'I should cocoa!' A mocking laugh indicated that Donald didn't expect Les to share confidences. 'But come in, come in!' He drew Brenda over the doorstep. 'Your hand is still bandaged, I see. And how's your gammy knee?'

'Not too bad, ta.' Brenda smiled brightly at stony-faced Hettie, entertained by the notion that Les's sister could give the famous Joan Crawford a run for her money. It was the steely, staring eyes that did it, and the firm jawline. Beautiful but dangerous.

The same might be said of Donald, except that there was a more masculine cast to his forehead and mouth. But still there was no doubt that he could have shone in the Hollywood firmament if he'd wanted to. Odd that two such exceptional-looking people could be found here, in this backwater. And it was puzzling that shy, self-effacing Les should belong to the same fierce brood.

He came down the stairs two at a time, apologizing and whisking her into a sitting room at the back of the house. 'I'm sorry, I didn't hear you knock. I was upstairs getting ready. I didn't realize the time.'

Brenda pulled a face. 'I was afraid I was going to get gobbled up.'

'By the Dragon?' Les grinned. 'Sorry, I

151

should've given her advance warning.'

'Will you please stop saying sorry?' Glancing around the room, Brenda saw that it was by no means pristine. The pale grey wooden panelling was scuffed in places and the floral covers on the two sofas were faded and frayed. And the rest of the furniture was out of date: heavy oak stuff belonging to the Victorian era. If she hadn't known better, she would have said that the once-wealthy Whites had fallen on hard times.

'Sorry,' Les said again then they both laughed. 'Let's get out of here.' He led her out through some French doors on to a stone-flagged patio edged with yellow rose bushes in full bloom. 'We can cut across the garden and walk into the village.'

Brenda linked arms with him. 'Is Donald on his way somewhere?' she asked when she heard a car engine start up on the front drive.

Les nodded. 'He's probably heading for Burnside — in my jalopy, by the sound of things.'

'Didn't he think to ask?' The engine roared and tyres crunched over gravel.

'Donald doesn't ask; he just takes.' Les shook his head. 'Anyway, he knows I'd have said no.'

'And you don't mind him taking a liberty?' She was still curious that the two brothers should be such opposites — not just physically but in their temperaments too.

'I used to, but not any more. Donald goes his own way and I've learned to go mine. And I'll bet you anything he's not going to have half such a good time with Doreen or whoever takes his fancy tonight as I am with you.'

They'd reached a garden gate that led on to a quiet lane with a square church tower ahead, visible above the hedges to either side of the road. An evening sun cast long shadows ahead of them — two figures walking arm in arm with the sun's rays warm on their backs.

'Thanks for suggesting this,' he said as they approached the village green. 'Here was me supposing you'd gone off me and now, abracadabra, here we are.'

'Don't thank me — thank Grace. She's the one who knocked some sense into my thick head.' Something about the warm, unfamiliar surroundings, the unseen river gurgling over rocks and the soft, golden light loosened Brenda's tongue. 'She said I should try letting my guard down once in a while.'

'Your guard?' He stopped her then sat her down on a bench by a bus stop. 'How do you mean?'

'This.' She gestured towards her chest with both hands. 'This shield I put up between me and the world. Oh, stop me — I'm talking rubbish.'

'No, I want to hear. And I know what you mean — we all need to protect ourselves. Take Hettie — she might look fierce but deep down she's soft as putty.'

Brenda nodded dubiously. 'She did a good job of cleaning me up last Sunday, I'll give her that. And she lent me a pair of her slacks that I forgot to bring back, darn it.'

'Next time,' he murmured. 'So what happens

153

when you let your guard down? Ought I to be worried?'

She smiled then was suddenly serious. 'I'm just not very good at getting close to people.'

'You're close to me now, aren't you?'

'Yes, but I don't always trust my own judgement.' Looking straight at him, she attempted another smile. 'Sorry. I don't mean to suggest . . . sorry.'

'Hang on — who's doing the apologizing now?'

'Me.' The look he gave back was deep and intense. His hand rested on her shoulder; she felt the warmth of it through her thin blouse.

'Brenda, I've said this before — I've seen something special in you. You don't mind me talking like this?'

She shook her head.

'And what I see I like. I picture us doing things together — listening to music, going to dances, chatting the way we are now. I want to spend as much time as I can with you.'

'That's nice,' she whispered. At that moment the word fell far short of what she felt. 'I mean it — it's marvellous.'

'Really?'

'Yes, but there's no rush, is there? Now that we know where we each stand, we can take things steadily.'

'Rightio.' Disappointment flickered across his face.

'We're both young. I'm twenty-one. How old are you?'

'Twenty-two.'

'You see — we have plenty of time.' Was this the right way to move things forward, slowly but surely? She wasn't sure.

He nodded. 'I won't rush you,' he promised. Even though he was head over heels and couldn't stop thinking about Brenda for a single minute, though he could even picture the ring he would buy her and her lovely face glowing with happiness as he walked her down the aisle. It was too early to say any of this out loud but it was what was in Les's heart. After all, he was lost to love, dwelling on foreign shores of rising, rushing, breaking emotions that he'd never experienced before.

For now, he placed his fingers on her soft cheek and felt her hand close over them and press them closer. He kissed her softly for a long time. The world turned and evening shadows lengthened.

\* \* \*

Just because Grace was married, her father didn't excuse her from her regular duties as stand-in barmaid at the Blacksmith's Arms. He sent her a message on the Saturday morning, saying that he needed her straight after she'd finished work at Horace Turnbull's because he would be busy in the forge. Lionel Foster was sending two of his hunters from Hawkshead for shoeing and when the Fosters wanted something doing you had to jump to straight away.

Grace had filled in behind the bar since she was fifteen so she managed to pull pints and

155

wash glasses almost without thinking. The afternoon atmosphere was relaxed. Bob and Maurice propped up the bar as usual while a couple of old-timers sat snug in a corner, enjoying the sunshine that streamed in through a nearby window. There was a background chink of glasses and hum of conversation, and in the gaps between serving, Grace pondered on the unresolved situation between Joyce and Edgar. She knew very few details, only that Joyce had at last replied to Edgar's letter, but in a careful, controlled way that was bound to have disappointed him.

'I didn't want to get his hopes up by saying too much about how I felt,' Joyce had explained, almost in passing. 'So I stuck mostly to what's going on in Burnside — Brenda's little spill on her motor bike, Alfie working for the Kelletts, the Italians coming back to Beckwith — that kind of thing. As I say, I didn't want to lead him on.'

'But you wrote back,' Grace had pointed out. 'He'll be pleased about that.' Joyce was Joyce: careful and considered. And the love letter from Edgar had been totally out of character so perhaps Joyce had been right to steer them towards calmer waters. Still, Grace had to admit that she'd hoped for more. Not wedding bells, exactly, but at least more than the exchange of village tittle-tattle.

'Two pints of John Smith's, please.'

A new order drew her out of her reverie. She nodded and smiled at two smart strangers at the bar — both in their forties, dressed in

156

navy-blue suits, wearing trilby hats and collars and ties. One had a thin, grey moustache, while the other sported heavy-rimmed glasses. She glanced over their shoulders and saw a black Morris parked in a position that blocked the entrance to the smithy. At the same time she noticed the arrival in the yard of the Fosters' Land Rover towing a spotless maroon horsebox. Her father came out in his leather apron, his bald head shining in the sun. He gesticulated his disapproval of the thoughtless idiot who had parked in the way.

'Is that your car?' Grace asked the bespectacled man who had ordered the beer.

He turned casually then nodded. 'Oops — someone's not happy,' he commented, seeing Cliff and the equally irate driver of the Land Rover. He took a long swig from his glass before sauntering out to remedy the situation.

'You just drove out here for the afternoon?' Grace asked the second customer. She assumed that the two middle-aged men were town types, possibly civil servants — but then again no, because they had too much swagger, and besides, lowly pen-pushers wouldn't be swanning around in a brand-new car. So maybe they were mill managers or munitions manufacturers from Bradford, responsible for churning out uniforms and arms for the forces and thus exempt from serving on the front line.

'That's the ticket,' the man readily agreed. The froth from the top of his beer left a thin white line on his moustache, which he ignored 'There's nothing like a breath of fresh air.'

Grace took up a tea towel and wiped some glasses. 'Have you come far?'

'No, not far.' He leaned across the bar and winked. When he spoke it was with uninvited intimacy. 'What about you? Do you live far away?'

'No — just across the street.'

'With some jammy fellow?' He'd spotted her wedding ring but his tone didn't change. When his companion came back, he winked again. 'What's your name, love? And what a shame that you've been snapped up by some lucky blighter before we turned up.'

'It's easy to see why,' his friend said with a suggestive nudge of his elbow as he appraised Grace from the chest upwards.

'Go on — tell us your name,' the first one continued. 'I bet you're a Gloria or a Miranda.'

'Grace,' she answered, eyes lowered and hoping that the men would soon find other means of entertaining themselves. When she looked up again, she was relieved to see Doreen breeze in through the door ahead of Donald.

'Hello, you two; what can I get you?' Grace called out before they'd reached the bar.

'I'll have a Dubonnet if you have one.' Unlike Grace, Doreen invited the attention of the two strangers. She pronounced the last two syllables of the drink's name as if it were something you wore on your head.

'*Doo-buh-ney*,' the man with the glasses corrected.

'Who cares? It all goes down the same way.' Her laugh filled the room as she tilted back her

158

head to take her first sip. She wore a rose-printed skirt and a white blouse with frills at neck and cuffs. Her white, sling-backed sandals had high, wedged heels.

Donald, meanwhile, took the pint of bitter that he'd ordered and quietly scrutinized the day's opposition. 'You're not from these parts,' he observed to the smaller of the two men — the one with glasses.

'Ten out of ten for that.'

'Are you here on a visit?'

'No.'

'So you're just passing through?'

'Yes.'

Donald got no more out of him than Grace had out of his companion.

Moments later, out of the corner of his eye, the taller stranger spotted a movement in the yard. He quickly downed his drink and indicated to his friend that it was time to leave.

'Where are they off to in such a hurry?' Doreen pouted.

'Why not go after them and find out?' Donald was in a sulk. It was all very well her dressing up to the nines for his benefit, but not at all the thing for her to toss her hair and use her throaty laugh to attract other male admirers. 'Go on, why don't you?'

'All right, I will.'

As fast as her heels would allow, she was out through the door, leaving Donald to pass the time of day with Grace. He deliberately kept his back to the window and acted as if he couldn't care less. 'How's married life?' he asked.

Grace's smile was self-conscious. 'It suits me very well, ta.'

'That's all right then.' A small muscle in Donald's jaw twitched until he clenched his teeth to stop it. Then he took a swift pull at his beer and went to join Maurice and Bob at the other end of the bar.

\* \* \*

The sun shone in Doreen's eyes as she left the pub. She shaded them and made out the Morris across the yard with its bonnet up and boot lid raised. Then she spotted three men bending over and peering at the engine.

'What's up?' she called. 'Shall I call the AA?'

All three turned to face her. She was surprised to discover that the third man was Alfie Craven and that none of them seemed pleased to see her. In fact, Alfie had the cowed look of a man whose past had just caught up with him. There was a tension in the air that she could have cut with a knife.

'No need for that. Run along now, there's a good girl.' The taller visitor spoke between clenched teeth while his shorter friend gave his jacket lapels a sharp tug. Alfie, meanwhile, gave her a distinctly nasty look.

'You heard him — run along.' The stockier one obviously expected Doreen to turn tail immediately.

But they hadn't reckoned on her digging in her heels over what she recognized as a slight. 'Oh, Alfie,' she cajoled as she sidled up to him;

the tall man went swiftly to the boot and slammed the lid. 'Aren't you going to introduce me?'

He gave a quick nod and seized her by the arm with an unexpectedly tight grip. 'Gents, this is Doreen,' he announced.

She held out her hand to the one with the moustache.

'Howard,' he grunted.

'Pleased, I'm sure.'

'Talk about, if looks could kill,' Doreen told Grace later. 'Alfie would be laid out in that yard, dead as a door nail!'

The stocky man gave his lapels another tug then shook her outstretched hand. 'Clive.'

'Charmed,' Doreen trilled. Then, before she knew it, Alfie was whisking her back the way she'd come.

'He frog-marched me right through the door!' she complained to Grace.

There was another slam as the bonnet closed then more activity in the yard. Grace's father led two newly shod hunters out of the smithy, closely followed by the Fosters' groom in flat cap, waistcoat and corduroy breeches. The horses backed away nervously from the Morris as its driver succeeded in choking the engine into life. The groom, who was dwarfed by his sturdy charges, took matters in hand by leading them round the corner out of harm's way. After some coughing and spluttering, the car eventually pulled away.

'Honestly, that Alfie doesn't know his own strength!' Doreen rolled back her sleeve to show her upper arm to Grace. 'I've got the bruises to prove it!'

⋆  ⋆  ⋆

'You're asking for trouble,' Grace warned Doreen as the afternoon wore on. She'd watched the way Doreen had played Donald off against Alfie, keeping them both dangling on the end of a string, smiling and laughing her way through three more Dubonnets until Grace had at last refused her what would have been her fifth. 'Have you seen the look on Donald's face?'

Out came the scarlet, pouting underlip. 'What's wrong? He often looks like that.'

Donald sat by himself in a window seat, staring glumly across the yard and ignoring Doreen and Alfie's recent antics at the bar.

'Sometimes wringing a smile out of him is like getting blood out of a stone.'

'Just now I don't blame him,' Grace persisted. Doreen might be right — Donald did have a morose, brooding look when you caught him unawares — but on this occasion she could understand why. So, while Alfie was making a quick trip to the Gents, she'd seized the chance to intervene. 'You can't go on the way you do and expect Donald to be happy about it.'

'Why not? I can talk to who I like, can't I?' Doreen's balance was unsteady. 'He's not my keeper.'

'Still.'

'Neither are you, Grace, so leave me alone.' Launching herself away from the bar, she stumbled against a table, to be steadied by Donald just in time to stop her from falling flat on the floor.

Donald muttered something under his breath then sat her down in the window seat as Alfie came back.

Grace beckoned him across. 'I'd leave them to it for a bit,' she advised. Alfie put up his hands in surrender then looked around for someone else to annoy. When he didn't find any other candidate, he settled on a stool close to the bar. 'So, Grace,' he began, 'how's marri — '

'Don't!' For once she was snappy and impatient to reach the end of her shift. 'Everyone asks me that and it really is none of their business.'

'Oh, touchy!' He stretched his lips into a smile that left his hooded eyes blank and dull. 'What's up, Grace, had your first argument with Bill?'

'No, and while we're at it, I've been meaning to have a word with you.' Taking off her apron, she hung it on a hook under the counter. She was tired, really tired. 'It's about Poppy. She told me what you did to her in the woods behind Fieldhead.'

Alfie burred his lips dismissively. 'What can I say, Grace? I'm just your average, red-blooded chap.'

'I don't want to hear it!' Her hand went up in warning. Here was her father at last, making his slow way out of the smithy and across the yard, not a moment too soon. 'All I'm saying is that Poppy has only just had her eighteenth birthday. She's struggling to cope with Land Army life as

163

it is, without you frightening her half to death. She almost ran back home to her mother because of you.'

He shook his head. 'Hark at St Grace,' he muttered, 'gathering up waifs and strays, taking them under her wing.'

Her hand tingled with a powerful urge to slap his fleshy cheek. 'Leave her alone, you hear? If you go near Poppy again, I'll call the police and you'll find yourself twiddling your thumbs in a prison cell!'

'My!' he said, top lip curled, dead eyes staring. That was all — nothing else.

'Now then,' Cliff said as he squeezed his bulk behind the bar then rested his hands on its copper surface. He glanced at his pale-faced daughter and a sneering Alfie. 'You look tired, Grace. Why not get yourself off home?'

★　★　★

Una had done as she planned and secretly swapped shifts so that she could be at the hen farm on the Saturday morning. She'd made the arrangement with Kathleen on the understanding that she wouldn't spread any gossip.

'Mum's the word,' Kathleen had promised once she'd understood Una's reason. 'Who am I to stand in the way of true love?'

For Angelo had answered Una's note. '*Cara mia*' and 'darling' were scattered throughout his reply like bright confetti. Yes, they must meet as soon as possible. His heart longed for her. He would wait for her in the woods behind Beckwith

Camp after supper on Saturday evening.

How she'd got through the day she didn't know. Her fingers were all thumbs as she collected eggs from the coops and placed them in a basket. She hadn't heard a word Elsie and Jean had said as they'd worked alongside her.

'Have you gone deaf?' Jean had bellowed over a cacophony of clucks and squawks as they finished their shift in the musty, dust-filled hen hut at Winsill Edge. It was twelve o'clock and she was impatient to get back to Fieldhead to begin her afternoon off. 'I said, get a move on if you're planning to cycle home with Elsie and me.'

Hardly recognizing the sound of her own voice, Una had told them to go on ahead without her then she'd sought out Thomas Turnbull, Horace's ancient father. She'd found him sitting on a stool outside the door to their poky cottage, smoking a pipe. Well into his eighties, Thomas was hunched and toothless, more of a hindrance than a help whenever he volunteered to work alongside the Land Girls in the hen huts. Hopelessly vague about the job in hand, one of the girls would be obliged to follow him with an extra basket to pick up the eggs he'd missed.

Despite the fluttering of her heart and her light-headedness at the prospect of the reunion with Angelo, Una had managed to lay these careful foundations for her evening visit to the camp. 'Mr Turnbull, is it all right for me to take this extra order of eggs for the Italian prisoners? I promised to save Horace the job of driving them over.' She'd shown him two trays of eggs

165

— four dozen in all — that she'd kept back specially.

No such promise had been made — indeed, the camp cook had no idea of his forthcoming good fortune. But Una relied on the old man's hazy understanding to execute the next stage of her plan.

Thomas had sucked on his pipe and nodded without comment. It was doubtful if he even realized that eggs were on ration these days. He would certainly forget to mention the under-the-counter arrangement to his son.

'Ta very much!' Una had cleared her conscience and been off in a flash, stashing the trays in the front basket of her bicycle before riding off at speed. She'd arrived at the hostel five minutes after Jean and Elsie, still breathless at her own daring.

Once in their shared room, Kathleen had taken a quick look at the contraband eggs then pretended to be shocked. 'Blimey, you'll soon be giving Alfie Craven a run for his money!'

'They're not for me,' Una had protested.

'I know they're not, silly.' One glance at Una's flushed cheeks and the hectic red patches on her neck had softened Kathleen and she'd gone over to the alcove where she, Una and Brenda hung their dresses. 'Come on, let's decide on what you're going to wear later on. How about your blue cotton with the white daisies? Or this? Or, if you like, you could borrow my pink and white striped? No, maybe not — it's a shade too big.'

And now the sun was sinking behind the elms and it was time. Una's thick auburn hair was

166

brushed to silky smoothness, her legs and arms were bare and she'd added a white belt and white canvas sandals to the daisy dress — Angelo's favourite from last year's Christmas show. At the last minute she remembered to pick up the two trays of eggs: the pretext for her visit.

'Don't you need a cardigan?' Kathleen suggested as Una took one last look in the mirror.

'I don't have one that matches.'

'Here — take mine.' No sooner said than done and Kathleen ushered her out of the door, all the way along the corridor then down the stairs. 'Good luck!' She leaned over the banister and called after her.

All was a blur — the lanes, the trees, the hills — as Una cycled away from Fieldhead, through the village then along Swinsty Edge. She was aware of nothing except the thumping of her heart and a vision of Angelo's face as they met in the shadows of the pine trees; how he would smile and his brown eyes would crinkle. His features would blur and his lips would be soft. The moors rolled ahead of her, the white clouds were tinged with pink.

After many twists and turns, dips and hollows, heathery moorland gave way to a sea of green ferns then to fields of ripening wheat until at last she turned into Penny Lane, into the full glare of the setting sun. And then the fear rose like a lion: would her lie about the eggs get her past the prison camp sentry? Might it be the same British Tommy who had seen her fall off the wall and land in the brambles? Worst doubt of all: would

Angelo be there to meet her as promised? Her heart pounded on and she gripped the handlebars more tightly than before.

Two Canadian pilots drove a grey Land Rover out of the entrance to the old isolation hospital, giving her a curious glance as she cycled on without acknowledging them. The guard on duty called out a friendly greeting. On she rode to Beckwith Camp.

⋆    ⋆    ⋆

Her worries proved groundless as the fresh-faced British corporal on duty prepared to raise the barrier without a moment's hesitation. He said that Una was a sight for sore eyes and wished that all deliveries could be accompanied by a smile like hers.

'It's a Saturday night. Shouldn't you be out with your pals, enjoying yourself?'

'Later,' she managed to mumble. Surely the sentry could hear her heart knocking against her ribs?

'Good for you. You know where the canteen is — in the hut behind the main house.'

Una nodded and cycled on between neat rows of long, low wooden huts. She saw the original building straight ahead — a large Georgian farmhouse with wide entrance steps flanked by pillars — and as she passed, she looked through the long, low windows to glimpse prisoners still at supper, heads bent over their meals. Sure enough, there was a Nissen hut behind the house, connected to it by a covered pathway

168

— the canteen and storeroom that the soldier had mentioned. But instead of stopping there to deliver the eggs, Una glanced over her shoulder to make sure that the sentry wasn't still watching then rode on towards the far edge of the camp.

*Almost, almost!* Angelo was within reach, quietly waiting for her in the lengthening shadows. She leaned her bike against a boundary wall then entered the wood. Her footsteps fell silent on the bed of pine needles.

'Una?'

It was Lorenzo who called her name, not Angelo. She saw his tall figure as it stepped out from behind a tree.

She ran to him. 'Where is he? Where's Angelo?'

Lorenzo laid a hand on her arm. 'He sent me to tell you — he will try to come.'

'But where is he? Why isn't he here?'

'He will do his best.'

'That doesn't answer my question!' Desperately she looked around, as if Angelo might materialize out of nowhere. The tall, straight trunks rose high over their heads.

Angelo's fellow prisoner took out a cigarette then lit it. He inhaled deeply. 'He is not well.'

'Not well — how do you mean?'

'He is not strong. But he wishes to see you.'

'How long has he been ill?' A different kind of fear clutched at her — not the hot, hammering at her heart as she'd cycled here but an icier grasp that made her shudder. Still she searched for Angelo among the trees.

'Today he is in the hospital hut. He has not

169

eaten.' Lorenzo studied Una closely, taking in the desperation in her eyes, which eased slightly as she took in these last few words.

'Oh then, he has a temperature — a stomach upset, maybe?' It couldn't be serious because she'd seen Angelo jump down from the truck with her own two eyes and then run to join the others. How many days ago had it been since the prisoners arrived? Three; yes, three.

Lorenzo shrugged and drew smoke into his lungs.

'Poor Angelo,' she murmured. She was on the point of asking which hut housed men who were sick when Lorenzo threw down the cigarette and pointed over her shoulder.

'So he is here after all. I go,' he muttered as he retreated with silent footfall.

Una spun around to face the man she'd longed to see, through nights of not sleeping and the web of days spent dreaming of this moment. He was as she'd imagined: smiling and walking towards her, opening his arms. She gasped and ran to meet him. His arms were around her just as she'd pictured, his cheek against hers as she hugged him back.

She sighed as he released her. 'Oh — oh!' Joy, joy — to be with Angelo, to touch his lips with her fingertips, to see in his eyes how much he loved her still.

He was as before. They were the same together; he taller than her, with browner skin, blacker hair, holding her close. She nestled against him and it was as if he'd never been in Scotland but had been here with her all the time.

'This . . . I do not believe . . . ' Lost for the English words, he came out with a rippling stream in his native tongue — *amore*, *piccola*, *tesoro* . . . He held her as if he would never let her go.

Coming to her senses, she gently pushed him to arm's length. 'How are you feeling? Lorenzo said you were poorly.'

'I see you,' he whispered. 'I am happy.'

Was he paler than before, and perhaps thinner? But then the work in the shipyards had been gruelling and less healthy than labouring outdoors in the fields, so this was hardly surprising. 'We don't have much time before the sentry begins to wonder where I've got to,' she went on hurriedly as her feelings bubbled over in smiles and sighs. 'I've kept all your letters and I never take this off, even at night.' She held up the gold cross round her neck — his parting gift on Christmas Day as the lorry had pulled out of the yard of the Blacksmith's Arms.

He'd leaned out to press the crucifix into her cold palm. He'd closed her fingers over it. 'Take! . . . I write. Every day, I write . . . *Ti amo*, *mia cara*.'

He smiled through tears. '*Carissima*, you love me — this is true?'

'Cross my heart.' Without shyness, she placed his hand where he would feel its strong, rhythmical beat.

She was soft and warm, full of life. How could he not kiss her and hold her as if she was the most precious thing in the world? After all, she belonged to him.

# 11

'Grace! Grace!' Bill flung down his hat on the kitchen table then ran to the foot of the stairs. 'Where are you?'

She came in from the back yard where she'd been watering her pots of parsley and mint. 'Here I am. What's up?'

'It's Jack!' His eyes shone with excited disbelief. 'There's good news! He's in Italy, in a camp. The Italian navy picked him up. He's alive!'

'Oh, Bill, that's marvellous!' She took his jacket and hung it over the back of a chair then sat him down and demanded details.

'The telegram came through earlier today. Esther delivered it to the Hudsons in person. News spread like wildfire around the village. The blast didn't kill him — somehow Jack managed to get off the ship in one piece.'

'How did you find out?'

'From Mum. She telephoned me at the workshop. Honestly, Grace, I couldn't credit it. She had to repeat it three times.'

Grace reached across the table and held his hands. 'What did the telegram say?'

'Not much — just bare facts. Jack's a prisoner of war. He's held near Rome, according to Mum, in a big camp where they plan to send hundreds of our boys captured at Tobruk. He'll be in good company.'

He paused for breath and Grace squeezed his hands tight. 'I wonder how long he was in the water before he was picked up. At least it's warm in the Med, that's one good thing.'

'Yes. We don't even know if he was wounded. But Jack's tough — he'll come through this all right, I know he will.'

She nodded. 'There'll be doctors in the camp. It's near Rome, you say?'

'North east of the city.' Bill sagged forward and let out a long sigh of relief. 'We just have to get through these next few months until Jack and all the other lads are released and sent back home for good. Russia's holding on to Sevastopol and we still have Suez. Hitler's not getting it all his own way.'

Grace was silent. They were yet to see the 'light which shines over all the land and sea' that Mr Churchill had promised them late last year and so far the dreadful bombing raids over Germany that Edgar was involved in had not weakened the enemy — in fact, the opposite: the so-called Pact of Steel powers were seemingly poised to take Egypt. And then, further afield, there was Hong Kong and Burma, not to mention the struggles in India.

'We will come out on top,' Bill vowed. 'Before long, we'll put Jerry in his place.' Raising his head to seek agreement, he saw doubt in her eyes instead of certainty. 'That's what they're saying on the news bulletins — that we're well on the road to victory.'

'Fingers crossed.' Grace would sometimes note the silences on the news rather than the

173

statements that the politicians regularly spouted. What about the damage to Canterbury, Bath and Coventry, for instance? There'd been no mention of that after the German bombardments, nor any attention paid to the recent back-pedalling in Libya. 'I'm just sorry that it's taking so long. And it must feel awful for Jack, being taken prisoner along with all the chaps who scrapped so hard in the desert. He'll be pretty cut up.'

Bill frowned. 'You can't talk like that. To win this war we all have to look on the bright side, otherwise we might as well throw our arms up now and surrender.' He resented the shift of mood and wanted to pull their attention back to his best friend's lucky escape. 'Anyway, I wouldn't be surprised if Jack tunnels his way out of this camp before too long. He's not the type to sit on his backside.'

'A lot of them do try to escape — so yes, I wouldn't be surprised either.'

Something was bothering Grace but she couldn't put her finger on what. Perhaps she was just tired after three days at Home Farm, weeding and rat-catching, milking and haymaking late into the evening, until tonight when she'd finally put her foot down and clocked off at teatime for a change.

'He'll be up and at 'em — unlike me.' Bill carried on with his train of thought, pulling his hands away and clenching his fists. 'Sometimes I wish . . .'

'Wish what?'

'That I didn't have to tinker around with tractors all day long.' He broke free abruptly then went to look out of the window where he saw Maurice closing and locking the door to his workshop. The green paint was peeling and there were weeds growing up through the cobblestones in the shared yard. 'It's not what an able-bodied bloke should be doing when there's a war going on.'

'The powers that be don't think that,' she reminded him. 'And it stands to reason — we need to make sure our farm machinery is in good working order to keep the war effort going. That's the way everyone looks at it.'

He shook his head without turning round. 'But if I was Jack or Edgar, I could hold my head up better. As it is . . . ' He shrugged then tailed off again.

In a sudden rush of sympathy, Grace joined him at the window. Maurice was opening the back doors of his van, whistling as he loaded a wooden crate containing car parts. There were only a few years separating the two men but the mechanic's waistline was already thickening and the bald patch on the top of his head did nothing to improve his baggy, down-at-heel appearance. 'You're not comparing yourself to Maurice?'

Her probing question opened the floodgates and three years of pent-up frustration poured out. 'When it comes to it, where's the difference? Not much, as far as I can see. Except that Maurice is a one-man band whereas I have three mechanics working for me, which frees me up to swan around in a suit and tie, drumming up new business.'

'So you'd rather be in navy uniform, standing in the bow of a boat waiting for a low-level bomber to drop torpedoes on you?' Aware that her exasperation would push them further apart in this their first disagreement of married life, frustration still got the better of her. 'What's got into you, Bill? I've never heard you talk like this before.'

'No, but on the quiet I've felt rotten ever since war was declared. I've known people were looking sideways at me, judging me. Why wasn't I volunteering? What made me so special?'

'I'm sure they haven't been,' she protested. 'Everyone knows that what you do is important.'

Bill ignored her. 'And if Dad had still been here, or if he hadn't had his bad heart, I would have volunteered as soon as war was declared,' he vowed. 'I'd have chosen the army and I'd have been proud to serve.'

'And what about me?' Where did she feature in this alternative version of events? Grace's stomach twisted into a knot as she waited a long time for him to reply.

Stony faced and standing by her side without reaching out to her, he stared across the yard. 'I'd still have married you.'

'Then I'd have run the risk of losing a brother *and* a husband.' It was selfish and she was ashamed the moment she spoke the words. But men had no notion of how it felt for the nation's women to snatch envelopes off the doormat the moment they fell through the letter box, desperately hoping for a letter from their loved ones addressed in familiar handwriting, dreading

176

the official telegram that would change their lives utterly.

His frown deepened and the gap between them widened. For the first time they would go to sleep that night without any loving caresses. 'I'm just saying,' he muttered. 'It bothers me; that's all.'

★  ★  ★

'Well, Joyce — thank you for writing back to me and I'm sorry if my last letter came as a shock. I promise that I'll be on best behaviour this time.'

She smiled briefly then read on in the quiet of the common room. All the others were already in bed and the old building settled and sighed towards a midnight silence.

'I'll stick to what I hope will interest you. First off, I've been sent to the barber's for my compulsory short back and sides, all over and done with in a minute and a half, start to finish. Last weekend we went for a refresher course in navigation and Morse code. I spent the Sunday evening back at base building a valve radio for use in the billet. Then I did my washing the Rinso way.

'There — how's that? I'm sure you're glued to the page and can't wait for the next instalment.'

Dressed in her pyjamas and curled in one of the big leather armchairs, with the window standing open and moon and stars reflected in one of the tall panes, Joyce's imagination carried her off into an unfamiliar men's world of barber's chairs and shaving cream, dot-dot-dash and the hum of valves and smell of molten solder.

'Seriously, though, there were many evenings prior to that when I was on operational duty, with no time for building radios or doing laundry. My name showed up on the battle order for five nights on the trot, Monday to Friday. Dicing tonight, as the saying goes. We get a briefing beforehand and a report from the Met officer, Navigational officer and Intelligence officer in that order. There's usually time for a few hours' kip before we fly out. Once out over the bomb line, we have to watch out for night fighters and try to avoid enemy flak coming up from below, doing our best to keep out of range of the searchlights.

'On the Wednesday night, something daft happened. We were instructed by Control to maintain height and turn two degrees east, steady away. There was an unidentified aircraft close behind us but we were not to alter course or speed. Bugger that, we thought (pardon the French) and we took evasive action. But guess what — Jerry had locked on to our wavelength and we spent the next five minutes exchanging fire and flinging swear words at each other in a mixture of German and English — bloody hilarious! (Again, excuse the language.)'

She smiled a second time then sighed. This follow-up letter from Edgar, so different from the first, echoed the tone of her own reply but she found herself disappointed. It could have been from any one of the thousands of RAF pilots currently in active service to any friend, male or female, left to serve on the Home Front; a letter in which they made light of the horrors of warfare and gave nothing away. There were only a few sentences towards the close that lifted Joyce's spirits.

'At the end of this week I'll have finished my current tour and will be due five days' home leave. I'll be more than ready, believe me. So, Joyce, if you can stand to be seen out and about with me with my newly scalped haircut (which will have grown a little by then), perhaps you'll agree to come out for a drink. Shall we say on Monday the 29th at half past seven? If you agree, I can drive out to Fieldhead. A yes from you would be a real pick-me-up. With very best wishes, Edgar.'

'Yes please, Edgar.' She wrote back without hesitating in forward-sloping, even handwriting. 'I'll be very happy to meet you when and where you say. I look forward to it very much. Love from Joyce.'

\* \* \*

Of all the work places they were regularly sent out to, Brigg Farm had quickly become Doreen's favourite. She got on well with the normally snappy, acerbic Roland Thomson for a start.

'Now then,' he called out to her with unaccustomed breeziness when she cycled into the yard with Una and Kathleen on the last Thursday in June. There was a drizzle in the air and little breeze to shift the heavy clouds clinging to the horizon. 'I hope you're ready to

179

roll up your sleeves and get stuck in.'

'Always!' she replied, propping her bike against the stable wall. 'What have you got in store for us today, Mr Thomson? I hope it's not thinning turnips in the top field like last time.' That had been a nasty, back-breaking job — down on their knees for hours on end, with sacks over their heads to keep off the rain.

'No, I want two of you down in Low Field, loading hay on to the wagon; the other one can lend a hand further up the hill, bringing in the spring lambs.'

'Us and whose army?' Doreen demanded, nudging Una when she spotted a tell-tale army Land Rover parked across the yard. Young Neville went to cadge a cigarette from the driver, who leaned his rifle against the wall while he offered him a light.

'Who do you think?'

'Would it be our Italian friends, by any chance?'

'Bull's-eye,' Roland confirmed.

'Una, the lambs will be your job for the day.' Kathleen winked at Doreen. 'Hayricks, here we come!'

The Tommy with the packet of cigarettes strolled across to join them. 'I have to walk up the hill with coffee for the Eyeties,' he told Una. 'All the gear is in the back of the Land Rover. You can help me carry it.'

Things were working out perfectly and Una beamed at Doreen and Kathleen. In fact, she'd spent the last week more or less in a state of ecstasy, boldly inventing more reasons to visit

180

Beckwith Camp and wangling secret assignations with Angelo. As the days went by she found that the other prisoners and even some of the guards would turn a blind eye whenever she left her bike at the gates and slipped out of sight.

Today, however, might turn out to be the first time that they would spend the whole day together. And even if he wasn't part of the group, she would surely be able to get a message to him to arrange their next meeting.

'It's a pity it's not a better day,' the Tommy observed as they slung bulky canvas satchels over their shoulders then set off up the steep, stony hill at the back of the farm. There was the chink of tin mugs and the slosh of coffee inside big vacuum flasks as they walked. 'My name's Cyril, by the way.'

'Una,' she replied.

Cyril recognized her as the regular visitor to the camp. 'This has made your day, eh?'

'What — walking out with you?' He was a jaunty lad, about the same age as her youngest brother, Geoffrey, and she felt able to tease him.

'You should be so lucky,' he joked back. 'Anyway, I don't think my sweetheart back home would be too happy about that if she found out.'

Una asked his sweetheart's name — Mildred — and all about her. She was eighteen and lived in Northgate and they were engaged to be married.

'When?' Una asked as they toiled up the hill past a limestone outcrop and over a ridge. A low mist clung to their faces, cutting down visibility to twenty or thirty yards, so that they could hear sheep bleating in the distance but could see no sign of them until they descended into the next valley and a new, mist-free vista opened out.

'The sooner the better.' Everything about Cyril was raw and eager — his voice and his smile, the way he strode out into whatever the future held. 'Mildred's mum is the only thing stopping us. She says we should wait a couple of years. I'm working on Mildred to make a stand and do it sooner — in secret if we have to. Once we've signed on the dotted line, her mother can't argue.'

Una paused and inhaled deeply. Ah yes, now she could see the sheep scattered over the hillside: ewes with their heads down to graze the short, sparse grass; lambs doing what lambs did — running and springing straight up in the air, racing to tug at their mothers' teats then skip off again.

Cyril waited for her to catch her breath. 'Who are you looking for? No, don't tell me — let me guess.'

Una's face grew more serious. So far she hadn't spotted the party of prisoners who had been sent to herd the sheep. 'Is he here?' she asked anxiously. 'I mean Angelo.'

'I know who you mean. And yes, your luck's in. I brought him and his pal Lorenzo and a couple of others. But you know what the Eyeties are like — they're a lazy bunch so they're probably taking a quick kip while they think no one's looking.'

Just then a black-and-white collie cut across the green slope and started to snap at the heels of one of the ewes, which raised its head then tottered unwillingly towards its two lambs, bleating loudly. The dog stayed low to the ground, ears pricked, intent on pinning down and holding the sheep.

Then two men appeared, dressed in the familiar grey uniforms. Una's heart skipped a beat as she recognized Lorenzo and Angelo. At the same moment they noticed her with the soldier. They exchanged a few words before they split apart — Lorenzo to carry on working the dog and Angelo to set off in her direction.

'No need to say anything — three's a crowd.' With an exaggerated wink, Cyril made himself scarce.

Una put down her satchel then ran down the slope. Before she knew it, Angelo's arms were around her and his lips against hers, bringing that swooning sensation she felt at every embrace.

For a while no words were spoken. It was enough to kiss and lean in close, to breathe each other in.

*So warm, so gentle.* He was everything she'd ever dreamed.

*So small and beautiful.* Her eyes shone with love.

She saw tears form in his deep brown eyes and gently brushed them away. 'You're not sad?'

'No — happy.'

*The exact timbre of his voice, like no one else's. The way a lock of his thick black hair curled down over his smooth forehead.*

There was space all around them — a misty

sky and green slopes folding into each other all the way to the horizon. They ignored the barking of the dog in response to Lorenzo's high whistle.

Una gestured towards the satchel perched on a rock further up the hill. 'We've brought coffee. I've been sent to help with the lambs.'

Angelo wrapped his arms tight around her waist. 'My wish is true.'

'Shall we tell Lorenzo and the others to stop for coffee?'

'After.' First they must smile and kiss again and again.

'Hey up!' It was Cyril's voice that broke them apart. He still carried his rifle but he'd put his satchel alongside Una's and now shouted down the hill. 'This is getting out of hand.'

Angelo blushed and let go of her. Una laughed out loud. 'Don't mind him.' She grinned. 'He's only jealous.'

But the mood was broken and as if by magic, two other prisoners materialized from behind one of the great, mossy slabs of rock that littered the slope while Lorenzo settled the dog to guard the huddle of sheep then joined them. Soon everyone sat cross-legged in a circle, tin mugs at the ready, while the flask of coffee was handed from one person to the next.

Una sat close to Angelo, exchanging smiles and listening to the rapid flow of Italian between the prisoners. Every so often, Cyril's blunt tones cut across the running rivulet of foreign sounds — 'nice weather for ducks' as the drizzle turned to rain, 'bloody things' when two ravens swooped down to peck at the jam jar containing sugar for the coffee. The birds flapped and squawked then flew off when Lorenzo tossed a stone in their direction.

Angelo noticed that Una had no coat. He took off his short grey jacket and wrapped it around her shoulders, leaving him in a thin white shirt that was soon soaked by the rain.

'Blimey!' Cyril raised an eyebrow but made no other comment. *Like flipping Walter Raleigh with his cloak,* he thought. *Mildred would never expect that sort of treatment from me. She wouldn't get it either.*

When the coffee was drained, Lorenzo was the first to stand. He looked to the heavens and smiled as he pointed to an area of cloud that had thinned, allowing a weak sun to shine through.

'Time to get a move on,' Cyril declared as he got up and dusted himself down. 'Let's round up the sheep over the brow of the next hill. Lorenzo, I'm putting you in charge. Una and I will stay here and collect the coffee cups.'

★　★　★

Back at Brigg Farm, Doreen and Kathleen rode on the back of Neville's cart to the hay field in the valley. They perched with pitchforks across their laps on top of a pile of folded tarpaulins, ready to cover the ricks at the first sign of heavy rain.

'We're all right so long as it doesn't chuck it down,' Neville called over his shoulder. 'We can work on in this.'

Kathleen tilted her head back to feel the warm

dampness on her cheeks. She enjoyed the swaying rhythm of the wooden cart over the rough track and the sound of Major's hooves clip-clopping along.

'When you say 'we', I suppose you mean me and Kathleen.' Doreen had got the farm lad's measure the first time she met him. 'Not that I'm calling you work-shy, young Nev!'

'Quite right — I'm a busy man.' With a self-important flick of the reins he urged Major on down the track. Hawthorn hedges in full bloom obscured the view of fields to either side. 'In fact, later on this morning I'll have to leave you girls to it and nip off to see to other business.'

Kathleen laughed merrily. Doreen prodded him in the back with the blunt end of her pitchfork. 'Ooh-er — other business!' she echoed, while Kathleen broke into an old Harry Champion song.

''Any old iron? Any old iron?' What are the words? Something about, I wouldn't give you tuppence for your old watch and chain?'

Doreen hummed the tune. 'That's about it, eh, Nev? You and your old horse and cart have entered the rag and bone trade.'

'Mock all you like,' he sulked, turning into a sloping field where hand-built hayricks awaited them. 'You'll be laughing out of the other side of your faces when you see me waltz your little friend Poppy off in a taxi to Northgate on Saturday night.'

'A taxi!' Kathleen cried in astonishment as she jumped off the back of the wagon then

186

immediately attacked the nearest rick with her fork.

'All the way to Northgate!' Doreen too got stuck in to the morning's task. 'Are we sure this hay's not too damp?' she checked with Kathleen.

'Neville's the boss,' came the reply. 'You heard what the man said — we have to work on until it pours down.'

Which it did after less than an hour's pitching, when the cart was only half full. The heavens opened and the girls were quickly soaked to the skin.

'Quick — tarpaulins!' Kathleen told Doreen to grab one side of a canvas sheet. Together they covered what was left of the first rick before sprinting on to the next.

'Come on, Nev, lend a hand!' Kathleen insisted. 'This hay is meant to see Major through the winter. It'll be ruined if we don't watch out.'

So they hauled and lifted as a threesome until the job was done. Then the girls insisted on a lift back to the farmhouse to wait for the rain to ease.

'Giddy-up, Major!' Doreen climbed up beside Neville and seized the reins. Before long they were clip-clopping up the lane with her in the driving seat. They arrived in the farmyard smiling but looking like drowned rats, according to Roland, who told them to take shelter in the hayloft while Neville unharnessed Major and he went into the house to make a pot of tea.

'Two sugars for me, please!' Doreen called after him.

'You'll be lucky.' Kathleen discovered a

wooden crate hidden under a heap of hay in a corner of the loft and sat down. It was only now that she realized just how wet she was — the corduroy fabric of her breeches clung to her thighs and her hair was plastered to her head.

Doreen took off her red headscarf and wrung it out. Then she tipped her head forward and shook out her dripping curls.

Down below, they heard Neville telling Major to stand still while he removed his harness. Then there was another voice that they couldn't quite make out.

'That doesn't sound like Mr Thomson coming back with our tea.' Doreen glanced down into the yard. 'Look who it isn't!' she said.

'Hmm.' Kathleen joined her and spotted Alfie wheeling his bike across the yard. There was a crate tied to the back of the saddle so she watched for a few seconds as he undid the straps then she tutted and went back to sit on her box without commenting.

Doreen, however, thought there was more fun to be had. She emerged on to the top step and stood, hips tilted at an angle, one hand placed lightly on her waist, waiting for Alfie and Neville to look up at her. When they did, she gave them plenty of time to study her statuesque pose.

Noticing that her wet cotton shirt and corduroy trousers outlined her figure perfectly, Alfie immediately took up the challenge. 'Hello, Doreen — that's quite an eyeful!'

'Why, hello to you too, Alfie. I take it that you've decided not to ignore me today.' She went down the steps languidly, with a provocative pout in his direction.

He grinned in an insinuating way then offered his hand for her to jump down the last two steps. 'When did I ever ignore you?'

'Last Saturday,' she reminded him. 'In the pub car park. You were too busy with your fancy friends to bother with the likes of me.'

Alfie glanced quickly at Neville, who seemed to take the hint to wheel Alfie's bike out of sight, round the side of the stable. 'Don't be fooled; they're not fancy and they're not my friends.' Tapping the side of his nose in a knowing way, he slid her arm through his. 'Anyway, I came into the Blacksmith's Arms with you, didn't I? I don't call that ignoring you.'

'Yes, you warmed up after a frosty start,' she remembered. 'You bought me a drink, right under Donald's nose, as I recall.'

'You didn't say no, though, did you?' He raised his eyebrows and pinched her arm lightly, appreciating her smooth, damp flesh, warm to the touch.

Seeing Roland emerge from the house complete with loaded tray, she withdrew her arm and led the way. 'Tea up!' she called to Kathleen and Neville. 'Mr Thomson, is there enough in the pot for an extra cup? Alfie has cycled all the way from Home Farm. The poor chap needs to wet his whistle.'

★　★　★

By midday the rain had stopped and herding the sheep and lambs resumed. Up on the fell, the four POWs and Una worked all afternoon to round them up. As they began to bring the flock down to the farm, Cyril gave her and Angelo the job of staying back to check for strays.

'Don't spend too long looking,' he advised with a knowing smile. 'You know what they tell Little Bo Peep in the nursery rhyme — leave them alone and they'll come home . . . '

'Wagging their tails behind them!' Convinced by now that her happiness was infectious, Una mouthed a lively thank-you. She recited the whole rhyme to Angelo then explained its meaning. ' 'Wagging' means wiggling — like this.' She shook her slim hips from side to side and made him laugh. 'Do you have any children's rhymes where you come from?' she asked.

He thought a moment then took her hands and swung her round as he sang some strange words. ' *'Giro, giro, tondo . . . Casca il mondo. Casca la terra, tutti giu per terra!'* ' On the last line he pulled her down on to a patch of long meadow grass with golden buttercups and pale milkmaids.

'Let me guess what it means,' she laughed as she clasped her arms around his neck. ' 'Everything turns, the world falls down . . . ' Then what?'

' 'The earth falls down, we all fall down!' '

'Like 'Ring a Ring o' Roses'!' The same rhythm, the same actions. But rolling slowly with Angelo down the slope and with the blue sky turning above them, her mood shifted without warning. 'The world won't end, will it?' she asked in a small voice. 'You don't suppose that the war will alter everything and there'll be no getting back to where we once were?'

Struggling to understand, Angelo pushed her hair back from her face then stroked her cheek. To him it was like a shadow coming over the sun. 'Do not be sad.'

'I won't,' she promised. But she couldn't escape a sudden, sharp awareness that everything was temporary — the petals of the buttercups were easily crushed, clouds would obscure the sun, rain would fall.

★   ★   ★

'Daft things!' Doreen had no patience with the hundred or so sheep and lambs bleating loudly in the stone fold next to the tumbledown sty where Lady M and Roland's other pigs were housed. The sheep stumbled and crashed into each other in their struggle to find a way out. 'They sound silly and they *are* silly. That's all there is to it.'

'I don't hear you complaining when you've got a nice, juicy lamb chop on your plate.' Ever since Alfie had put in an unexpected appearance, Kathleen had been subdued. The girls had drunk their tea then gone back to the hay field and carried on pitching without asking Neville the whys and wherefores of Alfie's visit. Now, though, as she and Doreen sat on the hayloft steps waiting for Una and Angelo to come down off the fell, Kathleen had to decide whether or not to open up the topic that had been bothering her all afternoon.

'Don't talk about food — I'm famished!' Doreen couldn't work Kathleen out. Sometimes, she was the life and soul of the party — at Grace's wedding reception, for instance, when she'd danced right through to the end. But at other times, like now, she seemed flat and deflated. 'What is it? Have you had bad news about a sweetheart?' she asked.

Kathleen leaned back against the warm wall and shook her head. 'No bad news. No sweetheart.'

Doreen rolled her eyes. 'You're kidding. I expected you to have at least two or three on the go.'

'At the same time?'

'Naturally. You can have the pick of the bunch with your looks. What did you do in Civvy Street, by the way?'

'I was a hairdresser in Millwood.'

'That fits. I mean, you've got nice hair. Is it permed or were you born with those curls?'

'Natural. How about you?'

'Hand on heart? The waves are natural but the colour isn't. I wanted to make changes after I got the telegram about Bernie.'

'Your fiancé?'

'That's the one. Changes, starting with my hair. That sounds like nonsense, doesn't it? The man I was to marry snuffs it so I dye my hair brunette. But that's me, take me or leave me.'

'It's not nonsense,' Kathleen argued. 'And I understand. Anyway, blonde isn't my natural colour either. By rights I'm mousy brown.'

Doreen laughed then busied herself by taking

out a cigarette and lighting it. 'We've got more in common than I thought.'

'You don't say. And while we're having a heart-to-heart, you might as well know that I went out with Alfie Craven a while back, when we both lived on Union Street.'

'Never!' Doreen's answer was accompanied by a fleeting but piercing glance at Kathleen's face through a puff of blue smoke. 'I take it you don't want him back?'

'No, never in a month of Sundays.'

'That's all right then.'

'Do you want to know why I dropped him? No, don't bother answering — I'll tell you anyway. It was for two reasons. First of all I learned that he'd been in prison.'

'What for?' Doreen's attention was now firmly fixed.

'Grievous bodily harm. It involved a knife — that's all I know for certain. And that he made a lot of enemies when he was in gaol and that he got out after three years.'

'Blimey. Does Ma Craven know?'

'I haven't a clue. I wasn't too keen on him after I found that out, but I might have considered him a reformed character and given him another chance if it wasn't for the second thing.'

'Let me guess — he was married.'

Kathleen remembered the exact moment when she'd learned this secret from a customer who knew someone who knew the wife, Maureen. 'With two nippers — a boy and a girl, apparently. He called himself Alf Watkins back then, so it was a big shock when he showed up in Burnside and I made the connection. I would've kept it to myself, except I've noticed the way he is with you.'

'And you want to stop me from getting my fingers burned?' Doreen stubbed out her cigarette then flicked it to the ground. 'Ta — I appreciate it.'

'Stick with Donald — that's my advice.'

'I said ta.' Pressing her lips together, Doreen turned her back.

'Because a leopard doesn't change its spots,' Kathleen insisted.

From her high vantage point Doreen spied Una and Angelo walking down the hill hand in hand. She jumped down the steps and hurried to fetch her bike, ready for the off. 'At long last, here they come — love's young dream!'

# 12

A blast of fierce heat struck Grace's cheeks as her father opened the furnace door then used a pair of heavy pincers to shove the curved blade of Joe Kellett's broken scythe deep into the glowing embers. She listened absent-mindedly to the sounds that had been part of her childhood — clinking metal and gusts of wind forced through bellows — accompanied by the smell of hot iron and choking fumes that caught the back of your throat as you breathed them in.

Cliff cocked his head sideways to peer into the furnace. 'I take it Joe wants his scythe back straight away?' he growled.

'Yes, he told me to wait until you've finished.' She glanced outside, wrinkled her eyes against the sunlight and was able to make out a regular customer leading his horse into the yard. 'Neville's here with Major. Were you expecting him?'

'No and I've only got one pair of hands,' her father grumbled. 'Tell him he'll have to wait.'

'I don't suppose he's in any hurry.' Neville was taking his time to tie Major's lead rope to an iron post before he sauntered in to announce his business.

Cliff raked more red embers over the rusty blade, his face glistening with sweat. 'This is the last time I can fix this; the steel's all but worn away. Joe needs to shell out for a new one, tell him.'

'I will, Dad.' Grace was enjoying the breather from hard labour that her visit to the smithy had afforded. She'd left Una and Brenda slaving away in Joe's ditches, digging up weeds and mud from the clogged channels. While her father got on with the repair job, she strolled outside to have a word with the newcomer.

Neville ducked under Major's head and walked slap into Grace.

'Good grief — what happened to your face?'

'It's nothing,' he muttered gruffly.

'Then how did you get those two shiners?' Neville's left eye was swollen almost shut, the right one not much better. And the skin on his cheek and forehead was scraped red raw. He moved stiffly, as if every joint hurt.

'Ran into a lamp post, didn't I?'

'Pull the other one.' She made as if to put a kindly hand on his arm but he winced and drew back.

'Bang into it, head first,' he insisted as he skirted around her. 'Wasn't looking where I was going.'

Grace refrained from asking more questions and followed him into the smithy.

'Hello, Mr Kershaw. Dad says have you got time to fettle a new shoe for Major — front left. He lost it in the mud after it rained.'

Cliff glanced at the lad's black eyes then offered a quick solution. 'Have you tried raw steak on them?'

'Where would I get that when it's at home?'

Grace took his point. These days, even in a farming community, every ounce of beef that the ration books allowed went straight into meat pies and stews, with no scraps left over. That was why the unexpected extras from Dale End had come as such a boon to every cook and housewife in the valley.

'Go and see what's in the larder,' Cliff instructed Grace, who went off into the house and returned with what was left of the week's ration of stewing steak. 'Slap a couple of pieces of that on your eyes — it'll take the swelling down.'

So Neville sat in a corner nursing his injuries while Grace waited for her father to pull the scythe out of the furnace, cool it in a bucket of cold water then sharpen it at the grindstone. Afterwards she fetched Major in for a spot of re-shoeing.

'Feeling any better?' she asked Neville before she set off for Home Farm.

He looked sorry for himself but didn't answer.

'Stop clucking over him; he'll be right as rain in a day or two.' Cliff sent her on her way.

'Now, lad, what did you tell your dad — was it the wall or a lamp post?' he asked Neville with a conspiratorial wink. 'Nay, I'll keep my nose out. As long as this horse of yours stands still and does as it's told, we'll have you out of here in two jiffies.'

★　★　★

Even up to her calves in mud, standing in a wet ditch, Una couldn't have looked lovelier. This was Angelo's opinion as he and Lorenzo worked alongside her for the second day running, slashing at brambles with his knife then heaving them out of the ditch to be carted away by Brenda. He was amazed by her energy and cheerful determination, wondering how a girl so small and slight could wield a spade so willingly. But here she was beside him, with her shirtsleeves rolled up and a leather belt fastened tight around her waist to hold up her breeches, digging for all she was worth.

'Stop looking at me.' She blushed and went on digging. 'You're putting me off.'

'I like to look.' He tried to slide his arm around her waist but she dodged sideways.

'Joe will catch us if we're not careful.'

The sour-faced farmer stood at the gate with eyes peeled.

'Una's right,' Brenda chipped in. 'A girl can't even stop to take off her pullover without the old so-and-so giving her a dirty look. What's the betting he won't let us stop to eat our sandwiches until we've dug the entire length of this field?'

Lorenzo caught the gist of her muttered comment and took it upon himself to organize the dinner break by striding up the hill to where the old man stood. He spoke and gesticulated for a while before whistling through his fingers and beckoning for Angelo, Una and Brenda to join them. The sound of his whistle brought three other prisoners up from a neighbouring field, and by the time Grace arrived with Joe's mended scythe their slave driver had retreated inside the house and they had settled down in a corner of the farmyard with a kettle boiling on a metal tripod over a fire of twigs and a coffee pot containing rich-smelling grounds at the ready.

There was a contented silence as they ate their sandwiches, broken only by Brenda's compliment about the coffee then the distant drone of three aeroplanes, which they more or less ignored until they were directly overhead.

Una was the first to glance up and spot the unmistakable swastika markings on the wings. 'Blimey, they're Jerries!' she cried in sudden panic. 'Get down, everyone!'

'Junkers,' Grace confirmed as the planes swooped low. She led the scramble for cover.

The small group split in different directions — Grace and Brenda towards the relative safety of the house, Lorenzo into the nearest ditch, leaving Angelo and Una to kick dirt over the fire then run towards the empty milking parlour.

They were just in time. From inside the parlour they heard the rapid rat-a-tat of machine-gun fire and bullets ricocheting from the corrugated iron roof over their heads. Angelo wrapped a protective arm around Una's shoulder to shield her from the filth and debris that dropped from the rafters.

'Why are they flying over at this time of day?' Una crouched low and waited for the firing to stop. 'They usually wait until night-time.'

He held her tight and gritted his teeth at this grim reminder of war. Often he could forget that Una and he were on opposite sides but this brought it home with a vengeance.

'I'll bet they've been split up from the rest of

their squadron and they're taking aim at anything they come across.' Home Farm stood on an exposed ridge, making it an easy target, especially with the smoke from the fire to draw the pilots' attention.

Another rattle of bullets strafed the roof and more rubbish showered down. Angelo put his hand to his mouth and coughed long and hard. By the time he'd stopped, the planes had passed over, leaving the farm in silence.

'Are you all right?' Una whispered. The wheezy cough came from deep in his chest.

He cleared his throat and nodded but was then caught up in another spasm. He spat on to the floor as he made his way to the door. 'It is safe,' he reported. 'Come, Una; they are gone.'

Sure enough, she found that Lorenzo had already climbed out of the ditch while Brenda and Grace stood in the porch with Joe and Emily. They congregated in the farmyard, cursing the enemy or keeping silent according to which side they were on, but all thanking their lucky stars that no bombs had been dropped.

'That's a bad cough you've got,' Brenda commented to Angelo as Joe ordered them back to work. 'Are you still feeling poorly?'

He shook his head but had to pause and lean on the gate as they entered the field.

'Are you sure? Una mentioned that you'd been to the doctor. You do look a bit peaky to me.'

'She means thin and pale,' Una explained as Brenda went back to digging. Small alarm bells sounded in her head — perhaps they'd been ringing for a while but now she found she couldn't ignore them. 'I've been thinking the same thing myself.'

'No.' He denied it point-blank. 'It is bad air inside cow house.'

But he was quiet for the rest of the day and didn't attempt to dig, only to slash through the thorns and nettles then bundle them up and carry them to a new bonfire that had been started at the bottom of the field. Una noticed that Lorenzo kept a careful eye on him throughout the afternoon. When it was time to pack up at the end of the day, Lorenzo seemed to remonstrate and try to usher Angelo straight into the Land Rover without saying goodbye. But Angelo argued back and came to separate Una from Brenda and Grace. He pulled her into the shade of a hawthorn hedge and held her tight. '*Arrivederci*, my Una. Soon I will see you?'

'Of course you will. Do you know where you'll be working tomorrow?'

He shook his head.

'It's my half day. Let's try to meet up later in the afternoon. I can come to the camp, like last time.'

'Good. I wait in trees.'

'I'll find you there.' A rising fear pecked at her insides and her smile of parting was less whole-hearted than usual. Still she went along with acting as if all was well as she waved him off.

'He is, you know — looking a bit peaky.' Brenda wouldn't let it drop, despite a warning glance from Grace.

Una frowned then nodded. She kicked with

the toe of her wellington boot at some chickweed growing up through the flagstones. Everything here was so neglected, it got you down. And Emily Kellett wasn't much more than a skeleton, a silent presence in the doorway as Joe stamped around bullying people. And by the way, where was Alfie? Typical of him to make himself scarce instead of lending a hand with the heavy work that had gone on today.

'Come on, cheer up.' Brenda was the first to fetch her bike. 'Angelo has probably got a bad cold, that's all. He'll be better in a day or two.'

'You're right.' Una mounted her bike and started to pedal.

Grace soon followed suit and the three women rode off along the lane.

'Look at Brenda — raring to go,' she said to Una to lighten the mood. 'My guess is that she's arranged to meet Les tonight.'

⋆　⋆　⋆

With the prospect of only a half day's work ahead of them, many of the Land Girls at Fieldhead set their minds on enjoying a good night out. It meant that there was a long queue for the bathroom on the landing that Poppy shared with eleven others and ablutions were restricted to a quick all-over sponge-down in cold water followed by a sprinkling with talc and a rapid brushing of teeth. Make-up was applied back in the bedroom. Hair was brushed and crimped, dresses chosen in a flurry of non-stop activity.

'How do I look?' Poppy twirled in a flared, peach-coloured cotton skirt and short-sleeved white blouse.

Doreen and Joyce scrutinized the effect.

'Pretty as a picture.' Sitting cross-legged on her bed in her work clothes, Joyce gave her seal of approval.

'That skirt needs a belt.' Doreen fished one out of her drawer and watched Poppy put it on. 'Good Lord, it's fastened on the tightest hole. Your waist must be tiny!' She spoke with a hint of pique then decided what she might lack around the waist in comparison with Poppy she made up for in the bust department. 'Which shoes will you wear?'

'These.' Poppy held up some well-worn white sandals. 'They're all I've got.'

'They'll have to do, I suppose.' Doreen herself was done up to the nines in her green satin sheath dress with boned bodice and off-the-shoulder straps. She'd saved up to buy it two summers ago, soon after she'd got her job in the department store and long before clothes rationing had come in.

Joyce glanced up again from her magazine. 'You must be going somewhere special — I see you're wearing your nylons.'

'Yes, and a new suspender belt.' She showed them a glimpse of her stocking tops, held in place by pristine elastic suspenders. 'I've got a lacy brassiere too.' She winked as she gave them a quick view of this as well.

Guessing at a black market source for Doreen's finery, Joyce hid her disapproval.

'Alfie's in for a treat.'

'Who mentioned anything about Alfie?' Doreen retorted.

'No one. I only thought . . . '

'Yes, they're presents from him. He likes to give me nice things but it doesn't mean he owns me.'

'Does he know that?' Joyce had begun to grow weary of the way Doreen constantly claimed centre stage. She wasn't jealous — it was more that Doreen never tired of putting herself first on every occasion. So she uncrossed her legs and drifted out of the room.

'Ooh-er!' Doreen hogged the dressing-table mirror while Poppy put her hair into a ponytail as best she could in a small hand mirror propped against the wall, excited at the prospect of Neville arriving in a taxi no less, ready to take them into town.

Soon, though, Joyce reappeared with a message for Poppy, passed on by Mrs Craven who had intercepted her in the main hallway. 'I'm sorry, Pops, Neville has telephoned to say he can't come after all.'

Poppy's face fell a mile while Doreen breezed out of the room. 'That's taken the wind out of her sails,' she remarked as she departed.

'Did he say why not?' Poppy asked with a heavy heart. Disappointment quickly turned to irritation — didn't Neville realize she'd been doing him a big favour by agreeing to go out with him? Who the heck did he think he was?

Joyce shook her head. 'Just that he can't make it and he's very sorry. Never mind, we two can have a cosy night in instead. We'll go downstairs to the kitchen and make cocoa, have a nice chat.'

Just then Brenda popped her head around the door. She was dressed in petticoat and skirt. 'Can anyone lend me a safety pin?'

Joyce took a sewing kit out of her bedside-table drawer. 'How big?'

'The smallest you have, please. It's for this petticoat strap — it's come adrift.' She took the pin and fixed the strap in place. 'What the eye doesn't see . . . ' she said with a grin before dashing off.

'Let's hope Les appreciates the effort Brenda makes for him,' Joyce said with a wry laugh. 'She's probably held together with half a dozen of those things. And she's bound to be an hour late at least. She'll turn up on Sloper, windswept as can be and, knowing him, he'll still think she's a fairy-tale princess.'

Poppy sighed and sat heavily on her bed. Why couldn't she be lucky enough to meet someone like Les who adored her and would never let her down?

Joyce saw that she was almost in tears. 'Would you rather go out to the pub?' she asked gently. 'I can throw on some decent clothes then we'll cycle into Burnside if you like.'

After some cajoling, Poppy agreed. *Forget about Neville*, she told herself, while Joyce quickly slipped into a cream linen dress and wrapped a gold and blue silk scarf around her neck. *He's too young for me anyway.*

By the time they set off on their bikes, Poppy was feeling better. It was a fine evening and they

205

soon caught up with other girls heading in the same direction, all chatting and laughing as they cycled along the lanes. They made fun of some of the farmers they had to work for: so-and-so is a right skinflint and have you seen the way so-and-so's wife carries on behind his back, and on like this until they came to the village and sighted three Canadian Air Force men parking their Land Rover on the street before heading towards the pub.

'See — things are already looking up,' Joyce whispered to a more cheerful Poppy, pleased to see that a cool breeze, the sun and exercise had worked wonders as ever.

★ ★ ★

'We can stay in tonight if you'd rather.' Les greeted Brenda with a kiss on the cheek. Despite his open-necked shirt, worn with slacks and a yellow cravat, he seemed on edge. 'The others have gone out so we've got the whole place to ourselves.'

As Joyce had predicted, Brenda had arrived late at Dale End and Les had stood fretting at the front sitting-room window. What if she'd changed her mind and gone out with the girls instead? Or suppose she'd had an accident on one of the narrow lanes? As soon as he'd heard the sound of her motor bike approaching the final bend, he'd rushed straight to the front door.

'Stay in and do what?' she asked, taking off the man's flat cap she'd put on to protect her hair.

She'd worn it at a jaunty angle, knowing that it and her heavy leather jacket were at odds with her pleated apple-green dress beneath. She shoved the cap into her pocket and looked past Les across the empty hallway. Several doors stood ajar but there was silence except for the ticking of a grandfather clock against the wall to her left.

'We could play some records,' he suggested.

'Your favourite Glenn Miller?'

'Yes, or whatever you want. Come in and I'll show you what we've got.'

She followed him into the faded sitting room overlooking the garden. For the first time she noticed a gramophone in a polished wooden cabinet in one corner of the room and in a side compartment a neat stack of records in their paper sleeves. Throwing her jacket over the back of the nearest sofa, she knelt down to make her choice.

'Drink?' Les opened the door to a corner cupboard to reveal a wide choice of whisky, port, gin and brandy.

'I'll have gin with a splash of tonic for a change.' She pulled out 'Boogie Woogie Bugle Boy' by the Andrews Sisters and handed it to him.

'Let's listen to this; I hear it's a hit with the Yanks.'

He abandoned the drinks cupboard to place the record on the turntable then gently lower the needle. After a crackle of static, the noise of bugles burst forth, quickly followed by foot-tapping saxophones that established a swing rhythm. Then three female voices harmonized in praise of the Boogie Woogie Bugle Boy of Company B.

'Well, Bren, what do you think?' He watched a slow smile spread over her face.

She nodded. 'I like it. It's livelier than Glenn Miller. Anybody could dance to this, even with two left feet.'

While he went back to the drinks, she took in more details of the room. True, the sofas were shabby and the panelling needed a lick of paint, but the brand-new gramophone must have cost a pretty penny and the rug covering the oak floorboards was the genuine, hand-made Persian article. Looking out of the French doors across a large garden laid out in carefully planned tiers, with pergolas and a circular fish pond complete with fountain as a centrepiece, she reckoned that the flower beds would have kept at least two men busy before the war had siphoned them off into one or other of the armed forces.

'Thanks for coming,' Les said as he handed her the drink and gazed directly into her eyes.

'I said I would, didn't I?' To deflect his attention, she turned to the question of horticulture. 'Who keeps your garden in such good nick?'

'These days it's mostly Hettie. I mow the lawns and dig the vegetable patch when she asks me to.'

'Back home in Northgate we had a pocket-handkerchief garden — no grass, just flagstones and a little strip of marigolds and petunias.' She felt no shame in highlighting how different their upbringings had been. 'It was row after row of terraced houses that I saw from my back window, rising up the hill behind us, mill chimneys belching out smoke, a railway track running right past our door. I loved to hear the chug-chug of the trains sending me to sleep every night.'

He raised his forefinger to her lips and pressed them softly then took her glass from her hand.

'Are you listening to a word I say?' she protested.

With the music gathering speed, he put both arms around her waist and would have kissed her except that she turned the embrace into a dance, putting her arms around his neck then leaning back and starting to move in time to the rhythm. When the record finished, there was the click of the needle in the final groove then an awkward silence.

And so the evening went on — Brenda fending Les off, choosing more records and avoiding the slow tunes, drinking occasionally, talking animatedly as usual — until in the end, he chose a record — 'The Anniversary Waltz' by Bing Crosby — then quietly sat her down on the sofa.

'I still don't know what to make of us,' he confessed with an exasperated sigh. 'I'm certain of how I feel but I need to hear it from you; am I wasting my time?'

'Like I said before: it's not you, it's me,' she replied, her head a little woozy after three gins. 'I'm sorry, I don't think I'm in the frame of mind for anything serious.'

Les frowned and looked thoughtful. 'So I gather. At least, that's the line you spin to me — and everyone else, for that matter. But it's not the whole story, is it?'

This time she didn't break away from his intense gaze. 'I'm sorry,' she faltered.

'Don't be sorry. Try to explain.'

She gave a stiff shake of her head. 'I don't know how to.'

'Why not? Whatever you say is between you and me. Not another soul will ever find out, I promise.' He could see confusion in her eyes and likened it to the reaction of a cornered creature in the wild: a fox or a deer, on high alert, working out which way to run.

'Grace says it's because of my bad scrape with Mack the Knife — that's the Canadian I crossed swords with last Christmas. That's when my guard went up and I haven't lowered it since.'

'Bad scrape?' The frown deepened.

'Don't ask,' Brenda told him, with the singer crooning in the background and the French doors overlooking the garden letting in fresh air and a scent of roses. 'Let's just say I came out of it in one piece, if you know what I mean. But it knocked my confidence. I couldn't help feeling that I'd brought it on myself. And people talked.'

'That's not fair,' Les insisted. He understood for the first time that her lively, sometimes devil-may-care personality hid something deeper and darker. The realization made him want to reach out and protect her but for now he would have to go carefully, one step at a time. 'But I don't blame you for holding back; it's only natural.'

She looked at him quizzically then thanked him.

'What for?'

'For giving me some breathing space. I mean it, Les, most men wouldn't.'

'I'm not most men.'

*No, you're not. You have a gentle, patient way with you. You like music and I bet you have your head stuck in a book every chance you get. You have nice grey eyes.* This last thought brought a smile to her lips.

'And you're not most girls.' He saw the smile and gained courage. 'The more you tell me, the more I see how true that is. You do what you want to do and you say what you think; I admire you for that. On top of which, you like to have fun but there's a serious side as well.'

She gave a small nod and felt a light-headedness that was more than a mixture of roses and gin. 'That's me to a T,' she murmured.

Then they did kiss for the first time that evening. His features blurred as he leaned towards her — the grey of his eyes mesmerized her and she responded to the soft touch of his lips. They sank back on to the sofa, closely entwined, both ready to give in to desire. Neither heard the click of the front door above the dying strains of 'The Anniversary Waltz'.

'Future years . . . A few little tears'. The sentimental words drifted out into the hallway.

'Les, are you there?' Hettie's footsteps approached the sitting room.

211

Les and Brenda sprang apart. Brenda sat up and smoothed her skirt while Les jumped to his feet.

'There you are!' Hettie took in the scene — the two empty glasses beside the gin bottle, cushions and clothes in disarray, the hiss of static on the record player. She tilted her head to one side as if demanding an explanation.

'You're back early.' Les glanced at his watch. It was half past eight. 'I thought you and Dad were playing bridge with the Fosters tonight.'

'I changed my mind and dropped in on an old friend instead.' Hettie didn't blink or budge. Her plum-coloured dress and spinsterish brogues made her seem more of a school ma'am than ever. 'Hello, Brenda. I noticed your motor bike parked outside.'

Here it came: the judgement that Brenda had come to dread — the stern narrowing of the eyes, the pursing of the lips. Her barrier slammed back into place. 'I have to be off if I want to get back to the hostel before dark,' she told Les hastily. 'Ta for a lovely evening.'

'You'll need your jacket,' Hettie pointed out, stony-faced.

Brenda doubled back to pick it up from the sofa but Les snatched it away. 'There's no rush,' he insisted. 'Hettie, why not join us for a drink?'

'No thanks. It seems Brenda has had enough already.'

Her unprovoked rudeness prodded him into action. He slung Brenda's jacket on to the nearest chair then caught her by the hand. 'Don't worry about the time,' he insisted. 'I can

212

always drive you home when Donald brings the car back.'

'No, I don't want to put you out.' *How can one woman whip the rug from under me with a single stare and a few short words? Stand up for yourself, for goodness' sake!* She looked from Les to Hettie then back again.

'This is not on, Hettie,' he protested. 'I think you should say sorry to Brenda.'

'What for? For speaking the truth?'

'What's it to you, anyway?' Shoving his hands deep into his pockets, Les paced the room. 'Why can't you mind your own damned business?'

'This *is* my business.' Without raising her voice or changing her expression, Hettie kept her gaze firmly on Brenda. 'She's playing with your affections — any fool can see that.'

'Oh!' Brenda gave an outraged gasp then grabbed her jacket from the chair and made for the door. 'Get out of my way,' she told Hettie. 'I won't stay where I'm not wanted — I'm off!'

'No, wait a minute.' Les came between the two women, pulled his sister into the room then closed the door. 'You can't go on doing this, Hettie — poking your nose in where it's not wanted. Not any more.'

Hettie let out a grunt of disgust. 'And I suppose you've become a sound judge of character all of a sudden? Well, let me tell you a few home truths.'

'What about, for God's sake?'

'About our Land Girl here. I'm sorry to be the one to break it to you but it's common knowledge that Brenda Appleby plays the field. Her name is mud, from here to Burnside and back!'

Brenda's eyes blazed with indignation. 'Believe what you please!' she shouted. 'But I'm telling you now, the rumour mongers are the ones who should hang their heads in shame, not me! And you too, Hettie, for believing them.'

With a look of smug satisfaction at having riled Brenda so badly, Hettie murmured under her breath a comment about the lady protesting too much.

'That's enough!' Les stormed. As Brenda tried to push past them both, he stayed her with his arm. 'Hettie, if you go on like this, I swear I'll — '

'You'll what?' For the first time, Hettie's expression showed a flicker of uncertainty.

'Nothing. I'm telling you to shut your trap. You have to get used to the idea of me taking Brenda out and that's the end of it.'

'Taking her out?' Hettie echoed scornfully. 'Is that what you call it?'

'That really is enough!' Les's face was red with anger. 'I'm warning you, Hettie!'

'Don't bother, I'm off!' As the situation spiralled out of control, Brenda pushed past him and wrenched at the door handle. She was halfway across the hall when Hettie called after her.

'By the way, has Les told you his latest news?' She was back to her coolest manner, looking over her shoulder at her brother. 'No, I see that he hasn't. Come along, Les, tell Brenda about the letter that dropped on our mat yesterday morning.'

Brenda's heart lurched. What did Hettie mean? Was it a love missive from a sweetheart that she didn't know about? No, that was more Donald's style than Les's. Was it something to do with the family business of renting out machinery? She froze and waited for his response.

'A letter in a brown envelope addressed to Mr Leslie White,' Hettie explained, circling slowly overhead, ready to drop the bombshell. 'With no stamp on it — just the Royal Crown printed in the top right-hand corner. I knew what it was the moment I saw it.'

Brenda knew too, from the careful description. She jutted out her chin then marched on towards the door.

'It was his call-up papers,' Hettie confirmed. 'Les is to join the Royal Navy and there'll be no getting out of it. They say Donald can carry on here as normal but Les has no choice but to join the fight for King and Country.'

# 13

'Aren't you coming to church?' Jean asked Doreen early the next day. She'd made an effort to spruce herself up in a royal-blue dress with a gored skirt and white piping around the neckline. She'd even waved her straight dark hair and pinned it up on top of her head. Now she was about to set off on her bike with Kathleen, Poppy and Una, who were also in Sunday best for the morning service.

Doreen sat on the front doorstep of the hostel, quietly smoking a cigarette. She was still in her dressing gown and slippers, with her face scrubbed bare of make-up and her hair uncombed. 'No, I'll give it a miss today,' she answered nonchalantly.

Brenda brushed past her from behind and took the steps two at a time. 'You'll have Ma Craven after you,' she warned. 'She likes us to show our faces at St Mike's at least every other week.'

Joyce followed at a more sedate pace, saying nothing as she joined the others.

'I'll think up a good excuse, don't you worry.' It was a mystery to Doreen why everyone at Fieldhead was so keen to toe the line. Doreen certainly had better things to do with her day off than to warble a few hymns and parrot the Lord's Prayer.

So she watched the girls cycle off then went

216

inside to revel in having time to herself. She pottered in the kitchen, making a hot chocolate and opening every tin until she came across a couple of broken rich teas. After that, she wandered out into the walled garden to see if the cherries were ripe then back into the house to flick through some weeklies in the common room. *The Land Girl* magazine, with its patriotic guff, knitting patterns and recipes, held no interest, however, and she objected to the musty smell of old books and furniture polish.

*Time to get dressed*, she thought with an idle sigh.

She'd reached the first landing when she heard her name.

'Doreen Wells — if it isn't my favourite Land Girl!' Alfie's muffled but unmistakable voice called.

Doreen leaned over the banister but the visitor was evidently lurking in the corridor leading to the kitchen. 'Alfie, is that you?'

'Who else?' He emerged into the hallway wearing the suit and trilby hat he'd first arrived in, walking with a limp and keeping his hat pulled forward.

She drifted down to meet him. 'Your mother's not in. She set off for church half an hour ago . . . ' She let her words tail off into silence as she noticed a deep cut about two inches long on Alfie's cheek. 'Blimey, what happened to you?' she said after she recovered from her shock.

'If you think this looks bad, you should see young Neville,' Alfie quipped. 'They laid into him good and proper.'

'Who's 'they'?' In fact, Alfie looked shocking. There was a bandage around his right hand and bruises on his left knuckles, besides a host of other hidden injuries, she shouldn't wonder.

'Never you mind. Let's just say I was ready for them and young Neville wasn't, worse luck.'

Mindful of the tittle-tattle about Alfie's criminal past that she'd picked up from Kathleen, Doreen walked full circle around him. 'This wouldn't have anything to do with those two spivs in the Morris Oxford, by any chance?' If so, she was confused — Alfie's injuries seemed to have been inflicted more recently than that.

Alfie laughed. ''Spivs' — that's not a very nice name.'

'They weren't very nice men,' Doreen retorted. 'Anyone could see that.' She remembered the tension in the air in the pub yard and the way one of the men had slammed the car boot shut to prevent her from seeing inside. 'And you couldn't wait to see the back of them, if I'm not mistaken.'

She was a smart cookie so there was no point in hiding the truth. 'Let's say that Howard, Clive and I had a small falling-out over a business proposition.' To be specific, Alfie had conned Clive Nixon and Howard Moyes out of a considerable sum of money — hence their persistence in tracking him down. 'Two against one — that's the only reason I came off worst.'

She circled him again. He was unshaven and the gash on his face was deep but clean — made with a sharp blade. It should have had stitches

218

but Alfie had obviously chosen not to go to hospital. 'How does Neville Thomson come into it?'

'That'd be telling.'

'At least he'll think twice about getting involved in your shady dealings from now on.' Did this mean there would be an end to her supply of stockings, lacy underwear and chocolate? she wondered.

'Neville will do as he's told,' Alfie contradicted sullenly before changing the subject. 'You say Ma's at church?'

'As per usual. She won't be back before dinner time.'

'Is there anything to eat in the kitchen?' He limped down the corridor and she followed. 'Emily Kellett is starving me to death. I've had cheese on toast three nights in a row, with a poached egg if I'm lucky.'

Doreen overtook him and went to the stove to lift the lid off a pot of stew. 'Boiled beef and onions in gravy with a few carrots and spuds chucked in. I can heat some up for you.'

He nodded then eased himself into a chair, admiring Doreen's back view as she turned on the gas, poured some stew into a small pan then set a place for him at the table.

'Never say I don't make an effort,' she said after she'd placed a steaming plate in front of him. But this was as much as she was prepared to do for the unexpected visitor so she made her excuses. 'Now, if you don't mind, I have to go and slap some cold cream on my face and put some curlers in my hair.'

* * *

Alfie wolfed down the stew and was finished almost before Doreen had reached her room. *She doesn't look up-to-much without her war paint*, he mused cynically. *But you can't pull the wool over her eyes, I'll give her that.*

His attention was neither fully on Doreen and the meal in front of him nor on the whereabouts of his mother, because he'd come to Fieldhead for a different reason entirely. Leaving the empty plate on the table, he scraped back his chair then limped off down the corridor and into the hallway, where he paused to recall which of the doors led to the office. He tried the common room then the door next to it, which opened up on to a small room with a telephone, a bookcase containing grey marbled box-folders and a desk covered in brown oilcloth. There was a blackout blind at the window and an electric light with a green metal shade hanging from an ornate ceiling rose in the centre of the ceiling. *Bingo!*

He approached the desk and pulled open the drawers, disturbing papers, a stapler and a hole-punch in one and a cardboard box containing paper clips and drawing pins in another. 'But no tin for petty cash,' he muttered out loud. He glanced at the window sill — a daft place to keep money, he knew. What about the bookcase? He drew a blank there too. So he went back to the desk and wrenched the drawers open to their full extent. There, hiding behind the box of paper clips, was the very thing he was looking for.

He took out the locked metal box and shook it. There was plenty of loose change inside and he could hear the rustle of banknotes too. But there was no key to the tin — again, even his mother wouldn't be stupid enough to leave that lying around. The answer was to take the whole thing with him, prise it open once he got back to Home Farm, then count out its contents. He needed twenty quid at the very least.

Alfie slammed the drawers shut and tucked the box under his arm. For a few seconds he visualized his mother's reaction when she discovered the theft. She would soon realize that only Doreen had been in the house when the money was taken. An innocent girl would stand accused and would snitch on him, no doubt. Or would she? Surely Doreen knew a good thing when she saw it in the shape of nylons, perfume and lipstick. And if she was as smart as he supposed, she'd straight away see the downside of turning him over to the police.

Anyway, what did he care? He would deny it, swear that he'd never set foot in the place. How could he, hampered as he was by the cuts and bruises that had forced him to take to his bed since Thursday? So he limped out of the office with the box rattling encouragingly under his arm, down the kitchen corridor and straight out of the back door to one of the empty stables where he'd stashed Emily Kellett's old boneshaker of a bike. Then he walked it through the wood at the back of the hostel until he came to a little-used lane, vanishing as quietly as he'd come.

Grace laid the table for tea with care. She was expecting her mother-in-law but was preoccupied by a short conversation she'd had with Una after church that morning. It had been about Angelo, of course. Una and he had arranged a romantic tryst for the previous evening but Angelo had failed to show up.

'He sent Lorenzo instead,' Una had explained with a worried expression. 'It turns out that Angelo's poorly again.'

'That cough of his won't go away?' Grace had surmised.

'That's right. The camp doctor ordered him to stay in bed. Lorenzo told me they had to dose him up with something that would make him sleep, otherwise he'd have disobeyed orders. By all accounts, he only stayed put once Lorenzo had promised to pass on a special message.'

'That he loved you?' Grace guessed rightly a second time. She'd pictured the heavy thud of disappointment that Una must have felt standing in the gathering dusk in the pine wood behind the camp and the icy fear that must have gripped her. 'Try not to worry too much,' she'd advised gently. 'Whatever's wrong with Angelo, doctors can work wonders with the medicines they have these days.'

But poor Una's face had been a picture of misery — pale with dark circles under her eyes after a sleepless night — and Grace wasn't as confident as she'd tried to sound. She wondered how much attention doctors in POW camps really paid to their patients and how good the treatment was. After all, what was one enemy prisoner more or less?

Still, she'd done her best to console Una and told her to keep her chin up. 'At least Angelo is safer where he is than out there in the desert alongside Rommel's lot, in daily danger of being blown to smithereens.'

Now, she laid a clean cloth on the table and methodically set out the best china in honour of Edith's visit. Bill was out but expected back at any time. There were scones in the oven and butter and home-made blackberry jam to go with them. Now all she had to do was put the kettle on and pour milk into the jug.

Edith arrived at four on the dot: upright and prim, with a crocodile-skin handbag over her arm and wearing T-strap shoes polished to perfection. As Grace opened the door to her, she removed her hatpin and took off her hat. 'I don't see Bill's car,' she commented as she handed the hat to Grace.

'No, he's not back yet.'

'It's not like him to be late.'

'I know. I'm sure he won't be long, though.' Grace led the way into the kitchen, with its welcoming smell of fresh baking. Anxious as usual to make a good impression, she hoped that Edith appreciated the effort she'd made.

'He's been looking a bit thin lately.' Edith sat down at the table, noticing every detail. 'I don't mean to find fault, Grace dear. I'm only saying that Bill has lost weight.'

'He's working very hard,' Grace admitted. Of

course she did feel undermined; it was as if her mother-in-law was saying that she didn't know how to feed her new husband properly. 'He's eating well, though.'

It was so hard to relax with Edith — Grace had always known this but she'd hoped that things would improve once they'd all settled in to the new situation. But there she sat with her ramrod-straight back, picking at the edge of the tablecloth, dainty as a small bird, without a trace of a smile on her carefully powdered face. A few minutes of ill-at-ease conversation passed before Grace was relieved to hear the sound of Bill's car drawing up outside the house, then the opening click of the front door. She stood up to welcome him.

The moment he appeared in the doorway, she could tell that he wasn't his usual self. He seemed on edge and reluctant to look at her or his mother as he took off his jacket and hung it over the back of his chair. When he sat down to tea, he ran his forefinger around the rim of his cup and stared unseeingly at the plate of scones on the table.

'Come along, Bill, out with it.' Edith was the one to break the awkward silence. 'What's on your mind?'

'Nothing.' He took a sip of tea then rattled his cup down into his saucer.

Grace was puzzled. She hadn't asked where Bill had been going when he set off straight after dinner, but wherever it was and whatever it had been about, he'd returned shrouded in gloomy unease. Perhaps he would work through his bad mood if she changed the subject. 'I had a chat with Una after church,' she told Edith. 'She was down in the dumps over Angelo, poor lamb.'

'I'm afraid Una has made a rod for her own back,' Grace's mother-in-law pointed out. 'She should have realized that her association with a POW would attract no sympathy in the long run.'

The two women talked through Una's difficult situation with one eye still on Bill, who continued to ignore his tea and stared out of the window. Then he got up from the table and went to stand at the back door, arms folded.

'Let's hope the doctors at the camp sort Angelo out,' Grace concluded.

Edith was less sanguine. 'But if they do have to send him to a hospital, Una will have to grin and bear it. It'll be a test of her mettle.'

'I drove Maurice out to look at the workshop.' Bill's interruption was unusually abrupt.

Edith looked quizzically at Grace. 'Whatever for?'

Grace's thoughts raced as she tried to make connections.

'Maurice knows his way around car engines. We agreed it won't be a big leap for him to start working on tractors.'

Edith gave an understanding nod. 'That's right. It always comes in handy to have an extra mechanic standing by.'

So why was Bill's expression so tense and his manner so preoccupied? Grace wondered.

'Maurice is a diabetic so there's no chance of him being called up at a later date.' His back was still turned, his crossed arms defensive.

Grace could stand it no longer. 'What's this really about?' she demanded. 'I know you; you haven't asked Maurice to stand by just in case, have you?'

He turned to them at last, his chin tucked in and looking out at them from under a furrowed brow. 'You're right; I've asked him to take over from me,' he confessed.

'Whatever for?' Edith sat stock still, staring at him. 'Oh Bill, you're not poorly?'

'No.' His flat voice disguised the pressure he was under. 'Grace, I hope this decision won't come as too much of a shock.'

She shook her head. *Of course, of course!* She'd closed her mind to it but this was exactly what she should have expected.

'Mum, Grace and I talked this through a while back — she knows how badly I feel about not doing my bit. It's on my conscience day in, day out — the fact that Jack and most of the other lads from the village signed up the minute they got the chance, yet what do I do? I stay behind and tinker with a few tractors, that's what.'

If anything, Edith's posture grew stiffer, her face more immobile. Grace, meanwhile, closed her eyes and let her head drop forward. *You didn't listen to a word I said*, she thought illogically. *I obviously don't matter to you.*

'Well, it stands to reason — any trained mechanic can do my job, apart from the book-keeping angle. I showed Maurice that side of things and he took it all in. That leaves me free to sign up — for the army, if I have my way, but

I'll go wherever I'm most needed.'

'You can't!' Edith gasped. 'Your father . . . I . . . You can't!'

Bill's face remained impassive. 'I can, Mum, and I will. First thing tomorrow morning, I'll drive down to the recruitment office in Northgate to enlist.'

★   ★   ★

'Your letter told me you'd be here on Monday after work!' Joyce dashed downstairs to greet Edgar with what sounded like an accusation. Since her heart-to-heart with Grace, she'd kept her own counsel about the letters passing between them and built up as calmly as she could to their arranged meeting, but she wasn't prepared for his early arrival. 'I'm sorry, I must look a proper mess.'

Edgar shook his head. Here she was, dressed in slacks and a short-sleeved blouse, her hair roughly pinned up, barefoot but beautiful as ever in his eyes. 'You look fine to me. But shall I go away and come back again tomorrow as planned?'

'No, stay!' She took his hand, not knowing whether to lead him into the common room or outside, where they might be more private. She glanced down at her feet. 'Wait here!'

He watched her run up the stairs, hovering uncertainly in his uniform, cap in hand, oblivious to the curious glances of other Land Girls as they crossed the hallway. He'd reached home only an hour earlier and hadn't even got changed, so keen had he been to drive out to Fieldhead and see Joyce.

'Where are you off to in such a hurry?' his father had grumbled. 'No, don't tell me — there's a girl in the picture.'

And yes, there was — much to Edgar's surprise. *Ask me six months ago and I'd have said, 'You must be joking!' Back then I was hardly managing to put one foot in front of another.* He hadn't given his father the satisfaction of a straight answer, however. It was early days with Joyce, very early.

She came back down with her hair loose and newly brushed, wearing flat shoes and a cardigan. 'It's a nice evening. Let's go for a walk.'

'Tea's at half six!' Kathleen's sly reminder came from the common-room doorway as they left by the front door.

Edgar hesitated on the top step. 'Honestly, I can come back tomorrow if you'd rather.'

'Ignore Kathleen. Mrs Craven's in a stew over a burglary that happened while we were all at church. My missing tea will be the last thing on her mind.'

'What got stolen?' He put on his cap, then offered Joyce his arm.

'Some petty cash. In fact the whole money box went missing with eleven pounds, seven shillings and sixpence in it. Mrs Craven keeps careful track of every single penny. She has to, with Mrs Mostyn to answer to.'

Despite the pitter-patter of her heart, Joyce was pleased that she could sound normal as she and Edgar talked of everyday things.

'What rotten sod would steal money from the Land Army?' Edgar was at a genuine loss. 'Were there any signs of a break-in?'

'Not so far as I know.' Standing on the gravel drive, Joyce decided which way they should go. 'Let's skirt around the side of the house, through the garden and into the wood. We can walk as far as you like up the fell at the back.'

Edgar hesitated. The last time he'd walked through the wood had been on the night the Jerry pilot came down on this very hillside and he'd been determined to join the search party. Dark memories flooded back of stumbling into snow drifts, hardly knowing where he was, bedevilled by sounds and visions of his recent dogfight; the rattle of machine guns, bullets tearing through metal and Plexiglas into Billy's chest. Billy, his best friend and co-pilot, had been mortally wounded as he sat at the controls of their Lancaster bomber. And now Edgar remembered the silence when the plane's engines had stopped and their pilotless plane had drifted down to earth.

'Or somewhere else,' Joyce suggested quickly.

'Where you said is fine.' He'd got over it, hadn't he? He'd fought through the nightmare, out of his alcoholic fog and wild wanderings on the moors. He'd been declared fit to return to duty.

So they headed around the side of the building, through the stable yard then into the walled garden, neatly laid out with fruit and vegetables. There were hoes and forks leaning against an apple tree and an upturned wheelbarrow standing nearby with a pair of mud-caked wellington boots perched on top. As they passed a row of peas, Joyce paused to pick a ripe pod and hand it to him. He shelled it and they shared the contents.

Edgar threw down the empty pod then walked a little way ahead, through the gate and into the shaded woodland area. 'You probably think I'm a silly fool, jumping the gun the way I did.'

'Not at all. You're only a day early,' she said with a laugh. A bright sun glinted through small gaps in the green canopy, though the heat of the day was already starting to fade. Ahead of them a fast-running brook tumbled over rocks: too narrow to necessitate a detour, though Edgar paused to offer Joyce his hand. 'It's all right; I can do it,' she assured him as she leaped across.

Then they were out of the wood and ascending the rocky hillside, shading their eyes from the sun, swishing through bilberry bushes, smelling peaty earth beneath their feet.

'I don't mean jumping the gun in that way,' he said, as if there'd been no lapse in their conversation. 'I mean making a fool of myself in my first letter.'

She walked on, feeling a flicker of doubt. Why had he mentioned it? Was he about to backtrack and settle for a straightforward friendship after all?

'It wasn't like me. I don't usually wear my heart on my sleeve.'

'No, I gathered that.' Letting him catch up with her, she overcame her doubts. 'It took me by surprise, that's all.'

'But you didn't mind?' As he watched the breeze lift her hair from her face and saw the flush in her cheeks, he hoped with all his heart that she didn't.

The love contained in his intense gaze swept towards her like a strong wave, threatening to lift her off her feet. 'I didn't mind,' she murmured. 'When you know me better, you'll realize that it takes me a while to work things out. I'm like Grace: neither of us acts on the spur of the moment. That's why we get along so well.'

'When I know you better?' he echoed.

'Yes, if all goes well.' She set off again with her hand in his. They climbed to a ridge from where the wreckage of the German plane was visible. It lay in rusting pieces beyond a drystone wall, among tall ferns, with one wing and the tail section torn off and the other wing sticking up at a ninety-degree angle. 'We can turn back if you like?'

'Not on my account,' he assured her. Flying, fighting, taking a direct hit, spiralling, crashing to the ground — these were the facts of life that had to be faced. *Every time we take to the skies, we dice with death.*

She squeezed his hand. 'I'm glad you're back on a better footing. And it was brave of you to write and tell me how you felt.'

They came closer to the wreckage. The twisted fuselage revealed a black swastika inside a white circle. One engine lay some distance away, beside a rock. Two rooks perched on the pilot's shattered cockpit.

'I'm better than I was,' he confirmed.

'But?'

'I won't ever be the same as I was before.'

'In what way?'

He thought for a long time. 'I've got scars down my left side and thigh, for a start. The docs patched me up as best they could, but now . . . Let's just say I'll never play centre forward for Leeds United.'

Joyce smiled as she turned away from the enemy plane and walked on with him towards the rocky summit.

'Those dreams are well and truly in the past. I'm only twenty-five, but sometimes it feels more like a hundred and twenty-five. Where's that carefree kid gone? What happened to him?'

'Likewise.'

Her brief, murmured reply made him stop close to a limestone outcrop and pull her towards him. 'Is it the war? Is this what it does to us?'

'We all lose someone,' she whispered.

'Who did you lose?'

'My fiancé, Walter.'

So she'd loved before, he realized. She'd lost. 'I'm sorry. I didn't know.'

'I did tell you about him last December, but you weren't in a good enough state to take it in. Anyway, I'll remind you. Walter was in the Royal Navy. His ship was torpedoed. It went down with all hands. That was when I lived in Warwickshire.'

'I see.' *And I'm sorry I was too wrapped up in myself to remember.*

'I did go to pieces for a while,' Joyce confessed. 'But then I realized I had to pull myself together. For me that means rolling my sleeves up and getting stuck into hard work. My dad lost the family farm through drinking too much, so in effect I was forced to make big changes. That's when the idea of the Land Army cropped up. I signed on the dotted line and was sent up here into the wilds of Yorkshire. I've never looked back since.'

'Never?'

'Not often. I do miss the old farm sometimes and I'm sad whenever I think of Walter. But I'm not cut out to play the tragic heroine; I've got too little imagination for that.'

'No,' he said quietly, his arms around her waist, remembering how Joyce had been the one to see his suffering and to understand it. 'I won't have that.'

'Well.' She studied his face more closely. Edgar's features were even and finely shaped, his brows straight and flat over pale grey eyes, his nose straight, his jawline firm. She'd noticed all this before, of course, but the thing that she saw for the first time was the way everything now combined to create a look of confidence and certainty. 'At least talking to you about Walter feels like a weight off my mind.'

'I'm glad you did. And thank you.'

'For what?'

'For putting your trust in me. I understand much better now.'

'I hope it hasn't put you off.'

'You mean, being the second love of your life,

not the first?' He let a slow, warm smile spread across his face.

She responded by tilting her head back then challenging him. 'Who says you're the second?'

'Am I?' *Say yes. Tell me you love me.*

His whispered words swirled around her and carried her safely to the shore. 'If I say yes, what then?'

'Then I'll go back to base a happy man.' Even though they had only five short days before them and it would be letters that would hold them together during the months of duty, the endless rosters and nightly forays over enemy territory, the hard struggle ahead. A long-distance love.

'Then yes, I love you.' She put her arms around his neck and took in the clouds flitting overhead. A kiss would seal it. Blue sky, white clouds, a setting sun.

He put his lips against hers and felt her respond softly. How sweet it was to discover that life's hard blows didn't break a man after all.

# 14

The news on El Alamein was better than expected. Though Rommel had been closing in on Alexandria, lack of ammunition had held up the German advance and a stalemate was reported on the wireless.

'It could be worse.' Hilda sat with Edith in her office on the Tuesday afternoon following the burglary, going through the ins and outs of what had been taken. A news bulletin had interrupted their conversation and drawn their attention to bigger things. 'We've got more American troops to back us up in Europe now and our RAF boys won't let up after Essen.'

'That's right,' Edith agreed, wishing nevertheless that they could concentrate on the matter in hand. That way she might be distracted from Bill's shock decision to hand over the business to Maurice. She hadn't slept for two nights and still hoped against hope that he would change his mind. She'd even taken him to one side and asked him to consider the effect enlisting would have on Grace and their marriage — an unusual step that had flown in the face of her determination not to interfere in the lives of the newly-weds.

He'd given her short shrift. 'That's between me and Grace,' he'd snapped and Edith had retreated with her tail between her legs. This was the general way of things for women of her and

Hilda's age: they'd had their own partings and sorrows at the start of the Great War but no one took this into account any more. The young ones thought only of banging the drum and being heroes, as if the world would change for the better this time.

The wireless carried other, less encouraging news. There was every likelihood that Sevastopol would soon fall and the Red Army would collapse in the Crimea. Now the opposition party was gunning for Churchill in the House of Commons, even though he'd flown all the way to America for talks with Roosevelt, and Eisenhower had arrived in London to become commander of their forces in Europe.

'You wait,' Hilda asserted as the bulletin ended and she turned off the wireless. She thought that Edith seemed even more pinched and on edge than usual, and that was saying something. 'Mr Churchill will come through all right. He'll turn things around before you know it then we'll all be singing his praises again.'

'Meanwhile, we have matters closer to home.' Until now Edith hadn't been directly involved in events surrounding the burglary. She'd let Hilda inform the police and deal with their visit to the hostel. She had, however, informed County Office and requested extra money to cover the shortfall. 'We're to receive five pounds to tide us over, which is more than generous under the circumstances.'

Hilda seemed satisfied. 'That'll pay the gas bill and the butcher, among other things.'

'And what are the police proposing to do?'

Edith's pen was poised, ready to jot down notes.

'They'll inquire if anyone in the neighbourhood heard or saw anything unusual. The trouble was, we were out at church when it happened, all except Doreen Wells.'

Edith looked up sharply and frowned. 'Doreen wasn't at church? Why not?'

Hilda shifted her weight backwards and gave an uneasy reply. 'According to her she had a headache. She was in bed when it happened.'

This was another black mark against the new girl, one that Edith wouldn't readily forget. 'So she didn't see or hear anything?'

'Not a thing.' There were rumours, of course. The word 'headache' was bandied around among the other girls with raised eyebrows and a roll of the eyes. Jean had mentioned to Hilda that Doreen had looked as fit as a fiddle when she'd seen her sitting on the doorstep smoking a fag before they left. But Doreen was sticking to her story and that was that.

Edith's frown deepened. 'It couldn't be . . . You don't suppose — '

Hilda cut her short before she could state the unthinkable. 'That Doreen had anything to do with the burglary? No, definitely not. I'd vouch for it in a court of law if need be.'

'I admire your loyalty, Hilda, but I'm not convinced.' Of all the recruits at Fieldhead, Doreen was Edith's main worry. 'I've noticed her flouting the rules here more than once. And I've watched her when she's out and about. She's too loud and brassy for my liking. Did you notice, at Bill and Grace's reception, how she jumped up and snatched the bouquet that Una was meant to catch?'

'So that makes her a thief, does it?' As a way of bringing their meeting to an end, Hilda began to pour the tea that had been stewing in the pot since before the news. 'This business has upset the girls no end. Until the culprit is found, they feel that the finger of suspicion points at each and every one of them. And they realize how easy it's been for an intruder to get in. Some of them have started to bolt their bedroom doors.'

'We must take care that morale doesn't drop.' For Edith this was even more important than catching the thief. 'What can we do to prevent it?'

Hilda passed her a cup of tea. 'We go on the same as always,' she insisted. 'We keep the girls well fed and happy and we put new locks on all the doors.'

★   ★   ★

By the end of the week, word was all around Burnside that Bill Mostyn had signed up for the Prince of Wales's Own Regiment and was waiting for a date to report for duty. Maurice went around with an unaccustomed spring in his step while Grace kept her head down and got on with her farm work.

'It must be hard for her,' the women said. 'What newly-wed is happy to wave her husband off to war?'

'About time too,' Joe Kellett commented to Horace Turnbull as they propped up the bar at the Blacksmith's Arms on the Friday evening.

'Keep your voice down or Bill's missis will hear you,' Horace warned.

Grace's ears burned as the old men grumbled and she went on wiping glasses. Luckily the pub was busy so she could switch her attention to serving Roland.

'What if she does?' Joe commented. 'Bill Mostyn's job is no different from Les White's — they both work at keeping farm machinery in good nick — and they say Les's call-up papers landed on his mat this past week. In fact, I reckon Bill has decided to jump before he's pushed.'

'That's just like you, to think the worst of the lad.' Horace prepared to go and sit with his father by the inglenook. 'What about Alfie Craven? I don't see you giving him a shove in the direction of the recruitment office.'

'Dodgy ticker,' Joe got in before Horace moved off. 'Or so he says. Anyway, I wouldn't care if the useless bugger did get called up — he's no good to man nor beast and that's God's honest truth.'

★   ★   ★

'Tho' you're tired and weary, still journey on.' As she rode Sloper along the twisting lanes into Burnside, Brenda couldn't get the old Harry Lauder song out of her head. 'Keep right on round the bend.' The wretched words and tune played over and over like a stuck record. They promised her all the love she'd been dreaming of, there at the end of the blessed road.

The way was definitely long; she'd give old Sir Harry that much. And not just literally either. For who would have thought, after the events of the previous Friday, that her heart would have taken so many twists and turns? She rounded a bend at speed and swerved to avoid a baby rabbit stranded in the middle of the road. *Crikey O'Reilly, slow down!* she told herself. The surface was slippery after a short, sharp shower and she'd had all on to keep the bike upright. Ahead, the clouds were inky blue and threatening.

*Tho' you're tired and weary.* It had been quite a week for Brenda, as she did her best to stay out of Les's way. He'd telephoned the hostel three times and on each occasion she'd persuaded someone to lie for her: I'm sorry, Brenda's out; she's washing her hair; she's working late. In the end, Joyce had demanded to know what she was up to — why was she avoiding Les? What had she suddenly got against him?

'Nothing. I'm steering clear, that's all,' she'd replied.

But, like the words to the song, she couldn't get Les out of her head. Or Hettie, for that matter. All through the week, she would pause from haymaking and lean on her pitchfork, only to imagine his face or to remember their conversation and kisses before they'd been so rudely interrupted. Or else she would cut off from the chatter around the dining table and relive the disastrous way it ended: the scent of roses drifting in through the French doors, the sound of Bing Crosby spinning his syrupy web of words, Hettie's face as stormy as the clouds that now lay on the horizon.

But tonight Brenda was determined to forget. She'd dressed casually in trousers and a white blouse, tied a red and white scarf turban-style around her head then set off to have some fun.

'We'll see you down at the pub,' Kathleen had called as she, Elsie and Joyce commandeered the hostel van, ready to drive into the village.

Friday night was invariably music night at the Blacksmith's Arms — someone would pull out the piano and start a sing-song. The room would be alive with the clink of glasses and bottles, laughter and general good cheer. Ah yes, the piano. That's when Brenda had really started to pay attention to Les: after she'd danced with him in the pub and he'd sat down at the piano to tinkle the ivories, as Donald had put it. There, amidst the whirl of skirts, shirts open at the neck and smiling faces, she'd been impressed by the way Les's fingers flew over the keys, by his straight back and broad shoulders and the exposed, soft vulnerability of the nape of his neck. *Damn!* Brenda thought as she slowed down at the junction leading into Burnside and saw the avenue of beech trees ahead. *I'm not cured of a serious case of Les White-itis after all.*

She'd reached the pub and pulled into the yard before she spotted the back end of his green MG Midget parked by the smithy. Then she saw Doreen perched on the low bonnet, talking to Donald. *That's all right then*, she told herself.

241

She could safely go ahead and join the other girls as planned.

So it took her by surprise when Les was the first person she bumped into when she got inside. She'd hardly walked through the door when he rushed towards her and took her by the arm.

'Brenda, come for a drive with me,' he insisted, eagerly steering her outside and quickly getting rid of Donald and Doreen.

Donald scowled and Doreen protested, but Les snatched the car keys from him and gave him a look that said he would brook no argument.

'Please,' Les said to Brenda as soon as they were alone. He held the passenger door open. 'Give me a chance to explain.'

'There's nothing to explain.' She sank into the leather seat with a sigh. Les started the engine and the car pulled away.

'All right, then; let me apologize.'

'What for?' He drove back the way she'd come but turned at the junction on to the road that would take them along Swinsty Edge.

'I'm sorry about Hettie for a start. She's been used to laying down the law ever since Mother died. I'm not sure she even knows she's doing it.'

'Oh, I think she does.' Brenda was convinced that Dragon-sister was in control every inch of the way.

'Anyway, she had no right.'

'To insult me or to drop the bombshell about your call-up?'

'Both.' Les gripped the steering wheel and

built up speed. In the distance the storm clouds rolled clear of the horizon, allowing a patch of blue to creep through. 'I would have told you myself if she hadn't come home early.'

'I wish you had.' After all, she'd been honest with him — more open than she'd been with any man since Mack the Knife — and all the while Les had harboured a secret that he knew must change everything.

'I wanted to find out how you felt about me first. Is that so wrong?' He spoke hesitantly and glanced at her. 'You might not have given two hoots about me going away; I wasn't sure.'

'I care,' she admitted. The wind stole her words and carried them over the heathery hillside. All was open space and speed.

'That's good to know, since I have to take the train up to Scotland this coming Sunday.' He slowed down and waited for her reaction.

'Sunday?' she repeated.

He nodded. 'The recruitment office has ordered me to report to a Petty Officer Warner at the James Watt Dock in Greenock, ready to begin training on Monday morning. I'll be issued with my kit and allocated my billet, ready for action.'

'This Sunday,' she said again, careful not to give anything away.

'That's why I had to see you and talk to you. I might not get another chance.'

*Don't say that; it frightens me, it really does.* Brenda took a sharp intake of breath and grasped the door handle as the car sped around a bend.

243

He saw her stricken look. 'I don't mean 'ever'. I mean 'another chance before I left'. But I'll be back on leave and driving out to Fieldhead to visit you before you know it.'

*And if you and I push ahead with this love affair, I'll be waiting, pestering the postman for letters, hanging on every word you write. Love between a man and a woman isn't freedom. It feels more like a prison that we make for ourselves. And yet . . .* Oh, she was too mixed up for words!

'Say something,' Les pleaded. He pulled off the road into a gateway leading on to the moors.

She surprised herself by starting to cry, then scrambled out of the car and tried to open the gate. When it stayed shut, she climbed over it and began to stride up the hill.

He ran after her, calling her name.

'Trust you, Les White!' she cried without looking back. 'Trust you to go and join the blinking Navy!'

'I didn't have a choice; you know that.'

She stopped to show him her wet cheeks. 'Look what you've done.'

There was nothing to say, nothing to do except put his arms around her and hold her until the crying stopped. Then he spoke softly. 'This is the real thing, isn't it? What's going on here is genuine. You'll miss me as much as I'll miss you.'

'Of course I will. But I'll write letters and tell you all the nonsense that goes on in the village: who's going out with who, who says what behind whose back.'

'You promise? Every day?'

She turned down the corners of her mouth and shook her head. 'I'm a busy girl. How about every other day?'

'Done.' He made a valiant attempt to match Brenda's light-hearted tone. 'SWALK, don't forget.'

'I won't.' For now they exchanged real loving kisses on the moor top.

'I want to carry on doing this for the rest of my life.' Les lifted her off her feet and swung her round. '*Our* lives,' he added.

There was such life in him — in his clear grey eyes and in the play of delight around his lips. How could she resist? So she kissed him again until they had to break away and breathe.

'Will you marry me, Brenda Appleby?'

The words tumbled out and she saw him prepare to go down on one knee. She stopped him by seizing his hands and grasping them tight.

He laid his heart at her feet instead. 'Will you, Bren? Will you wait for me and write to me and stay true?'

'Yes,' she whispered with sudden, out-of-the-blue certainty. 'I swear, hand on heart, that I will.'

★ ★ ★

Poppy resisted the lure of a Friday night at the Blacksmith's Arms and kept a promise to deliver Joe Kellett's note to Brigg Farm.

'It'll save me the cost of a stamp if you take it.'

The old miser had thrust a sealed envelope into her hand as she clocked off from a day's hard labour.

He'd picked on her as the Land Girl most likely to agree.

So while Elsie and Kathleen had cycled back to Fieldhead to spruce themselves up, Poppy had pocketed the letter and taken a different route, thinking her own thoughts as she rode along and sheltering under an oak tree during a short, sharp shower.

*I hope I don't run into Neville.* She watched the rain pelt down on to the tarmac and tried to dodge the overhead drips. *If I do, I'll let him know that he can't stand me up and still hope for us to be friends. He definitely won't get a second chance with me.* Her determination hardened as she watched the rain. Anyhow, *if all goes according to plan, I'll take the bus into town tomorrow afternoon, be home by teatime and then have the whole of Sunday with Mum back on Albion Lane. Goodbye, Burnside; goodbye, Neville blinking Thomson, and good riddance!*

A couple of large drops landed on her bare head then trickled down her neck. But at least the rain was easing off and she soon got back on her bike and rode the final half-mile to the Thomsons' place. As she turned off the road on to the lane leading to the farmhouse, she tapped her pocket to check that the letter was still there, making up her mind to deliver it and make as quick a getaway as possible.

And it seemed she was in luck. The farmyard

was deserted and the only movement came from Major, who stuck his head out of the stable door at her approach. A breeze drove stray wisps of straw across the stone flags and Poppy heard the clunk of the horse's heavy hooves against the door and the muffled snorting of pigs from the sty behind the stable. Quickly she leaned her bike against the hayloft steps then ran up a short path to the farmhouse door. Within seconds, Joe's note was slipped through the letter box and she was on her way back to collect her bike.

'Ah, if it isn't Little Miss Tell Tale!' Alfie Craven stood at the top of the stone steps, hands on hips, staring down at her. He was in dark blue suit trousers, held up by braces. His white shirtsleeves were rolled back and there was a partly healed cut on his cheek.

As he came down the steps two at a time, Poppy darted for her bike. But Alfie was one step ahead of her. As she reached for the handlebars, he grabbed them and stood astride the front wheel, blocking her way. Major looked on from his doorway, his great head looming dangerously close to Poppy's shoulder, his warm breath on her neck.

'Why did you have to go and spill the beans about us to Grace?'

She tried to wrench the bike away. 'I didn't! Let go! Leave me alone!'

'Yes, you did.' He thrust his face towards her and kept firm hold of the handlebars. 'You gave her the wrong end of the stick about our little tête-à-tête in the woods.'

Poppy pulled in vain — his grip was strong,

247

the muscles in his arms taut. 'I only told her the truth!' she cried.

'Hmm.' Alfie let go with one hand to demonstrate that he was still more powerful than her. 'The truth according to who? There wasn't anyone there to back you up. It's just your word against mine.'

There was no point arguing and Poppy felt desperate to get away. She looked wildly around the yard, judging that if she were to abandon her bike, she might be able to sprint back to the house and knock on the door for help. But what if it was as she thought and no one was in? Wouldn't it be better to make a run for it, straight down the lane and out on to the road?

'The same as today.' His slow, low threat crept over her like a dense fog. 'We're alone again, just you and me.'

No, she wasn't having this! He wasn't going to touch her or breathe over her. 'Keep your hands to yourself!' She raised her voice and sprang away. She was quicker than him at least, easily able to outrun him, so she sprinted across the yard, up the path towards the house.

The door was flung open before she had time to knock. One glance at Poppy's pale, frightened face and the sight of Alfie lurking at the gate told Neville all he needed to know.

Once it was clear that the rotten sod had tried it on with Poppy and reduced her to tears, Neville's shaky allegiance fell away. He pulled her inside the house then confronted Alfie. 'Bugger off out of here, or else!'

248

'Or else what?' The childish threat amused Alfie. He pushed at the gate and started to advance up the path.

Neville stood his ground. 'I'm warning you. I'll send you packing.'

'You and whose army?' This was too ridiculous for words: a floppy-haired, bruised and battered whippersnapper playing at being a knight in shining armour. Still, Alfie was riled by not getting his own way so he kept on advancing. 'Stand aside, sonny,' he ordered.

Neville braced both arms against the door jambs, aware of Poppy tugging at his shirt from behind.

'Come inside, close the door!' she gasped.

He ignored her. 'What are you doing here, anyway?' he challenged. 'Why are you trespassing?'

'I'm looking for something that's mine by rights. No, not her, stupid.' He laughed as Neville glanced uncertainly over his shoulder. 'The girl would have been a bonus, I admit. But that's not what I was after, not really.'

The way Alfie spoke about her, as if she was a thing, not a person, made Poppy's skin crawl and it infuriated Neville, who launched himself from the doorstep, fists flailing. He landed a punch right in Alfie's bread basket and heard him expel air with an 'Oof!' Then he felt a fist land smack in the middle of his face. There was the snap of knuckle against cheekbone.

The two men crouched with fists up, pausing to size each other up. Neville's confidence grew. Alfie might be heavier and stronger than him, but he was past his prime. And if he aimed his next punch at the nasty cut on his cheek, he could definitely make it count. Alfie saw that the lad meant business but it didn't matter; he would knock him clean off his feet with a single blow. Then he'd be down on the ground and a few hefty kicks would finish him off.

'Back off,' he snarled. 'I can eat two of you for breakfast.'

Poppy's heart was beating so fast that it practically jumped out of her chest. She dashed out after Neville and tried to come between the two men, only to be thrust aside by Alfie.

Neville threw himself at his opponent and lashed out again, landing a couple of lucky punches that Alfie absorbed with ease. He smiled and beckoned him on. 'Come on, sonny; have another go!'

Blind with fury, Neville ran straight into an upper-cut, a blow to the chin so hard and swift that it floored him. He felt his knees go to jelly and his head snap backwards before the sky whirled and he was down.

Alfie gave a satisfied grunt and prepared to kick. He would aim for the head. But Poppy was back on her feet. She saw Alfie, one leg off the ground, ready to lash out and so she charged, succeeding in toppling him sideways. Alfie crashed to the ground and felt a searing pain. He knew it was a broken rib the moment it happened. He ought to have known his body wasn't up to fisticuffs after the beating he'd taken from Nixon and Moyes, and now this one little push had done for him. He groaned as he rolled on to his front then raised himself on to his knees.

'Neville, wake up!' Poppy crouched over him and cradled his head. His eyelids flickered open. 'Get up, get up!'

Alfie tried to suck in breath then groaned again. No good, he was buggered. He reckoned that as long as no one tried to stop him, he could just about make it up on to his feet and stagger off. That was his best bet. He could reach the road and thumb a lift from a passer-by. Where he would go after that he had no idea.

Poppy was still busy with Neville. Aware that Alfie was crawling away, she hitched both hands under Neville's armpits and raised him to a sitting position. 'It's all over. We won, we did it!'

Neville stared at her face with an unfocused gaze. 'Did I knock him out?'

'No, you idiot. He knocked you out. But I pushed him sideways and he fell over. I heard something crack — a rib, I think.' She checked to see how far Alfie had got. He was halfway down the lane but in no shape to come back and take up where he'd left off, so she gave Neville time to recover.

He fingered his chin and winced, predicting another massive bruise to add to the ones he already had. But the jaw wasn't broken, so he got up on to his feet and dusted himself down, saying nothing as Poppy followed him into the house.

'Where's your dad?' she asked, taking in the typical men's mess in the kitchen and adjoining living room. There were dirty pots piled up in

251

the sink and crumpled laundry slung over a drying frame above the old-fashioned stove. The table was covered by a stained brown oilcloth and the floor was in need of a good scrub.

'Out.' Neville was embarrassed by two pairs of his father's long johns hanging from the frame. It would draw attention if he snatched them down so he left them where they were and sat down groggily at the table.

Poppy sat opposite him, determined to get to the bottom of things. 'So what did Alfie mean by looking for something that's his by rights?'

Neville shrugged and touched the tender spot on his chin.

'Don't you try to make me feel sorry for you, Neville Thomson. I want to know what's going on. Why are you and that man covered in cuts and bruises? I don't understand.'

'Believe me, it's better if we keep it that way.' He tried to wriggle but, like it or not, she was intent on pinning him down. It turned out that Poppy was like a fierce little terrier when she needed to be.

'Answer me. What have you got to do with Alfie?'

'All right, all right. If I let you in on it, you have to promise not to tell Dad — or anyone else, for that matter.'

She nodded.

'I mean it; you have to promise.'

'I've said yes, haven't I?'

'All right then. I made an arrangement with Alfie to keep some of his things up in our hayloft.'

'Without your dad knowing?'

'Yes, I had to agree to keep it quiet. Dad only ever goes up there once in a blue moon, so I reckoned it was the safest place to stash them.'

'What sort of things?'

'I don't know. I didn't ask.'

'Neville!'

'Just oranges and chocolate and other stuff.' He looked down at his hands, up at the ceiling, anywhere but at Poppy.

She stared at him in disbelief. 'What other stuff?'

'Women's stockings and underwear, scent, watches, lipstick. I didn't open all the boxes. I hid the small ones up in the rafters without looking inside. I knew enough to realize they were all things that you can only get on the black market.'

'And Alfie paid you to look after them?'

'Not a lot. But yes. It was all right for a while; no one bothered about them. Then last week two blokes turned up here out of the blue. They claimed it was their stuff, not Alfie's, and I had to hand it over, or else. They scared the living daylights out of me, so I did as I was told.'

'Yet they laid into you.' Suddenly Neville's failure to show up the previous Saturday made sense. He'd been beaten black and blue by two strangers.

'Yes. They said some money had gone missing. It belonged to them. They wouldn't leave without it.' Neville's mouth was dry, so he stood shakily and went to the sink for a glass of water.

'How much money?'

'Seventy-five quid.' He took a swig from the glass.

'That's a lot!' Poppy gasped. 'Didn't you tell the men that Alfie was the one who had it?'

'Course I did. I stuck to my story and told them I didn't know anything about their seventy-five lousy smackers. In the end they believed me and left.'

'So did Alfie have it stashed away in his room at Home Farm?'

Neville stared shiftily out of the window. 'That's what I wanted them to think.'

The penny dropped as Poppy studied the back of his head. 'Neville, turn around and look at me. Who really had the seventy-five pounds — you or Alfie?'

Without saying a word, he went to a set of shelves in a niche next to the fireplace and stood on a foot-stool to reach for a rusty tea caddy in the furthest corner. He stepped down from the stool and unscrewed the lid. With shaking fingers he took out a fat roll of five-pound notes held in place by a rubber band.

Poppy's eyes widened. 'You didn't!' she gasped.

'I did.' He swallowed hard. 'Now Alfie's on to me and sooner or later I'm sure those other two brutes will be back.'

'I see.' She felt her blood run cold.

'Do you?' Neville came towards her with a look that was part forlorn, part hopeful. 'Then can you tell me what to do now? Because I honestly don't have a clue.'

# 15

There was comfort to be found in keeping to the busy, chatter-filled Friday-night routine. Behind the bar at the Blacksmith's Arms, Grace pulled a pint for Roland while her father talked to Maurice about recent events in Egypt. Brenda sat with Les, diverted by the usual competition between Kathleen and Doreen to win the attention of a group of laughing Canadian pilots. Joyce and Edgar held hands across the table in a quiet corner of the room. For two of the couples, the weekend would bring a sad parting, while for Grace and Bill the same fate lay not too far ahead.

The door was open, letting balmy air into the smoky room. As the evening wore on and the noise grew more raucous, Les had to shout above the racket to order another Dubonnet for Brenda and a half of bitter for himself, while one of the Canadians sat at the piano and struck up a tune. There was pushing and shoving and moving of furniture to make a space where couples could dance; the inevitable high spirits, the normal din.

'Ready to leave?' Edgar asked Joyce as he tilted his head in the direction of the open door.

She nodded and picked up her handbag to follow him outside. Five days in Edgar's company meant that she'd grown used to his shorthand way of speaking: never two words

255

where one would do. It was actually one of the things she liked best about him.

'That's better,' he said as he breathed in fresh air. 'What now?'

She slipped her arm in his and they strolled across the yard towards his car. 'What would you like to do?'

'This is our last night. You choose.'

'We could go for a little walk.'

He stopped to look through the open doors of the smithy. It was a space full of boyhood memories: of his father in his prime raising a muscular arm to beat red-hot metal, of the hammer ringing out, the roar of flames, the hiss of steam when he dipped a horseshoe in the bucket of cold water. Suddenly Edgar's heart felt too full.

Joyce looked at his face and guessed what he was thinking. She pressed his arm then smiled.

He smiled back. 'Let's go for a drive instead.'

So they drove out of Burnside towards the wild places beyond Swinsty, soon leaving civilization behind. Eventually they came to the stark, dark bulk of Kelsey Crag, a massive cliff that rose vertically out of the valley, and they passed under the deep shadow of its overhang. Emerging on the far side, they climbed high on to the hilltops once more. Here, close to the tarn, Edgar stopped the car.

'Remember this?' he asked.

Joyce gazed out over the smooth, black water to the far shore, where glints of white limestone amongst the thick heather caught the dying light. Three swans glided silently towards them, carrying their heads erect, causing scarcely a ripple. 'How could I forget?' *Edgar at his worst, lost and lonely, striding into the frozen wilderness with death on his mind.* The image would stay with her for ever.

'You saved me,' he murmured. 'I wouldn't have carried on living if it hadn't been for you.'

She said nothing, only looked at the swans as they circled slowly then swam away.

'I don't mean I'd have chucked myself in the water and finished it that way. More likely I'd have drunk myself to death or gone back to flying Lancasters, not caring if I lived or died. Then you came along.'

'I didn't do anything special.'

'Yes, you did. You listened. You didn't pass judgement. You believed in me.'

'And you in me.' It hadn't been one-sided, she reminded him. 'I was in a bad way myself. After I met you, all the misery over losing Walter gradually slipped away. It was like a new day dawning for me, like letting the sun in again. Not that I showed it, in case you didn't feel the same way about me. It took that first letter for me to be sure.'

'Ah yes, the letter.' For a moment he was embarrassed. He turned awkwardly in his seat so that he could look straight at her. 'And now this.'

For Joyce, 'this' meant five days of working in the fields, while for Edgar there'd been endless hours of tinkering about and doing repair jobs for his father in pub and forge, but they had each known that they would meet afterwards in the pub or out at the hostel and make the most of the long, light evenings. They'd walked their legs off: Edgar showing Joyce his favourite boyhood haunts, where he'd built dams across a stream or made a den in the woods, Joyce pointing out ditches she'd helped to dig and drystone walls she'd recently mended. They laughed together about how their burgeoning romance might look to others — no candlelit dinners, no spooning in the back row of the cinema, no expensive gifts by which to measure their affection.

'That's not us,' Joyce had told him as they'd sat perfectly still at twilight in the copse behind Fieldhead, watching a family of badgers forage in the undergrowth. 'We don't need any of that.'

Edgar's arm had been round her shoulder. She'd been nestled against him. Their kisses had grown stronger until passion had taken hold and almost swept them off their feet — almost but not quite. The lights of the nearby hostel had glinted through the branches; what if one of the girls had wandered into the woods and seen them? Joyce had pulled away just in time. Then, after she and Edgar had said goodnight, she'd lain awake for hours, regretting her decision.

'Now this,' she repeated at Kelsey Tarn as she put her arms around his neck. He kissed her hard without any of the usual soft build-up then suddenly broke off and swung open his door. He strode round the car and opened the door on Joyce's side, offering her his hand. 'Will you come?'

She took his hand and let him lead her along the shore of the tarn. A magnificent sunset turned the clouds bright pink, edged them with

258

gold and lit up the mirror-bright surface of the tarn. There was no wind, no movement other than the gliding motion of the swans, no sound except for the lapping of water and the piercing, two-tone cry of a curlew high above.

'There's a shepherd's shelter just over here, a little stone hut.'

She saw it as he spoke: a tumbledown affair with part of the roof missing and the rafters exposed. There was no door to stop them entering. He showed her the shadowy interior. A smooth green carpet of moss had grown over the original mud floor and there was an empty fireplace and a rough wooden platform where the shepherd had once slept. 'Is this all right?' With her heart in her mouth, Joyce nodded.

'You're certain?'

She answered with an embrace then led him slowly towards the platform. There was a faint, lingering smell of woodsmoke coming from the hearth as they sat down. 'I'm sure.'

That lovely voice! It got him every time; rich and soft, from deep in her throat. Her skin was pale as she let down her hair then started to unbutton her blouse. From this point there was no going back.

'Very sure,' she told him.

The blouse slid from her shoulders. He eased her arms and hands free. Her skin was smooth and warm, glowing in the half-light. Her eyes were softly dark as she removed her white under-slip.

He put his lips to her shoulder and felt her shudder. Then she lay back and he sank down

259

beside her, the length of their bodies touching. She ran her fingers over his rough scars then over the smooth skin of his belly, a soft stroke as he kissed her throat and the hollow at its base. She arched her back and pressed herself against him.

He was everything she'd known he would be, not rushing on regardless, but gentle and patient, tender but strong, arousing her in a way that she'd never experienced before. And she loved every moment of it and every inch of him, his eyes on her face as she enfolded him and ran her hands down his back, the depth of his gaze. She looked up through the rafters at the open sky, felt the strong beat of Edgar's loving heart.

⋆  ⋆  ⋆

Saturday at Fieldhead dawned cloudy and with a damp chill in the air. A report on the wireless told listeners about preparations for a scaled-down Fourth of July celebration in America in light of losses in the Far East and the ongoing struggle to push the last of the German U-boats clear of the Atlantic coast. There were dour comments around the breakfast table along the lines of, 'Those johnny-come-latelies should think themselves lucky they've got anything left in their larders to celebrate with', or, 'At least their food convoys are still getting in and out', and so on. As usual, Jean was chief of the moaners, with Doreen coming in a close second.

'What's up with you this morning?' Brenda asked as she offered to clear away her empty porridge bowl. She'd been amongst the earliest to sit down at the table and was the first to finish. So far, she'd not felt like saying anything to anyone about accepting Les's sudden proposal of marriage. She wasn't able to work out a good reason why not, only to acknowledge to herself that her previous night's certainty seemed to have vanished like morning mist. A puff of wind and it was gone.

'Everything,' Doreen grumbled. 'I've run out of shampoo for a start. And I need to wash my hair.'

Brenda sent out an SOS: 'Call out the cavalry — Doreen has run out of shampoo!'

'Oh, dearie me!' came the ironic chorus from all directions.

Brenda offered false comfort. 'Never mind, you can always get Alfie to track some down.'

Elsie winked at her then offered to lend Doreen some of her shampoo after they came back from work. 'Here, Bren, give me those dishes. I'll take them to the kitchen for you.'

'And last night Donald left the pub early, drat him,' Doreen went on, giving voice to her major grievance. 'He said he'd only be gone for a few minutes but I waited a full hour before the penny finally dropped that he wasn't coming back.'

Brenda sat down beside her. 'Maybe he was in a bad mood because Les wouldn't lend him the car?'

'Oh yes, I saw you two canoodling together. Where did you slope off to after you left?'

'Nowhere much.' Brenda shrugged.

'Don't give me that. I bet that was the last

time you'll see Les before he sails off into the sunset. You wouldn't want an audience for your final few minutes together.'

Across the table, Joyce caught the drift of the conversation between Brenda and Doreen. The latter's world-weary tone bothered her so she moved away to sit with Una and Poppy.

'As a matter of fact, I'm planning to go over to Dale End after church tomorrow to say goodbye.' Brenda had noticed Joyce give Doreen the cold shoulder and was about to follow suit until Doreen caught her by the wrist.

'Don't get me wrong, I wouldn't blame you and Les for making the most of your time together. We all have to wring what we can out of these situations. I know I do with Donald.'

Brenda frowned. 'But Donald isn't in the same boat as Les, or as most of the men round here. He's avoided the call-up, hasn't he?'

'So far.' Doreen agreed without letting go of Brenda's arm. 'But who knows what's round the corner? Anyway, I still say we women have to get the most out of our menfolk while we can. Take that whichever way you like.'

'Ta, I'll remember that.' Feeling an uncomfortable twist in her stomach, Brenda made as if to stand up. 'Would you mind letting go of my arm, Doreen? I've got a load of laundry to sort through before I set off for Winsill Edge. Then it's my morning for egg collecting and doing my best to keep out of old Horace's toothless clutches.'

Doreen loosened her grasp but she stood up and followed Brenda out of the dining room. She caught up with her at the bottom of the stairs. 'I mean it. Make the most of what you've got is my motto. Take it from me, these looks won't last and men are fickle at the best of times. So God knows what happens when we get the odd grey hair and a wrinkle here and there, eh, Brenda?'

Back at the table, Joyce too kept quiet about events of the previous night. But unlike Brenda, her silence came out of deep, settled knowledge that she loved Edgar with all her heart and that he loved her back. She kept this glittering diamond of certainty polished and hidden away until she was ready to share it — perhaps in a quiet moment with Grace as they cycled home from Henry Rowson's farm out by Kelsey Crag. They were both due to work there this morning, along with Una, who at this moment looked as if she also needed cheering up.

Joyce sat down beside her. 'Still nothing from Angelo?'

'No, I haven't seen him for a whole week.' Una's face was a picture of woe: pinched and pale, with dark shadows under her big brown eyes.

'But you've heard from him?'

'Yes. Neville brought me two notes: one on Monday, then one yesterday afternoon. The doctor says they must wait and see. In the meantime, he's to stay in bed. Poppy, what's Neville done to his face, by the way? How did he come by those two shiners?'

'Don't ask me.' Poppy gulped down the last of her porridge then made a hasty exit. Her plan for the weekend had changed in light of the previous night's events at Brigg Farm. Albion Lane would have to wait, she'd decided. She needed to stay at the hostel and give herself time to consider what Neville had revealed.

'So how is he?' Joyce asked Una, eager to hear more about Angelo.

'He's up and down. The doctor didn't let him go to work this week because he wanted to keep an eye on him.'

'There you are, then. Sometimes it takes longer than you think to get over a bad chest, but by the sound of things they're allowing him to take it easy.'

Una wasn't so quickly reassured. 'I'm not sure. Angelo has written me nice letters but he hasn't asked to meet up. I'm beginning to wonder if — '

'Listen!' Joyce patted her hand. 'He's probably worried that whatever he's got is catching, that's all. He wants to keep his germs to himself.'

'Perhaps,' Una faltered. 'Oh, Joyce, I was so looking forward to him coming back! I thought everything would be exactly the same as before.'

'I know you did. But nothing ever is, believe me. That doesn't have to be a bad thing, though. Look at it this way: Angelo being poorly is a kind of test. It means you have to be patient and find a way to stand by him even if you're not seeing him as often as you did.'

Una seized on the optimistic advice. 'How do I do that?'

'I don't know. Maybe make Angelo something that he'd really like. A card with some pressed flowers and a message saying how much you love him, an embroidered bookmark — something like that.'

'I will.' Una's eyes lit up and she rose from the table with fresh determination. 'I'll do it this afternoon, ready to give it to him after church tomorrow.'

'If he's there,' Joyce cautioned.

'He will be!' There was no doubt in Una's mind. 'Come along, Joyce, we'll be late for work if we don't get a move on. And the earlier we finish at Kelsey, the sooner I can get back and make my present for Angelo.'

★ ★ ★

Sunlight flooded in through the stained-glass window above the altar in St Michael's Church. The rich reds and blues lit the faces of the congregation: Canadian pilots in full dress uniform, Land Girls in smart civvies, Italians in grey POW garb and assorted farmers in tweeds and flat caps, which they wore for church whatever the weather. Towards the end of the service, Esther Liddell pulled out the stops for 'Abide with Me' in the vain hope that volume would mask her lack of skill.

As the organist played the opening notes of the dirge, Brenda leaned sideways to whisper to her neighbour, Squadron Leader Jim Aldridge: 'The vicar must have been in a gloomy mood when he picked today's hymns. 'The darkness deepens', and all that.'

''Earth's joys grow dim'.' Aldridge nodded

then added in a stage whisper, 'So where's death's sting, then?'

'Just what we need, Vicar!' Brenda faced ahead and mouthed the words of the first two verses. 'It's no good,' she sighed and leaned in again. 'Call me a terrible sinner, but I don't feel like singing about death and decay on a glorious day like today.' Instead, she looked around at her fellow worshippers. She spotted Emily Kellett on the front row, without Joe at her side. Mrs Mostyn was there, of course, next to a tense-looking Grace and Bill. Then there was Ma Craven minus Alfie, who, as far as Brenda knew, hadn't been seen for a day or two. Turning her head towards the door, she saw Bob Baxendale, whose job as caretaker at the Institute overlapped with his role as church warden. He stood in stiff collar and ill-fitting suit, ready to re-stack the hymnbooks as people filed out. Finally she gave Una a small nudge with her elbow as she spotted Angelo amongst the group of prisoners near the back of the church. 'Guess who's here!' she hissed.

'I know!' Una breathed. 'I spotted him when he arrived.' She felt in her pocket to make sure that the card she'd made was still there. Talk about being on tenterhooks; she'd hardly been able to breathe throughout the whole service. The vicar's drone as he delivered what seemed like the longest sermon on record had been a special torment.

'In life, in death, O Lord, abide with me.' A sigh of relief was almost audible throughout the church, and people muttered a final prayer before filtering out of the pews and down the aisle.

'So how is life treating you, Squadron Leader?' Brenda engaged in light conversation as they shuffled out of the church.

'Please — call me Jim.' He stood aside to let her pass through the door. 'I'm doing just fine, thanks for asking. How about you?'

'Fit as a fiddle, ta.' Brenda looked up to the Canadian commanding officer in more ways than one. He was six inches taller than her, for a start; well set and muscular, his wide shoulders and broad chest enhanced by his slim-fitting uniform. Also, she admired him for his honesty and directness. 'I take it all's well on Penny Lane since the POWs moved back to Beckwith Camp?'

'Some of our guys have had to stay on there so it's a little too crowded, to tell you the truth.' Out through the porch and into the glare of the sun, Aldridge appeared happy to stay a while and talk. 'We've kept two of the Nissen huts for our newest trainees while they settle in but that means the Italians have to squeeze in to the remaining eight. They're none too happy with that situation.'

'But they're not in a position to make a fuss, I take it?' Privately Brenda thought that beggars couldn't be choosers.

'Right,' he confirmed with a nod. 'They should take a look at some of the camps in their own back yard. Our boys in the Trieste and Mantua dulags are lucky to have proper sanitation and one decent meal a day.' Seeing his men pile into the back of the lorry that had brought them to church, he shook Brenda's hand and took his leave. 'It's been good talking with you, Brenda.'

'Likewise.' Firm handshake, a look straight in the eye, leaving with a smile — she appreciated all of that. As she lost sight of Jim Aldridge and made her way across the road to pick up her motor bike then drive over to Dale End, she had to thread her way through the group of POWs assembled in the pub car park, close to their green lorry with a canvas roof that had seen better days.

'What's happened to Bachetti?' a rough-voiced Tommy called from the driver's cab.

The good-natured soldier called Cyril, armed with a rifle, had begun to usher prisoners into the back. They climbed in slowly, muttering in Italian and deliberately taking their time. 'He went for a — ' Aware of Brenda's approach, he corrected himself. 'Sorry. Bachetti had to answer a call of nature, Corporal!'

The driver grunted. 'Couldn't he tie a knot in it till we get back?'

'Steady on. The bloke's been poorly. He'll only be a couple of minutes.'

The sympathetic private, along with a few of the prisoners, had picked up clues that Angelo had an assignation with his pretty Land Girl but he'd decided to turn a blind eye provided he was away no more than five minutes.

'I'll spin things out here,' he'd promised. 'But don't take too long about it.'

Brenda lingered to watch the men being

loaded into the lorry. '*Ciao*, Lorenzo,' she called to the last in line.

He turned and flashed her a broad smile.

Summer suited him. His face was deeply tanned and he looked almost absurdly handsome with his thick, slicked-back hair, square jaw and white teeth. The prisoner's grey uniform with the large white circle on the back did nothing to diminish the effect of a Roman god. Rome was where Lorenzo came from, she remembered, hence his air of worldly sophistication even in these diminished circumstances.

Brenda thought on her feet. She too had guessed where Angelo really was and reckoned that it would work well for Una if she could distract the driver and keep him talking, so she sauntered towards the cab. 'I didn't see you in church, Corporal,' she said with her brightest smile.

'That's because I wasn't there.' He tapped the steering wheel and glanced down at her.

'Lucky you. It was the longest blooming sermon ever. I snatched forty winks in the middle of it but it didn't help. The vicar was still rabbiting on about love thy neighbour when I woke up.'

The corporal took a second look and decided that here was someone he didn't mind passing the time of day with. He reached into his top pocket, took out a packet of Woodbines and offered one to Brenda. 'I had a quick kip too,' he admitted as he held out a light. She tilted her head back and inhaled. The end of the cigarette glowed red. 'I heard enough in Sunday school about loving my neighbour to last me a lifetime, ta very much.'

★　★　★

'We don't have long.' Una could scarcely believe that Angelo's arms were around her. She kissed him and breathed him in. They talked in short bursts then kissed again.

'My Una, I miss you.'

'And I miss you. So much,' she said with a deep sigh.

'I long for you.'

'Here I am — at last!' But they had five minutes at the most round the back of the forge, before Cyril came looking. And so much to cram in. 'Here; I want to give you this.' She drew out the card with an arrangement of dried wild flowers on the front — golden buttercups, white milkmaids and purple vetch — and a loving message on the inside. 'Read it later. Keep it safe.'

'I put it here.' He nodded then slipped it into his top pocket, which he tapped. 'Near my heart. Always.'

Her whole body tingled with joy. Angelo loved her as much as ever. How could she have doubted it? 'Are you better now? You must be, if the doctor let you come to church.'

'Yes,' he said. 'I have no cough.'

'So when will they let you go back to work?'

'Soon, I hope.'

*And yet* . . . Una shook the nagging fears out of her head. 'That makes me happy too. We'll be

270

'able to spend whole days together like we used to.'

'Today the sun shines,' he assured her, laughing as she stood on tiptoe to plant kisses on his cheeks and forehead. 'The trees are green. You are with me, my Una.'

Heaven itself couldn't outdo this. Her heart was full to bursting. 'I'll always be with you.' She ignored the sound of footsteps crossing the pub yard, coming ever closer.

Angelo heard them and held her close. Soon they would be parted, so every moment was precious. 'Remember this,' he whispered.

She gazed up at him. Now she heard the footsteps and Cyril's voice.

'It's time to call it a day, Bachetti.'

Una couldn't bear to let go. It was Angelo who took her hands and gently pushed her away.

'That's a good lad.' The private winked at Una, who blushed and looked as if she was about to cry. 'My corporal's on a short fuse this morning; otherwise I'd have let you have a bit longer.'

'Goodbye, my Una.' Tapping his pocket then blowing her a last kiss, Angelo allowed himself to be led off by Cyril.

Una moved her lips as if to reply but no sound came out. She stood silently, watching the two men walk away.

⋆   ⋆   ⋆

Brenda had done her best to keep Corporal Bellyache happy but the scowl had reappeared

271

before they'd finished their cigarettes and he'd barked an order for Private Atkinson to go and fish Bachetti out of the privy. So she'd retreated to the back of the lorry for a quick word with Lorenzo. 'Tell Angelo that this has made Una's day — her whole week, as a matter of fact.'

'He knows this.' Lorenzo leaned out to see his friend returning, quick march. 'But I will also tell him.'

'She's been worried about him.' Brenda glanced over her shoulder at the two figures heading towards the lorry and was shocked. 'I'm not surprised. Angelo looks like death warmed up.' Compared with Lorenzo and the other prisoners, he was pale and gaunt, his posture stooping as he struggled to keep up with Atkinson. She approached him with a worried look.

He walked past without looking her way, then had second thoughts and called after her. 'Brenda, you will care for Una?'

'You bet I will.' It went without saying. 'We always keep an eye out for one another.' She turned and followed slowly, watching Lorenzo and another prisoner haul Angelo up into the lorry.

'If I go, you will care for her?' he asked again.

'Go where?'

'Please?'

'I've already said I will.' Brenda was seriously alarmed. All she could think was that she'd guessed right about Angelo being at death's door.

'Lorenzo, what is he talking about? Is he more

272

poorly than he's letting on?'

'He is sick.'

Brenda's eyes widened. 'How sick?' she demanded. 'Why is Angelo talking about leaving? What exactly is the matter with him?'

'The doctors do not say.' The reply was guarded as Lorenzo raised a warning finger to his lips. 'They will do a test. Do not say to Una. He does not want her to know.'

Brenda heard the guard climb into the cab and the slam of his door. The driver started the engine. 'What kind of test?' she demanded. His energy spent, Angelo let his friends manhandle him into a comfortable position towards the front of the lorry then slumped sideways against his neighbour.

'You promise?' As the lorry crawled out of the yard, Lorenzo leaned forward to hear Brenda's reply.

She wrenched the words out unwillingly and heard them drowned by the growl of the lorry's engine. 'Yes, I promise.'

They were gone and she stood in a plume of blue exhaust smoke, turning to Una as she emerged in tears from behind the smithy and walked blindly across the yard.

'Don't cry, love.' Brenda put an arm around her shoulder and searched for whatever kind words she could find. 'It's not as bad as all that.'

Una brushed her wet cheeks with the back of her hand and smiled. 'I'm not sad,' she explained. 'These are happy tears. Angelo loves me and he swears he always will.'

# 16

Brenda knew she was hopeless at saying goodbye. She didn't know why it was, but she had a history of it. When her older brother, Robert, had emigrated to America five years before, she'd stood behind her parents on a Liverpool dockside, waving him off without enthusiasm, anxious for the ship to set sail and for it all to be over and done with. It had been the same when Nancy Barker, a favourite cousin who had married a southerner, had gone to be a fisherman's wife on the North Devon coast. Brenda had turned up at Nancy's leaving do to wish her well but had been sure to make herself scarce before the round of hugs and tears at the end of the evening.

And now she had to face the most important farewell of her life so far, to her new fiancé as he set off for Greenock, into a future so uncertain that it didn't bear thinking about.

*How will I get through this?* she asked herself as she rode her motor bike over the moors, her stomach churning at the prospect. I only hope I don't do or say anything stupid. Then she berated herself for not putting Les first. *Imagine how he must be feeling right this minute. His bag is packed and he's leaving his old life behind for who knows how long. He has to say goodbye to everything he's ever known: his home and the dale he's lived in since he was born, not to* mention his father, brother and dragon-sister. And me.

Without being aware of it, she eased off the throttle and dawdled along the final stretch of road, gritting her teeth as the grand old house came into view.

Dale End sat in the valley, bathed in mid-morning sun, its weathered stone making it seem a part of the natural landscape. Behind the mansion stood vast, newly built barns that housed the family's farm machinery and beyond them a river snaked peacefully through green fields where sheep and cattle grazed. It was a way of life that had gone on for ever, disrupted now by the demands of war.

*And here's me, a newcomer, also doing my best to rock the boat.* Brenda had a sudden glimpse of what Hettie must think of her. *She probably had a nice, settled girl from the village lined up for Les; someone who would make a steady farmer's wife, not a shop girl from a smoky mill town who happens to have seen a bit of the world and has a different notion of what she wants out of life.*

The idea didn't make her feel any more confident as she turned into the drive and saw Hettie standing in the doorway talking to Arnold and Donald.

'Look out, here comes trouble,' Donald quipped as Brenda pulled up and killed her engine. Two shotguns were propped against the stone pillar and he swung three dead rabbits in her direction, only narrowly missing her as she came up the steps.

'Give me those,' Arnold barked at him before disappearing round the side of the house.

Hettie tutted. 'You and Dad were cutting it fine,' she muttered at Donald while staring steadily at Brenda. 'Les has to leave for the train station in fifteen minutes. A taxi is due at half twelve.'

'That gives us all plenty of time to say our fond farewells, eh, Brenda?'

She shrank back under Donald's gaze then briskly took herself in hand. 'Has Les told you our news?' she asked Hettie as she brushed past Donald and entered the hallway. Les was on the landing at the top of the stairs, suitcase at the ready. 'Have you?' she called up to him.

He dropped the case and took the stairs two at a time. 'Have I what?'

'Announced our engagement.' She slid an arm around his waist to await the response.

Hettie stepped in quickly. 'Of course he has; he did it over breakfast.'

'And didn't he make a meal of it!' Shaking his head in amusement, Donald sauntered into the study. 'Dad practically choked on his toast and marmalade.'

Hettie nodded towards the study. 'Go in and say your goodbyes while I have a word with your fiancée,' she told Les as she drew Brenda into the sitting room.

*Here they come: the dire warnings, the downright disapproval, the refusal to let it go ahead.* Standing with her back to the French doors, Brenda steeled herself once more.

But Hettie surprised her. 'Don't worry, I'm

not going to ask you to break the engagement. Les has made his choice and that's that.'

'Oh, I thought — '

'It doesn't matter what you thought — or what I or anyone else thinks, for that matter.' Hettie folded her arms and eyed Brenda calmly. 'What matters is that Les is happy. And he is. Any fool can see that.'

Brenda gave a sigh of relief. 'You're probably of the opinion that it's happened too fast, though.'

'Like I said, that's not the point. And we all know everything is different these days. So I'll say this quickly before I leave you two to say whatever you have to say.'

Brenda met Hettie's gaze but she still felt a tightness in her chest.

'It's this: you have to promise me to do right by Les while he's away.'

'What do you mean?' Brenda's eyes widened and a spurt of anger forced its way out. 'Of course I'll do right by him. I've said I'll marry him, haven't I?'

'It won't be a case of out of sight out of mind?'

'No! What do you think I am?'

'Stop a second. I'd say the same to any girl, so don't think that I'm getting at you in particular.'

'Of course you are. You've already made it quite plain that you believed the nasty rumours about me and I've told you that you'd no right to say them to my face.'

'Listen to me. I'm sorry I did that. I've been mulling things over since then and gone back over the dealings I've had with you. So now I'm sticking my neck out and backing this engage-ment of yours.'

'That's good of you!'

'No need to be sarcastic.' Hettie sighed and started to back towards the door. 'Put yourself in my position. I'm only doing my best for my brother. When push comes to shove, I can learn to like you, Brenda. And I hope you and Les will be very happy.'

'You hear that?' Les cried as he burst through the half-closed door and immediately scooped Brenda into his arms. 'We have my sister's blessing; that's quite something.'

Hettie closed the door behind her as she left.

'What about your father?'

'Dad will take his lead from her.' Les lowered his voice and held her tight. He put his cheek against hers and waltzed her slowly round the silent room until they came to the doors out into the garden. 'I can practically hear the seconds ticking away,' he whispered. The sun fell on Brenda's smooth, dark hair, streaking it with strands of rich chestnut. Her dress felt light and silky as it brushed against his legs.

'I wish — '

His kiss stopped her. But yes, the clock was ticking and he had more to say. 'You wish what?'

'That you didn't have to go. I know you have to, but I wish we had longer.'

'I'll write as soon as I can,' he promised. 'And before I go, I want you to have this.'

Brenda watched him dip his hand into his pocket and draw out a small, dark blue velvet box. He flipped the lid open with his thumb and she saw a cream silk lining. When he tilted the box towards her, she gasped.

He took the ring out of its silk nest and held it out. 'This was Mother's engagement ring. She left her wedding ring to Donald and this one came to me.'

'Oh no, I can't take it!' A big sapphire surrounded by small diamonds, exquisite jewels set in rose gold.

'Wear it for me while I'm away.'

'No, I can't.'

'Please.' Taking her left hand, he slid the ring on her finger. 'Make this do for now. I'll buy you a new one as soon as I get the chance.'

'It's not that. This is too beautiful, too precious.' It sat snug on her finger, sparkling in the light. It didn't belong.

But Les kissed her again and made her agree.

'All right, but I won't be able to wear it every day.' The ring was real. Wedding bells sounded faintly in her head.

There was a knock on the door. 'The taxi's here,' Hettie's muffled voice announced.

'Let me come with you to the station,' Brenda pleaded on impulse.

'No, I'd rather say our goodbyes here in private.'

Les held Brenda tight for a few seconds more then released her. Before she knew it, he was gone and she was left with the sun streaming in and the ring glittering brightly on the third finger of her left hand.

\* \* \*

The days and nights of living like a tramp had brought Alfie lower than ever before. It beat even his time on the run before he went to prison, when at least he'd been able to hole up in a disused barge on the Millwood canal with enough food to see him through. He'd had high hopes of escaping justice, until Maureen, his former wife, had dropped a hint to the coppers and they'd eventually hunted him down and thrown him in the clink for armed robbery. But out in the country there were no handy bakeries or grocer's to break into, no mazes of terraced streets to throw pursuers off the trail. Here there were only wide-open expanses and farmers with shotguns. And besides, it hurt like hell every time he moved.

In some ways, the rib was the least of his problems. The last visit to Brigg Farm hadn't produced the desired result, thanks to the little Land Girl with the fair hair and forget-me-not blue eyes who had turned out to be tougher than she looked. If it hadn't been for her making a fuss, Alfie would have squeezed the seventy-five quid out of Neville, no bother. That pipsqueak had conned them all out of the money, Moyes and Nixon included. Without a shadow of a doubt Neville had it stashed away but even a beating from the two experts hadn't convinced him to give it up. After that they'd turned on Alfie and kicked him half to death. And that hadn't been the end of it; they'd cursed at him and given him forty-eight hours to stump up the cash. Alfie had done a deal to find them thirty quid as a first instalment and hand over the rest a week later — a hard-driven bargain that Moyes and Nixon had been forced to accept. The problem was, unless Alfie could prise the seventy-five out of Neville, he had only the eleven pounds plus loose change from Fieldhead to his name, plus the Kelletts' five pounds, leaving him well short of the required thirty. And so he'd stumbled away from Brigg Farm to find shelter where he could, in ditch and barn, wherever he ran the least risk of being spotted.

By Sunday he'd made it as far as Winsill Edge but he was growing desperate. His clothes were in a filthy state from when he'd slid down the bank of a stream into muddy water. All he'd had to eat for three days were scraps thrown down for the pig at Henry Rowson's place and, first thing that morning, raw eggs stolen from the hen farm. In constant fear of Moyes and Nixon's return, Alfie had steered clear of the roads and used back lanes instead, ready to jump into a ditch or crouch down behind a hedge at the sound of any approaching car.

But now exhaustion and hunger made him desperate. He needed somewhere safer to hole up until his rib healed, a place where he wouldn't be discovered and where he might gain access to a better supply of food. Hunkered down behind some straw bales shoved up against the back of the hen hut, well out of sight of the farmhouse, he eyed a few stray hens pecking at seeds in the long grass, racking his brains and discounting first this hiding place then that.

The sound of thick, chesty coughing and of footsteps shuffling towards the hen hut and opening the door brought Alfie back to the here and now. He ducked down low as hens squawked and flapped, running into the yard from all directions towards the hut and a night's safe roosting. Eventually the door slammed and the squawking died down. The coughing faded. Alfie's strength was almost spent but he managed to shift a couple of bales to form a windbreak around him. This would have to do for the night, he told himself. Tomorrow he would move on and find somewhere more permanent, wherever that might be.

★    ★    ★

'Have you seen Poppy anywhere?' Joyce had looked all over the hostel. The last place she tried was the kitchen, where she found Kathleen and Elsie on their hands and knees scrubbing the floor as a favour to Hilda. There was a strong smell of carbolic soap and the brisk swish of bristle over flagstones.

Elsie glanced up. 'Not lately — why?'

'She skipped dinner and she's not in our room. I'm wondering where she's got to.'

Kathleen raised a greenish-white lather by scrubbing methodically in a circular motion. 'Have you asked Doreen?'

'Yes, but she was no use. She kept her head stuck in her magazine.'

Elsie rested on her heels to think back through the day. 'Was Poppy at church this morning? I can't remember.'

'She was. She had a ride back in the van with

me and Jean. That's the last I saw of her.' Joyce was genuinely worried. 'She's been looking peaky and down in the mouth all weekend. I hope she's all right.'

'Is she going down with something?' Kathleen wondered.

'I don't think it's that. It looked to me as if she had something on her mind, poor lamb.'

'Perhaps she's missing home.' Elsie wrung out a dripping floor cloth then wiped up a patch of suds.

'Or else there's a boy in the picture,' Kathleen suggested.

Joyce was about to leave them to their scrubbing when she happened to glance through the window and saw the very person she was looking for.

'Sorry, girls,' she said as she tiptoed hastily across the wet floor. 'I've just spotted her.'

She ran out through the back door and caught up with Poppy in the vegetable garden. 'There you are — at last!'

'Hello, Joyce.' Standing in the shade of the cherry tree, dressed in blouse and skirt, with her arms folded tight across her chest, Poppy tried not to look as if she'd just been crying.

Joyce wasn't fooled. 'What's up, love?'

'Nothing.'

'It doesn't look like nothing to me.'

'I don't want to talk about it.'

'All right, I won't ask. But come for a walk with me anyway.' Sliding her arm through Poppy's, she strolled with her past the gate into the wood. 'Aren't you starving after missing

283

dinner? I know I would be.'

'I wasn't hungry.' Poppy had struggled through the weekend, unable to get Neville's secret store of banknotes out of her mind. Saturday morning had been manageable because helping Doreen and Elsie to herd Henry Rowson's sheep and lambs off the fell had kept her busy. The afternoon had seen her wandering into the village under orders from Mrs Craven to deliver a batch of newly laundered tea towels to the Institute. But she'd turned round when she'd reached the signpost at the junction and retraced her steps without ever completing her mission. In the evening she'd stayed quietly in her room but Neville's desperate plea had replayed itself inside her head like a gramophone needle stuck in a groove. *Can you tell me what to do now? Because I honestly don't have a clue.*

She'd had no answer then and none late on Saturday night as she sat on her bed darning the heels of her work socks. She could have said, 'Give the money back to Alfie right now, this minute!' or, 'Tell your dad what you've done, tell him everything!' But she hadn't; she'd remained shocked and silent, staring at Neville's bruised face for a full thirty seconds before turning tail and fleeing. She hadn't looked back, just grabbed her bike and cycled off, praying hard that Alfie wasn't lying in wait somewhere and only catching her breath once she was safely down the hill and coasting through the village. By the time she'd arrived at Fieldhead, she'd convinced herself that her best course of action was to say nothing to anyone. Silence:

that was the answer.

She kept her resolution at breakfast on Sunday and afterwards at church, but then the effort became too much. If she stayed one more minute in the company of other people, she would blurt out the truth about what she'd seen. *Neville's stolen Alfie's money! It wasn't really Alfie's to begin with. Now he doesn't know what to do.* She might say it to anyone: to Doreen stretched out on her bed reading a magazine, to Mrs Craven as she wheeled the dinner trolley along the kitchen corridor and now to Joyce who had collared her in the vegetable garden.

There was no wind. The wood was calm and peaceful. You could lose yourself amongst the tall trunks and spreading branches.

'It feels good to stretch my legs and get a breath of fresh air,' Joyce commented. 'I've been cooped up most of the afternoon, composing a letter to Edgar. His leave finished yesterday.'

'That's a shame. I didn't realize.'

'We didn't make a song and dance. But I will miss him.' More than she could say.

'Neville's got himself into a hole.' The words spouted from Poppy's mouth like rain spilling from a gutter. 'He's stolen some money.'

'You don't say!' Joyce stopped in her tracks.

Poppy drew a deep, jagged breath. 'He showed it to me on Friday. It was in a tea caddy on the top shelf.'

'What money?' It took Joyce only a few seconds to see where this was going. 'It couldn't be connected to the burglary last Sunday, by any chance?'

The cat was out of the bag. There was no putting it back. 'I don't think so. There was much more than eleven pounds and some silver — lots of five-pound notes — seventy-five pounds altogether.'

Joyce shook her head. 'Neville, of all people!'

'But Neville didn't steal it. He found all the money hidden in the hayloft, amongst the boxes that belonged to Alfie. Only it seems Alfie didn't really own the boxes . . . or the seventy-five pounds, as it turns out . . . '

'Stop!' Joyce put up her hands in dismay. 'Have you told anybody else about this?'

Poppy shook her head. 'You're the first. What'll happen now? Will I get into trouble?'

'What?' There seemed to be much more to this than Joyce had thought. Poppy was petrified for a start, trembling all over and looking around as if she expected to be pounced on at any moment. 'No, of course not. But if the cash isn't Neville's and it isn't Alfie's either, who on earth does it belong to?'

'The two men who . . . I don't know. There are some men Alfie knows.'

Joyce sucked air in through her teeth as she tried to connect the threads. Neville was in wrongful possession of some ill-gotten gains that had something to do with Alfie Craven and something to do with two other men. Word was all around the village that Neville had taken a mysterious beating. Alfie had disappeared from Home Farm and hadn't been seen for days.

'Come on!' She turned Poppy around and walked her back towards the house. 'Doreen knows more about this than she's been letting on. We need to talk to her.'

★ ★ ★

They found her still in their room, the magazine closed, her dress lying crumpled on the floor, sitting on the bed in her underwear and subjecting her reflection to close inspection in a small handbag mirror. She scarcely looked up as Joyce and Poppy burst into the room.

Poppy shrank back as Joyce launched into her speech. 'Doreen, you were here last Sunday when the burglary happened, weren't you?'

Doreen dabbed at a small red pimple with a wad of cotton wool. 'What if I was?'

'Did you see anything?'

'No. I've already told Ma Craven that. I said the same to the nice policeman who came to interview me. I was in bed with a headache.'

'Are you sure?'

'Why would I lie?' Doreen made it plain that the state of her skin was far more interesting than Joyce's unwelcome questions.

'Because you have something to hide, that's why.' Once Joyce had her teeth into something, she refused to let go. And there was no point beating about the bush with Doreen; a direct attack was necessary. 'Come clean now: admit that you made up the story about the headache.'

'Dearie me.' Reluctantly Doreen put down her mirror and tried to outstare Joyce. 'You do go on.'

'What are you hiding? Who did you see?'

'I told you: no one.' A faint shadow of uncertainty clouded Doreen's expression. 'In any case, we're only talking about a few measly quid. Nobody got murdered, did they?'

'Not yet. But if you stick to your story and the culprit gets away with this, somebody easily could.'

Doreen snorted and tossed her head, then hummed a few chords of threatening music — the sort that played in the background of a murder mystery at the cinema. 'Who done it? Is it the countess or the maid?'

'Neither,' Joyce said quietly but firmly, refusing to blink. 'In this case I'd put my money on Alfie Craven.'

The name made Doreen jump up from the bed and start pacing the room in exasperation.

'You knew he was trouble but you were still happy to take presents from him.' Joyce stood by the door in case Doreen tried to flounce out.

'What's wrong with that, for heaven's sake?' Reaching for a packet of cigarettes on her bedside table, Doreen found that it was empty and threw it down in disgust. 'I don't look a gift horse in the mouth, not like some people round here.'

'So let's get this straight. Alfie turned up here last Sunday. You saw him. What then?'

'Who says I saw him?'

'I do. Come off it, Doreen, you might as well come clean.'

'So I saw him! Have either of you got a fag?'

Still backing away and wishing she was any-where but in the room, Poppy shook her head.

'No,' Joyce said. 'Carry on.'

'All right, Alfie was here. We had a chat then he said he was hungry so I took him to the kitchen and gave him something to eat. Then I left him to it. What was wrong with that?'

'Nothing. But that's not what you told the police. Or Mrs Craven, for that matter. I want to know why not.'

Doreen paced again then sat down on her bed. Her voice changed to a low murmur, ending in a sigh. 'Because, as I keep on saying, you take what you can get in this life but you don't cross a man like Alfie. I learned that the hard way a long time ago.'

'I see.' Until now it hadn't occurred to Joyce that Doreen might be afraid. 'You say you left him in the kitchen?'

Doreen nodded. 'And I wasn't lying: I did have a headache that day. I went straight up to bed and I have no idea what he got up to after I left.'

'Or why he needed the money that he stole?'

'Not a clue. Or about what's happened to him since. Good riddance to bad rubbish is what I say.'

'Except now Mrs Craven needs to be told.' Joyce's face settled into a deep frown while Doreen's resumed its brittle, mocking smile.

'I'll leave that part to you, Sherlock.'

'The sooner the better,' Joyce decided. 'Poppy, you stay here while I go and find her.'

# 17

Hilda listened intently while Joyce talked. They were in her office with the door locked so that no one could disturb them. The blackout blinds were down and they sat in a pool of yellow light cast by the overhead electric light.

'I can't tell you how sorry I am,' Joyce said when she came to the end.

'Don't be.' Hilda's hands rested on the desk and her face showed no emotion. 'It's not your fault.'

'But still.'

A heavy silence descended.

'It explains a lot,' Hilda said at last. Though ignorant of Alfie's affairs, she'd long suspected the worst and now that worst had come to pass. Her son's early pattern of petty theft had continued unabated and now it had come to this. 'It explains why Alfie showed up in Burnside after so long — he was desperate to get away from whatever trouble he was in. But the plan backfired, didn't it?'

'Apparently.' Joyce's heart went out to the stoical older woman sitting across the desk from her. She'd just learned that her son had sneaked into her office and stolen Land Army cash. Not only that, he was caught up in shady, black market business with violent men. And yet Hilda didn't show any sign of losing her dignity or her self-control. That took a lot of strength.

'I knew he was up to something, I just didn't know what.' She leaned heavily on her desk as she stood up. 'Thank you, Joyce. Thank you for letting me know. You can reassure Poppy that she hasn't done anything wrong and please tell Doreen that she must go to the police station first thing tomorrow to put the record straight. I'll take her off the work rota for the morning.'

Joyce stood up too. 'I'm sorry,' she said again. 'I truly am.'

Hilda unlocked the door and walked into the hallway towards the coat stand by the front door. 'I can't help thinking things might have turned out differently for Alfie if Willis hadn't died when he did,' she said with her back turned to Joyce. 'Of course, my lad was always headstrong, even as a small boy. That's why he needed a firmer hand than mine.'

'Don't blame yourself. I'm sure you did everything you could and more.'

Hilda shook her head. 'I was too soft. Alfie was our only son. In the early days I tied him to my apron strings. I spoiled him.'

The idea of smooth-talking, burly Alfie Craven as a mummy's boy was hard for Joyce to imagine. Much easier to picture him as the wayward youth, readily led astray. 'Where are you going?' she asked as Hilda put on her coat.

Hilda felt in her pocket for her keys. 'It's late but I'm going to drive over to Home Farm.'

Joyce understood that the warden needed to do something other than sit and brood, so she followed her through the door. 'If it's to find

Alfie, he isn't lodging there any more. He left a few days ago and only Poppy and Neville have seen him since. I'm afraid he was in a bad way.'

'I'll go anyway. Maybe Joe or Emily can tell me more.'

Joyce made a quick decision. 'Wait while I fetch my coat. I'll come with you.'

'Thank you.' Hilda walked purposefully towards the van parked in the drive. The sun had sunk behind the high fell to the west and the violet sky was rapidly fading to black. 'I won't let the matter drop,' she muttered as she sat in the driver's seat, grasped the wheel and waited for Joyce to join her. 'I intend to sort this out once and for all.'

★　★　★

'It's a month ago today that we were married.' Bill had woken early and watched Grace asleep beside him for a long time before she opened her eyes and he murmured the words. 'Does that count as an anniversary?'

She smiled sleepily and turned on her side to look at him. 'A whole month.'

*A lifetime.* Already the details of his single life were a blur: the Friday nights out with the lads before the war got in the way, the Saturday football matches, day trips to the seaside on the lookout for girls — all ancient history.

As she came fully awake, Grace's smile dimmed. 'It's six o'clock; I'd better get a move on.'

Bill put his hand on her shoulder. 'No. Stay

here a while.' *In the warmth of this bed, close to me.*

She resisted his touch. 'No, really, I have to get up. I'm due at Home Farm in an hour.'

'Please, Grace.' Four weeks had gone by in what might have been perfect harmony if only he hadn't made the rash decision to enlist. He imagined a month of uninterrupted kisses and sunshine, him and his new wife taking tea together in their cramped kitchen with the light streaming in, watching her get dressed into her Land Army uniform in the morning and undressed at night, lying without any clothes, her body so smooth and curved. The soft touch of her fingers on his chest. 'We have to talk.'

Grace sat up and swung her legs over the side of the bed. 'Not now, Bill.'

'Then when?' Reaching out for her hand, he turned her towards him. 'Tell me how I can put things right.'

*By not leaving me*, she thought with a sharp pang. *By not taking the risk of getting yourself killed.* But this was wartime and a wife couldn't say such things. All she could do was sigh and shake her head.

'I have to go, Grace.'

'I know that.'

'I have to do my bit.'

She looked at him through sudden hot tears. 'Oh, Bill!'

'I understand,' he murmured. 'I don't mean to hurt you, and you know that deep down the last thing I want to do is to leave you.'

'Then why?'

'Because this is the way of the world right now. Would you rather I stayed here and felt the shame of it for the rest of my life? Think about it. How would I hold my head up when Jack comes home at the end of the war, or Les or Edgar for that matter, knowing that I'd been a coward and chosen not to fight? I couldn't, could I?'

Faced with this reasoning, Grace felt the arguments she'd rehearsed slip away. 'I'm being selfish, I know.'

'No, it's only natural. And it's bloody hard for me as well.' *To tear myself away, not to hear your voice every day, to give all this up for who knows how long.*

Grace wiped away her tears and struggled out of her own misery. She turned towards him. 'I know and I'm sorry. I've let you down.'

'How?'

'By not taking your feelings into account. How could I be so selfish?'

'Grace, Grace.' He reached out for her and she sank against him. 'I love you.'

'And I love you,' she whispered. It would happen; Bill would join the army and the fears she'd felt for Edgar ever since he joined the RAF would be doubled and trebled by every passing plane, every wireless bulletin and newspaper report. How would she bear it? By putting one foot in front of the other, by working hard and soldiering on, she told herself.

They embraced and kissed sweetly and sadly, then got up and dressed. Bill went downstairs and picked up a letter from the mat. He opened it and read that he'd passed his army medical and been accepted into the second battalion of the Prince of Wales's Own Regiment. He was to report for duty on Monday, 20 July at eight o'clock prompt.

★ ★ ★

'Here we are: the old gang together again!' Brenda was happy to be working alongside Joyce and Grace at Home Farm. Their company made even Joe's gripes and grumbles bearable, as well as the presence of a small team of POWs headed by Lorenzo. Their job for today was to carry on with the drystone walling that had been begun a month or so earlier and continued on and off ever since. The wall that needed rebuilding ran along the back of the cowshed and dairy — a stretch of about thirty yards that had been neglected for years.

It was hard, back-breaking work that went on amidst the constant chip of hammer and chisels against stone and the occasional bursts of Italian conversation. Two Tommies with rifles — Private Cyril Atkinson and one they didn't know by name — supervised the prisoners while chatting and flirting with the three Land Girls.

'Joe was in a terrible mood when we got here,' Grace remarked to Brenda and Joyce. It would soon be time to take a much-needed break. Hopefully Lorenzo and his lot would have brought along some good coffee. She saw signs of this happening as Cyril ordered his charges to down tools.

'As per usual.' Brenda chose a heavy stone

from the nearby pile then scraped away the moss and dirt. 'But if Joe thinks he can get away with passing nasty comments and constantly moaning about the way we do things, he's got another think coming.'

Grace took the stone and positioned it carefully on the half-built wall. 'He's got worse, if anything, since Alfie vanished.'

'Ah yes, about that . . . ' Though Joyce had been intending to bring the others up to date with the latest developments, she'd held fire until after they'd all settled into work. After all, she had to watch what she said about last night's events because they involved other Land Girls, namely Poppy and Doreen.

Brenda looked closely at Joyce's face. 'Come on, out with it.'

'As a matter of fact, I was here in this very yard last night.'

'Who with?' Brenda demanded.

'Not on a social visit, surely?' Grace said simultaneously.

'No, actually I came with Ma Craven.'

'Ma Craven?' they echoed.

Lorenzo passed close to them as he went to the army lorry to fetch a small primus stove, his coffee pot and some tin mugs. He said a polite, quick hello in English instead of the usual friendly *ciao*.

Brenda was the first to reply. '*Ciao*, Lorenzo. No Angelo this morning, I see?'

He shook his head and hurried on, as if unwilling to answer questions.

'So, Joyce, what's this about Hilda and you

paying Emily and Joe a visit?' Grace wanted to know.

Joyce framed her reply carefully and without drama. 'There's been a development regarding the burglary. Ma Craven needed to talk to Alfie.'

'Mysteriouser and mysteriouser!' Brenda's face was flushed from two hours of heavy lifting. 'What was so urgent that it couldn't wait?'

'It was something that Doreen told Poppy and me that I had to pass on straight away. It'll all come out soon enough so you might as well hear it from me. The fact is we got Doreen to admit that it must have been Alfie who took the cash box.'

'Ha!' Brenda gave a cry of triumph as if she'd suspected this all along, while Grace's thoughts flew to the warden.

'Oh dear, that's bad news,' she said with a sigh.

'A lot's happened since, to do with the two men seen hanging about in the pub yard a couple of weekends ago.'

'Yes, I remember them,' Grace said quietly.

'Now Neville's been dragged into it too.'

Grace and Brenda looked at each other with furrowed brows.

'Leaving that to one side for now, that's the reason we came to pay Joe and Emily a visit. Alfie wasn't here, of course, and Joe was none too happy about opening the door to us so late at night.' In fact, he'd taken one look at his visitors through a chink in the door and slammed it shut.

A minute or so later, Emily had opened it again, keeping Hilda and Joyce standing on the doorstep while she'd answered their questions. No, she had no idea where Alfie had got to, she'd insisted. And she didn't care either — the lazy so-and-so had been eating them out of house and home. 'Sorry, Hilda,' she'd said, 'but that son of yours is no good to anyone.' She and Joe weren't the only ones who held that opinion. In fact, Alfie had managed to ruffle someone's feathers so badly that he'd been given a good thrashing.

Hilda had listened with gritted teeth then turned and set off down the path. 'Ta, Emily. If Alfie does turn up here again, can you let me know?'

'He won't.' Emily hadn't meant her reply to sound so curt but she was never one for beating about the bush. 'And if he does, he'll be lucky if Joe doesn't take the horse whip to him. Or, worse, take a pot shot at him with his gun.'

Hilda had carried on without a word.

Joyce had lingered on the doorstep. 'Why would Joe do that, Emily?'

'Because there's five pounds, two shillings missing from our bureau drawer, that's why.'

The door had slammed and Joyce had followed Hilda to the van. 'Perhaps it's for the best,' she'd suggested on the drive back to the hostel. 'Now you can hand over this whole thing to the police and let them get on with their job.'

Hilda had looked resigned but said nothing to Joyce all the way home.

'It's her I feel sorry for,' Joyce said now to Brenda and Grace.

'I agree,' Grace said. 'This is a hard pill for her to swallow.'

'Now then, girls, less of the chinwagging.' Cheery Cyril broke into their conversation. 'There's coffee on the go, if you fancy a cup. And try to put smiles on the faces of our Eyetie friends while you're at it. For some reason they've all got out on the wrong side of the bed this morning.'

★   ★   ★

Lorenzo and co. had not been their usual chirpy selves, Grace, Brenda and Joyce acknowledged as they cycled towards Burnside after a long day at Home Farm.

'No laughing and joking, no singing — nothing.' Brenda sighed.

'And no wonder,' Grace observed. 'Lorenzo's obviously on edge about Angelo.'

Joyce agreed. 'He definitely clammed up when we asked him how his pal was. And of course they must all feel the strain of life in a prison camp. It can't be much fun — being away from home for so long, missing your loved ones, and so on.'

'Let's keep schtum as far as Una is concerned,' Brenda suggested. 'She's worried enough already.' The exhilaration of freewheeling down the hill into the village was refreshing so she eased off the brakes and whizzed ahead.

'Watch out!' Joyce cried as Maurice's van edged out of a narrow side road.

Brenda saw it just in time, braked and screeched to a halt. The back wheel of her bike slewed to the left and she lost control and landed in a bush.

'Blithering idiot!' she cried after Maurice, who had slowed down to make sure she wasn't hurt then given a casual wave and driven on. She was disentangling herself from the brambles when Joyce and Grace arrived.

'Who? You or Maurice?' Joyce's wry expression elicited a snort from Brenda.

'Him! It was my right of way.'

Grace said nothing but gave her a meaningful stare before offering her a hand. She'd glimpsed a white ribbon peeping out from under Brenda's Aertex collar. 'What's that you're wearing around your neck?' she asked. Brenda's hand shot up to conceal the ribbon.

'Come on, Bren; what have you got there?' Having set her bike upright and checked it for damage, Joyce was as curious as Grace.

Brenda sighed before raising her ring into full view and dangling it from the ribbon. The sapphire and diamonds caught the light and sparkled beautifully. 'Les gave me it yesterday, just before he left.'

'Oh, I say — an engagement ring!' Grace gasped.

'Yes, top marks.' Brenda laughed uneasily. 'I wish I had a camera. Your two faces are a picture.'

'Les wants you to marry him?' Joyce said.

'Don't look so surprised. He asked me and I said yes. What else was a girl to do?' Blushing furiously, Brenda tried to wrest her bike back but Joyce held on to it.

'Yesterday, you say? You kept that close to your chest.'

'No, I didn't!' The wrestle to gain control of the bike continued. 'Not on purpose.'

'So why not wear the ring on your finger and show it off?'

'For drystone walling? Are you mad?'

'That's fair enough,' Grace said quietly as she came between them. 'Congratulations, Brenda. I'm over the moon for you. I mean it. And it's a lovely ring.'

'I said yes.' Brenda repeated this as if she still couldn't quite believe it. 'Did I do the right thing?'

'If you love Les; yes, of course you did.'

*Do I? Do I love him, really and truly?* The question squirmed away beneath the surface. 'He caught me off guard.'

'In any case, you've sent him off to Scotland a happy man.' *All these goodbyes,* Joyce thought with a pang of sadness.

It was left to Brenda to make the comparisons. 'Now we're all in the same boat, aren't we? Edgar and Les have already gone and Bill is about to leave too.'

'Two weeks today,' Grace confirmed. 'His call-up papers arrived first thing this morning.'

They stood in thoughtful silence at the side of the road; three women in corduroy breeches, leggings and cotton shirts thinking about sad partings. They all put on a brave face that hid undercurrents of doubt and self-doubt. Would Grace's pride in Bill's brave decision to go to war overcome her fears? Would Joyce's new, deep delight in Edgar's love be stolen away by a cruel turn of events? And did Brenda believe in herself

301

enough to keep her promises to Les? These were the questions they asked themselves as they stood on the grass verge at the bottom of the hill, looking ahead to an uncertain future.

★  ★  ★

The best places for Alfie to sleep were the isolated hill barns, used for storing hay and housing livestock during the long, cold winters. In summer they were rarely visited by the farmers, meaning that he could bed down and get a good night's kip then be up at dawn and on the move again, scavenging food wherever he could. He drifted on like this from hour to hour and day to day without a long-term plan.

But as the pain in his ribs began to subside, he grew more decisive. At dusk on the Monday he risked a return to Winsill Edge for more fresh eggs and even crept into the Turnbulls' kitchen when he caught sight of both Horace and his father at the far side of the farmyard, irritably rounding up their scatterbrained chickens and shooing them into the henhouse for the night. He stole half a loaf from the bread bin and was gone before he heard the two men returning to the house, grumbling and bickering over signs that a fox had been near. He chewed hungrily at the crust as he walked on. Then, finding that he was heading in the direction of Burnside, he decided to keep well out of sight by skirting around the back of the woods and following the river along the valley bottom until he came to one of the barns he favoured for night-time accommodation. A glance towards the road told him that he'd reached Peggy Russell's farm about half a mile from Fieldhead. He gave a satisfied grunt; Peggy was a doddery old widow who lived alone and rarely ventured out after nightfall. True, she owned a vicious dog that strained at its chain and barked at any passing car or bike, but that was to Alfie's advantage since it would alert him as well as its mistress to any unwanted visitor.

In fact, the dog set up a racket as Alfie stood in the barn doorway assessing the situation. He heard a car in the distance — possibly a visitor to the hostel, which lay at the end of the lane — so he stepped further into the shadows while it passed. It took its time, cruising along at low speed, driving Peggy's dog into a frenzy as it drew near. Then it stopped and Alfie got the shock of his life.

Howard Moyes switched off the car engine then stepped out. He narrowly avoided the frantic dog then knocked on the farmhouse door. His tall, stooped figure and gleaming black car were unmistakable. Besides, no one else in the dale dressed in a navy-blue blazer and yellow cravat or wore his trilby at that cocky angle. A closer inspection showed Clive Nixon sitting in the passenger seat, idly tapping the dashboard and watching the conversation going on between Moyes and the old widow.

Alfie swore and retreated into the barn. He climbed the steps into the hayloft and found a narrow slit in the stonework that let air circulate. His breath came in short gasps as he peered through the spy hole and waited for the car to drive on towards Fieldhead.

★ ★ ★

'Doreen, you've got two visitors.' Una flew up the hostel stairs and caught sight of her in her petticoat going into the WC. 'Jean answered the door to them and I overheard them asking for you.'

'Are you sure?' Doreen's day had begun with a trek into town to visit the police station and confess her sins — it had meant two changes of bus then a grim half-hour being interrogated by a portly desk sergeant instead of the wet-behind-the-ears constable who'd come to Fieldhead to investigate on the Monday after the burglary had taken place. She'd ummed and ahhed and pretended to have forgotten about bumping into Alfie Craven that morning; she'd had a splitting headache so her memory had been hazy, etcetera. The sergeant had noted everything down without believing a word. Then he'd flipped his notebook shut, aimed a slow look of contempt that had travelled down her body from head to foot and sent her on her way. Now all she wanted to do was to keep out of everyone's way and not answer any more questions.

'I'm sure,' Una insisted. 'Why, aren't you expecting anyone?'

Doreen frowned. 'What do they look like?'

'Two men in suits. No, on second thoughts, the tall one's wearing a blazer. The smaller one has specs.'

Doreen's heart thudded and lurched — one heavy beat then onwards in a skittering, rapid race. She only had a foggy idea of why Alfie's so-called friends might seek her out, but she sensed danger ahead. 'Tell them I'm not in,' she said.

Too late. Jean followed Una up the stairs, talking in a loud voice. 'Ah, there you are, Doreen!' She stopped to shout back down the stairs to the visitors. 'Your luck's in. She has to make herself decent but she'll be down in a minute.'

So there was no other option but to face the music unless she climbed down the drainpipe to escape. The madcap notion was gone in a flash and Doreen tried to control her nerves as she went to her room to put on her tight-fitting green dress and white shoes. After applying a slick of lipstick, down she went to bluff it out for the second time that day.

'They're waiting for you in the common room.' Jean had stood eager guard at the bottom of the stairs. The two men looked like trouble to her so her curiosity was piqued.

Doreen swished by and entered the room in style. 'Well, well, this is a nice surprise,' she trilled as she closed the door behind her.

'Hello, Doreen.' Moyes's easy manner didn't over-ride the look of harsh suspicion in his eyes. He'd taken off his hat and held it in front of him. 'It's nice to see you looking so well.'

'Likewise, Howard, Clive.' She knew precisely the weapons she had in a situation like this and she employed them by standing between the men, shoulders back, chest thrust forward, one hand on her hip. 'I'm sure this isn't a passing visit so how can I help you?'

'My, you have a good memory,' Moyes said with an insincere smile.

'Oh, I never forget a name, especially when it belongs to a man who drives a nice new car. I take it this has to do with a certain mutual acquaintance?' Attack was the best form of defence, so Doreen looked expectantly from one to the other.

'Oh yes, our Alfie!' The girl had plenty of nerve; Moyes gave her that. 'That's exactly why we're here. We've been looking all over the shop for Alfie Watkins but he seems to have vanished into thin air.'

'And I'm the magician's assistant, am I?' She sounded a light 'pah!' with pouted lips and tossed her hair behind her shoulders. 'You're waiting for me to pull the rabbit out of the hat?'

Moyes enjoyed Doreen's performance more than Nixon, who chewed at the skin at the side of his thumb and eyed her impatiently. 'Not necessarily. But we think you might be able to remember when you two last met.'

She held his gaze. 'Oh, not for weeks. In fact, probably not since he introduced us outside the Blacksmith's Arms. Why do you want him? Does he owe you some money?'

'Bingo!' Moyes said with an intensification of the steely glint. 'We've asked him 'nicely', of course, but so far no luck. Now we might have to be less polite.'

Doreen shrugged then walked to the window.

'I'm sorry I can't help you. I would if I could but, like I say, I haven't clapped eyes on him.'

'That's a pity.' He stroked his clipped moustache as he came up behind her. 'We came all the way out here, sure that you'd still be the first in the queue for any little luxury our friend might slip your way.'

'No such luck, I'm afraid.' The skin at the back of her neck prickled and she tried to edge away. But Nixon advanced too and between them they cornered her in the window bay. 'By the way, he answers to the name of Craven in this neck of the woods.'

'He does, does he?' Nixon showed no surprise.

'You will be a good girl and tell us the next time you see Mr 'Watkins', won't you?' The question from Moyes contained an unmistakable threat. 'We'll be waiting for your call.'

Nixon slipped a hand into his breast pocket and drew out a small piece of white paper that he thrust at Doreen. 'This is our telephone number,' he explained in a voice that was surprisingly light and lilting. 'We'll need the exact details so we can follow it up straight away.'

'Please,' Moyes added with mock politeness. 'And pass the word around that this is the number to ring if Alfie *Craven* is spotted hereabouts.'

Doreen pushed the scrap of paper down her cleavage and managed a conspiratorial wink that was as false as Moyes's 'please'.

'Good girl,' he crooned, coming so close to her that she felt his breath on her face. 'I can see why

307

you're Alfie's favourite. He has taste if nothing else.'

*How much longer can I keep this up?* she wondered as every nerve ending strained against the man's proximity. She took in his narrow, small face and the five o'clock shadow on his chin, a deep pock mark between his straight, dark brows.

He sneered then stepped back, eyes fixed on her face. 'But do you find that your looks sometimes attract the wrong type? I would say they might, wouldn't you, Clive?'

Nixon was bored by Moyes's games. The woman had been unable or unwilling to tell them anything useful and he was left feeling frustrated and impatient to continue the search. 'Do as we say,' he warned her as he snatched the car keys from Moyes then strode towards the door. 'Be sure to keep your eyes and ears open for us, especially if you fancy your chances in a beauty contest in the near future, if you catch my drift.'

★ ★ ★

At six o'clock next morning, Joyce was on her way to the bathroom when she heard the faint sound of the telephone ringing in the warden's office. She leaned over the banister to see if anyone was available to answer it, wondering who on earth could be calling at this hour. No one else was awake, it seemed, so she raced downstairs to take the call.

She picked up the receiver. 'Hello, this is

308

Field-head Hostel. Who's calling, please?'

'Hello, this is the operator at the Northgate exchange. I have a call for you from a Squadron Leader Aldridge, in charge of the Royal Canadian Air Force base on Penny Lane. Will you take it?'

'Yes, thank you.' Joyce's thoughts raced through various possibilities, each one more far fetched than the last.

'Hold the line, please. I'll put you through.'

There were several clicks on the line then Jim Aldridge's voice came through. 'Apologies for the early call,' he began. 'But this is an emergency. Who am I speaking to, please?'

'This is Joyce Cutler. Would you like me to find the warden for you?'

'No, it'll be quicker if you can pass on a message for me. I have a dozen other calls to make. Do you have pen and paper?'

Joyce reached across the desk. 'Yes. Fire away.'

'OK, write it down exactly as I tell you. There's been a break-out from Beckwith Camp. Eight prisoners have escaped.'

'Eight.' She steadied her hand and wrote down the number.

'All from the same hut. It happened overnight. When the guard carried out his early morning patrol, he found that eight of the beds hadn't been slept in.'

'Did anyone see what happened?'

'If they did, they're not saying. I got a call fifteen minutes ago from the sergeant in charge. We think they escaped on foot so they can't have got far. That's why we're both manning the telephone right now, putting calls out to everyone in the neighbourhood.'

Joyce scribbled as fast as she could with a dawning realization of the repercussions. 'Do you have a list of names? Should I write them down?'

'Names and numbers,' he confirmed. 'Ready?'

'Yes, ready.'

'OK. Ricci, number 4701; Bianchi, 3276; Marino, 4396; Bachetti, 3840 . . . ' She went on writing but her mind was fixed on 'Marino' and 'Bachetti'. Lorenzo Marino, prisoner number 4396; Angelo Bachetti, prisoner number 3840.

Aldridge brought the list to a rapid conclusion. 'You got that? Good. Tell everyone to report any possible sighting immediately. This is going to cause one hell of a stink, so the sooner we recapture every last prisoner the better.'

'Got that,' Joyce said hurriedly. 'Thank you, Squadron Leader. I'll do as you say.'

There was a click and the line went dead.

Joyce replaced the receiver. For a few moments she didn't move.

Hilda had made her way from the kitchen at the sound of the phone. She burst into the office then clutched at the bib of her apron when she saw Joyce's shocked expression. 'Alfie? Have the police arrested him?'

'No, it wasn't that.'

'What then?'

'The POWs. Eight have gone AWOL.' Joyce pushed the list across the desk. 'Angelo is one of them. I'd better go straight up and tell Una.'

She took a deep breath and crossed the

hallway. Her feet dragged as she mounted the stairs, walked along the landing then knocked on the door of Una's room. She walked in without waiting for an answer. Brenda and Kathleen were still asleep, Una was sitting up in bed, looking at her with a bleary frown.

'What is it, Joyce?' She sat bolt upright and waited for the axe to fall. 'It's something very bad. I can see it in your face.'

# 18

There was scarcely any time for Una to recover from the shock. The morning routine demanded that she get dressed and go down to breakfast before her whirling thoughts and feelings had settled, so she found herself sitting at the long table, staring down at her bowl of uneaten porridge and surrounded by fellow Land Girls whose sole topic of conversation was the dramatic overnight happening at Beckwith Camp.

'It takes some nerve to go on the run like that,' Kathleen said to Elsie and Brenda. 'To give up a comfortable billet where they know they're going to be fed and watered and make a bid for freedom.'

'Yes, it's risky,' Elsie agreed. 'But that's exactly what I'd do in their position — try to escape and get back to my own country where I could rejoin the fight. So I can't say I'm surprised.'

Though concerned for Una, Brenda couldn't resist joining in. 'That's right. I watched a story on Pathé News recently about our brave boys tunnelling their way out of camps in Germany and Poland. That makes getting out of Beckwith a piece of cake by comparison.'

'Our chaps end up as heroes.' Like most patriotic citizens, Kathleen felt pride in such achievements. 'They go through hell and high water to get back into Allied territory and rejoin the fight.'

Una heard but didn't take it in. Everything was a jumble. All she could hold in her mind was that Angelo had left without saying goodbye.

Joyce leaned across the table and spoke softly to her. 'Eat your porridge. You need something to line your stomach to help you through the day.'

She shook her head. 'I'm not hungry.'

'Try to eat anyway.' Fortunately Joyce would be able to keep an eye on Una as they worked at Peggy Russell's together. The farm was close enough to the hostel to bring her back at lunchtime for soup and a sandwich if necessary. She must let Hilda know that she might do that.

'You're sure Angelo's name was on the list?' Una clutched like a drowning man to a last straw of hope.

'Absolutely certain. Lorenzo's too, if that's any comfort.'

'What do you mean?'

'Lorenzo has always looked out for Angelo. We can rely on him to carry on doing that.'

'I thought . . . ' *Angelo hasn't been well. He's been missing from work. I saw him on Sunday; he never said a word. He told me he was better. He made promises. I gave him the card I made especially for him . . .* 'Oh, I don't know what I thought!'

'Hush!' Jean gave Joyce a nudge and all heads turned towards Hilda as she entered the room.

Standing where everyone could see her, the warden rapped a spoon on the table to attract attention. 'Listen, everybody. You all know by now that some POWs have gone missing from

313

Beckwith Camp. What you might not know is that this was planned well ahead.'

An expectant murmur went around the room as everyone waited to hear more.

'From what I gathered during my phone call to the camp just now, the remaining prisoners were in on it. They deny it, but the guard on duty says he was called to a different hut soon after midnight to sort out a scuffle over something and nothing. The men made a big fuss so it took him quite a few minutes to settle them. He thinks that's when the escape must have happened, while his back was turned.'

Kathleen raised her hand to ask an obvious question. 'Didn't he suspect anything was amiss?'

Hilda shook her head. 'According to the sergeant in charge, the guard put it down to Italians getting over-excited, the way they do. Anyway, it's not our place to point the finger. Our job is to keep our eyes peeled for any sight of the missing prisoners.'

In her distraught state, Una was sure that the warden's eyes had rested on her as she made her next pronouncement.

'Each and every one of us has a duty to make sure that they don't get far.'

'That's right,' Jean agreed in a loud voice, fixing Una with a suspicious glare. 'We can't let them get away with it. If they do, every prisoner in the county will be bound to follow suit.'

There was a loud buzz of agreement before Hilda went on. 'You must report any sighting immediately. Is that clear?'

'Yes, Mrs Craven.' Answers came from every corner of the room and the news gave rise to a general air of animosity that seemed to be directed at Una.

Sitting next to Una, Brenda patted her hand. 'Everything will be all right. We'll have them all back in camp before you know it.'

Una pressed her lips together and nodded without believing it.

'Even if it's only gossip, you should pass on what you hear to me. Who knows, a rumour may turn out to be true.' Hilda had got through her speech. She'd had to put aside all thoughts about Alfie to concentrate on the latest emergency, but as she left the dining room and retreated to her office, it struck her that the urgent search for POWs might also turn up clues as to her son's whereabouts. She sat at her desk to contemplate the shame she would be bound to feel if Alfie were to be discovered. He would be arrested, tried for burglary and found guilty. What mother would want this for her son? Would she simply have to stand by and let it happen?

Hilda shuffled papers around her desk then went to stare out of the window, then to her desk again, where she tried to concentrate on the rota for the day. In the hall and out on the drive, girls' voices were calling out goodbyes as they set off for work. There was washing up to be done, housework to get through, a phone call to be made to bring Edith Mostyn up to date with events.

*This doesn't feel right*, she thought as she

made her way to the kitchen, eager to immerse herself in everyday chores. She had no one she could talk to, no husband to lean on, not a single friend in the village who would offer her a scrap of sympathy about this. So she took her dilemma to the dirty pots piled high on the draining board and to the hot, soapy water in the sink. *I gave a fine speech about everyone doing their duty, yet all the while I'm backing away from the notion of handing Alfie over to the police. I'm a hypocrite when all's said and done.*

★   ★   ★

Hours after Una had arrived at Peggy Russell's farm with Joyce, she was still hollowed out with shock and trying to recover from the hostile looks that many of the girls at the hostel had cast in her direction. She went about her work like a zombie, unseeing and clumsy, slow to carry out the orders that Peggy shot at them from the moment they began.

'The brambles in the ditch behind the house need cutting back, then after that I want you to put fresh straw down for the pigs.' The frail-looking widow — all skin and bone, with thin grey hair and tough, leathery skin — fetched two sickles from an outhouse next to the pigsty and pushed them at Joyce and Una with an instruction not to turn their backs on the biggest of the two sows when they eventually entered the sty. 'Ivy's not so bad but Ruby doesn't take to strangers,' she warned.

Joyce thanked her then kept a wary eye on

316

Ruby and her six piglets as she led Una round the back of the house, where they climbed a stile into a rough, tussocky field that had been left fallow for two successive summers. They found that the ditch running alongside the wall was badly overgrown with nettles and ferns as well as brambles — so much so that rainwater couldn't run freely and instead stood in deep, muddy pools that overflowed into the field.

'It's a good job we're wearing wellingtons.' Joyce stepped gingerly through a muddy patch of ground before lowering herself into the ditch. 'This job will take up most of the morning by the look of it.'

The dazed expression lingered on Una's face as she stepped down into the ditch and, side by side, they slashed and cut. When she did finally speak, it took Joyce by surprise. 'Why did he do it?' she demanded.

'Who — Angelo?' Joyce had just added to the heap of thorny, tangled blackberry stems that they'd piled up in a corner of the field. It would be left to dry out before being set alight. Now she stood over Una, hands on hips.

'Yes. Why did he make me promises he knew he wasn't going to keep? Why not give me a clue?'

'Perhaps he did but you didn't pick it up.' Joyce recalled Lorenzo's evasiveness when she'd last encountered him at Home Farm. It had been out of character and she remembered now that all the Italians had behaved differently and she'd put it down at the time to them being homesick and fed up with prison-camp life, no more than that. 'I was with Lorenzo all day recently and I didn't suspect a thing. Try not to blame Angelo too much, though. Elsie spoke the truth: any self-respecting POW of any nationality would attempt to do what the Italians have just done.'

Una didn't listen. 'Angelo told me he missed me, that I was near his heart always.' She remembered every word of their last meeting.

'Did he say when he'd see you again?'

'No. He told me he was feeling better, though.'

Painful as it was for Una, Joyce knew that she had to come to terms with what had happened. 'Doesn't that show you that the plan to escape had already been hatched and last Sunday was his way of saying goodbye?'

Una refused to believe it. 'He promised to take me to Pisa. He carved a little wooden box with our initials. I wear his necklace.'

'Then, who knows? Perhaps you'll still see Italy after the war has ended.' Seeing Peggy approaching the stile, Joyce offered a hand to haul Una out of the ditch. 'Try to forget about it for now. Let's go and see what the old girl wants.'

*He gave me his gold crucifix.* Una felt the mud suck at her boots as Joyce raised her up. *It was the very last thing he did before he left for Scotland.*

★   ★   ★

Like many of the farmers who employed Land Girls, Peggy was a hard taskmaster. She was unreasonable about how fast she wanted jobs done and was quick to criticize their methods and standards if they fell short of expectations. 'In my day, we weren't frightened of putting in a good day's work', and 'You youngsters don't know you're born', were constant refrains as she stood with arms folded, watching Joyce and Una pile up debris from the ditch then later muck out the pigsty before they laid fresh straw.

Una was nervous as she pushed the wheelbarrow into the pigs' cramped pen. She kept a wary eye on Ruby, whose enormous bulk took up one whole side of the sty. The pink sow lay with legs stretched out, swollen teats angled for her piglets to suckle, following Una and Joyce's every move with her red-rimmed eyes. Meanwhile, Ivy came snuffling up to Una for treats.

Avoiding the piglets that ran squealing between her legs, Una retreated to the far side of the barrow and had scarcely begun to help Joyce to lift soiled straw before Peggy poked her nose in.

'It doesn't take two to do that job. Why doesn't one of you collect three fresh bales while the other one stays here and mucks out?'

'Where do we get the new bales from?' Joyce asked.

'From the barn in the far field. There's an empty barrow there to wheel them back.'

'You go,' Joyce said to Una. 'I'll carry on here.'

Glad to be away from the stinking pen and out from under Ruby's baleful stare, Una climbed the stile into the field where they'd been working

319

earlier. Her hand went up to touch Angelo's cross, a gesture designed to convince herself of his enduring love. 'He will come back,' she murmured as she jumped down from the stile and hurried across the rough ground towards the isolated barn. 'I have to carry on believing that, whatever happens.'

Angelo would return and all would be well. It didn't matter how long he was away or where he'd got to, just as long as he was safe.

The barn door was ajar and three swallows flew out of one of the narrow windows as she approached. They swooped down to head height then suddenly curved upwards into a clear blue sky. Una stood for a moment to watch them soar then she entered the barn. Her eyes adjusted to the shadows and she made out a barrow propped against the far wall.

Up in the hayloft, Alfie crouched behind a tower of baled straw. Until the startled swallows had flown from the rafters, he'd been sleeping the day away, so had no warning of the girl's approach. But now he could hear her moving about below then the sound of her foot on the bottom rung of the ladder leading up to the loft. He held his breath and waited.

Una climbed the ladder then seized the nearest bale of straw. It was heavy for her to shift, but she managed to drag it into position then tilt it and tip it over the edge on to the ground below. Peggy had instructed her to fetch three bales, so she turned to do the same again.

Alfie squatted down in the far corner. He

didn't move. With luck the girl wouldn't venture this far. If she did, he was ready for her.

The second bale thudded down. Una watched it land then turned again. Dust had got up her nose so she sneezed then rubbed it to stop it itching. Another sneeze came and then a fit of small, quick ones that made her sit down on the nearest bale to catch her breath.

*Not a step closer, young lady; not if you want to leave here in one piece.* Alfie waited with bated breath.

'Last one,' Una grunted as she stood up and shifted the bale she'd been sitting on. She suspected that the dust in here was giving her hay fever so the sooner she was out and breathing fresh air again the better. The final bale landed on top of the first two and she quickly descended the ladder to pile all three on to the barrow and push it out of the barn.

'Get a move on,' Peggy shouted from the yard gate. 'No need to take all day!'

⋆   ⋆   ⋆

'Eight men can't vanish into thin air.' Neville echoed the opinion that the majority of villagers held about the POWs' overnight break out. He was there to welcome Poppy and Brenda as they rode into the yard at Brigg Farm. 'They're bound to nab 'em and cart 'em back to camp, kicking and screaming.'

'Una for one certainly hopes so.' Brenda leaned her bike on the wall of the hay barn and prepared to follow Neville to the top field where

Arnold White's straw-baling machine was waiting for them. 'But so far they've shown a clean pair of heels.'

'Trust me — it won't be long.' As Neville chatted to Brenda, he glanced anxiously at Poppy. Then, as soon as they arrived in the field and Brenda joined Roland to learn how to operate the mechanical monster, he pulled her to one side. 'What did you say about the money?' he asked. 'Did you tell anyone?'

Poppy squirmed under his gaze, doing her best to avoid commenting on his cuts and bruises. 'I'm sorry, I had to. Joyce knew something was up and she winkled it out of me.'

He ran a hand through his hair and bit his bottom lip. 'What exactly?'

'That you had some money that didn't belong to you and that Alfie was involved.'

Neville groaned. 'Then what?'

'Then Joyce had it out with Doreen and after that Alfie's goose was cooked. Mrs Craven got to know and now the police — '

'Every bleeding blighter!' Neville groaned again.

Poppy could see only one way ahead. 'You have to give the money back,' she insisted. 'Go to the station yourself, hand over the seventy-five pounds and tell them everything — '

'Shut up!' He cut her off vehemently. Making sure that his father and Brenda were still busy, he walked Poppy further away. 'I can't do that!'

'Why not? If you don't, those two men will force the truth out of you. Or else Alfie will be back. Either way, isn't it far better to go to the police?'

'I can't, I can't!' The skin on his neck was a patchy red, his swollen features twisted in angry frustration. 'You can say it till you're blue in the face, it won't make any difference.'

'Neville, you're not listening to me!' Poppy balled her hands into fists and stamped her foot. 'It's time to own up. Give it all back.'

He squeezed his eyes shut then opened them again to rock back on his heels and stare up at the sky. 'I can't,' he said in a suddenly flat voice. 'I didn't know which way to turn after you left here on Sunday so I shoved the whole lot on the back of the fire and held it down with the poker until every last note went up in smoke.'

★   ★   ★

The working day ended in stifling heat. There was no breath of wind blowing through the dale; only baking air and a low sun so bright that the girls had to pull down the brims of their hats and cycle slowly home, perspiring under its rays. Once at the hostel, they gathered in the shade at the back of the house to exchange the latest snippets about the escaped prisoners — still no sightings. It was developing into a big mystery, but surely someone would spot them in due course.

Joyce didn't join in with the speculation. Instead, she took a letter addressed to her from the hall table and went straight upstairs to her room. She took off her hat and jacket then sat on the bed to compose herself before slicing the letter open with the blade of her pocket knife.

'Dearest Joyce, I hope this letter finds you well,' she read. Edgar's words danced before her eyes so she started again. 'Dearest Joyce, I hope this letter finds you well. I'm fine as I write it. Picture me on my top bunk, pen in hand and shining a torch on this paper while three chaps around me snore in their sleep. No dicing tonight — touch wood — only a quick trip over Normandy to drop supplies earlier in the day. So I've made myself a cosy nest of pillows and blankets and have all the time in the world to remind you how much I love you and am thinking of you.'

She paused to take a deep breath before reading on.

'Somehow it doesn't seem awkward to write this down; in fact, it feels like the most natural thing in the world. When I come home I want to shout it out from the top of St Michael's steeple — 'I, Edgar Clifford Kershaw, love you, Joyce Cutler!' Do you have a middle name, Joyce? If so, write and tell me what it is. I'd like it to be Rose because a rose smells sweet and feels velvety soft to the touch. Am I embarrassing you? Do you mind that I've gone soft in the head?

'Remember, you have to make allowances and understand that now the door of the cage is open and this bird can fly free at last, there'll be no stopping me. I'll be tapping my beak at your window and tweeting and chirruping morning, noon and night. 'I love my Joyce, tra-la!''

She paused again, her whole body suffused

324

with the power of Edgar's passion; warm, soft, silly, intimate — sharing words that were for her eyes only, that she would keep secret and close to her heart.

'My dearest Edgar,' she replied before she went down to supper. She wrote in her quick, fluent hand on her best Basildon Bond writing paper. 'My darling, picture me in turn sitting on my bed overlooking the woods at the back of Fieldhead. The room is quiet and the low sun is shining through the branches. Though you can't be here with me, I have your letter in front of me, making me at this moment the happiest woman alive.'

⋆　⋆　⋆

Alfie knew from bitter experience how to play the waiting game. He'd learned it in prison, when he'd spent months plotting his revenge against Ron Jackson, the man who had pointed the finger at Alfie for a series of house burglaries that they'd planned and carried out together. Jackson had got off scot-free but in the end, after Alfie had served his time, he had got his own back in a skirmish involving knives in which Jackson had lost two fingers on his right hand. Sit tight, wait with steely determination and then act; that was Alfie's motto. So, though a secret dawn visit to Fieldhead on the Tuesday morning to see if he could find out from Doreen the reason behind his enemies' visit hadn't produced the desired result, he'd simply made his way back to Peggy Russell's barn to wait out the rest of the day. From there he would keep watch and pounce on Doreen on her return to the hostel then drag out of her the facts behind Nixon and Moyes's visit. A close call with the Land Girl sent to fetch straw had been the only drama of the day; otherwise, he'd smoked his last two cigarettes to quell the hunger pains and tried to sleep through the heat of the day.

By five o'clock he was back on the alert, listening to the rough bark of Peggy's dog at every approach and spying through the narrow slit until at last Doreen appeared, hatless and with her shirtsleeves rolled back, cycling alone towards the hostel.

Alfie's luck was in. He went straight into action: down the ladder in a flash and taking a stealthy short cut across fields towards Field-head, reaching the gate into the walled garden at precisely the same time as Doreen wheeled her bike across the yard towards the stables. He jerked back out of sight then risked another surreptitious glance around the yard to check that there was no one else in sight. Satisfied, he ignored the ever-present pain in his ribs and walked swiftly up the garden path in time to see Doreen emerge from the stable, about to close the door behind her.

Doreen saw him out of the corner of her eye but had no time to react before he knocked her clean off her feet, back into the stable where she collided with the bike that she'd just propped against the entrance to a stall. He stood astride her and mocked her in his slow, calculating way. 'Fancy that — three visitors for you in the space of twenty-four hours. Someone must be popular.'

'What are you on about?'

Alfie remained convinced that he was on the right track. 'Come off it, Doreen — Nixon and Moyes were here yesterday, large as life. What did they want?'

'Don't ask me.' Her prevarication earned her a sharp kick in the ribs. 'All right then — yes, they were here. And yes, I did talk to them.'

She rolled on to her side and tried to stand but he thrust her back with his foot, which he kept pressed against her chest. 'Let's not waste time. You'll tell me what Moyes and Nixon wanted then you'll nip inside and fetch me some grub. You won't say a word. Got it?'

She nodded and he lifted his foot, allowing her to scramble to her feet. 'Cut out the rough stuff, Alfie. I'm on your side, remember.'

His eyes were narrow with mistrust. 'The only side you're on is your own.'

Moodily she brushed straw and dust from her trousers. 'So what? A girl has to look out for number one.'

'So what did they want?'

'They asked me if I'd seen you lately. I swore that I hadn't clapped eyes on you since the day in the pub yard. There, is that good enough?'

He gave the slightest of satisfied nods. 'And what did they say back?'

Doreen fished in her trouser pocket and drew out the scrap of paper with the telephone number written on it. 'They told me to keep my eyes peeled and to tell the other girls to do likewise. If any of us sees you, we're to ring this number.'

'Give me that.' He snatched the paper, screwed it into a ball, then threw it to the ground.

She ducked down to retrieve it, gasping out a protest as he stamped on her hand. 'Please yourself. I know it off by heart anyway.'

'Leave that alone and listen to me. Straight after you've fetched me my grub, you'll go ahead and call that number. You're to tell Moyes that you saw me catch a bus earlier today. It pulled up at the village stop; a number fifteen to Northgate.'

'I won't be able to do any of that at this rate.' With her hand still trapped, she spoke through gritted teeth.

He stepped away then pulled her roughly upright. 'A number fifteen. I was carrying a suitcase.'

'All right, all right, I'll do it.' She would play along for now. Later she would take her time to think everything through.

He swung her towards the door then pushed her into the yard. 'Bread and cheese, some cold meat. Not a word!'

So she ran to obey, waiting by the kitchen door until she heard the warden wheel a trolley laden with plates and cutlery down the corridor towards the dining hall. Then she darted inside and took whatever she could lay her hands on: bread and cheese as requested, plus a jar of fish paste and half a roast chicken that she found under a glass cover in the larder. She wrapped the chicken in grease-proof paper before stuffing everything into a hessian shopping bag hanging from a hook on the door. She was gone from the kitchen before the warden returned.

She found Alfie where she'd left him: a sorry-looking figure in his crumpled suit, minus his collar and tie, cowering as he held one arm across his ribs. *Not such a big cheese after all,* she thought as she thrust the bag of food at him. *He's no match for Moyes and Nixon.*

Perhaps he spotted the contempt in her eyes. In any case he saw something that made him lash out with the knife concealed in his free hand. The blade flashed towards her and she jumped backwards just in time. *That'll teach her!*

'What was that for?' Doreen demanded, trembling all over and with her eyes fixed on the knife. *Never underestimate the underdog* was the lesson she'd just learned.

'Because!' he snarled back. He closed the blade of the flick-knife with a sharp click then pocketed it. Hearing voices at the front of the house, he realized it was time to make himself scarce. 'Don't let me down,' he warned before he backed out of the yard then through the gate into the garden.

'Who was that?' Brenda asked Doreen as she and Poppy wheeled their bikes into the yard.

'No one.'

'That's funny. I could've sworn I heard you talking to someone.'

Doreen shook her head and hid her grazed hand behind her back. 'That was me singing.'

'It didn't sound very tuneful, did it, Pops?'
Brenda wheeled her bike past Doreen into the
stable.

'Tone deaf, that's me.' She set off towards the
house. 'Now, if you'll excuse me, I have to go
and get changed. Donald's picking me up at
seven o'clock sharp.'

# 19

'Do you know how they saved Canterbury Cathedral?' Twelve days before Bill was due to join his regiment, Grace was keen to concentrate on the few positive stories that had been reported in recent weeks. 'The Dean there gave orders for criss-crossing ladders to be laid across the whole roof so that firemen could run over it and sweep off any incendiaries that scored a direct hit. It said on the News that it worked a treat.'

Bill held her hand as they walked by the side of Kelsey Tarn. What could be more peaceful than to look out over the calm water at the sun setting on the spectacular limestone escarpment? 'They could do with having the Dean stationed in Bath or half a dozen of our cities that Jerry blitzes on a nightly basis. Someone should tell Mr Churchill as much.'

'I'm sure he already knows.' To Grace, this whiff of criticism of the Prime Minister seemed disloyal. 'In any case, he has to concentrate on Libya and Rommel for the time being.'

'I can't argue with that,' Bill agreed. Looking ahead and reading between the lines, he expected his unit to be among those trained in desert warfare before being shipped out to North Africa, but the less said to Grace about that the better. 'Changing the subject, I hear that the police have been stopping all buses in and out of

Hawkshead, Attercliffe and Burnside, searching for the POWs. They think they might be heading for one of the aerodromes to the north-east of York. That's too far for them to reach on foot without being spotted.'

'But that doesn't make sense. They'd be even more likely to be caught if they tried to catch a bus.'

'Not if they split up into twos and threes and got out of their uniforms into some sort of mufti. Anyway, it's a shame all round. Until now the Italians had a good name with farmers up and down the dale.'

'They were champion to work with,' Grace agreed. 'Poor Una still sticks up for them, of course.'

'She'd have them back like a shot, no doubt.' From a distance Bill found it hard to sympathize with Una's predicament, though she was bound to be torn between loyalty to her country and heartbreak. 'I reckoned she was on a sticky wicket from the start. I told Mum as much when she first got in tow with . . . what's his name?'

'Angelo.' Grace didn't want to pursue this subject either. Her real desire was for the two of them to make the most of their remaining precious time together, soaking up the sun's last rays, watching concentric ripples appear on the still surface of the tarn as fish rose to the surface to catch flies. The rings widened and faded, one after the other, until the sun finally disappeared and it was time to drive home.

'Shall we call in at Mum's?' Bill suggested on the way back.

It was agreed, so he drove into the village and drew up outside his mother's house. Hand in hand once more, he and Grace walked up the path.

Edith came to the door with a worried look. 'What's the matter? Have they caught Alfie Craven?'

'Not yet, as far as I know.' Bill gave her a peck on the cheek and stepped inside. 'The problem is he knows the lie of the land better than most. He could hold out for weeks if necessary.'

Edith drew Grace over the threshold. 'Give me your hat. Go into the sitting room. Is this to do with the prisoners, then?'

'Mother, sit yourself down. Nothing is wrong. We thought it would be nice to drop in, that's all.'

'It's not too late, is it?' Grace suspected that Edith was struggling to appear hospitable as she went to a cabinet and took out a bottle and three cut-glass sherry glasses. 'We don't want to keep you up.'

'No, it's lovely to have company.' Below the polite surface ran a torrent of unexpressed emotions; it was the effort to conceal them that put such a strain on her. Terror was uppermost. It tugged at her and almost swept her away. Terror of Bill going away to war and never coming back, of him facing enemy fire, of bombs scoring a direct hit, of shrapnel tearing into his dear flesh, of his lifeless body lying in the desert sand. Such nightmares surfaced only at night as Edith slipped in and out of sleep. 'How is Maurice coping with learning the business?' she asked with ill-concealed strain.

'Pretty well. It's quite straightforward and he's a quick learner.'

Grace tipped her glass and felt the sweet liquid trickle over her tongue then hit the back of her throat with sudden warmth. She and Edith must join forces to support Bill in his decision, she realized. 'Maurice knows he'll have you to turn to if something goes wrong.'

'Oh, I know nothing about tractors.' Edith's lady-like disclaimer harked back to the days when Vince had been in charge of all things practical and financial. But she was grateful to Grace nevertheless. 'Have you heard how Hilda is managing?'

'She's coping well, considering.'

'She's not letting things slip?' Edith had been too busy to visit Fieldhead since fresh news about the burglary had broken and she'd had to put in several further requests to County Office for extra funds; she'd had to fill in official forms and make seemingly endless telephone calls to explain events. 'The girls are being properly looked after?'

'Yes, according to Joyce there's no need to worry on that score. You can always rely on Hilda.'

'Let's hope so.' Edith's memory went back to the early days when young Alfie had been attending the village school. 'But everyone has a weak spot, Hilda included. I'm afraid Alfie is hers.'

'What's your weak spot, Mum?' Bill said with a wink at Grace. 'Would it be me, by any chance?'

Edith sipped her sherry then sighed. 'You say that, son, but I hope I didn't spoil you when you were little. I always insisted on good manners and being kind to others. You were never rude.'

Grace teased him about this later that night, when they were in bed with only a cool cotton sheet to cover them. 'I remember you at school. You were the class monitor in the year above. I thought you were the bee's knees.'

'But now you know better.' There was enough daylight to make out her dark grey eyes with their long lashes and fair eyebrows arching elegantly above. He followed the irresistible urge to kiss her lips.

'No, I still think so.' She smiled as she pulled away then her face took on a wistful expression. The days and nights were sliding by. Bill would soon be gone. 'Nothing you do will ever make me change my mind about that.'

★   ★   ★

Working with pigs had to be the worst job going and Poppy was miserable as Roland set her and Una the task of turning his four beasts and their eighteen piglets out of their ramshackle, tin-roofed sty into a paddock behind Major's stable. To add insult to injury, it was raining heavily and they were both soaked to the skin.

''This little piggy went to market.'' Una poked one of the fat piglets with a long stick and sent it squealing through puddles after its mother. Others scattered across the yard.

Poppy tried in vain to herd them towards the

fenced paddock. One of the sows broke away from the wriggling, squirming group then set off at an absurd gallop down a recently planted field of wheat, her barrel-shaped body rolling from side to side, her sharp trotters digging deep into the soft earth.

'There goes breakfast for the whole of Burnside,' Roland commented wryly as Poppy followed Lady Macbeth and he lent Una a hand to usher the remaining three sows into the paddock. Then he took a handful of potato peelings from a bucket stationed by the gate post and scattered them. 'You watch; this will soon sort them out.'

As predicted, the sows and errant piglets came charging for the food — all except for Poppy's runaway, who proved to be more interested in digging up roots in a hedge bottom than in rejoining the others.

A stout stick was the answer, Poppy decided. As Lady M grubbed in the ditch, she seized a forked branch lying nearby and gave her backside a sharp poke. The pig ignored her so she jabbed again. 'Nasty, horrid thing!' she said out loud as the pig carried on digging without batting an eyelid. 'Just you wait. From now on I'll be eating bacon every chance I get!'

'Here, try this.' Neville offered her a carrot. He'd appeared seemingly out of nowhere, though in fact he'd been waiting all morning for the opportunity to talk to Poppy alone. From the hayloft window he'd seen her chase after Lady Macbeth and taken a different route down the hill, coming up behind her as Poppy jabbed ineffectively at the muddy sow.

'Here, nice piggy!' Suspecting that Neville wanted to corner her for another heart-to-heart, Poppy fended him off by crouching at the edge of the wet ditch to thrust the carrot under the pig's snout. 'Ta, Neville. I can manage now.'

But he hung around with a hangdog look, letting the heavy rain fall on to his bare head, watching her slowly tempt the sow up the slippery bank. 'No one's come back for their money so far,' he muttered.

'Who do you mean?'

'You know.'

She did, of course, but she wanted to stay out of it. 'That's a blessing,' she said in an off-hand way.

'Everyone says Alfie daren't show his face.'

'I'm not surprised.' She kept her answer deliberately short.

'Here, give me that.' He snatched the carrot then tossed it over his shoulder. In a flash Lady M was out of the ditch and grubbing after it amongst the green wheat. Then Neville seized the stick from Poppy and started to herd the sow up the hill to where his father and Una stood waiting at the gate. Poppy trailed a few steps behind. 'What I told you about shoving the whole lot on the fire . . . I hope you haven't mentioned it to anyone.'

'For Pete's sake, Neville!' She ran to catch up, slipping and sliding as she went. 'I don't know why you let me in on it in the first place. It's got nothing to do with me.'

He gave Lady M's backside a whack. 'I've got

no one else to tell, have I? And I must have got the wrong idea. I thought you cared about what happened to me.'

'I do,' she protested.

He stopped to stare at her.

'But only in a friendly way.' She felt her face go red and saw how crestfallen he looked as his shoulders slumped and he turned away again. 'I'm sorry if I gave you the wrong impression. I didn't mean to.'

'Friends,' he mouthed. First Una and now Poppy; this was the second time in quick succession that Neville's case of calf love had gone unrequited. That was it; he made a resolution to give up on the romantic front from now on.

Poppy watched his head drop forward and the rain drip down his face. The bruises and cuts from Nixon and Moyes's visit had started to fade at last but still he looked a picture of misery. But what could she do? Neville was too young for her, and anyway he wasn't her type. However, she was soft-hearted enough to run after him and help shoo the bad-tempered sow towards the gate. 'I still say if you're scared those two men will come back and do their worst, go to the police,' she insisted. 'Make a clean breast of everything. It's the only way out.'

★ ★ ★

By the end of the afternoon the rain had eased and a watery sun shone through the dispersing clouds. Shortly after Poppy and Una had breathed a sigh of relief and set off on their bikes on their homeward journey, they met Elsie and Kathleen on the road into the village then Jean, Joyce and Grace on their way from Winsill Edge. Each swapped stories of the day as they cycled. Kathleen told of Emily Kellett's kitchen being overrun with rats yet again, while Jean grumbled about being pestered all day long by Horace Turnbull. 'He had the cheek to tell me I wouldn't be bad looking if only I had more meat on my bones. I said that it was a shame I couldn't say the same about him.'

'At least it's stopped raining.' Joyce came alongside Una, who'd stayed silent and solemn as they'd cycled along.

'Thank heavens.' Una murmured her reply. These last two days had been agony for her, wondering every minute of every hour how far Angelo and the other POWs had got and thinking of the endless dangers they might find themselves in.

'How are you bearing up today?' Joyce asked quietly. The church steeple was in sight and as they rounded the bend into the main street, she noticed two Land Rovers parked in the pub yard.

'I'm all right so long as I keep busy,' Una replied. 'It's the evenings and nights that I've started to dread.'

At the head of their little group, Grace turned into the yard to have a few words with her father, who stood talking to Squadron Leader Aldridge and an army sergeant.

Cliff called her across. 'Have you heard the

latest? They've picked up two of the Eyeties out near Braffield aerodrome.'

Una's heart missed several beats as she veered off the road into the yard. Joyce and the other girls stopped too.

'Which ones?' Grace asked Aldridge, who turned to the sergeant for information.

'Prisoner numbers 4701 and 3276.' The British NCO delivered the information in a clipped, no-nonsense voice. He was a chest-out, firm-jawed type with a trim moustache, who wore his stripes with cocky self-importance. 'They were picked up by three of our RAF boys on a back road a mile from the airfield.'

4701. 3276. Una held her breath and looked to Joyce for help.

Joyce raked through her memory. 'Ricci and Bianchi, if I remember rightly.'

Aldridge picked up on Una's reaction. Unlike the other girls, who had greeted the news with smiles of relief and praise for the eagle-eyed RAF men, she'd hung back and looked miserable. 'The other six will be hard on their heels,' he promised. 'My bet is that we'll have them all back in camp by this time tomorrow.'

'See?' Joyce squeezed Una's arm. 'That's not long to wait, is it?'

Jean butted in with a bull-in-a-china-shop comment of her own. 'You see, Sergeant, Una takes a special interest in one of the escapees.'

The soldier's shoulders went back a fraction and he shot Una a suspicious glance. 'Name?'

'Never mind,' Kathleen said, pulling Jean away.

'Name and number?' the sergeant insisted.

Una found herself stuttering a reply. 'Bachetti, number 3840.'

The soldier jerked his head towards Aldridge. 'That's the one with TB that I was telling you about.'

*TB? Tuberculosis.* Una's head spun.

Again Aldridge saw the effect on her. He drew Una and Joyce towards the entrance to the smithy and explained quietly. 'I'm afraid it's true. The army doctor received the result of the test he carried out on Bachetti. He made his diagnosis at the beginning of the week. That's one reason why it's so important for us to bring him back.'

Joyce too was shocked. The word 'tuberculosis' brought to mind skeletal figures with lesions on their lungs, coughing up blood and dying a lingering death. 'Angelo needs to go to hospital.'

'Right away,' Aldridge confirmed. 'TB is an infectious disease. He should be in isolation. They'll have to test all the POWs that Bachetti has been in contact with — it's likely that others have contracted the illness too.'

'TB.' Una was hardly able to whisper the dreaded name. Her heart felt squeezed almost to the point of being unable to breathe. *My Angelo. My love.*

Aldridge offered what little comfort he could. 'It's a wonder what clean air and rest can do to keep it at bay, provided it's detected in its early stages. And the doctor tells me there's an antibiotic medication they may be able to give; something new that's being developed.'

'That's good,' Joyce said cautiously. Her mind stuck on the contagious aspect of the situation. Never mind about poor Angelo, what if he'd passed on the illness to Una?

*I didn't see it coming! I thought he had nothing worse than a cough and an upset stomach. I should have known the moment I saw him!*

'Una!' Joyce said softly and urgently. 'Squadron Leader Aldridge is busy. We must let him get on.'

He put a hand on her arm. 'I truly am sorry.'

She gazed at him with unseeing eyes.

'Come away, Una,' Joyce said. 'Let's get you home.'

★  ★  ★

A ride on Old Sloper was the only way to clear Brenda's head of the anxious thoughts buzzing round and round inside her head. Monday, Tuesday, Wednesday and now Thursday had dragged by with no letter from Les. *Am I banking on it too much?* she wondered as she kicked the bike into action. *He only arrived in Greenock late on Sunday. I should give him more time to write and tell me how much he's missing me. Then again, he did promise to write to me as soon as he could.*

The real question in Brenda's mind had been: how much was she missing Les? For the first twenty-four hours she hadn't been certain, but as time went on and she pictured him in his uniform in his new surroundings, she felt sharp pangs of loss and loneliness. She would be pitching hay or feeding pigs and she would suddenly stop to wonder what Les was doing at that moment. Or else she would lie on her bed in the evening, remembering things that he'd said to her, the way he'd looked when he'd said them. *Yes, I miss him*, she thought with a sigh as she kicked Sloper into action.

'Keep a lookout for those Eyeties!' Doreen called after her as she passed Brenda on the drive. 'They've picked up two of them; did you hear?'

'Yes, Joyce told me.' Mention of her friend once more reminded Brenda that she wasn't the only one to be dashing home after work to see what the postman had brought. Joyce was in the same boat and soon Grace would be too. They were three women in love caught up by wartime events, longing to hear from their men. As for Una and her consumptive Angelo, that was a different kettle of fish.

'Where are you off to in such a hurry?' Doreen's voice was almost drowned by the roar of Sloper's engine.

'I haven't a clue!' she called over her shoulder. 'Anywhere. It doesn't matter.'

Just to be out on the open road was the thing, with swallows swooping in and out of Peggy's barn, the dark bulk of Kelsey Crag on the horizon and eventually a decision to be made over whether to head into the village on the chance of a quiet chinwag with Grace or instead to head over Swinsty Moor and create that feeling of riding along on top of the world. She

343

chose the latter and opened the throttle. There was nothing like soaring over the hills, free as a bird.

Until she met Les's green sports car speeding towards her with the top down and Donald at the wheel.

He recognized her bike and braked hard. 'Hello, Brenda. We must stop meeting like this!'

'Hello, Donald.' He'd left a gap wide enough for her to ride through and she had every intention of carrying on.

'Have you heard from our jolly Jack Tar?' he asked as she eased past.

She stopped short. 'If you mean Les — no, not yet. Why, have you?'

'Hettie had a phone call from him . . . when was it? Tuesday night.'

Brenda felt an unexpected pang of jealousy. 'And?'

'He says learning the ropes is tougher than expected but so far he's still in one piece. Funny, I thought he'd at least let his fiancée know how he's getting on.'

'Oh, I expect he's too busy to write before the weekend.' Determined not to show Donald that she was disappointed, she steered the bike through the narrow gap. 'Cheerio and thanks.'

'For what?' He twisted round in his seat with a knowing smile.

'For passing on the news. And say hello to Hettie and your dad for me. Ta-ta!'

On she went, her heart plummeting as she rode into a dip then up a steep, slow hill. She tried to reason with herself. It was true, Les was bound to be kept busy from dawn till dusk. He would want to sit down and write a proper letter, not just dash off a scribbled note. There wouldn't be much privacy in his crowded billet and there was even a chance that he had written but the letter had been held up in the post. But still Brenda's heart was sore. Then she grew angry at herself. *It's as I feared; I've turned into a different person since I agreed to marry Les,* she thought. *Someone I never thought I'd be in a million years. I'm not carefree, take-me-as-I-come Brenda Appleby any more. What on earth is happening to me?*

She twisted the throttle to increase her speed, oblivious to the fact that Donald had turned his car around in the nearest gateway and was following her. She only caught sight of him in her wing mirror when the village of Attercliffe came into view.

*What now?* she thought with rising irritation.

He overtook her as she approached a bend. Then he braked and idled down the hill towards Dale End.

'Idiot!' she muttered to herself. *What's he playing at?*

Donald stuck out his right hand and indicated with a circling motion that he was about to stop in the middle of the road.

There was no alternative; she had to pull up behind him and watch him step out of the car.

He walked breezily towards her in an open-necked striped shirt and dark blue slacks, still with the confident smile 'I just had a thought. Since you're in this neck of the woods, why not drop in at our house for a drink and a chat? Hettie's at home. She can tell you more about how Les is getting on.'

The old Brenda would have said, 'No, thanks; I'm enjoying riding Old Sloper too much to stop,' and would have sailed on. But the new, engaged one found herself saying, 'Ta very much. I think I will.'

So she and Donald arrived at Dale End and went into the house together, with no sign that anyone else was there.

'Here, I'll take your coat and gloves,' Donald offered, spotting but not commenting on the ring on her left hand as she gave them to him. 'I've always fancied one of these leather jobs,' he said as he hung the old RAF jacket on the hall stand. 'Come into the sitting room. I'll get you a drink.'

She followed him into the familiar lounge, hoping to see Hettie out in the garden, tending her roses. There was no one out there and she felt increasingly uneasy as she watched Donald pour her a glass of Dubonnet.

'See, I remembered your favourite tipple,' he said with a wink. 'Sit down anywhere you like and tell me more about yourself, Miss Brenda.'

'There's nothing to tell.' *Idiot!* she said to herself this time. *What have you let yourself in for?*

He came and sat with his own drink on the arm of her easy chair. 'A little bird tells me different.'

'What do you mean?' She stood up abruptly and walked towards the French doors.

'Keep your hair on. I'm only saying I've heard

346

plenty of interesting things about you.'

'Who from?'

'From Les, for a start.'

The idea of the two brothers discussing her behind her back made her frown. She kept her face turned away from him.

'He's biased in your favour, of course. But I can see for myself that you're never going to bore the pants off a bloke the way some women do.'

*Enough!* She turned to face him. 'Where's Hettie?' she demanded. 'You said she'd be here.'

Straddling the chair arm, he swilled whisky around the bottom of his glass. 'She must have popped out. Never mind, it means we can have a cosy chat.'

Resisting the urge to rush from the room, Brenda raised what she hoped was a sophisticated eyebrow. 'About what, pray?'

'About my brother's sudden rush to the altar.'

'Les and I are not rushing anywhere.'

'I must admit, I was surprised. I didn't think you were his type.'

'I'm not anybody's type.' She put down her glass on a side table and strode angrily towards the door. 'Now, if you don't mind . . . '

He arrived there before her. 'Whoa! Me and my big mouth. I didn't mean to upset you. I'm pleased for Les. He's done well for himself.'

'I have to go. Let me pass, please.'

Donald put his hands up in surrender and stepped to one side. 'You can't blame us for being taken aback,' he said as he followed her across the hall. 'It's not just me. Hettie's another — you could have knocked her down with a feather when she heard the news. And Dad's the same. When Les told him about the ring, there was an almighty bust-up.'

'What do you mean?'

'Let's just say my brother packed his bag and went off to Greenock in a huff.'

Brenda pulled on her jacket. 'Why are you telling me this?' she demanded. 'You can't change what's happened. Les and I are engaged and that's that!'

'I'm only saying.'

'Well, don't. And listen to this, Donald White. From now on, keep your distance. Don't ever try it on with me again, do you hear? I've had enough of your snide remarks and nasty, insinuating looks. You ought to be ashamed.'

'Of what?' he exclaimed. 'Of being attracted to my brother's fiancée? A chap can't help that, you know.'

'For God's sake!' Brenda opened the door. 'You're meant to be going out with Doreen. Think of her, if no one else!'

'Doreen?' he repeated with raised eyebrows, leaning casually against the door post and watching her storm off.

'It's not funny!' Brenda glanced over her shoulder in time to see Hettie push past Donald then follow her on to the drive.

'Your gloves,' Hettie said, handing them over and speaking with calm deliberation. 'They were on the hall stand. I couldn't let you leave without them.'

# 20

Late on Thursday evening, Doreen was up to her elbows in soap suds in the hostel laundry room. She was keeping a low profile, torn in different directions over the problem concerning Nixon, Moyes and Alfie, which she'd stewed over for two days but still reached no conclusion. Should she bow to Alfie's threats by telephoning Moyes and dropping in the red herring about the number 15 bus? Or was she more afraid of where that would leave her if Moyes and Nixon discovered the truth? Then again, if she followed Moyes's orders to the letter and he and Nixon returned for Alfie, their victim might slip through the net and come after her to exact his revenge. Round and round she went in ever decreasing circles.

*All over a couple of pairs of nylons, a lace brassiere and a bottle of cheap perfume!* She laid the sleeve of her work shirt flat on the draining board and scrubbed hard at a grass stain, as if to take out her frustration. *I had no idea what a low-down, dirty rat Alfie Craven would turn out to be. If I'd have known, I wouldn't have touched his presents with a barge pole.*

The stubborn stain refused to shift.

*It serves me right.* Doreen plunged the shirt into a bowl of clean water then wrung it out over the stone sink before slinging it over a clothes line next to her corduroy trousers and two pairs of socks. *If I'd had any common sense, I wouldn't have got myself into this mess in the first place.*

'That's it!' she said out loud as she stood back and surveyed the dripping laundry. 'I've made up my mind.'

She dried her hands then marched along the corridor, straight to the warden's office. 'Knock, knock,' she said through the half-open door.

There was no reply so Doreen stole into the room. She picked up the telephone and, when the operator came on the line, she quietly gave her Moyes's number and asked to be put through. There was a succession of clicks then Nixon's voice answered.

'Who is that?' he asked, short and not so sweet.

'Hello, Mr Nixon. Doreen Wells here. I have some news for you about Alfie Craven.'

'You do? Then spit it out.'

'He was seen getting on to a number fifteen bus to Northgate.'

'When?'

'On Tuesday morning. I only got to hear about it an hour or so ago. That's why I haven't been in touch before now.'

'Who saw him?'

'I don't know. But whoever it was can't have realized Alfie was on the run because word didn't get round straight away. Oh, and he had his suitcase with him.'

There was a pause while Nixon weighed up the information. 'Anything else?'

'Yes. There's only one bus a day from

Burnside into town. It leaves here at half nine, arriving in Station Street around eleven.' Pleased with herself for delivering a convincing performance, Doreen waited for Nixon to sign off with a thank-you and a pat on the back.

'Very good.'

That was it. Then a loud click followed by silence.

When she put down the receiver and turned to leave, Hilda was standing in the doorway.

'Half past nine on Tuesday morning,' she repeated slowly and steadily. 'That's news to me.'

'Mrs Craven, you made me jump!'

Hilda didn't blink. 'You might have thought to mention it to me before you dialled 999. After all, I am his mother.'

'999: the police? Oh, yes.' Doreen felt the situation spin out of control once more. How could she fib her way out of this one? 'I was meaning to but you weren't here when I knocked. So I went ahead anyway.'

Hilda didn't blink. 'Alfie, with his suitcase?'

'Yes, so I heard.'

'Tuesday morning.' Straight away she realized that this didn't stack up. As the person in charge of the kitchen as well as every other aspect of life at Field-head, Hilda was only too well aware that food had gone missing on Tuesday evening — half a chicken, a loaf of bread, fish paste and some cheese, to be exact. She'd discovered the theft straight after dinner but hadn't plucked up the courage to make it known. For she knew with sickening certainty that Alfie must be the thief. Deciding to keep quiet, she prayed that this would be the last time that her wastrel son would turn up on her doorstep.

'Are you certain?' she asked Doreen, who had backed up against the desk.

'Quite sure.' She took a deep gulp of air. 'You can relax; Alfie's out of your hair. I've handed everything over to the police.'

'Thank you.' Hilda squashed down her anger as she held open the door. Who was Doreen to take matters into her own hands — worse still, to tell her how to react? And in any case, it made very little sense. On top of the matter of the missing food, a return to his enemies' stronghold of Northgate was as good as putting his own head in the noose. Alfie of all people knew better than that.

'You're not upset with me, I hope?'

'Of course not.'

'Good. That's a relief.'

Hilda's keen gaze penetrated deep below the surface though her words were bland. 'Go up and get a good night's sleep, Doreen. You're on early morning milking duty at Home Farm tomorrow. You won't want to be late.'

★   ★   ★

'Alfie was spotted getting on a bus.' Now that the die was cast, Doreen saw no harm in broadcasting the lie. On her way up from the warden's office, she resolved to cover her tracks by making an anonymous telephone call to the police station first thing in the morning. Meanwhile, she was happy to share the false information with Poppy and Joyce. *Why not? I'm a dab hand at this fibbing lark*, she told herself as she walked into the room to find them on their beds, wiling away the time until she joined them for lights-out.

When? Why? Who?

She answered their quick-fire questions with airy nonchalance.

'Good Lord!' Poppy's thoughts flew to Neville and the question of whether Alfie's departure improved or worsened his situation.

Joyce picked up on her reaction. 'What's wrong, Pops?'

'Nothing. I'm flabbergasted, that's all.'

'So was Ma Craven when I told her.' Doreen took her night things out from under her pillow: a pair of mauve silk pyjamas with white piping around collar and cuffs. She was half-undressed when Brenda burst into the room.

'Donald White is the absolute end!' she cried, her face white with anger. She hadn't even taken off her gloves and jacket before running up the stairs two at a time. 'How can you stand him?' she accused Doreen. 'He makes me want to run a mile!'

'Why? What's he done now?' Doreen pulled up her pyjama trousers then took off her petticoat and brassiere without seeming to mind that all eyes were on her.

'Such cheek!' Brenda fumed. 'He tried it on with me. I'm engaged to Les, for goodness' sake! I love that man with all my heart.'

'Sit down.' Joyce made room on her bed.

'And Donald's not free himself.' She flashed a

meaningful look in Doreen's direction.

Slowly and methodically, Doreen put on her silk jacket and fastened the buttons.

'What exactly did he do?' Poppy held her breath.

'He only sat on the arm of my chair and came this close!' Brenda held up her forefinger and thumb. 'Making remarks, breathing his whisky breath all over me.'

'Where and when was this?' Joyce invited Brenda to talk it out fully.

'At Dale End, just now.'

For the first time Doreen showed a flicker of annoyance. 'What were you doing there?'

'He invited me! To talk to Hettie — only she wasn't there, of course. Well, she was, but she left Donald to it as a test of my loyalty to Les.'

'Left him to do what?' Poppy grew more alarmed. Had Les's brother actually laid hands on Brenda?

Brenda ignored the anxious question. 'His sister kept out of the way until the very last minute. I'm sure she knew that Donald would try it on with me; I could tell by the look on her face. And this happened after she allowed me to think that she'd accepted me into the family — a big miscalculation on my part, as it turns out.'

Joyce recognized that Brenda felt especially let down by this. 'You think Hettie deliberately left you to Donald's tender mercies?'

'Yes, it was as if she was trying to prove a point.'

'And did she?' Doreen asked sharply.

Brenda was furious. 'No, of course not. What

do you think I am?'

With a toss of her head, Doreen turned down her sheets.

'Don't pretend you didn't hear me. I want to know: do you actually think I would go behind Les's back and yours too, for that matter?'

'You can please yourself. I don't care.'

Brenda appealed to Joyce and Poppy. 'Tell her I wouldn't!'

'What's that old saying about protesting too much?' With calculated carelessness, Doreen took her sponge bag from the drawer of her bedside cabinet. 'Now if you don't mind, I'm off to brush my teeth.'

Brenda rushed to block the door. 'Doreen, listen to me. You might not care, but I do. You need to know what Donald gets up to, the way he carries on with other women.'

'Oh Brenda, pipe down. You're not telling me anything I don't already know.' Unable to shove Brenda out of her way, Doreen retreated and flung the bag down on her bed. 'I'm not stupid. Donald likes to be seen out with me once in a while and he likes me for other things as well, but nothing goes deep with him. It's all on the surface.'

The surprise confession took them all aback.

Doreen gave a short laugh. 'Put your hands over your ears, Pops, you're too young to hear this. Donald White made it plain right from the start: I'm good for one thing and one thing only.'

Joyce spoke first. 'And you're happy to go along with that? Why?'

'Why not? It's a way to get on in this world.

Look at the nice treats I can get my hands on, for a start.'

'Like what?'

'As many free drinks as I want, rides in a sports car with the roof down and the wind in my hair.'

'You don't mean it.' Brenda's anger was replaced by profound disappointment. 'You must know that you're worth more. We all are!'

'Are we?' Doreen sank down on to her bed. 'I mean, let's be honest. Isn't that what it's all about — the sex thing between a man and a woman? Everything else — the wedding dresses, the promises to love, honour and obey — is just a fairy tale we tell ourselves.'

'You're wrong,' Joyce argued earnestly. 'There's so much more. At the risk of having you throw it back in my face, there's listening and learning to know the heart of a man, to see the goodness in him that lies hidden far beneath the surface, not to mention the fears and doubts, the darkness within. That's what a woman loves. There, I've made my speech!'

'Yes, Joyce, bravo.' Doreen filled the silence with slow, ironic applause. 'I've yet to see goodness in any man and I've had plenty of experience.'

'And look where it's got you.' Brenda didn't hold back. 'I'm sorry, Doreen. At one time I might have agreed you had a point but now I'm well and truly on Joyce's side.'

'Bully for you.' Doreen took the pins out of her hair and let it fall loose around her shoulders. 'But ta anyway, both of you, for trying to steer me on to the straight and narrow. And honestly, Pops, you should probably listen to them, not me.'

'Why are you crying?' Brenda turned her attention to the junior member of their group. 'I'm sorry if it was hearing me shout and stamp about.'

'No, It's Neville.' Poppy looked at all three in mute appeal then was overcome by a fit of sobbing.

Another confused silence fell in the small, cramped room. Outside in the wood, rooks went to roost and a solitary owl hooted.

'Neville?' Doreen and Joyce chorused.

'Yes. He's burned Alfie's money.'

'Is this the same money that you told me about?' A puzzled Joyce felt her way towards the truth.

Poppy nodded and cried harder.

'Hush. There's no need to be so upset.' Brenda sat down beside her.

'What do you mean, he burned some money?' In Doreen's world, nobody in their right mind set fire to hard-earned cash. 'Has he gone soft in the head?'

'No. He was scared of another thrashing.' Poppy explained through her tears, jumping from one fact to another. 'It wasn't Alfie who gave Neville the beating; it was two other men.'

Doreen was suddenly enlightened. 'Clive Nixon and Howard Moyes. But don't worry, Pops; Alfie was seen catching a bus out of the village so they'll soon be hot on his tail. We're not likely to see any of them again in the near future.' The lie was already so deeply embedded that she was scarcely aware that she'd made the whole thing up. *I'm only telling Poppy what she wants to hear*, she thought. *Where's the harm in that?*

'A bus to where?' Brenda asked suspiciously, the guarded look on Doreen's face telling her that all was not as it seemed.

'To Northgate. Like I said before we were so rudely interrupted, I just broke the news to Ma Craven. She's cut up about it, as you can imagine.'

'Thank heavens. I can tell Neville he's safe from now on.' Poppy attempted to smile.

'Only if Alfie did actually catch the bus,' Brenda pointed out. 'Come off it, Doreen. You're up to something.'

There was a stunned silence.

'I know you; you made the whole thing up,' Brenda insisted.

Doreen felt her cheeks flame bright red. 'Oh yes, Brenda, you're Gypsy Rose Lee all of a sudden. Where's your crystal ball?'

Brenda ignored the taunt. 'Why have you gone red? I know it's a big fat lie. But why?'

Out of the blue Doreen felt a sudden, strong prick of conscience. 'Don't all look at me like that!'

Poppy and Joyce couldn't help staring. As Brenda pursued her quarry, they braced themselves for more.

'What do you have to gain by pulling the wool over our eyes?'

Doreen gave in with a loud sigh. 'All right, it's

a fib. I was in a jam. I made it up because Alfie told me to.'

'You made it up?' Poppy echoed.

'He had a knife in his hand. I was sure he'd use it if I didn't do as I was told.'

'Which was what?' Joyce intervened.

'He said I had to telephone Nixon and Moyes and lie about him getting on the bus.'

'A knife,' Brenda muttered through clenched teeth. This was where mixing with black market crooks got you.

The cat was out of the bag and there was no putting it back in. Doreen sat down next to Poppy and took her hand. 'Listen to this, Pops. I was trying to cheer you up, but the fact of the matter is that Alfie is small beer in comparison with the dreaded Nixon and Moyes. And now Neville's gone and burned their profits. You can see where that might lead.'

Poppy swallowed hard then looked to Joyce and Brenda for comfort that never came.

'And you've told them a deliberate lie,' Brenda reminded the culprit. She glanced at Joyce, who nodded in agreement. 'The whole thing is a mess. And you two seem to have landed right in the thick of it.'

⋆　⋆　⋆

Betty Gates was by far the most popular woman in the remote villages where she delivered the Royal Mail. People hung out of their bedroom windows awaiting the morning post. They ran out and threw their arms around her when she brought long-awaited letters from across the seas or from naval, army and air force bases throughout the land. Mothers, daughters, wives and sisters cried tears of relief as they tore them open and shared their contents with a patient Betty, her curly brown hair hidden under a headscarf, face ruddy and legs strong after months of cycling up hill and down dale.

'Here's a letter for you,' she informed Brenda as she handed over Friday's delivery.

Brenda was up and dressed, ready for action at Peggy's farm. Her hands trembled with anticipation as she opened the letter and her eyes went straight to the signature. 'Your loving fiancé, Les xxx. PS: SWALK. You see, I didn't forget.'

*At last!* Brenda clutched the longed-for letter to her chest as she vanished into the common room to absorb it.

'And one for you.' Betty held up a letter for Joyce, who had just come down the stairs.

Joyce took it and recognized Edgar's handwriting. 'Ta. I'll save it for later.' Knowing that tingling anticipation of an event was often as pleasurable as the experience itself, she slipped the letter into her pocket then went into breakfast with the broadest of smiles.

'I'll leave the rest with you,' Betty said to Hilda, who had just emerged from the office.

As the post woman fastened her canvas satchel and departed, Hilda began to sort through the pile — two letters for Poppy, one for Elsie, three for Kathleen. She laid them out carefully on the narrow hall table then turned to find Doreen eyeing her nervously from the bottom of the stairs. 'What's wrong?' she bristled. 'Why aren't you at breakfast? You're not poorly again?'

'Not exactly, no.' She wasn't feeling too hot, it was true. 'I didn't get much sleep, though. I had a lot on my mind.'

'Ah, Alfie!' Sixth sense told the warden what this was about.

The usually upbeat, confident Doreen was close to tears as she nodded. 'I made a mistake, It turns out he didn't get on that bus.'

'You don't say.' Hilda's tone showed that she wasn't surprised.

'And I didn't telephone the police either.'

'I see.' She'd heard enough. 'Spare me the excuses and the crocodile tears, Doreen. Remind me who you're working with today.'

'With Jean at Home Farm again.'

'Very well. Eat your breakfast then get yourself off at the double. But be warned; you haven't heard the last of this.'

* * *

Morning routine at the hostel overrode all these ups and downs: the porridge, the toast with a scraping of butter, the clattering of dishes and cutlery, the dashing upstairs to take out hair curlers and don head-scarves or hats, the checking of the weather outside, the cheery goodbyes.

Then the working day took over. Sacks were heaved, hay was forked, curds were separated then strained, fields harrowed and seeds planted.

'I'll see you at the Institute at seven o'clock,'

361

Grace called to Poppy and Joyce as they split off after a shift at Winsill Edge.

'Why, what's happening?' Poppy had assumed that her day was done and that she could spend a quiet evening reading a magazine and trying to put Neville to the back of her mind.

Grace had dismounted from her bike and was wheeling it through her front gate. 'They're showing a Ministry of Information film, telling us how to improve yields, et cetera. The pressure is on ever since Jerry invaded Russia.'

'Do we have to go?'

'Afraid so.' Joyce waved Grace goodbye. 'The last thing any farmer round here wants is a bad grade from a government inspector, so we're obliged to keep up to date with the various ways to make silage and which wood to burn to make the best ash fertilizer.'

'I can't wait.' Poppy sighed. 'Honestly, though, it'll send me to sleep. I'm worn out as it is,' she complained as they cycled on.

Grace, meanwhile, went into the house to lay the table for tea. Looking at her watch, she saw that she had time to nip across the road into the wood at the back of the pub to forage for firewood ready for winter — you could never be too well prepared for the cold months, she knew. So she took an empty sack from the bike shed then made her way across the road into the pub yard, waving at her father still hard at work in the smithy. 'I forgot to leave a note for Bill,' she called. 'If you see him, tell him I'm collecting wood. I'll be back by six.'

She went on across the field with a pleasant

362

feeling that she would enjoy the cool calm of the trees. The grass here was due for scything, she noticed, and there was a stretch of wall that needed repairing. She would make sure that her father mentioned it to Lionel Foster, who owned both the field and the area of woodland which she climbed a stile to enter.

A light breeze lifted the leaves of the birch trees straight ahead. The ground was soft underfoot. This had been a grand idea, she realized: half an hour in the dappled light, sorting through fallen branches, choosing ones that she could carry back home. She breathed in the damp, peaty smell of leaf litter and the sweet scent of a wild rose bush growing up around the trunk of a tall, straight elm. Ahead was a dense thicket of rhododendron bushes still in bloom, their dull, spear-shaped leaves rising to head height, silently inviting her in.

There was plenty of wood here; in fact there was a pile of old logs almost hidden by low branches, so Grace stooped to fill her sack. Hearing a sudden movement, she glanced up but saw nothing. She worked on until the sack was almost full then tested its weight to see if she was able to carry it. There was another sound of a twig snapping underfoot. A badger perhaps, but then it was the wrong time of day. Too heavy for a fox or a dog. A deer, then?

Grace parted the leaves to peer into the centre of the rhododendron thicket and came face to face with Alfie Craven.

'Good Lord!' she exclaimed. The whites of his eyes stood out in the shadows, a gash on his cheek seeped pus and blood.

'Oh no you don't!' He caught hold of her before she could step back. She used her weight to drag him from his hiding place but she couldn't shake him off. 'Alfie, you look like death. Let me go. What are you doing?'

'What's it look like?' He kept tight hold of her arm and swung her against the nearest tree trunk, where he trapped her by shoving his shoulder against her chest and bringing his face close to hers. 'I'm saying hello to my old friend Grace Kershaw.'

'Grace Mostyn now. Alfie, let go of me!'

'No chance.' Days of living like an animal had heightened his proclivity for violence. He thrust his forearm against her throat, blocking her windpipe and watching her struggle for breath. 'Not until you answer a few questions.'

She nodded desperately and he released the pressure.

'One, have you got anything to eat with you?'

'No.'

'Can you get me something?'

Another nod.

'Good girl. Bread, cheese, ham, whatever. Bring it here.' As she tried to pull free, he shoved her back against the trunk and threatened to throttle her once more. 'Two, has Doreen spread the word about me leaving Burnside?'

She resisted the pressure on her throat. 'I don't know. I'm not living at Fieldhead, remember. I don't always pick up what's going on there.'

'A fat lot of good you are!' He took out his

frustration by shaking her then shoving even harder than before. Grace's back thudded against the tree, forcing air out of her lungs.

'Three, any sign of Moyes and his sidekick?'

'Who?' she pleaded, trying to hook her hands under his arm and prise herself free.

'Two blokes in a Morris Oxford: one tall and thin; one small and thickset, wears glasses. You can't miss them.'

'No, I haven't seen them.' If only he would let go and let her breathe properly, she might be able to reason with him. As it was, she felt helpless.

His eyes blazed with fury. 'Listen. This is what you're going to do. First, the grub. Bring it here and leave it hanging from this tree. I'll pick it up when I know the coast is clear. Second, do what I asked that useless tart Doreen to do. Make up a decent story about me leaving the area. Got that?'

*Anything to get away from you, from your nasty, unshaven face, your savage eyes.* She tried to gasp air into her lungs.

'Third — '

Bill crept up from behind and hooked his arm around Alfie's throat, dragging him backwards and releasing Grace.

She gave a choking cry and watched the two men stagger backwards, lose their balance and fall in a heap.

Alfie landed on top. He was first on his feet, taking out his flick-knife and brandishing it in front of Bill, who crouched with arms out-stretched like a wrestler in a fairground ring.

'Here comes the cavalry in the nick of time!' With the knife in his hand, Alfie assumed a mocking control. 'The stakes are a tad higher now, eh, Grace?'

Bill edged towards her until Alfie slashed the blade through the air and drove him back. He came between Bill and Grace, turning his head and talking over his shoulder. 'You see the problem? Bill hasn't got a knife. He's the underdog.'

'Stop it, Alfie. What good will this do?'

'Suppose I agree to put this knife away, what then? No, don't bother; we all know what happens next. You and your brand-new husband trot off out of this wood and find the nearest telephone. Before we know it, the coppers are crawling all over the show.'

Bill raised both hands to shield his face. He'd got home from work to find places set for tea but no sign of Grace. He'd crossed the road to the smithy and learned from Cliff where Grace had gone. He'd followed her into the wood and discovered Alfie bloody Craven attacking his wife. Knife or no knife, he would charge the bugger, knock his block off, stamp on him until he was dead.

'Oh no you don't!' Alfie lashed out again as Bill launched himself. The blade met solid flesh but even as Alfie pulled the knife out, Bill kept on coming, taller and stronger than him and with no thought for his own safety, only for Grace and what Alfie had put her through. He overpowered him and wrestled him down to the ground, grasping for the knife.

Grace saw that Bill was bleeding. A dark patch appeared high on his chest and spread rapidly, staining his white shirt crimson.

'Drop it!' He grasped Alfie's wrist and banged his hand against a rock. 'Drop the knife.'

Alfie resisted. He too saw the blood.

'Alfie — Bill, please!' How had it come to this? What should she do?

Alfie felt Bill's grip weaken. He disentangled himself then rolled, knife still in his hand. Bill made a desperate lunge to catch hold of his leg. Then Grace was between them, down on her knees, pulling them apart. Bill gave a long, loud gasp and sank against her. Alfie broke free.

'What now?' She cradled Bill's head and looked up to challenge their attacker. 'Do you intend to kill us both?'

'Quiet!' Back on his feet, Alfie tried to assemble his thoughts.

'It's either that or run.' Bill's wound was wide and deep; Grace needed to stop the bleeding with anything that came to hand. So she tore off the scarf she'd been wearing around her head and pressed it hard against his chest. 'Run, Alfie, while you have the chance!'

Whatever fix he was in, he didn't want two dead bodies on his hands. Where would he hide them, for a start? The notion of burying them here in the wood struck even Alfie as absurd. He stared at the knife then down at Grace and Bill.

'Quickly — go!' Her hands were covered in Bill's blood. 'Stay awake,' she pleaded with Bill, as his eyelids started to flicker and close.

He heard her and tried to speak. 'Grace . . .'

'Grace?' A voice shouted from the stile at the edge of the field. It was her father, on his way to find them.

'Grace, where are you?' Cliff called from the birch trees that fringed the wood. 'Did Bill find you?'

'Dad! Dad's coming,' she whispered to Bill. 'We'll get you to hospital.'

His eyes closed again.

'Here!' she called out strongly. 'Dad, we're over here!'

Alfie heard bushes being pushed aside and a heavy tread approaching. With a last glance at Bill sinking into unconsciousness and at Grace holding him in her arms, he flicked the knife shut and melted away.

# 21

'It's not like Grace to miss work.'

Joyce and Poppy had arrived at Brigg Farm to discover that Grace wouldn't be joining them as planned. Joyce made the comment to Roland as they leaned their bikes against the hayloft steps then turned to him for further information.

'She was listed on the rota,' Poppy told the out-of-sorts farmer. 'Isn't she feeling well?'

'It's not her, it's Bill' Roland had caught up on events the previous night, when he and Neville had called in at the pub and found Cliff manning the bar. The place had been unusually quiet for a Friday night; no Land Girls, no Canadians, only the old-timers from the village and surrounding farms. The atmosphere had struck him as odd the minute they'd walked in.

'Where's your lass?' he'd asked as his pint was pulled.

'At the hospital.' Cliff had offered no further explanation.

Maurice, standing nearby, had been the one to enlighten Roland. 'Haven't you heard? Bill Mostyn's at death's door. Alfie Craven stuck a knife into him in the woods at the back of here. From what they say, he's hanging on by a thread.'

'Bloody hell.'

If the news had sent shock waves through Roland, the effect on Neville had been as if his world had come to a sudden, catastrophic end. His face had turned ashen and he'd gone weak at the knees. Maurice had only just placed a stool under him before his legs had turned to jelly and he'd slumped against the bar.

Maurice had relished his role as imparter of dramatic news. 'Cliff here called the ambulance, didn't you, Cliff? By the time it arrived, everyone in the village had heard what Alfie had done. Edith and Grace went off in the ambulance with Bill, A few of us went searching for the lunatic before it got dark, but no luck.'

'So that's where Grace is,' Roland reported to Poppy and Joyce now. 'At Bill's bedside. You two girls will have to do the work of three. You can start by harnessing Major and taking the wagon down to Low Field. Those last hayricks need bringing in before the skies open and it pours down.'

It was hard to concentrate on the task but they did their best to knuckle down. Poppy led the shire horse out of his stable then held him steady while Joyce put on his tack. The most difficult part was making Major stay in position long enough to hitch him up to the cart. He obviously had his own ideas for the morning, which didn't include pulling heavy hay loads up a steep hill, so he stamped his feet and tossed his huge head, refusing to stand still while Poppy and Joyce tackled the job in hand.

'Where's Neville this morning?' Joyce grumbled while Roland stood by and smoked his pipe.

'Don't ask me. I heard him tossing and turning all night long but when I went to turf

370

him out of bed at half past six, he was already up and gone.'

'We could have done with him here to lend us a hand.' Joyce swerved a swift kick from an irritable Major. 'Stand still, you brute!'

*Where can Neville have gone at that hour?* Poppy's mouth went dry but she said nothing.

'Hold the reins tighter; keep Major's head steady.' Roland took the pipe out just long enough to instruct her. 'Don't let him get the better of you.'

At last the horse was hitched and Joyce could climb up on to the driving seat. Roland went to tend his pigs while Poppy hopped up on to the cart and, with a flick of the long whip, Joyce drove out of the yard, down the green lane to the bottom field, where they rolled up their sleeves and began to fork hay on to the wagon. They'd almost transferred the first of the two remaining ricks when Poppy had to stop to lean on her fork and catch her breath.

'I'm bothered about Neville,' she confessed once she'd rested.

Joyce glanced up at a bank of clouds hovering low over their heads. 'Personally, I'm more worried about Bill. Aren't you?'

'Of course. It's awful. But he's in good hands.'

'Let's hope so.' Joyce imagined what Grace must be enduring. 'I try not to think too far ahead, just in case.'

Poppy took her point. 'Yes. Poor Grace.'

'And poor Mrs Mostyn.' Taking care to steer clear of Major's clodhoppers, Joyce took up her pitchfork and began to toss more hay on to the wagon. 'Poor everyone, for that matter.'

They fell silent and worked on. Despite sharing Joyce's worry over Bill and his family, Poppy couldn't rid her mind of the picture of Alfie Craven still on the loose, creeping along hedgerows, hiding in barns, attacking Bill with his knife. *Neville must be frightened out of his wits,* she thought. *That's why he's made himself scarce — in case Alfie shows up here again.*

Joyce hoisted the last forkful of hay high into the muggy air then dumped it on top of the pile. One more rick to go; she and Poppy had best get a move on if they wanted to get all Roland's hay safely into the loft before it rained. 'Once we're finished here, I'll go back to the village and make a telephone call,' she told Poppy.

'Who to?'

'Edgar.' Although only too well aware that he already had plenty on his plate, on balance she felt he should hear about the latest trouble. 'He is Bill's brother-in-law, after all.'

\* \* \*

Edgar's world as a fighter pilot had everything to do with duty rosters and dicing with death, with propellers and crankshafts, bomb loads and moving targets on radar screens. It had nothing to do with affairs of the heart. So when his gunner, Tommy Wright, sauntered into the common room soon after midday, Edgar looked up from the map spread out before him, expecting to learn details of their upcoming raid.

'Where are we headed next, Tommy lad? Is it

372

Dresden; or Essen for a change?'

'Neither. Guess again.' They spoke casually, as if choosing between venues for a Saturday night out.

'Not Hamburg?'

'No, let me put you out of your misery.' Tommy sported a brand-new, David Niven style moustache: straight and thin, clipped to within an inch of its life. He wore a Fair Isle jumper and his brown hair was brushed back from his forehead and slicked down with Brylcreem. 'This isn't about Dresden or Bremen or any of them. No, old chap, I've come to let you know there's been a telephone call for you.'

'Bloody hell, why didn't you say?' Edgar sprang from his seat, almost tipping over his chair as he did so. 'Who is it? What do they want? Man or woman?'

'I haven't a clue. Better run and find out.' Tommy grinned from ear to ear. He could see from Edgar's sudden eagerness that what the lads gossiped about was true: his flying pal, once so morose and turned in on himself, had fallen head over heels for a girl back home.

Edgar dashed out into the corridor then back again. 'The phone call — office or telephone box?'

'Public phone.'

He sprinted out of the barracks, across the drill yard to the red call box, where he found a fellow pilot, Frank Ellison, talking ten to the dozen down the line. He frowned then rapped sharply on the glass pane.

Frank didn't want to be disturbed. He made a

V-sign then turned his back.

Edgar slammed the glass with his palm. He wrenched the door open. 'What the bloody hell are you doing? I had a call; someone was hanging on for me.'

Frank cupped his hand over the receiver. 'Keep your hair on. I've got my missis on the line.'

Edgar slammed the glass a second time. 'Who was calling me, do you know?'

'She said her name was Joyce. I told her to ring back in five minutes.'

'Christ!' He let go of the door. *Bloody Frank Ellison, bloody Tommy Wright. Idiots, both of them!*

★   ★   ★

Joyce stood in the phone box outside the post office on Main Street. She hardly noticed Esther pull down the dark green blind then come out on to the pavement in her coat and hat, ready to lock the door. Doreen and Ivy cycled by, with Kathleen close on their heels. Poppy had already gone on ahead, glad to have the morning at Brigg Farm over and done with.

'I won't be long,' Joyce had promised. 'I just need to make a phone call.'

She'd entered the box, coins at the ready, phoned the exchange and asked to be put through to Edgar's base. Did she want to call the office number or the public call box in the grounds, the operator had asked in that precise and patient way they had. Making the connection had taken an age and meanwhile Joyce's palms had grown sweaty and her heart had raced. A person called Tommy had picked up the phone. 'Hang on,' he'd said, 'I'll try and find Edgar for you.' Precious seconds had ticked by. The pips had sounded, she'd put more money in the slot then a voice she didn't know told her to hang up while he had a cosy chat with his wife. Give him five minutes, he'd said, then try again.

Five minutes passed and Joyce changed her mind three times. Yes, she would talk to Edgar and explain about the knife attack on Bill. No, she ought not to worry him. Better to wait until there was more definite news from the hospital. Then finally yes, she would ring again and bring him up to date. In the end, she looked at her watch and saw that it was time to make a second call. The same operator connected her. 'Better luck this time,' she said kindly as she put Joyce through.

Fat drops of rain began to fall as Joyce inserted the money then listened to the clicks. The drops splashed on to the grey pavement slabs and dripped down the glass panes, slowly at first then gathering speed. Her heart was in her mouth as Edgar came to the phone at last.

He spoke first. 'Hello. Is that Joyce?'

'Yes, it's me.'

He felt his heart leap. 'Oh,' he said, 'it's marvellous to hear your voice. Are you well? Tell me what you've been up to.'

'Yes, I'm well. And you too, I hope.'

'All the better for talking to you. I miss you, you know.'

'Same here.' His voice sounded thin and distant, interrupted by crackles on the line. Outside, the rain pelted down. It bounced off the pavement and bubbled and streamed along the gutters. The street was deserted.

'Joyce, is everything all right?'

'It's Bill,' she told him hesitantly. 'Something's happened.'

'I know. Grace mentioned it in her last letter. He's only gone and joined up, the daft blighter.'

'No, not that.'

Edgar glanced out of the box at the short queue forming in the canteen doorway: three more chaps eager to ring their loved ones during their afternoons off. 'Not that I blame him,' he rattled on. 'Joining the war effort is definitely the right thing to do. I do feel for Grace, though.'

'Edgar, Bill is in hospital.' Talking over him, she wasn't sure if he'd heard.

'Hospital?'

'Yes. Alfie Craven stabbed him. Grace was there. I haven't spoken to her yet; she's still at the hospital.'

'How bad?' he asked.

'Pretty bad. It was quite a while before the ambulance arrived. I imagine Bill lost a lot of blood.'

'But will he make it?'

'It's touch and go, apparently.'

'Right,' he said, as if struggling to get a grip on his reaction. 'Leave it with me. I'll talk to my squadron leader.'

'Will you come home?' *For Grace's sake and because you're the person we can all rely on.*

376

'I'll try,' he promised. 'Hang on, Joyce. I'll do my very best.'

★   ★   ★

Grace and Edith had a strong aversion to hospitals. Both were reminded of recent events they would rather forget. For Grace it was her visits to the place they called a convalescent home near York where Edgar had been sent after his plane had been shot down over Brittany. A gracious stately home on the outside, complete with timbered gables and tall Tudor chimneys, inside it had been converted into sterile wards for soldiers whose faces had been disfigured by grenades and for airmen without limbs, the sound of whose crutches clicking along the ancient gallery she would never forget. Edith shrank from disinfected wards because of Vince's final days in this very hospital, when he was tended by nurses in starched aprons and caps. They were efficient but distant as her husband's heart gave in and he slipped away before her eyes. Fewer than four months had passed since then and the familiar smell of the ward, the sound of shoes squeaking across the lino, the sight of patients lying immobile on their beds had brought back the loss in vivid form.

Now she and Grace had stayed at Bill's bedside overnight, keeping silent vigil. His wound had been cleaned, stitched and bandaged. The doctors said that the knife had entered his chest two inches below the collarbone and penetrated his left lung, which had collapsed and caused him to be short of oxygen. Because of this and the drastic loss of blood, there was no sign yet of him regaining consciousness.

By morning, Edith was woozy from lack of sleep. Her face was drained of colour, her skin creased, her hands trembling.

'Come and have a cup of tea in the canteen,' a young nurse suggested solicitously.

Edith didn't have the strength to object. She was led by the arm into the corridor, leaving Grace alone with Bill,

'My love.' Grace reached out her hand and rested it on his. The sheets were turned back to expose his bare chest and broad, strong shoulders and heavy bandaging. His eyes were closed. 'I'm still here,' she whispered. 'I'm waiting for you to wake up.'

There was no reaction, only the shallow rise and fall of his chest as he breathed.

'I won't leave you,' she promised.

In the next bed, an elderly patient, skeleton-thin and with deep, dark eye sockets, lay with deathly stillness, his glittering gaze fixed on her.

'Don't give in,' she begged. 'Please, Bill, please!'

★   ★   ★

'Why don't we take Old Sloper out? It'll perk you up a bit.' As Brenda sat with Una in their shared bedroom after a heavy morning's work, she saw that her companion was in desperate

378

need of distraction. 'It's better than sitting here all afternoon fretting and fidgeting.'

Una was so worn out that all she wanted to do was flop on her bed. Yet she knew she wouldn't rest. 'What for?' she asked with a weary sigh. 'I don't feel like going on a jaunt.'

'I realize that, silly.' Brenda pulled her up from her bed then thrust her hat into her hands. 'Put this on. Now here's your jacket. This won't be a joyride. This will be us forming our own little search party for your precious Angelo.'

Una felt her heart skip a beat as she slid her arms into her sleeves. 'But where will we look?'

'We could start at the spot where they picked up the first two.'

'But it's miles away, close to Braffield air base. The sergeant at Beckwith Camp reckons they planned to steal a plane.'

'That makes sense. Do we know if our boys carried out a proper search of the rest of the area?' Brenda led the way along the landing then down the stairs.

'Yes. Mrs Craven keeps in close touch with the camp. They looked but they didn't find any other prisoners.' Una caught up with Brenda as they ran along the kitchen corridor, heading for the back door. 'The thing is, I don't believe Angelo can have got that far.'

'Why not?' Lately Brenda had been so caught up in her own affairs that she hadn't paid much attention to Una's plight. In fact, she hadn't even asked her why she was moping about the hostel so much in the evenings instead of joining in the search for the missing prisoners.

Una hesitated and bit her bottom lip. 'Hasn't Joyce told you?'

'Told me what?'

'Angelo's poorly.'

Brenda frowned as they went out into the yard, where her motor bike was parked. 'Yes, I know. He has a bad cough and cold.'

'TB.' As Una said the word, her pent-up worries escaped like a thousand fluttering moths into the hot, still air.

Brenda stopped short. 'Never!'

'It's true.' She drew a jagged breath.

'I see.'

'Squadron Leader Aldridge said that these days there's a medicine they can give him.'

'A cure?' Though Brenda hadn't heard of this, she certainly didn't want to dash Una's fragile hopes.

'Yes. Rest and fresh air, and what do they call it — an antibiotic?'

Brenda quickly absorbed this piece of information. 'Then we'd better find him,' she decided then and there. 'Come along, Una, hop on the back and let's get started.'

⋆   ⋆   ⋆

Following Una's rationale that a man as sick as Angelo couldn't get very far on foot, Brenda first rode the bike along familiar lanes and tracks, with eyes peeled, stopping at each farm to enquire if anything had been seen of the missing POWs. Peggy Russell gave them a definite no. Maurice, whom they stopped in his van on the edge of the village, scratched his head and thought a while.

'Wait, let me have a think. I was expecting you to ask after Bill; you've heard he's been stabbed?'

'Yes, the news has spread like wildfire.' Everyone in the dale was talking about it and taking a gloomy view of the eventual outcome. 'There's not a person within a thirty-mile radius that isn't after Alfie's blood.'

'Quite right too. That's what I've been up to this morning. I've been out with Roland and Joe trying to track him down. Did you know that he stole five quid from the Kelletts? Joe swears he'll shoot on sight if he spots him.'

'Better watch out, Alfie!' Brenda had no doubt that Joe would carry out his threat and moved quickly on. 'I suppose this means you'll have to step into Bill's shoes sooner than expected. I hope you're up to scratch with the inner workings of Fordsons and Field Marshalls.'

'Bill mainly works on Fergusons.' Maurice assured her he was ready for the challenge.

'So, any sign of our Italians while you were out?'

*At last!* Una had kept silent, itching for them to continue their search.

'Not a whisper. Wait a second, though. Henry Rowson did say something about food going missing from his larder a couple of days back, while he was up on the fell. A loaf of bread, a tin of bully beef. It could have been a tramp — there are plenty of those around during these summer months. Or Alfie. Or your Italians. That's the only clue we came across.'

There was no question that this was where they should head next. So, having said goodbye to Maurice, Brenda and Una set off for Henry's isolated farm under Kelsey Crag. It took them half an hour to get there.

'No one at home.' Brenda knocked at the door three times before admitting defeat.

Una stared up at the two small first-floor windows in the squat, square house then scouted around in the lean-to outhouse attached to the side, where she found the farmer's old bicycle. 'He can't have gone far,' she reported back to Brenda. 'His bike's here.'

'So let's take a look on the fell. There's a good chance he's busy with his lambs.'

Within seconds they were back on Sloper, following the green lane that ran up the side of the crag on to the hilltop. Here, the land levelled out and the tarn stretched out in front of them.

'We're on foot from here.' Brenda parked again and surveyed the wild, deserted landscape.

Una, meanwhile, turned away from the lake and looked back the way they'd come. She thought she'd heard the sound of an engine on the road close to the crag so wasn't surprised to see a black car emerge from under its shadow, only paying attention when it slowed down then drew into a gateway as a green sports car approached from the other direction.

'Brenda, look!' she called excitedly. 'That's Les's MG!'

Brenda's heart sank as she ran to join her. 'Yes, with Donald at the wheel.'

Together they watched the sports car stop

alongside the black saloon. The two drivers talked without getting out.

'What the heck is Donald doing so far off the beaten track?' Brenda craned this way and that for a better view of the man at the wheel of the bigger car. 'You can be sure he's not driven all the way up here for the sake of his health. Did you recognize the other driver?'

'No. I only caught a glimpse. He was wearing a hat.'

'What kind of a hat?'

'A trilby. He had a passenger with him.'

This was enough to make Brenda return to Sloper. She kicked the bike into action then yelled for Una to hop on behind. They set off at full tilt down the grassy slope.

Una held on tight as Brenda's unzipped jacket and red scarf flapped in her face. They rounded a bend then approached the gate that closed the lane off from the road, only to find that the black car had gone on its way.

Brenda gave Una a moment to slip off the pillion seat before hurriedly ditching the bike and launching into a conversation with Donald. 'Who was that?' she demanded, gesturing down the road.

Wearing a broad smile, Donald vaulted out of the car without bothering to open the door. He walked jauntily towards the gate. 'Brenda, I didn't think you were talking to me!'

She didn't respond. 'I asked you who that was.'

'Just a bloke wanting to know the way back to the main road. I told him he was way off track and gave him a few directions.'

'And what are you doing up here anyway?' Brenda felt her confidence seep away. It happened every time she came into contact with Donald, despite all her efforts to prevent it. 'I didn't have you down as a fell-walker or a fisherman.'

'You're right there.' The infuriating grin didn't shift. 'What are my brother's fiancée and her little pal doing out in the wilds, for that matter?'

'We're looking for the missing POWs — ' Una blurted out. Then, at a sharp elbow jab in the arm from Brenda, she stopped.

'Is that right?' Donald kept his gaze locked on Brenda. 'Why bother? They can stay missing, as far as I'm concerned.'

With the closed gate acting as a barrier between them, Brenda stood her ground. 'So you haven't come across them?'

'Nope. I say the same about Alfie Craven; why waste time and energy? Let him fall down a cliff or drown in the lake. No one will be any worse off. You heard what he did to Bill Mostyn, I take it?'

Brenda nodded.

He leaned on the gate, close enough to Brenda for their shoulders to touch. 'So then, let's talk about something more interesting instead.'

His familiar tone took Una aback. With a distinct sense that two was company and three was a crowd, she glanced quickly at Brenda's flushed cheeks and took a few steps back.

'How's Brenda since we last met?' he asked softly. 'Not wearing your ring today, I see?'

'Brenda is fine, thank you.' She would not, not, *not* be intimidated or worn down by him! She would keep Les's image to the forefront of her mind and gather strength from that. 'How's Hettie?'

'Tickety-boo, ta.'

'And your father?'

'Likewise. Come on — where's my mother's ring?'

'None of your business.' In fact, it was hanging from the ribbon around her neck, out of sight.

'Aah, why so touchy?' He could see her weakening. She had that flickering look of uncertainty that women displayed when about to give way. They couldn't help themselves. 'I've written and told Les what a lucky man he is. I said not to worry, I'll keep an eye on you and make sure you don't get up to mischief.'

'You said what?' She was within a split second of slapping his chiselled cheek but instead she unbolted the gate and swung it hard against his abdomen. 'Sorry about that,' she muttered through gritted teeth, all doubt gone, eyes blazing.

*Whoops, wrong move.* 'I only meant that I'd look after you while he's away. I mean to be a good brother-in-law if you let me.'

'Champion!' Brenda snapped, wheeling her bike through the gate. 'Now, if you don't mind, Una and I have to get on.'

He followed close on her heels, leaving not enough room for her to swing her leg over the saddle. 'And do what?'

*Give nothing away. Don't trust him an inch.*

She kick-started the engine — once, twice, three times. 'Ignore what Una said; we're looking for Henry Rowson but we haven't had any luck.'

'I'll tell him if I see him.' *So tantalizingly near to getting what I'm after and yet so far. Still, there's always a next time.* Donald took a step back and bumped into Una, who was about to take her place on the pillion seat.

'Aren't we going back up to the tarn?' Una whispered as Brenda revved the engine.

There was no answer. Brenda eased the bike out on to the road without looking back while Donald stood on the grass verge, arms folded, wearing the same smile and watching them go.

★ ★ ★

Did she feel better after hours of fruitless searching? Una wasn't sure. She and Brenda had covered many miles, even riding into the neighbouring dale to Attercliffe then back over the tops to resume the search for Henry Rowson. They'd spotted him on the crag and waited on the road until he came down the shepherd's lane with two dogs at his heels: Border collies obedient to every command. The dogs had sat by the gate at Henry's instruction while he'd answered Una's questions. Yes, some food had gone missing but the thief had been long gone before Henry had realized. But no, the POWs weren't responsible so far as he knew. Why would they trek all the way up here? The road didn't lead in the right direction and it didn't make sense to head north if they were intending to go

386

east to one of the half-dozen airfields located close to the coast.

So it had been a frustrating afternoon and Brenda hadn't been on good form. The conversation with Donald had left her cross and taciturn and Una could hardly blame her; he was the type to leave a nasty taste in most girls' mouths. Not Doreen, though. Una realized that she was the exception that proved the rule.

Anyway, they were back at the hostel now and Una strolled alone in the walled garden after dinner, trying to compose her thoughts. What if Angelo's illness wasn't as serious as the camp doctor had indicated? Perhaps the TB was still in its early stages, in which case Angelo could in fact have made it to one of the aerodromes with his group of escapees. He could be out of the country already. How would she feel about that? The question was left unanswered as her thoughts raced on. On the other hand, he'd been too poorly to work in the days leading up to the escape. And something told Una that Angelo knew deep down how sick he was. She recalled the way he'd said goodbye to her behind the Blacksmith's Arms, as if he knew it might be the last time he would see her. No, she refused to believe that! She was reading things into the situation that hadn't been there. Oh, she was confused and sad, filled with dread yet still clinging on to a thread of hope.

She left the garden and walked on into the wood. The dazzling green of the leaves overhead and the softness of the ground underfoot gave her surroundings a floating, dreamlike feel — a state where unexpected things could happen without her questioning them. So when Lorenzo approached her through the trees, she didn't show any surprise.

'*Ciao*, Una,' he began. 'I have been waiting.'

She walked quickly up to him. 'Where's Angelo?'

'Listen. I wait each night, hoping you will walk in here. I dare not come to the house. I have to be sure you are alone.'

'I am. Where's Angelo?'

'Close to here. We could not walk far. He has a fever, he is too sick.'

'You stayed with him?'

Lorenzo nodded. '*Mio amico*. He is my friend.'

'Take me to him.' Una felt swamped by a sudden wave of fear.

Lorenzo took her by the hand and walked her deeper into the wood, towards the stream and the steep hill beyond. 'I try to bring him food. He does not eat. He does not sleep. He does not wish to leave. We walk here, slowly, slowly. We do not escape with others.'

'Quickly!' she urged.

They broke into a run and jumped across the stream, emerging from the shady wood into full sunlight. Nothing seemed real to Una; it was too much to take in.

But Lorenzo didn't slacken his pace. He strode up the hill with her, through green bracken towards the wreckage of the German plane. 'Be quiet, be gentle,' he advised as they drew near the twisted, rusting metal. 'He is my

388

friend. I do all I can.'

Una's heart stuttered almost to a halt. There was the wing with its mangled propeller, lying separate from the fuselage. The cockpit windows were crazed, making it impossible to see inside.

Lorenzo climbed up, stood on the remaining wing and held out his hand. 'Come.'

She let him pull her up to join him but at first she couldn't bear to look inside the belly of the plane.

'*Eccola qui*,' he called softly to his friend as he made room for her to enter. '*Arrivederci, amico mio. Dio ti benedica!*'

Una didn't notice him slither down the rounded fuselage on to the heather then run swiftly down the fell.

'Angelo?' she whispered after she'd lowered herself but before her eyes had adjusted to the darkness inside the plane.

He heard her voice and saw her outline through a mist of pain. He could scarcely breathe, let alone move towards her.

She found him propped against some oxygen tanks, the white of his eyes gleaming and then the outline of his dark head and shoulders. He wore his grey prisoner's uniform with the jacket open and the buttons of his white shirt undone. Suddenly calm, she went down on her knees and clasped his hands. 'My darling, my dearest!'

'My Una.' He smiled and his hands returned the pressure. 'I wait many days.'

'Hush. I'm here now.' She pressed her lips against his cheek

Angelo felt the gold cross of the necklace he'd

given her swing lightly against his throat. 'Do not cry. I am happy.'

'Don't ever leave me again without telling me where you're going,' she pleaded. 'I can bear anything just so long as I know.'

'I will not leave. I am here.' But tired, unable to hold on to her, he let his hands drop and his head fall back against the cold grey metal of the fuselage.

Another wave of panic swelled then broke over their heads. 'Angelo, you must eat and rest. Lorenzo, tell him!' She called up out of the belly of the plane, expecting him to back her up.

'He is gone,' Angelo explained. It was harder and harder for him to draw breath. 'He joins the other men now.'

*Arrivederci, amico mio. Dio ti benedica!*

'This is good. All is good.'

'Hush, my dear. Don't try to talk.' She looked around in desperation then took off her jacket and folded it to make a pillow for his head. What should she do now? She couldn't leave him, yet she wasn't strong enough to move him. How would she get help?

'Every moment I see you I am happy. Do not cry.'

'Angelo, I love you more than the whole world. Do you hear?'

'I know this.' He smiled at her then gathered enough energy to clasp her hand.

With the darkness surrounding them, the plane was a cold, comfortless cave. Then sounds from outside entered their small world: two women's voices and the swish of footsteps through the heather.

'Una, are you in there?' Joyce called. 'It's me and Brenda.'

Brenda was the first to reach the plane. 'We met Lorenzo. He told us where to find you.'

'Yes, we're here,' Una replied. She pressed Angelo's hand and smiled back. 'See,' she whispered. 'My friends have come. Soon you'll be safe.'

# 22

'Our hands were tied. What else could we do?' Joyce's face conveyed a keen sadness as she stood with Brenda at the front door of the hostel and watched Angelo being carried on a stretcher into a waiting ambulance. Light was fading and a big, pale moon rose in a clear sky.

Brenda was silent. *Yes, there was nothing else. Once we saw the state he was in, we didn't have any choice. We had to telephone the camp and tell them to send a doctor asap.*

Joyce had waited inside the plane with Una, who clung to Angelo's every breath, willing him to live, while Brenda had run down the fell and made the call. 'Come quickly. He doesn't look as if he can last much longer without your help,' she'd told the army doctor.

'We'll be thirty minutes,' he'd promised before he put down the phone. Just enough time for Brenda to carry blankets and a flask of tea laced with brandy up to the wreckage. She and Una had kept Angelo as warm as possible and he'd taken a few sips of the liquid. Una had held his hand throughout. His valiant smile had slowly faded but he kept his eyes on Una's face, even when they'd heard the approach of the doctor and his helpers.

The doctor had climbed up the fuselage and shone his torch down on the huddled group. 'Move aside,' he'd told Brenda, Joyce and Una as he'd lowered himself inside; a young man still wet behind the ears, in army uniform with a stethoscope suspended from his neck. 'Now then, Bachetti, sit up, there's a good chap. Let's take a look.'

Brenda and Joyce had clambered out of the wreck and shaken hands with Atkinson and another soldier they didn't recognize, but Una had refused to budge. She'd watched the doctor listen to Angelo's chest then give a quick shake of his head. He'd felt the patient's pulse and checked his temperature, asked Una about the contents of the flask. Everything had been done at speed and a quick decision made. 'Send the stretcher in,' he'd yelled at Atkinson. 'You bring it and, Haynes, you stay put, ready to take the weight at one end as we hoist him out.'

The order had been carried out and Una pushed aside. The tearing sensation of loss she felt as Angelo's hand slid from her grasp would stay with her for a long time.

But, as Joyce and Brenda told her repeatedly, there was nothing else she could have done. Angelo needed to be in hospital. The soldiers had to carry him down the fell into the waiting vehicle. She must accompany him to the door of the army ambulance then let him go.

'Where will you take him?' Joyce asked the doctor after he'd finished talking to Hilda and she had made a careful note of everything that had happened.

'To Clifton House. It's an isolation hospital just south of Leeds. I've given the warden the address.'

'What can you do, Doc? Is there any way you can help him?'

Brenda's no-nonsense question was met by a sharp glance and an answer that was to the point. 'We can bring down his temperature for a start. Then, if he accepts food, we can gradually build his strength back up.'

'But?'

'Can he be cured?' The doctor shook his head. 'Not unless you believe in miracles.'

Una stayed with Angelo, even as Atkinson began to close the ambulance door. Then he had a change of heart. 'I'll give you another minute then you'll have to step aside,' he told her gently.

She leaned over to whisper in Angelo's ear. 'You must do as the doctor tells you. I'll visit you as soon as I can.'

Her voice broke through the muddle of disconnected sounds and swaying, jerking movements. Angelo locked his gaze on to hers one last time.

'You hear me?' she repeated. 'I'll visit you and we'll make plans for when you're better, for when the war is over.'

He gave a deep, uneven sigh.

'Italy. Pisa. Sunshine. That'll be us, my dearest.'

'Hurry up now,' Atkinson muttered as the doctor said goodbye to Joyce and Brenda.

'*Ciao, Angelo. Ti amo, ti amo!*'

'I love you,' he whispered back as the doors finally closed.

★　★　★

*What a day!* Brenda gazed at her reflection in the bathroom mirror as she brushed her teeth. It was only now that she had time to recall her encounter with Donald in the shadow of Kelsey Crag and wonder again about the effect he had on her. There was no one like him for pure, strutting arrogance. Perhaps it came out of him being so strikingly good-looking; women must fall at his feet as a matter of course and, with a combination of looks and wealth, he was able to lord it over men too. *But he's a big fish in a small pond,* she told herself. *It would be different in a town or a city. He'd soon come up against cleverer, more sophisticated types who wouldn't hesitate to put Donald White in his place.* She spat into the basin then rinsed out her mouth, taking her time to replace her toothbrush in her washbag as she heard Doreen give an impatient rap on the door and order her to get a move on.

'What's the hurry?' she asked when she stepped out on to the landing. 'Do you want to get to bed? Are you short on beauty sleep?'

'Miaow!' Doreen came straight back at her.

She'd swept into the bathroom and Brenda was halfway along the landing when a light bulb went on inside her head and she stopped dead. 'Of course!'

'Talking to yourself now, eh?' Elsie's door stood open and she called out to Brenda.

'I just realized something.' Glued to the spot, Brenda began to work it all out. Donald hadn't been on a joyride that afternoon, any more than she and Una had been. He'd driven out to Kelsey specifically to meet someone: the driver

395

of the black Morris. 'Howard Moyes, no less.' She backtracked to the bathroom and knocked on the door. 'Doreen, I want to ask you something.'

'Not now. I'm having a wash,' came the short-tempered reply.

'It's important.'

Brenda heard Doreen pull the plug and listened to the water gurgle away. When she opened the door with a towel in her hand, the skin on her face was shiny and scrubbed.

'Always rinse in cold water,' she advised. 'It tones everything up nicely.'

'Doreen, listen. This is about Donald.'

'Not that again.' She was about to close the door when Brenda put her foot in the way. 'I've told you: Donald does what he wants when he wants. I'm not his keeper.'

'It's not you and him I'm interested in. This is something different. I'm convinced I saw him earlier today, having a secret powwow with Howard Moyes and Clive Nixon.'

Frown lines appeared on Doreen's forehead. 'So? There's no law against it, so far as I'm aware.'

'But is Donald friends with those two men? I need to know.'

Doreen let go of the door and allowed Brenda to step inside the cold bathroom, where a row of towels hung on hooks next to an old Victorian sink with cast-iron brackets and dripping brass taps. 'Why's that, Brenda? Why are you always so interested in your fiancé's brother?'

'Forget about that for a second. I'm not trying

to get one up on you, all right?'

'That makes a change,' Doreen said sulkily. 'Anyway, if you must know, I have no idea who Donald's friends are because he never introduces me to any.'

Still intent on working things out, Brenda sat down on the edge of the bath. 'So help me, please. Do you remember any of the evenings when he promised to meet you and then backed out at the last minute? Or when you were with him and he would vanish without warning?'

'Of course I do. I don't need reminding, ta.'

'And were Moyes and Nixon sniffing around Burnside at the time?'

Doreen shook her head in genuine puzzlement. 'I have no idea. Why?'

'Because I want to work out how far back those three might go. And, if they do know each other, how and where did they first come across each other? What do they have in common that would make them want to meet in secret at a place where the chance of anyone seeing them was slim?'

'Like I said, don't ask me.' It was once bitten, twice or thrice shy as far as Doreen was concerned. She'd got far too close to Alfie and almost paid a heavy price. Every day she woke up and went about her business in dread of a second unwelcome visit from the two men that Brenda was asking about. 'I don't want any more to do with them — or with Alfie Craven, for that matter.'

'No one does,' Brenda interrupted. 'Not after what he did to Bill.'

'Exactly.' Doreen had made her point and had no more to say. 'Now go away and leave me alone.'

★ ★ ★

Within twenty-four hours, every join in the dark brown lino and every finger mark on the pale green walls of the ward where Bill lay had become familiar to Grace. She knew the exact times when the nurses came in to take his temperature and renew his dressings, the hours when they changed their shifts and when the beds were made, what was for breakfast and the name of the orderly who wheeled in the trolley. She'd resisted every attempt by the nurses to make her break her vigil.

'I'd rather stay here,' she insisted quietly when Edith tried to take her place. It was midnight; exactly twenty-six hours since the ambulance had brought Bill to the hospital and there was still no sign of him waking up, 'You go home and get some rest. There's no point two of us sitting up all night.'

'Perhaps you're right.'

'I am. Take a taxi if you'd rather not drive. I'll telephone you if there's any change.'

'Very well.' It was Grace's right to choose and Edith conceded gracefully. *Oh, my son!* She sighed to herself as she trod the silent corridors and left by the main door. *My son!*

Grace gazed at Bill's face. His eyes were still closed, his mouth slightly open, chin shadowed with dark stubble. But hope was there

398

somewhere. Not in the paraphernalia of tubes, charts and dials surrounding his bed, not in the discreet, brief chats between doctors and nurses, nor in the pale, motionless features of the man she loved. Hope and faith came from somewhere else, from deep within her. It rested in her heart's core if only she could find it.

*I believe you'll get better, I do! I know how strong you are and how brave. You'll come back to me and we'll carry on living and working together, being husband and wife.*

She remembered the church bells that had rung out for their wedding, how nervous she'd been as Brenda and Una had helped her to get ready and Joyce had handed her the bouquet. She remembered Bill waiting for her at the end of the aisle, turning to her and smiling.

'We have so much to live for.' Her lips touched his cheek as she murmured the words. 'Come back to me, Bill. I need you.'

★   ★   ★

St Michael's Church was unusually full for morning service on the second Sunday in July. Even intermittent worshippers like Maurice, Horace and Joe had made the effort to attend on an unseasonably cool morning with rain clouds threatening.

'This will please the vicar,' Maurice commented as he filed in through the porch then took a hymn book from Bob. 'Church is bursting at the seams.'

The brothers were aware that it had nothing to

do with a sudden attack of Christian piety among the Burnside parishioners. 'No one wants to miss vital information, that's why,' Bob said with a wink.

Maurice nodded then shuffled into the back pew as organ notes filled the crowded interior. He sat between Cliff and Hilda, who had visited Edith at home before church to ask about Bill.

'Cheer up,' Joe growled at Roland, who sat down next to him in a pew near the front. 'It might never happen.'

'It already has.' Roland had given up expecting Neville to return home and had come to the service in an attempt to distract himself. 'My lad's scarpered, I've got no idea where.'

'Or why?' Joe's memory was jolted back to the time when his son Frank had disappeared, never to return. For once he felt a grain of sympathy for his neighbour's plight.

Roland shrugged. 'He's sixteen and old enough to look after himself. It's up to him if he decides to take off for the weekend without telling me. I'm only his dad, when all's said and done.'

As Esther turned to a fresh sheet in her dog-eared collection of scores and began an almost identical slow, solemn tune, the Land Girls arrived. Bob handed Brenda and Kathleen a hymn book each and pointed to a couple of spaces close to the front. He asked a quick question about Bill and they told him that so far as they knew there was no fresh news.

'What about Alfie?' Brenda wanted to know. 'Any sign of him?'

'Nothing.' Bob kept on methodically handing out books.

'They did pick up one of the POWs, though,' Jean was quick to inform him. 'Una's chap, no less. He was at death's door so they carted him off to the isolation hospital double quick.'

Whispered word filtered from one pew to the next: still no Alfie, but one more POW had been recaptured. No good news about Bill, apparently. But did you know that Edgar Kershaw had applied for twenty-four hours' leave and was on his way back to Burnside right this minute? Standing between Doreen and Elsie, Joyce tried not to react to this particular rumour. Edgar had told her on the phone that he would do his very best; since then, she'd heard nothing.

The organ notes wheezed to a halt as, in the small, damp vestry, the vicar pulled on his white surplice then adjusted it before entering the church. All heads turned towards the altar as nine choristers of various ages and sizes filed into the choir stalls.

★ ★ ★

On the way to church in the van with Joyce and Doreen, Poppy had made a daring plan. The idea had come to her as she got dressed but she hadn't finally decided to go ahead with it until Joyce had parked in the pub yard and Poppy had noticed Roland entering the church alone.

*I'll skip the service but not tell anyone,* she thought as the others stepped out of the vehicle, straightened their dresses then went ahead. *It'll* take some nerve but *I'll do it anyway.*

'Are you coming, Pops?' Doreen called over her shoulder.

'I'll just be a minute.' She pointed towards the pub toilets.

It was a good enough excuse and she was soon alone in the yard. Now came the bit that took courage. She'd banked on finding Grace's bike in the place where it was always left, leaning against the outhouse beside the smithy. Good, it was where it should be. Poppy told herself she was only borrowing it and would be back before the service ended, once she'd cycled out to Brigg Farm and discovered once and for all whether or not Neville was lying low. *If I do winkle him out, I'll have one last try to talk some sense into him. And if he's still too scared to go to the police station, I'll come back here, wait outside the church and tell his dad exactly what's been going on. I'll hand it all over to Mr Thomson. He'll know what to do for the best.*

Poppy hadn't read many books as a child, but as she set off on Grace's bike, she felt she could be a character in a modern adventure story: the young heroine who breaks the rules and rescues her younger brother from the baddies. Of course, she knew that in real life a happy ending wasn't guaranteed; she only had to bear in mind what had happened to Bill to realize that. Still, Neville had taken a shine to her from the beginning so she felt duty-bound to try to help him, undeterred by spots of rain on her face and bare arms and the fact that the wind was against her as she cycled up the hill to Brigg Farm.

She arrived out of breath, with her thin cotton dress thoroughly soaked. *I'm here now so I'll see it through*, she decided as she entered the farmyard, to be greeted by the usual sight of Major craning his neck over the stable door and the sound of Roland's pigs.grunting and jostling inside their sty. Rain had already formed muddy puddles and was overflowing the gutters, while dejected pigeons stared down at her from the newly installed telephone wire overhead.

*I'll try the house first*, she decided, taking care to avoid a nasty nip from the shire horse's teeth as she parked Grace's bike under the stone steps to the hayloft. She backtracked across the yard, opened the garden gate and hurried up the front path then gave a loud knock on the farmhouse door without expecting any answer. When she tried to turn the knob, she found that the door was locked. 'Neville!' Cupping her hands around her mouth, she yelled up at the bedroom windows.

Again, no reply.

'Neville, it's me, Poppy!' *I look a sight! What am I doing? How did I ever think that I'd get anywhere by doing this?* Exasperated, she turned and walked back down the path.

'Neville!' she cried at the top of her voice from the gate, turning in all directions to call his name.

Her voice drifted down into the valley as the rain set in. There would be no let-up for a while.

*For heaven's sake, this is a waste of time!* Angry with herself, she stormed into the yard, intending to retrieve the bike and cycle back to the village. Then again, perhaps she ought to take shelter and wait five minutes for the rain to ease. Yes, that's what she would do. She chose the only dry place she could think of: the loft above the stable.

She mounted the stone steps, sighing as she went in out of the rain, and sank against the slippery stack of hay that she and Joyce had carted up from Low Field the previous day. There wasn't much room, but at least it was dry and so she began to shift some of the hay further to one side to create more space. She paused to shake moisture out of her hair then took a handy pitchfork and got back to work.

The low rustle of hay and its sweet smell eased Poppy's frustration and she carried on for a minute or two, tidying and building up the heap until a good third of the rough wooden floor was visible. It was only then that she paused to put down her pitchfork and take a closer look at a dark, damp patch that she'd exposed. She bent down to touch it. The stain was sticky and when she examined her fingertips she saw that they were dark red.

She recoiled into a corner, staring at her fingers. This was blood. She looked again at the congealed stain, steeling herself before creeping forward to lift more of the hay. The irregular patch extended a long way towards the back wall. Without realizing that she was holding her breath, she cleared a larger area, until at last she touched something solid and with a loud exhalation went down on to her knees. With mounting horror she brushed aside the last of

404

the hay to reveal Neville's face.

He lay on his back with his eyes closed. Blood had poured from a deep wound on his right temple, soaking his hair. More blood had trickled from the corner of his mouth on to the floor, where it had formed a dark pool. She touched his cold cheek then brushed aside more hay to discover that Neville's final act had been to clutch at his assailant's shirt and tear away part of the collar. He'd held on to it in his death throes. The hand holding the starched fabric was flung wide of his body, the other rested across his chest. His long legs were spreadeagled. One boot was missing.

Poppy would never rid herself of the overwhelming feeling of absence inside the hayloft. All that was left of Neville once the spirit had departed was bloodied flesh and solid bone. Long ginger lashes curved over waxen cheeks, the mouth was slack. There was no breath, not the slightest movement. The person she knew was gone.

Rainwater splashed from the gutter on to the stone steps. Poppy rocked back on her heels and sobbed.

# 23

Twenty-four hours was all the leave that Edgar had been able to squeeze out of his commanding officer.

'You're making a habit of it,' Acaster had complained on the Saturday evening, looking up sharply from his desk and staring at Edgar over the top of his half-moon glasses. 'But since it concerns a serious assault on your brother-in-law, I'm willing to grant the request.'

The form was duly filled out and signed. Edgar had driven out of the base shortly after dawn next day. He'd gone straight to the hospital and joined Grace at Bill's bedside. After her initial exclamation of surprise, he'd held her hand and she'd shared what little information she had from the doctors. Bill was holding his own. His heart was strong but they weren't sure if he'd lost too much blood to make a full recovery.

'I can't agree,' she'd told Edgar firmly. 'They don't know Bill the way I do.'

'That's right.' Edgar hadn't picked up any hopeful signs on the charts and monitors but he'd known that his role was to shore up his sister. 'He'll fight every inch of the way.'

He'd stayed with Grace until Edith had arrived with pink roses from her garden. Then he'd sought out a doctor and discussed Bill's case. The elderly medic, a veteran of the First

War, had shown respect for Edgar's uniform and told him outright how much he admired the Spitfire boys who flew missions night after night without considering their own safety. He'd given no promises as far as Bill was concerned, but agreed that youth and strength were on the patient's side. 'It's a waiting game,' he'd confided as he'd accompanied Edgar to the door. 'We've sewn him up and done all we can. Now it's in the lap of the gods.'

*What have the gods got to do with it?* Edgar had felt irritated as he got into his car. *It's science and good nursing care that we have to trust.*

He was still weighing up Bill's chances of survival as he stood under an umbrella on the pavement outside St Michael's, waiting for the service to end. Feeling helpless was the worst thing about this damned situation but he resolved to take his lead from Grace and think positively. His sister was weathering the crisis as only she could: calmly, with courage and with something that for a while he couldn't put his finger on. It came to him as the church door opened at last and notes from the organ drifted out. *With faith*, he thought, suddenly jettisoning his belief in science. *Grace has faith that Bill will live, and by Jove, I think she'll be proved right!*

He watched the congregation emerge from the arched porch and spill out on to the path. Despite the heavy rain, no one seemed in a hurry to leave — he made out Joe and Emily talking to Roland in the porch then noticed Hilda usher out a bunch of Land Girls. She urged them to take shelter under a yew tree until the rain eased. Joyce wasn't among them. Perhaps she hadn't attended church this morning after all. Edgar would give it another couple of minutes, then if he didn't spot her he would drive straight out to Fieldhead to find her.

Joyce, meanwhile, lingered inside the church to ask if Doreen and Elsie wanted a lift home. They glanced outside at the rain then said a quick 'yes please'. 'Has anyone seen Poppy lately?' Joyce enquired as she looked around the almost empty nave.

'Not since she went to spend a penny,' Doreen admitted. 'Uh-oh, naughty Pops! Something tells me she found better things to do with her Sunday morning.'

Last to leave the church, the three girls heard Bob close the door behind them.

'At last!' Edgar took a few steps forward then halted, uncertain whether Joyce's look of stunned surprise meant that she was pleased to see him. Bareheaded and without a coat, she pushed her way through the crowd then fell into his arms. 'Don't say anything!' she begged. 'If this is a dream, I don't want anyone to wake me up!'

He hugged her tightly. 'It's real,' he assured her. 'I told you I'd come if I could, didn't I? I've got twenty-four hours, that's all.'

'You're here. That's all that matters.' Smiling and reluctantly withdrawing from his embrace, she noticed that Kathleen was among the group sheltering under the yew. 'Catch!' she called before throwing a set of ignition keys. 'You'll have to drive the van back to the hostel.'

As the rain eased off, Hilda began to organize the chattering gang: who else needed a lift, who was cycling back, and so on.

'I came on Sloper,' Brenda told her. 'I'll make my own way.'

'What about you?' Edgar asked Joyce, though it was a question that could only have one answer.

'I'll come with you. But where to?'

'I promised myself that I'd do my damnedest to track down Alfie Craven. It's the least I can do for Grace and Bill.'

'Count me in,' Joyce confirmed quickly. But as they hurried out on to the pavement, Joyce noticed Poppy cycling up the street. She knew in a split second that something awful had happened.

'Mr Thomson!' Poppy wailed as she saw Neville's father cross the road with Joe and Emily. The two men were deep in conversation and at first Roland didn't hear her call his name. She wobbled to a halt and let Grace's bike crash to the ground as she ran towards him. 'Mr Thomson, you have to come home quick!'

Joyce left Edgar's side and ran to join them. Poppy's hands and the hem of her yellow dress were stained red.

'What's going on?' Roland asked slowly as he looked her up and down.

'Please, you have to come!' She took hold of his jacket sleeve and tugged.

'Calm down, Poppy,' Joyce urged, though her own heart had started to race. 'Tell us what's wrong.'

'Neville,' she sobbed incoherently. 'Underneath the hay. I saw the blood. Neville!'

'He's dead, isn't he?' It was Emily who dropped the simple, devastating sentence into the ensuing silence. Emily Kellett, who had suffered the loss of her own son and would continue to feel the keen knife of grief until her last breath.

Poppy sank against Hilda, who had hurried to join the group along with a growing crowd. 'Oh, Mrs Craven, it's true. Neville's been killed. There's blood everywhere.'

Where? When? Who did it?

'Alfie.' The name sprang to everyone's lips. A lad was dead. The police must be called.

'Why? What had Neville got to do with Alfie?'

Hilda took Poppy's weight to stop her sinking to the ground. *Alfie, and again Alfie!*

Roland stared at the girl weeping hysterically in the warden's arms. He broke free from the group, his face expressionless, and walked to his Land Rover.

'Wait. You can't tackle this by yourself,' Joe insisted as he limped after him. He laid a gnarled hand on his neighbour's shoulder. 'You'll need someone to come with you.'

★ ★ ★

While Hilda and Elsie took Poppy into the pub to revive her and Kathleen telephoned the police, Edgar and Joyce set out on their mission. They drove out of the village in grim silence, their minds fixed on bringing Alfie to justice.

410

'If I don't strangle him with my bare hands before-hand.' Edgar gripped the steering wheel. 'First Bill, now this!'

'I'm partly to blame,' Joyce admitted. 'Poppy found out that Neville was mixed up in Alfie's dealings. She took me into her confidence. I shouldn't have relied on him to go to the police station and own up of his own accord, I should have done it myself.'

'No, this is Alfie's fault and his alone.' Edgar's mind flew back through the years to the occasions when Hilda's son, always a bully, had got on the wrong side of the law. At first it had seemed like a laugh to the other village lads, scrumping for apples with him or uneasily watching him throw stones at pigeons. But then it had got out of hand. At the age of thirteen he'd put his hand in the post office till while Esther's back was turned. Then, in the year when he'd been due to leave school, he'd set fire to a broom cupboard in the Institute and been sent off to Borstal, only to come back worse than ever. And so it had gone on downhill from there, to this terrible, tragic point. 'We'll catch him and make him pay the price,' he promised.

A trial before judge and jury. A hangman's noose.

*  ★  *

It was no good; they could do nothing to stop Poppy crying. She collapsed on a bench next to the fire-place in the Blacksmith's Arms, her

411

hands covering her face, weeping and wailing, a pitiful sight.

'Poppy, dear, try to pull yourself together.' Hilda sat down next to her. 'This isn't doing you any good.'

'The police are on their way.' Kathleen drew Brenda to one side. 'Honestly, of all the people who could have found Neville's body it had to be Poppy.'

'I know.' Brenda nodded thoughtfully. 'It's hit her hard. And Ma Craven as well. Think what she must be going through.'

'Yes, it's an awful mess.'

'And here we are, standing around doing nothing.' Brenda left Kathleen and made a beeline across the bar towards Doreen. 'Come outside,' she ordered. 'I want a word.'

For once Doreen didn't argue but trailed after Brenda into the yard.

'Look where doing nothing has got us,' Brenda began without preamble. 'It's time for action.'

'I don't know what you mean.' Doreen's instinct was, as always, to stay out of it. 'I told you, I've already washed my hands of Alfie Craven.'

'Easier said than done, worse luck.' She drew Doreen towards Sloper, parked in the smithy doorway. 'Look, we're not the only ones who've worked out the connection between Alfie and our two friends from the city but we can take it a step further, you and I. We can make a link between Moyes, Nixon and Donald.'

'Donald!' Doreen's scornful tone was accompanied by a sulky toss of her raven locks and an

412

intended return to the pub. 'Says you!'

Brenda swiftly blocked her way. 'What does it take to make you put others before yourself? One person is in hospital and another has died, for heaven's sake!'

'And what do you expect me to do?' The question exploded from Doreen's lips. 'Do you think I don't care about Bill Mostyn? Or about Neville? Of course I care. I just don't see how we can alter it.'

'We can find Donald and make him admit that he met up with Moyes yesterday.'

'Then what? Donald is never going to . . . what's the word?'

'Incriminate himself. That's true.' The logic of this defeated Brenda and she fell silent.

'So I'm right, there's no point.'

Still Brenda refused to take this line. She gestured towards her motor bike. 'You won't even come with me to Dale End and try?'

'Bull's-eye!' Doreen congratulated her as she flicked her hair behind her shoulder, sidestepped Brenda and walked rapidly across the yard. 'At last, the penny drops!'

★   ★   ★

Una waited at the gate to Beckwith Camp, carefully watching the comings and goings. She'd been there for more than an hour so the sentry had long since stopped paying her any attention.

'She says she wants to talk to the doctor,' Haynes told his sergeant, who was behind the

413

wheel of a Land Rover and had noticed Una on his way in. 'I told her she couldn't enter without a pass.'

Una ran eagerly towards the vehicle.

The sergeant nodded briskly at Haynes then put his foot on the accelerator. He was gone before Una could reach him.

'Sorry, love.' The soldier shrugged as he lowered the barrier, went back into his box and closed the door.

She reached her hand through the open window and took hold of his cuff. 'Please; I only want to find out from the doctor how Angelo is.'

'No can do,' he repeated, pulling free. He felt sorry for her, as he had done when they'd brought Bachetti off the fell side the previous day, but he couldn't help her.

Then she would try something else, Una decided. There was always the unofficial way: along the public footpath and over the wall into the pine woods at the back. From there she could keep watch until she caught sight of a prisoner going about his business. With luck, it would be one of the men who knew about her and Angelo.

She was on the point of carrying out this plan when a more sympathetic figure walked down the rain-soaked drive. She recognized Squadron Leader Aldridge in his smart Canadian uniform and heard him hail her from a distance of fifty yards.

'Hi there. I thought it was you,' he began as he came within speaking distance.

Curiosity aroused, Haynes kept watch from

414

inside his sentry box.

'What can we do for you, Miss . . . '

'Sharpe. Una Sharpe.' There was a catch in her voice and her heart was in her mouth. 'I've come to ask about Angelo Bachetti. They've taken him to — '

'To Clifton; yes, I know.' *These Land Girls*, he thought with a faint smile. *They arrive in the backwoods from city soot and smoke without a clue what they're letting themselves in for. They're thrown in at the deep end. Sometimes they swim, sometimes they sink.* 'As it happens, I just talked on the phone with Dr Jones, one of the Clifton doctors, and he gave me an update. He says Bachetti is comfortable and doing as well as can be expected.'

Una was desperate for more. 'But did he sleep? Is he eating?'

Aldridge's gaze was fatherly. 'One step at a time. First they have to control his fever and let him rest. That's the key.'

'Has he mentioned me?'

'Honey,' he murmured, 'your guy is very sick, you know that. There, don't cry.' He offered her a clean handkerchief and went on observing quietly.

'I'm sorry.' She blew her nose then breathed in deeply. 'Did they say how soon I can visit him?'

'Not for a while, that's for sure. But you can write as often as you like.' Aldridge paused to ask himself how much information Una would be able to take in. She seemed terribly young, but she also had a look of fierce determination so he decided to go ahead. 'In a case of TB this bad the doctors might decide to go ahead with surgery in order to drain fluid from the lungs.'

'They can make him better?'

'For a while at least. Good food will help too.'

'And fresh air?' Una clung to Aldridge's every word.

'Yes, that's essential. And they're finding new treatments all the time. I know this for a fact. My sister back home is acting as a guinea pig for the latest trials. She takes a cocktail of pills to keep the tuberculosis at bay.'

The confession silenced Una. 'I'm sorry,' she repeated when at last she found her voice.

'Annette is twenty-one. She's had this illness since she was fifteen. So far she's holding her own. In fact, there are times when no one would guess she was sick.'

As Una listened, she inched towards a pinprick of light at the end of the tunnel. Angelo might have to have an operation. With the right treatment, some people with TB lived for a long time. 'Thank you,' she murmured.

'You're welcome.' Aldridge continued to look her steadily in the eye. 'Now go home, Una. Write your boyfriend a nice long letter.'

'I will.'

'Wait for him to write back.'

'I will, I will.' She had the rest of the day to commit her feelings to paper. She would write truthfully and pour out her heart.

'And be patient.' *Easy to say, hard to do.* He gave her arm a sympathetic squeeze before walking up Penny Lane to his quarters. *Will this be one that sinks or will she swim?* He hoped the latter but knew that only time would tell.

★ ★ ★

'Donald isn't here.' Hettie spoke before Brenda could state her business. 'But come in anyway. There's no need to stand on ceremony.'

They went straight to the sitting room and from there through the French doors on to the terrace overlooking the rose beds and the fish pond beyond.

'Let's sit.' Hettie pointed to a nearby bench.

Brenda took off her hat and put it down on the seat. The swift ride from Burnside had left her mouth dry but she waved away Hettie's offer of a drink. 'Do you know where he is?'

'Donald?' The response was vague, not at all like the Dragon's usual fiery self. 'I have no idea. Oh, wait a minute. The dogs aren't here and the guns are gone from the boot room, so he must be out shooting with Dad.'

'How long will he be?'

'I don't know. Why?' Hettie's hackles had risen the moment she spied Brenda's motor bike turn into the drive. It hadn't helped that the atmosphere at Dale End had been dreadful since her last visit, with Donald refusing to answer questions about why Brenda had been so upset and their father firing off an angry letter to Les, which he'd ordered Hettie to post. 'Don't you think it would be best to keep your distance from Donald, all things considered?'

''Things' — what things?' Brenda's temper

flared. She was in no mood for Hettie's underhand insults. 'It's him you should be worried about, not me.'

Hettie stood up from the bench. 'Brenda, really . . . '

Brenda too jumped up. 'What's the matter, Hettie? Don't you want to hear some home truths? That Donald has no respect for his brother, for a start? That he can't keep his hands to himself? And there's plenty more that's wrong with your precious brother, if you'd only open your eyes!'

'That's enough.' Gun shots interrupted the women's argument — proof that Hettie had guessed right. They echoed up and down the valley, scaring crows in the fields behind the barns. 'Brenda, I think you should leave.'

'Gladly!' she retorted. Of course Donald's sister would remain blind to his faults. What else could Brenda have expected? So she stormed into the sitting room and out into the hall, where she bumped into Arnold, who had emerged from his study, gun dogs at his heel and newspaper in hand.

'What's all the shouting?' he demanded of Hettie, who had pursued Brenda to the front door. He ignored the visitor and backed his daughter towards the bottom of the stairs. 'Well?'

'Dad . . . ' Hettie grasped the top of the newel post to steady herself. 'Where on earth is Donald? I thought you two were — '

'Well?' The black spaniels ran hither and thither while Arnold's voice rose to a new pitch. 'Are you going to tell me what's going on?'

His back was turned, the newspaper rolled into a tight scroll that he wielded like a baton. Brenda grimaced as she took in the angry scene then slipped away.

# 24

She made a split-second decision: a choice between riding off on Sloper or finishing what she'd come here to do. Brenda dug the toe of her shoe into the gravel close to where the bike was parked, shot a quick glance back at the house and opted for the latter.

*Call me an idiot*, she thought as she cut across the front garden then climbed a wall into the neighbouring field, *but I'm damned if I leave without having it out with Donald first.*

She didn't notice Hettie come to the door and follow her progress across the valley bottom.

Brenda judged that Donald had fired the shots from low on the hillside overlooking the Whites' farm. She had to cross the river to reach its lower slopes but she didn't let this hold her up, simply taking off her white canvas shoes and wading through. Then she tied the laces together and slung the shoes around her neck. There was boggy land ahead so progress would be quicker if she went barefoot for now.

As soon as the spongy, soft grass gave way to coarser heather and fern and the land began to rise, Brenda stopped to put her shoes back on and give herself breathing space to look around. It seemed clear from this new vantage point that Donald wouldn't have carried on climbing towards what became an almost sheer limestone cliff but would have veered off to the right towards a stretch of rough grassland interspersed with gorse and hawthorn bushes that would be ideal territory for rabbits. There he would simply have to stand and wait, gun at the ready, for the little blighters to raise their heads out of their burrows then bang, bang, bang!

At the moment of visualizing this scene, a real gun was fired not far away from where she stood, then there was a short silence followed by three more shots. Echoes ricocheted along the valley towards the narrow, uninhabited end of the dale.

Brenda recovered from her surprise then set off at an uneven run towards the open meadow, arms spread wide to help her balance and occasionally losing her footing on loose shale. At one point she felt the surface give way under her. She halted her slide by grabbing on to a bush before running on again, convinced that at any moment Donald would step out from behind a rock, take aim at more rabbits and fire again.

Sure enough, she spotted two men with their backs turned, levelling shotguns and aiming across the rough meadow. *Drat, he's brought a pal along! That wasn't part of the plan.*

The thought was only half-formed when she was thrown to the ground and bundled out of sight behind a rocky ledge. She found herself flat on her back, staring up at Donald and unable to speak.

'What the bloody hell are you doing?' he hissed, his hand clamped across her mouth. 'For God's sake, Brenda, are you mad? Do you want to get yourself killed?'

Trapped beneath him, she managed to shake

her head. His face was livid; spittle flew from his lips in his fury. The pressure of his hand made it difficult for her to breathe.

With his other hand he gestured in the direction of the two marksmen. 'Those are the two bastards who stole my guns.'

'Stole them?' Her eyes widened as she grabbed his wrist and tried to speak.

'You hear me? They sneaked into the gun room and helped themselves.'

*A brief back view of two men dressed in suits and brimmed hats. Of course!* The image of Moyes and Nixon standing with guns raised was etched in Brenda's mind.

Donald saw that the look in her eyes had changed. 'You know them,' he guessed, pressing down harder than before.

She gave one nod. Sharp stones dug into her flesh. He was far heavier and stronger so she stopped struggling and stared.

'Stay down. Don't make a sound.' Slowly he released the pressure. Another shot split the silence.

'Don't pretend you don't know them too!' she hissed as soon as she was able to speak.

'What are you on about?' He pushed her shoulders back against the ground.

'Moyes, Nixon. Come off it, Donald!'

His upper lip curled as he took hold of the front of her jacket, wrenched her up into a sitting position then shoved her out of sight behind the ledge. 'What's this? You know their names?'

'Yes and so do you!'

'No. I got a quick look at both of their faces;

I've never clapped eyes on them.'

'Moyes. Nixon,' she repeated slowly. 'You talked to them at Kelsey. I saw you.'

'I've never . . . Ah, you mean the blokes who asked for directions!'

'And that wasn't the first time. You saw them outside the pub one Saturday afternoon as well.'

'I did?' Donald's blue eyes narrowed in genuine confusion. 'Sorry, I don't recall.' He smiled nastily as he leaned forward and cupped Brenda's chin with his hand. 'But since you're so clever, why not tell me what the hell's going on?'

★  ★  ★

Nixon and Moyes had had a couple of busy days. They'd seemed not to mind that they stuck out like sore thumbs in the villages where they stopped the Morris Oxford and pressed locals for information about the fugitive, Alfie Craven. They even spent time in the pub in Attercliffe on the day after they'd put paid to the ginger-haired farm lad. Nixon had done the honours on that occasion and it had been a doddle: hardly any resistance, only one ruined collar. A handy stone lay nearby. There'd been two quick blows to the skull and that was the finish, end of story. Messy but effective. No regrets.

But they still had Alfie to sort out, which is what took them to Attercliffe on the Saturday where they got chatting over a pint of bitter to a couple of off-duty Tommies who were willing to talk about the missing POWs and this led nicely into conversation about various searches that had been carried out in the area.

'We've gone over the whole of Burnside with a fine-tooth comb but so far not a sniff,' one of the soldiers volunteered. 'Sarge says we'll start in this neck of the woods come Monday. Tomorrow's Sunday: a day of rest.'

'With a bit of luck we'll have the coppers to back us up,' the other added. 'They're after a local villain — Albert, Alfred . . . '

'Alfie Craven.' His pal supplied the full name. 'He stabbed a bloke. If you spot him, steer well clear — he's still got the knife.'

No respecters of the Sabbath, Moyes and Nixon returned to the village the next day to continue their own search. They made no secret of the fact that they were looking for Alfie, allowing a rumour to spread that they were plain-clothes police officers hot on his trail. They heard of a tramp given a rude awakening in the bus shelter first thing that morning and of another man scrounging food at the back door of the pub. Both incidents suggested that they were closing in on their quarry. And then, finally, there was an actual, unmistakable sighting by a woman on her way to church.

'I saw the man you're looking for round the back of Dale End — the big house as you come into the village.' Their informant seemed uneasy. Neither Moyes nor Nixon looked like an arm of the law. But she told them what she'd seen: Alfie Craven acting suspiciously, crouching to fill a bottle from the stream. They thanked her and she hurried on.

Within minutes they'd worked their silent way

round the back of the house to find a gun-room door conveniently open and two shotguns complete with a box of ammunition within easy reach. From there they slipped unnoticed into one of the barns. If Alfie was in the vicinity, it was likely that he'd approach from the back in search of food and shelter.

★　★　★

Alfie drank water from an empty milk bottle, making sure not to be visible from the house. His bones ached with cold and weariness; his skin itched after yet another night of sleeping rough. But he was doing all right, he reminded himself. A few more days of this and he would have shaken everyone off.

Thirty, forty miles from here, there was little chance that he'd be recognized. Then he'd be able to use some of the money that he'd stolen from Fieldhead and the Kelletts to catch a bus to the coast — to Saltburn or Filey — where he would pick himself up and start a new life.

But still he had to take the utmost care not to be spotted.

The water was refreshing. He kept out of sight and made a plan to spend part of the day in one of the Whites' barns. There were plenty of them, facing on to a big yard, with a handy copse of silver birch between the river and the nearest building. If his luck held out, he could approach one of them without being seen.

★　★　★

Nixon and Moyes had chosen the smallest barn furthest from the house, where one of the Whites' tractors was stored. Once inside, they squeezed past it then found a stepladder leading to a disused loft. There, amongst cobwebs, dismantled machine parts and years of dust, they secured a vantage point overlooking the yard and a small copse beyond. They propped the shotguns against the wall. Moyes set up a careful watch while Nixon relaxed and smoked a cigarette.

Less than half an hour into their vigil, Nixon took his turn as lookout. The light was tricky; bright sunlight had broken through the thick cloud that had brought rain earlier that morning. The sun shone directly into his eyes so he wasn't sure at first if the movement he'd spotted at the edge of the wood was simply a breeze lifting the branches and creating dappled shadows. He had to check three times before convincing himself.

★   ★   ★

Alfie had judged the distance between the edge of the trees and the nearest barn, uncertain whether or not to risk crossing the open space. He checked and re-checked his surroundings until he was sure that he wouldn't be spotted. Then he set off.

He was twenty yards from safety when Moyes came down from the loft, stepped into view and levelled his gun. Nixon followed. They fired at Alfie, who dropped straight to the ground. Unhurt, he got up and made a crouching run for cover. Pellets ripped into the trunks. He dodged, dropped into the long grass, rolled and got up again. Nixon and Moyes were lousy shots. They'd fired and missed, fired again. If he could make it back to the wood, he'd be home and dry.

★ ★ ★

Concealed behind the rocky ledge, Donald demanded an explanation. 'Come on, Brenda, I can see that they're not here to shoot rabbits.'

'You honestly don't know?' It was as if someone had tossed an almost complete jigsaw into the air and the pieces had scattered in all directions. 'You're not involved in any of this?'

'Any of what?'

'Stockings, perfume, under-the-counter goods.'

'We're talking black market?' A glance over the ledge told him that the two marksmen were still stalking their quarry. 'Yes, that makes sense.' Even from a back view, he got the men's measure from their off-the-peg, pin-striped suits, broad at the shoulder, wide in the leg.

Brenda signalled assent with her eyes.

'And you thought I was caught up in that malar-key?' He gave a short, sardonic laugh then relaxed his grip. 'Do me a favour. But carry on, I'm all ears.'

'They've got a grudge against Alfie.'

'Doesn't everyone?'

'Listen to me! They're the reason he came back here in the first place. He got himself into a jam by stealing goods and cash from them, so he was forced to lie low.'

Seconds were ticking by and Donald gradually made sense of her story. 'That's quite a jam,' he muttered. 'Perhaps we should leave those two clowns to finish Alfie off. What do you think?'

His callous suggestion sent her head into a new spin. 'We can't do that. Whatever Afie's done, this is no way to solve things.'

He released her, then shifted his weight and sat down next to her, his back to the rock, legs splayed. He took out a cigarette and lit it with a slim, silver lighter. 'Rough justice — what's wrong with that?'

'No, we can't!' Free to act at last, she raised her head above the ledge. Moyes and Nixon had vanished but a pair of partridges had been disturbed lower down the hill. They clattered and whirred away in the direction of the farm. Immediately afterwards, there were two new shots and more birds rose from the heather.

'We can.' Donald inhaled deeply. 'I can, at least. You go ahead and risk your flipping life if you want. I'm staying here.'

'You really won't help?' she demanded. 'Then you're as bad as Doreen.'

'Worse, much worse,' he taunted. 'If you only knew.'

Contempt rose in her throat. There was more gunfire. 'Donald White, I don't know how you live with yourself.'

'Easy.' He aimed a thin funnel of smoke up into the air. 'I look after number one. Every one else can take a running jump.'

Contempt turned to pure loathing, which drove her on. 'I've got nothing else to say to you,' she exploded. 'Not now, not ever!'

With this as a parting shot, Brenda left the shelter of the ledge and ran recklessly across the rough meadow, following the direction of the startled partridges and the sound of renewed gunfire.

★ ★ ★

The woods hadn't saved Alfie after all. Nixon and Moyes were too hot on his heels for him to hide so he kept on running, ever more hampered by his sore ribs. He avoided another shower of pellets which flicked harmlessly off rocks and tore through leaves but they kept on coming as Alfie ducked and dived, raising game birds as he staggered on. Ahead was a deep hollow then the rough, open stretch of land where it would be well nigh impossible to find cover so, as he dipped out of sight, he backtracked and found a boulder to hide behind. He held his breath as his pursuers passed his hiding place and carried on up the hill. But impatience spoiled his tactic; he broke into the open too quickly in a bid to double back to the wood. Nixon heard him and swung round. He fired.

Now it was chaos: all three men running, tripping, stumbling. Moyes yelled his name. Alfie didn't stop. *Shoot me in the back, damn you*, he cursed to himself. *Get it over with*.

Nixon and Moyes stopped to reload. Alfie gained ground. He reached the wood with its tall, white trunks then ran on towards the Whites' barns, a glimmer of hope propelling him

429

towards the biggest of them. Surely he would find a dark corner where no one could winkle him out. Meanwhile, people would come out of the house to investigate the ruckus on the hillside. They would challenge Moyes and Nixon and send them packing.

He fled into the barn to be confronted by two threshing machines with their open metal maws and mighty steam-fired engines. They towered over him but there was just enough space to squeeze between two of the chutes then slither down and find a safe hiding place underneath the biggest machine. He wormed under the belly of the beast, across the oil-stained floor, using his elbows to ease himself forward.

'Which way?' Nixon's high-pitched voice reached Alfie from the edge of the yard.

'Try in that first building. I'll stay here and keep watch.' Moyes was short of breath.

There was the sound of footsteps followed by a creaking door then silence.

'Nothing,' Nixon reported back.

Moyes swore. 'The bastard's here somewhere. Try the stables.'

More footsteps. Alfie breathed in engine oil and coal dust. He waited.

⋆   ⋆   ⋆

'Brenda, why are you still here?' Hettie shouted from the terrace of the main house. 'I ordered you to leave.'

Brenda had waded across the river. Her plan to skirt the copse and take what she thought was a short cut had been spoiled by Hettie. 'Quiet!' She pointed towards the barns. 'Wait there. I'll join you.'

Hettie ignored her. She came down from the patio, along the garden path and out into the field to confront Brenda.

'Stay down!' Brenda ran the final few yards, caught hold of Hettie and attempted to pull her back into the garden when she spotted Moyes and Nixon, guns at the ready.

'Both of you, stay where you are.' Moyes had followed the sound of women's voices and brought Nixon with him. Together they stood, legs wide apart, aiming at Brenda and Hettie.

Hettie had lived with shotguns all her life and was having none of it. She broke loose from Brenda and walked steadily towards the two men. 'My family owns this farm. I'm the one who dishes out orders around here. I'll thank you to return those guns to their rightful owners.'

Brenda steeled herself to join Hettie. 'Be careful,' she whispered.

'I said, stay where you are,' Moyes threatened.

'And I said, give me those guns.'

From his filthy hiding place, Alfie smiled to himself. Not only were his town-based enemies lousy shots, they were on the point of being ejected from the premises by a pair of women. He almost laughed out loud as he prepared to roll out from under the threshing machine.

Moyes stared at Hettie from under the tilted brim of his hat; a church-going type in a maroon dress with her dark hair primly pinned behind her ears. He took his time to run through his options.

'If you please,' she insisted.

For a moment Brenda imagined that Moyes would pull the trigger at point-blank range. Nixon too would have fired in the blink of an eye.

'All right, you win.' Unexpectedly Moyes let the gun drop to his side. Nixon frowned and held his aim until Moyes reached out to tilt the barrel towards the ground. 'Forget it, Clive,' he muttered as he handed his own gun to Hettie. 'It can wait.'

Alfie grinned again. He wriggled out from under the machine and stood up, rubbing his oil-stained palms on his trousers. His shoulder knocked against a handle that opened the cab door. It swung wide and hit the side of the neighbouring vehicle with a loud metallic clang.

Quick as a fox, Nixon turned and darted towards the barn. He flung back the wide wooden door, raised his gun and aimed at Alfie, who was trapped between the two threshing machines. He fired from a distance of ten yards.

Moyes reacted by charging at Hettie, knocking her over and sprinting up the garden then round the side of the house on to the drive, where he found an open-topped car sitting on the drive complete with ignition key. He had no idea if Nixon had hit his target. Anyway, for once, the idiot would have to get himself out of a tight spot. He, Howard Moyes, wasn't willing to stick around and help. So he vaulted into the driver's seat and started the engine. Within seconds he'd pulled away without a backward glance.

Brenda stooped to help Hettie up but Hettie pushed her away. 'What are you waiting for? You've got your motor bike. Go after him.'

It was enough to send Brenda racing up the path. She heard the car engine roar into life and the rattle of gravel spat up by its tyres. Rounding the corner, she ran for her bike and kicked it into action. Moyes had reached the road and turned up the hill, accelerator pressed hard on the floor, racing up the gears as he approached the blind bend.

He braked late and felt the car swerve, fought to right it, but the centrifugal force of the spin flung his hands from the steering wheel. He lost control.

Brenda saw it from a distance of fifty yards: the screeching swerve, the spin, the roll of the car on to its bonnet, the impact as it mounted the verge and hit the wall. She stopped the bike, dismounted and walked slowly towards Les's MG.

A second car approached the scene of the crash. Edgar and Joyce had witnessed it from the top of the hill. Arriving less than a minute after the event, they approached on foot to see if they could help. They found Brenda crouched by the upturned wreckage, saw the wheels turning in the eerie silence.

Brenda looked up and shook her head.

The driver was dead. There was nothing anyone could do.

# 25

'You should have seen Les's car.' Brenda spoke to Una in the quiet atmosphere of the hostel common room. They'd shut the door on the bustle outside and basked in the evening sun that slanted through the windows. 'I warned Hettie; I doubt if it can ever be mended.'

'No need to think about that now.' Una wondered why this appeared to matter so much. 'As long as you're all right, that's what counts.'

'I am,' Brenda assured her. 'But the front end was smashed to pieces. The bonnet was torn off and the whole engine section shunted back by the impact. They say that's what killed Moyes — when the steering column hit him full force in the chest.'

Una nodded and sighed. It was less than half an hour since Edgar and Joyce had driven Brenda back to Fieldhead and the other girls were still noisily coming to terms with what had happened. Meanwhile, she made it her job to make sure that Brenda hadn't suffered too many ill effects. 'You don't need to talk,' she said gently. 'We can just sit here.'

'I knew he was dead before I got off the bike and went to look. I wasn't the least bit sorry.'

'Brenda, you don't have to — '

'Should I have been?'

'No. I understand.'

'Neither were Joyce and Edgar. We left him there for the police to deal with and walked back to the house.'

'You did the right thing.'

'Mr White had dialled 999. They were already on their way.'

Una drew down the blind to shield Brenda's face from the sun. 'Are you sure you wouldn't like something to drink?'

'No, ta. And as for Hettie, it turns out that I was right about her all along.'

'The dragon-sister?'

'Yes. She practically breathed fire when she stood up to Moyes, even though he was pointing a gun in her face. Goodness, Una, you've never seen anything like it. Then, after Nixon shot Alfie and Moyes ran off, it seems she grabbed the nearest thing to hand — a garden fork — and charged in like the cavalry. She discovered Alfie in the barn lying in a pool of blood.'

'But no sign of Nixon?'

'As a matter of fact, yes. The police picked him up when he tried to scarper. Luckily for Alfie, he was only winged. I dread to think what Hettie and her father would have done to him if Edgar hadn't separated them.'

Una waited until Brenda had talked herself out. 'It's a blessing you weren't hurt in amongst all that shooting.'

'I know it.' She stood up in sudden panic. 'Les! I ought to phone him about the car!'

'You can do that later.' Una knew that the warden hadn't come back to Fieldhead after church and that these days the office would be locked. 'The main thing is everything's under control.'

Brenda sat down again, letting her gaze drift over the bookshelves and threadbare carpet as if uncertain where she was. 'No thanks to Donald,' she said wearily. 'When it mattered, he was nowhere to be seen.'

It seemed to Una that nothing she'd said so far had had much effect, so she grew more forceful. 'Brenda, you ought not to dwell on the details. It won't do you any good. The best idea is to sit here quietly for a while.'

The change of tone worked and Brenda looked directly at her. 'You're right. I'll do as I'm told.'

'For a change.'

The remark drew a faint smile. 'I'm sorry, Una.'

'What for?'

'For everything. For not always being as good a friend as I ought.'

'But you are. You, Grace and Joyce are my best friends. I wouldn't have settled in Burnside without you. I wouldn't be a Land Girl.'

'So here we still are, by the skin of our teeth.'

A narrow shaft of sunlight crept under the drawn blind, falling across Una's shoulders and on to the back of her leather chair. She and Brenda sat together in warm silence until they heard a car come up the drive then Una went to lift the blind and peer out.

'Ma Craven's back,' she said. 'She'll unlock the office then you can make that phone call.'

★　★　★

'Poppy's gone home to her mother.' Hilda sat down heavily then leaned her elbows on the desk. 'I drove her there straight from the church, after the police had talked to her.'

Brenda and Una stood by the office door, lost for words.

'It's for the best — for the time being, at least.'

'But will she come back?' Brenda remembered her last sight of Poppy in her bloodstained dress.

'I'm not sure.' Hilda had delivered her charge to Albion Lane, into her mother's arms. The uncontrollable weeping had begun all over again. 'We'll have to wait and see. Meanwhile, I'll ask Doreen or Joyce to pack her suitcase then send it on.'

'How was Poppy when you left?' Una asked.

'A bit calmer. She seemed glad to be home.' Once Hilda had explained events to Mrs Gledhill and advised her that Poppy would receive at least two weeks' leave of absence, she'd sat with them for a while. 'Her mother told me she was never sure about Poppy signing up for the Land Army. She didn't think she was cut out for it. Not everyone is.'

'We'll look after her if she does come back,' Una promised. Then it struck her that the warden could have no idea about what had gone on that afternoon and she turned uncertainly to Brenda.

Brenda interpreted the look. 'That's right . . . ' she began. Then she drew a sharp breath. What was the right way to tell a person that their son had been arrested on a charge of attempted murder?

'Alfie's been found.' Una picked up the thread then dropped it again when she saw Hilda's weight sag forward and her head go down.

'What Una means to say is that he's been taken to hospital. I was at Dale End when it happened. Clive Nixon shot him but he's not badly hurt.'

Hilda raised her head and took a deep breath. 'Shot, you say?'

'In the shoulder.'

'Which hospital?'

'The King Edward's, I expect. The police made Nixon confess that he killed Neville, so Alfie's in the clear over that at least. He'll have to answer the charge of stabbing Bill, that's all.'

'It's enough.' Hilda let the facts sink in. An unexpected feeling of calm mingled with the shame that had threatened to overwhelm her. 'Dale End is the Whites' farm,' she murmured. They'd come full circle, from Willis's death at the hands of Arnold White's threshing machine through Alfie's troubled childhood to this point of no return. With the deepest of drawn-out sighs, she prepared to shoulder her burden of responsibility and carry it with her for the rest of her life.

The jarring ring of the telephone interrupted her thoughts and she picked up the receiver.

'Hello, this is Hilda Craven. How can I help?' She listened to the caller's message. 'Leslie who?'

Una exchanged astonished glances with Brenda. Before she knew it, Brenda was talking into the receiver, her tongue tripping her up as she tried to explain. 'Les, my dear, how did you

know? . . . Hettie rang you? . . . Yes, I'm fine
. . . Yes, perfectly all right . . . Dearest, your car's
a write-off, did Hettie say?'

★   ★   ★

It was only later, in the privacy of her bedroom,
that Brenda thought through her conversation
with Les and what he'd said to her after Hilda
and Una had left the room.

'I'm alone,' she told him. 'We're free to talk.'
Then suddenly, out of the blue, she'd begun to
sob and say sorry over and over.

'No need,' he told her quietly. 'But cry away
and get it out of your system.'

'Oh Les, I'd give anything to see you,' she said
through her tears. 'To have you at my side.'

'I wish I could get away but I don't see how.'

'I know. I'm sorry.'

'That word is not allowed.' Les pretended to
be stern. 'Listen, I could apply for leave and see
what happens.'

'No.' She dried her eyes. 'No, you stay where
you are and finish your training. I'll manage.'

'I know you will. It was for my sake as much
as yours. But you're right — we'll keep smiling
through like we always do.'

*Typical Les!* The words of the Vera Lynn song
brought a trembling smile to her lips. 'I love you,
Les White, did you know?'

'I did actually.' The line crackled and his voice
was faint. 'And I love you too.'

This was how they went on, talking over each
other, quoting songs, going from tears to smiles

439

and back to tears in seconds.

'I'll tell you one thing I know.' Brenda issued a warning before she rang off. 'After what's gone on today, your brother and I will never see eye to eye.'

'I'm glad to hear it.'

'Honestly, Les, I mean it. I wouldn't care if I never saw Donald again in my entire life.'

'I'll see what can be arranged . . . '

'You're chalk and cheese.'

'Thank heavens.'

'And as for your dragon-sister.' She paused for maximum effect before delivering her verdict. 'I may have changed my mind.'

'You don't say.' He heard the lilt in her voice, imagined the old sparkle in her eye. 'You're saying that you and Hettie will get along after all?'

'I wouldn't go that far,' she cautioned. 'But I might just get used to her, given time.'

★ ★ ★

The sun had begun to set when Una walked alone in the woods behind the hostel, rehearsing the letter she would write to Angelo. She wouldn't hold back. She would use English words that he might have to ask the nurses at Clifton for help with. It didn't matter who read them and saw how much she loved him.

*Dearest Angelo, I am glad you're safe and being well looked after. You must do as the doctors say. I picture you tucked up in bed with clean sheets and a soft pillow, or out on a sunny balcony, breathing in all that fresh air. They say the countryside is pretty where you are — not so rough and rugged as here. What can you see from your window? Are there hills and woods and birds in the trees? Do they give you interesting things to do to help pass the time? I mean, reading or sketching. Do the nurses know that you can carve boxes and musical instruments out of wood? Don't let any of them fall in love with you, by the way. But then how can they help it? I'm only joking (I think). Are you smiling as you read this? In any case, you know that I think of you morning, noon and night. I see you resting and eating properly, getting better day by day, especially if they do the operation I've been told about. Do the doctors say if this will happen? Please write and let me know. In the meantime, rest, rest, rest! Darling, I love you. I love you.*

Una paused to look through the trees at the red sky: shepherd's delight. The air was calm, scarcely a rustle in the leaves. She would draw hearts around the edge of her letter and rows of kisses at the bottom.

*Write to me please and tell me everything that happens in the hospital. Then describe sunny Italy to me, especially Pisa and its leaning tower, and the grapes and olives growing on the hillsides. Think of the time when we will be there together, you and me. I imagine the war ending and you being strong enough to travel. We'll sail away on a boat. Picture that, Angelo — you and me standing arm in arm on the deck, waving goodbye to the white cliffs of Dover. I long for it, my dearest love.*

She walked on through the trees, weaving a web of dreams strong enough to carry them through the darkest days of war and separation.

*For now goodnight, my Angelo. Sleep well. All my love — your Una.*

★   ★   ★

'Be prepared,' Edgar warned Joyce as they walked along the hospital corridor. 'Remember, the doctors are cagey about Bill's chances. Grace has stayed by his bed non-stop.'

She pressed her lips together and nodded, stepping aside as a nurse emerged from a sluice room carrying a tall stack of kidney-shaped dishes and bed pans. In a ward to their left, an elderly patient cried out for help. Joyce frowned and quickened her pace.

'Slow down. It's this one on the right.' Edgar pushed the door open and let her enter before him.

There were twenty beds in the ward, most surrounded by visitors, so it took Joyce a while to scan the rows and make out Grace sitting on a tubular-steel chair with her back to them, still dressed in her Land Army uniform of Aertex shirt and brown corduroy breeches. Strands of fair hair had escaped from the bun at the nape of her neck — the only sign of how long she'd been keeping her vigil.

Joyce approached slowly and quietly, concentrating on Grace and doing her best to ignore the metal stands and charts around the bed. She

442

caught a glimpse of Bill lying motionless, his eyes closed, face ashen, and his shoulder and chest heavily bandaged. His hair looked jet black against the crisp white pillow. Joyce's heart jolted; she hesitated then propelled herself forward.

Grace heard footsteps and turned her head. 'Hello, Joyce.'

Joyce accepted a chair from Edgar and sat down next to Grace, taking her hand and murmuring a soft reply. 'Hello, my dear.'

Grace glanced up at her brother. 'Hello, Edgar.'

He gave a silent nod.

'How is he?' Joyce whispered. *Pale, unmoving, lost to the world.*

Grace stood up then motioned to Edgar to take her place. 'Come with me,' she whispered.

She and Joyce walked down the ward and through the wide swing doors, out into a long, windowless corridor. 'Well?' Joyce asked again.

Grace's pale, oval face gave nothing away until, out of nowhere, her grey eyes filled with tears.

'What is it?' Joyce whispered.

She gave a small gasp. 'Bill opened his eyes.' The tears of relief ran freely down.

'Oh, my dear!' Joyce squeezed her hand. 'That's marvellous.'

'An hour ago. He heard the tea trolley, opened his eyes and said he was thirsty. The nurse gave him a drink through a straw. He's sleeping now. I was afraid our talking would wake him.'

'Wonderful.'

'I know.' Grace smiled through her tears. 'I know!'

'You were there at his side?'

'Willing him to wake up. I believed he would and I was right.'

'You were, my dear.'

'Oh, Joyce!' *Willing him and wishing, hoping, praying. Bill looked at me and smiled.*

'All will be well,' Joyce promised. 'He's young and he's strong. You'll soon have him home.'

*Strong and faithful.* The church bells had rung out for them on their wedding day: four rhythmical notes, *strong and faithful*, repeated as she'd entered the church and made her wedding vows, for better or for worse. *Strong and faithful*; *one-two, three-four.* Like the regular beat of a heart.

★   ★   ★

'Bill woke up again while you and Grace were away,' Edgar told Joyce as he drove her back to Fieldhead. 'He hadn't a clue what had happened to him. The last thing he remembers is rugby-tackling Alfie. After that, nothing.'

She gazed out of the window at a spectacular, flaming sunset. Deep pink clouds edged with gold clung to Kelsey Crag, which lay in dense shadow.

'I hope you didn't tire him out.'

'You're joking; I couldn't get a word in edgeways. Bill was pestering the nurses, asking how long he'd be laid up for and how soon he'd be fit to join his battalion.'

'It was meant to be a week from tomorrow.'

'Well, that won't happen. I'd say a couple of months, the end of the summer at the earliest.'

'Good.'

He glanced sideways. 'Who for, Grace or Bill?'

'Both. They'll have two months to enjoy being married. And who knows? A lot can happen in eight weeks. The army might not need him after all.'

'Don't bank on it.' Edgar drove on without elaborating. The hours were ticking away. Once he'd dropped Joyce off, he would have to drive like a bat out of hell to arrive back at his base on time. He didn't relish the parting from Joyce or what lay ahead tomorrow and the day after: more reconnaissance flights followed by incendiary attacks, a follow-up to the bomber raids on Bremen. 'Sorry, I didn't mean to sound so glum.'

'No, you're right.'

Back to the base and his narrow bunk bed, writing letters to Joyce by torchlight, dicing nightly, counting Spitfires out and back in again, watching his pals take a nosedive out of the black sky, trailing white smoke, exploding in an orange flash when they hit the ground. 'Will you marry me?'

She looked straight ahead. 'Yes.'

'You will?'

'Yes.'

He pulled on to the grass verge and switched off the engine. 'I haven't got a ring or anything.'

'I don't need one,' she said in the evening silence. She saw the outline of the hostel ahead,

445

the elm wood behind it, the fell rising steeply to the black horizon. 'Or the white dress or the bridesmaids. A registry office will do.'

'No faff. Just us and two witnesses?'

'Three: Grace, Brenda and Una.'

It was simply said. Edgar and Joyce would marry without fuss as soon as the war was over.

Their hearts were full as they watched the fiery sun sink behind the crag. They both knew without needing to speak the words that no goodbye on earth could lessen their love, that they were bound to each other with ties that would never break.

★　★　★

'Engaged?' Brenda's voice rose above the Monday-morning breakfast hubbub. She sprang up and stood on her chair. 'Girls, listen to this: Joyce is engaged to Edgar!'

The chatter and the clatter ceased and all heads turned.

'It's true!' Brenda declared. 'He proposed last night and she said yes. Tell them, Joyce.'

'I did.'

'See!' Brenda pulled her to her feet and slapped her enthusiastically on the back. 'This is a grand start to the week. Smile and look happy, Joyce, for heaven's sake!'

'I am — I'm smiling.' But blushing too and shrinking from the attention that her news had created. She extricated herself from Brenda's embrace then sat back down next to Una, who nodded and smiled broadly.

'Fools rush in,' Jean muttered to Kathleen and Elsie.

'Pipe down!' they said as one.

Excited questions poured down on Joyce's head. Where was the ring? Had they set a date for the wedding? How long before Edgar's next leave?

'First Grace takes a trot down the aisle, now Joyce.' Doreen's voice rose above the rest. 'Line up, line up; who's next?'

'Brenda, how about you?' Kathleen cried from the far end of the table. Cutlery was rattled against the boards and a chorus set up.

'Brenda! Brenda!'

'Not me — not until after the war has ended. Les and I intend to look a long time before we leap.' She laughed as she held up her hand to display the ring. 'But don't worry, you'll all get an invite as soon as we name the day.'

'Una?' Elsie asked. 'Has Angelo popped the question?'

Brenda stepped in with a rapid deflection. 'Give the bloke a chance. The army has only just rounded him up and sent him to hospital, remember.'

Una gave her a grateful smile. 'Ta, but I don't mind,' she said quickly. 'I love Angelo and he loves me. That's all that matters.'

'Doreen, how about you?'

Brenda's question drew new shouts from all sides.

'Yes, Doreen!'

'You and Donald!'

'When's the big day?'

'Never,' she replied as she took her time to stand up, stroll to the trolley then ladle porridge into a bowl. 'I'm single and free as a bird.'

There were cries of disbelief. Brenda raised her eyebrows at Joyce and Una.

'I am,' Doreen insisted with the customary flick of her raven mane. 'And what's more, girls, this particular little bird is about to fly the Land Army nest.'

'Wait for it!' Brenda warned. 'Come on, Doreen, what have you done now?'

Head held high, she carried her bowl back to her seat. 'I've only gone and joined ENSA.'

'You've done what?' Jean's incredulous question broke the stunned silence. 'You're leaving Fieldhead to tread the boards?'

*Singing and prancing about, Doreen's name in lights alongside Vera Lynn. Perfect!* Brenda jumped up again and started to clap, inviting the others to join in. 'Bravo!' she cried.

'Yes, bravo!'

'Give our regards to our boys on the front line!'

'ENSA. 'Every Night Something Awful'!'

There was laughter and praise, high spirits all round.

'Good for Doreen,' Joyce said to Una and Brenda as they finished breakfast then put on their jackets and hats.

'Yes, ENSA will suit her down to the ground,' Una agreed.

'Good luck to her,' Brenda said as they went to collect their bikes from the stables and set off together down the drive. It was a fine day, the start of a new week. 'Meanwhile, ladies, let's roll up our sleeves. We have serious work to do.'

We do hope that you have enjoyed reading this large print book.

Did you know that all of our titles are available for purchase?

We publish a wide range of high quality large print books including:
**Romances, Mysteries, Classics**
**General Fiction**
**Non Fiction and Westerns**

Special interest titles available in large print are:
**The Little Oxford Dictionary**
**Music Book**
**Song Book**
**Hymn Book**
**Service Book**

Also available from us courtesy of Oxford University Press:
**Young Readers' Dictionary**
**(large print edition)**
**Young Readers' Thesaurus**
**(large print edition)**

For further information or a free brochure, please contact us at:
**Ulverscroft Large Print Books Ltd.,**
**The Green, Bradgate Road, Anstey,**
**Leicester, LE7 7FU, England.**
**Tel:** (00 44) 0116 236 4325
**Fax:** (00 44) 0116 234 0205